EVERY GIVEN DAY

Also by Cathy Gohlke

William Henry Is a Fine Name

I Have Seen Him in the Watchfires

Promise Me This

Band of Sisters

Saving Amelie

Secrets She Kept

Until We Find Home

The Medallion

Night Bird Calling

A Hundred Crickets Singing

Ladies of the Lake

This Promised Land

EVERY GIVEN DAY

CATHY GOHLKE

Tyndale House Publishers
Carol Stream, Illinois

Visit Tyndale online at tyndale.com.

Visit Cathy Gohlke's website at cathygohlke.com.

Every Given Day

Cover design by Dean H. Renninger

Interior design by Cathy Miller

Edited by Sarah Mason Rische

Published in association with the literary agency of Natasha Kern Literary Agency, Inc., P.O. Box 1069, White Salmon, WA 98672.

Scripture quotations are taken from the *Holy Bible*, King James Version.

For information about special discounts for bulk purchases, please contact Tyndale House Publishers at csresponse@tyndale.com, or call 1-855-277-9400.

Library of Congress Cataloging-in-Publication Data

A catalog record for this book is available from the Library of Congress.

ISBN 979-8-4005-0859-2 (HC)
ISBN 979-8-4005-0860-8 (SC)

Printed in the United States of America

32 31 30 29 28 27 26
7 6 5 4 3 2 1

For Aimee and all the resilient and courageous
who navigate life with diabetes . . .
For Elisabeth and Tim and all the compassionate and
committed who provide daily support for loved ones . . .
For the dedicated and determined who will not
stop searching until a cure is found

"And I will love thee still, my dear,

While the sands o' life shall run."

ROBERT BURNS

PART ONE

1

PARADOX, PENNSYLVANIA
SEPTEMBER 1918

Gwendolyn Armstrong's heart beat a staccato rhythm as she approached the principal's office. She'd waited until Friday afternoon, when she was certain all the children had gone and even the school secretary had left for the day. By the time she raised her hand to knock on Herman Sapp's door, her throat had gone dry, and her heart had all but stopped beating.

"Come." The voice beyond the door sounded all business. But then Herman's eyes lit as they often did when falling upon Gwen. He quickly stood from behind his desk and donned his jacket, adjusting his eyeglasses and tie, smoothing his hair. "Miss Armstrong—Gwen! A most pleasant surprise." His smile stopped when she did not return his greeting. "Am I mistaken?"

Gathering her courage, she handed him her folded letter. "A surprise, certainly. I'm not sure you'll find it pleasant."

His eyes swept her letter of resignation. "No." She watched the protrusion in his throat rise and fall, the line of his mouth straighten as he dropped the letter on his desk. "Not pleasant at all. Why?" The word held recrimination, anguish—anguish she'd predetermined to ignore.

"I've received a letter from my sister, in New York. You remember Marion."

"The sister who deserted you for fame and fortune."

She ignored his dig. "Marion needs me. She suffers from tuberculosis."

He stepped around his desk. "I'm sorry. As did your mother. You see, I recall."

Gwen determined to ignore that too. "Now that Father no longer needs me, I'm free to go. I'm sorry to leave so early into the school year. I know it's not an ideal time—not convenient—but the letter came recently, since Father's funeral. I really must go." She stopped, breathless.

"Surely there is someone there to care for her. She has a husband . . . or did." Was there accusation in his voice?

"A husband, and two children—children she now needs my help with."

"For whom she could hire a nanny."

"She's asked me to tutor them at home. She doesn't want them in school, exposed to the epidemic. It's raging in New York. Much too dangerous—for her, and for them. They've not closed the schools there as so many big cities have—as we might soon. With Father gone, I've no reason to refuse." *Not that that is any of your business. And who are you to speak into my family's affairs?* But she knew who he presumed to be.

"I'd expected, after your father passed, that you'd reconsider my proposal—that you'd consider *us* a reason to stay. Gwen"—his voice softened—"I've asked you . . . more than once." There it was again, the anguish in his voice.

She didn't want to insult him or hurt him, but she didn't love him, had told him so and tried in a dozen ways to ward him off. "Herman, you know I've never given you reason to expect that. In any case, Marion needs me now."

"*I* need you, Gwendolyn. The children here need you. What about your class?"

Gwen looked away. She'd known he'd play on her sympathies; the children were the one thing that gave her pause.

Herman went on. "The school year is well underway and there's been no decision made to close—even temporarily. With the uncertain outcome of the war and so many children's fathers away, with the imminent danger to every household from the Spanish flu . . . These children have formed strong attachments to you. You're their anchor, a mainstay in their formative years. A mainstay for me. You must understand why I cannot accept your resignation."

Before she'd gathered her wits, he stepped closer, reaching for her hands.

Gwen turned away, wishing she'd left the door open, a clear means of escape. *Duty, guilt, the privilege of sacrificing for those less fortunate—those considered worthy*. She knew every nuance, had lived her entire life caring for those who needed her.

But laced into this need of her sister's was also, at last, a chance to escape provincial Paradox, and to escape her employer's cloying advances. She would not allow Herman Sapp or anyone else to drive one more nail into the coffin of her soul.

"I'm giving two weeks' notice. That should be sufficient time to hire a substitute—until you find a full-time teacher. You may not even need someone soon if the mayor decides to close schools until the epidemic passes. In any case, I'll leave detailed notes concerning each student, and of course, my curriculum guides."

She made for the door, but he was faster and leaned against it, crossing his arms.

"You're blocking my path."

He didn't move. Her heart's thrumming became louder, but she spoke softly, firmly. "Please. Step aside, Mr. Sapp."

"Can you look me in the eye and tell me you feel nothing for me, for the school, for the children here?"

She cared mightily about the school and the children she'd taught and mentored through the years. They were the only children she might ever claim. But they weren't her children, weren't her family.

Gwen lifted her chin, determined to stare him down. "What I feel has little to do with this. My sister needs me."

"Ah, yes." He smiled, now resorting to condescension. "The sister whose needs you supplied for years after your mother's death. The sister who deserted you." He seemed determined to drive the point home. "You want to see the world, as I recall. But you won't do that by tutoring youngsters in your sister's home, now will you? Do you not see history repeating itself?"

Gwen winced. She wished she'd never revealed that corner of her heart to Herman, to anyone, but what he said was true. *What I want—what I've always wanted—is to escape, to travel. I want to find love—to be loved. To see and experience the world, not just read about it, not just teach the details of its existence.*

For years she'd felt betrayed by Marion, had struggled with that betrayal. But Marion was her sister, and she needed Gwen now, as their mother had before. Besides, going to New York provided the first opportunity Gwen had seen in twelve years to change the trajectory of her life. She would take it, would grasp it with both hands.

"Open the door, Mr. Sapp. Consider your reputation, and mine." She spoke quietly, firmly, but it was a gamble. His reputation would not suffer from being behind a closed door with a spinster teacher. She refused to look him in the eye, refused to give him the power of any reaction he craved.

"You deserve a family of your own, Gwen. We could—"

"Open the door. Now." Her voice grew louder, her jaw hard. She waited, fists clenched at her sides, pressure building behind her eyes and in her temples. A shred of doubt in his decency ran through her brain, but she stood her ground.

He took one step closer. "Consider carefully what you are doing, Miss Armstrong. My offer of marriage stands. You have these two weeks to reconsider. Know that if you abandon your post, you cannot expect to return. No other school will have you . . . I promise. My offer won't be repeated."

It seemed forever, but at last the door opened, and Gwen, head held high and legs trembling, walked through it.

Gwen bought her train ticket and wrote to her sister of her travel plans the following morning, knowing she might not receive a reply. *Marion can be unresponsive, but at least she'll know I'm coming.*

She waited to tell her students of her leaving until her last afternoon. She'd never been good with goodbyes. Prolonging the experience would not help them or her. There were pleas not to go. Gwen told them truthfully that her sick sister needed her. She assured them that Mr. Sapp, whom she'd done her best to avoid for two weeks, would find them a good teacher, a kind teacher, and that all would be well. She hoped her promises proved true.

Gwen had arranged to let her cottage out to a second-grade teacher for the remainder of the semester, a young woman in her first year of teaching. In January they would review terms with the hope that their arrangement might continue indefinitely.

While she believed she would not return to Paradox, especially knowing Herman would make certain she could never teach in the town again, Gwen dared not sell her small house. It was the only thing left to her by her father, the only thing standing between herself and poverty. She'd learned the hard way not to count her chickens before they hatched, and not to burn her bridges. Her younger sister had taught her that in spades. Gwen could only hope, as Herman predicted, that history would not repeat itself.

2

By the time Gwen donned the gauze face mask recommended by the US Public Health Service as a precaution against the spread of the influenza and boarded the train—known itself to be risky for infection—she'd still received no reply to her letter alerting Marion of her arrival date and time. Gwen didn't consider that strange. While she was a planner, a plotter, a detail person, Marion was more of a live-in-the-moment and respond-in-the-heat-of-the-moment type—at least that's how Gwen remembered her. Marion had seldom written since her marriage—mostly Christmas cards, announcements of her children's births, and in response to their father's passing coupled with her plea for help.

She only hoped Marion would send the promised car to pick her up once the train arrived at the New York City station. She'd promised a great deal in her letter—a great deal that Gwen was now counting on. Was she holding too much hope in her sister's words? She hadn't seen Marion in twelve years—not since Marion fled Paradox to marry Russell Bennett.

Gwen dug her sister's letter from her purse, once more searching its contents for clues.

Dearest Gwen,

Thank you for your letter telling me of Father's passing. I'm sorry for how long he suffered, and for how you have borne the brunt of that suffering.

I hope he found it in his heart to forgive me for leaving all those years ago. If not, he now knows I've paid times over for my misdeeds. Perhaps he'll find some satisfaction in that.

I'm following in Mama's footsteps, Gwen—consumption. Though I've put it off—and will continue to do so for as long as possible—Dr. Callahan, our family doctor, urges me to go to the sanatorium to rest and take the cure. Only, as you and I know, there will be no cure. While I'm tired of this wasting body, I cannot bear to think of leaving my children for even the month he prescribes without a strong hand at the helm of their uncertain ship.

So, I must ask you, Sister—will you come to me? I know you stand on the threshold of gaining your own life at last, but I've nowhere else to turn. Russell is away much of the time, consumed with business and all that entails. With your help and support, I feel certain I can get stronger, better. We could have the time together we've never shared as women.

You will have read that New York, like so many places, is ravaged with the Spanish influenza, and yet the schools here remain open. Our mayor believes there is greater danger of the influenza's spread in keeping children home in confined houses than in classrooms.

Influenza would prove more than my body can take, and I refuse to send my children to school, to put them at such risk. They need a tutor. They need their aunt—the one person I can trust not to toy with their affections or with the eyes of my husband. I need my sister.

Of course, you will have your own bedroom and sitting room here at Bennett Place, a substantial salary, and a day and a half each week to yourself. You will love New York,

Gwen, once this horrid influenza subsides, as it surely must. There is so much to do and see here, and although I cannot share in those outings, I can introduce you to wonderful people. Living in New York, even for a few months, could open doors you've never dreamed of, perhaps even doors that lead to romance.

Write soon. Say you'll come. I'll send a car to meet you at the station.

Above all, please pray for me.

Your sister,
Marion

Gwen hoped she wasn't making a gigantic mistake. As a girl, Marion had been known to detail all kinds of wonderful, exuberant plans that rang with the joy of possibility—and then to let them drift away, like so many leaves after a violent summer storm, before she was on to the next exciting thing.

Gwen, on the other hand, had been the steady one. She'd had no choice. When their mother had been transferred to the sanatorium, Gwen had quit school to keep house for her father and care for her little sister. She'd done it willingly, only able to return to her education once Marion was older. She'd barely finished normal school, had taken some college courses and begun teaching her first class, when her sister—the one who'd pledged to take up the gauntlet at home as soon as she finished school—flew into marriage.

But that was before Marion had borne children . . . before consumption. *Surely those things have changed her, haven't they? Her letter sounds sincere, desperate even. And she asked for prayer, something I can't remember Marion ever doing.*

Gwen shifted her face mask so she could better breathe, then shifted in her seat, trying to find a more comfortable position. She checked her wristwatch. Two more hours to New York. *Have I been too quick to jump, so eager to leave my life that I've not been discerning?*

I should have waited for Marion to reply to my letter. What if she's had a change of mind, a change of heart? Or . . . what if she's remembered that I carried a torch for Russell all those years ago . . . and, I thought, he for me? Is that what she means about trusting me not to toy with the eyes of her husband? Is that a warning, innuendo?

Gwen's head ached. She kneaded the back of her neck. *Marion was so young and self-absorbed, so smitten with Russell in those days, she probably never took to heart how I loved him, had my hopes set on him. But he knew. Does he remember?*

Her throat went dry. She was on her way to live in the home that she'd once hoped might be hers, to teach the children of the man she'd once believed might be her husband—until his eyes fell on her younger sister. Now that she was about to step into that fire, Gwen wasn't at all certain she should.

Dusk fell as the train slowed to a stop, but there was no station by the side of the tracks. A hubbub of speculation ran the length of the car until a porter stepped up to announce a momentary irregularity, apologizing, asking for everyone's patience.

Trains were often delayed because of the war effort and the movement of troops, so there were low expectations for on-time arrivals and few gripes. Still, Gwen prayed the delay wouldn't be long. She didn't want to keep Marion's driver waiting, and she hated wearing the mask for hours at a time, necessary though it was deemed to be.

Half an hour later, the porter reappeared, less comfortable with his announcement. "Sorry to say we've encountered a bit of engine trouble, folks. Should be fixed shortly. Please sit back and relax."

Now there were gripes, expletives. Out came cigars and cigarettes. Several men lit up, puffing through holes worked into their masks, filling the car with the dense smoke of tobacco. Gwen could hardly breathe and opened her window to a myriad of grumbles and complaints that it was too cold for such nonsense. She closed the window.

There was speculation that smoking cigarettes prevented contagion. She didn't believe it.

Two hours later, a weary and smoke-saturated Gwen stepped down from the train in New York amid a sea of passengers doing the same, only they hurried away, seeming to know exactly where they were going.

She searched the faintly lit length of the platform for a familiar face or at least a printed sign bearing her name or the Bennett family name. Seeing nothing, she checked the empty waiting room, then searched in vain for a night clerk at the information desk. There was no chauffeur or anyone at all waiting for Gwen, the station finally empty of all but a few characters she didn't dare approach. She checked the platform once more.

Awkward. And frightening. Do I just show up on their doorstep? How would I even do that? Has Marion not told Russell that she's invited me? Begged me to come? Surely, he would have sent someone to meet me. Gwen's temples began to throb. *It would be just like Marion to come up with this idea, plead her case, then toss it to the wind. I've given up my job, for pity's sake!*

"Can I help you, miss?" A last masked porter leaving the train tipped his cap, startling Gwen.

"What?" Gwen could hardly focus.

"You look like you could do with a bit of help, miss. Are you lost?" His voice came muffled from behind his mask.

"No. I'm not lost. I'm just not found." Gwen sighed.

He cocked his head, questioning.

"I think I need a cab. Can you direct me to a cab?" Gwen was tempted to confide in the first person who looked in any way kind or interested or sympathetic but, knowing better, held her tongue.

"Bit late for that. Cabs, like everybody else, are running in shifts these days. We might find one. Right this way, ma'am. Let me carry that bag for you." He hefted Gwen's heavy case as if it weighed nothing and strode the length of the platform, into the station, and up a flight of stairs to the darkened street. Gwen followed, uneasy but grateful for someone else to do the heavy lifting, to take charge, even if it was only to help her find transportation.

The porter hailed a lone taxi waiting half a block outside the station. He placed Gwen's case in the trunk of the car, opened the back seat door for her, and tipped his cap.

"Thank you. Thank you very much." Gwen had hoped she'd feel a competent woman stepping into New York, but in truth she felt like a ten-year-old girl, overwhelmed by the night, the looming city, and the newness of it all.

At least she had the presence of mind to slip the man fifty cents, then wondered if that was enough, or too much. She pasted on a smile, thanked him again, and digging her sister's envelope from her purse, gave the driver the address.

That settled, Gwen leaned back into the leather seat, clutched her purse, and tightened her mask across her nose. Her school hadn't required masks, though most schools and many cities did. Gwen didn't know if New York was one of those. Still, she'd not take chances in going to her sister's house. *Influenza mixed with tuberculosis would be deadly.*

So many questions. So many things she didn't know. Gwen closed her eyes, and before falling asleep, much against her will, reminded herself of the admonition her mother had repeated in one of the last letters she'd sent Gwen from the sanatorium.

"It doesn't matter if you're afraid, my girl. We're all afraid. Remember, you can't go anywhere until you open the door and take that first step. Once you've mastered that, take another."

"This is it, lady. Sure you've got the right address?"

Gwen pulled herself together. The masked cabbie searched her eyes in his rearview mirror. *Eyes are now the main body language. Surprising how much you can tell from eyes alone.*

Gwen looked out the window. She knew that her sister had

married into Russell's family's money, but the house that loomed at the end of the long drive ran beyond Gwen's imagination, and she'd always had a good one. An iron gated entry bore a sign: *No Admittance—Quarantined.* The entrance led down a straight drive to the imposing house—more a mansion—standing three stories above street level. Closed drapes covered every floor-to-ceiling window, except one, which glowed with electric light, a beacon in the darkness. *We don't even have electricity at home.*

"Lady?" The cabbie looked concerned—or irritable. Gwen wasn't sure which.

She checked the address on her envelope against the plaque by the gate, barely illuminated by the streetlight. "Bennett Place. Yes, yes, this is it. Please see if the gate is locked. They're expecting me."

Reluctantly, she thought, he left his cab and pushed open the gate. *At least it's not locked. That's a sign I'm expected, surely.*

"Right." He drove in, hopped again from the cab, and quickly pulled her case from his trunk, setting it atop the landing by the door. Taking a deep breath, she stepped onto the walkway, ready with his payment.

He tipped his cap, raised his eyebrows, as if to say, *You sure about this?* and left as quickly as he could.

Gwen walked slowly up the steps to the front door. Not having seen Marion or Russell in twelve years, she pictured them as she'd last seen them, back in Paradox. He, devilishly handsome, taller even than she, dark hair, dark eyes, and a smile that would charm the roller skates off a child, or the wits from a grown woman. Marion—petite, a waist so small Russell could nearly encircle it with his two hands, curves that called for attention, flaming red hair, and bewitching green eyes. *They certainly bewitched Russell, even after I thought we'd formed an understanding, or the beginning of one. Marion took after Mother in her looks—all the McGurty women were delicate, beautiful. Marion's not only a classic McGurty, she was born a classic McFlirty. Russell certainly fell hard for her the moment she teased him with those "bewitching green eyes."*

Gwen shook herself from more than the early October night's chill. *This will never do. That was all so long ago—ancient history. Get yourself together, my girl. You're here to help your sister, your very ill sister, and to get to know your niece and nephew, to teach them. For no other reason. No other reason.*

Gwen straightened her shoulders, tugged her coat into place, moistened her lips, and turned the bell by the door.

"What do you mean Mrs. Bennett's no longer here?" Gwen could not quell the panic rising within her or lower the springing octave in her voice. Standing in the middle of the grand foyer, beneath a gigantic crystal chandelier and a ceiling that loomed three stories above, she dizzied, forced herself to breathe—barely, before nearly tripping over her case. *Did she go quickly in the end, like Mother?*

The older woman standing before her in night wrap and curlers looked as if she had no clue as to Gwen's near hysterics.

"Mrs. Bennett mentioned some weeks past that she planned to write to her sister in Pennsylvania, but gave no indication that arrangements were made. They took her . . . oh, it must be ten days past. As you can imagine, having left no directions, we've all been in a bit of a state, trying to piece things together as she'd wish to have done."

"Please. Did she suffer? Did my sister suffer?"

"I beg your pardon?" The woman's Scottish accent came strong.

"Did she pass peacefully? I've just buried my father . . . now my sister? Please tell me, did she suffer?" *Dear God, say it isn't so. Please.*

"Pass? Oh, no, I'm so very sorry, ma'am. Mrs. Bennett's gone to the sanatorium, for a rest, to take the cure. She's ill, but still very much alive." The woman looked distressed, surprised to have been misunderstood, and reached a steadying hand to Gwen. "I never meant to give such a fright."

Gwen's heart nearly stopped. Her legs so quivered in relief that she thought she might not stand. She might cry.

"Come, come into the drawing room. The fire may not have died altogether. It's likely still warm there."

The woman led Gwen into the first room on the left, a room so huge Gwen briefly closed her eyes. *My entire house could fit into this one room.*

"Let me take your coat. Sit here, by the fire, Mrs.—"

"Armstrong. Miss Armstrong, Marion's sister. She wrote to me, asked me to come, to be with her, to tutor the children. She promised to send a car to the station. Oh, have I already said that? I'm sorry—"

"You're weary from your travels now, Miss Armstrong, and I've given you a terrible shock, though surely I never intended to. Shall I bring you a cup of tea and a wee bite to eat?"

"Yes, please. I'm famished. The train was delayed, and there was no seating in the dining car."

The woman grimaced slightly, and Gwen realized that requesting food and drink at ten o'clock at night might be inconvenient. The woman, after all, appeared to be in her late fifties or early sixties, and was dressed for bed.

"Oh, please, never mind. I'm quite all right until morning."

"Nonsense. You must have something. Let me fetch tea and then we'll sort things through. Rest now. That's all that matters in the moment." The woman hesitated by the door. "I'm Mrs. Barrie, housekeeper for Mr. and Mrs. Bennett. I'm sorry there was no one to meet you. Our chauffeur took ill a week past . . . He was buried on Monday. The influenza."

"Influenza? Has anyone else—"

"Not in this house. We're most careful. He'd gone home to check on his family and never came back, poor man."

Her mind reeling, Gwen nodded, and obediently sank into the deep leather armchair nearest the ebbing fire. *Yes, poor man. A wicked death.*

The heat soothed Gwen's bones even as her mind circled the points of the compass. *If Marion left ten days ago, she may not have received my letter . . . so neither she nor Russell knew I was coming. With Marion gone, how can I stay in the house with Russell? But I'm likely more needed than before. Dear God, please watch over Marion, and please, step into this conundrum. I can't fix this; only You can sort this through.*

Gwen startled as Mrs. Barrie set a small table by her chair containing tea and toasted bread and cheese cut into triangles. "Oh. I can't believe I fell asleep." She tried to shake the fog from her brain.

"You've suffered a long day," Mrs. Barrie soothed, pouring Gwen's tea. "I'm afraid it's not much, just a bit of Scots rabbit this time of night. Cook's off to bed. Cream? Sugar? One lump or two?"

"Sugar only—one, please." Gratefully, Gwen accepted the cup and even more gratefully the warm cheese toast. *Scots rabbit? Like Welsh rarebit?*

"All the way from Paradox, you said?"

"Yes. I wrote my sister. Now I wonder if she received it before she left."

"Letters have arrived for Mrs. Bennett, but since she'd gone, they're awaiting Mr. Bennett's return."

"He's not home?"

"Away on business." Mrs. Barrie's mouth straightened again in disapproval, but disapproval of what, Gwen wasn't sure.

"Please, Mrs. Barrie, is there some way I can see Marion, talk with her?"

Mrs. Barrie sighed. "Not tonight, surely. Even tomorrow, I don't see how that will be possible. Dr. Callahan left word that only Mr. Bennett is allowed to visit—when he's here—and that but once a week on Sunday afternoon. It's best, he said, that Mrs. Bennett rest."

Gwen bit her lower lip and shook her head. "Then, how am I to—"

"She can receive letters, and the post here is very good. It should only take a day to reach her." Mrs. Barrie's forehead wrinkled. "Are you staying nearby?"

Gwen nearly dropped her teacup. "My sister said she'd have rooms prepared here for me—a bedroom and sitting room." She couldn't mention the promised "generous salary" to Marion's housekeeper. That wouldn't be proper, but the salary was imperative.

Mrs. Barrie's brows rose. "Did she, then? I see."

But Gwen wasn't at all certain the woman did see. *Should I show her Marion's letter? This situation is untenable. How advanced is the disease that Marion couldn't put off the sanatorium?*

"We'll see to the rooms directly, Miss Armstrong, if you don't mind resting here for a bit. I'm sure Mr. Bennett will sort everything upon his return."

I'm sure he will, but what does that even mean? "When do you expect him?"

"Well, of course we never know for certain, but I expect within the fortnight."

"Two weeks?" Gwen gasped, setting down her teacup.

"Possibly sooner. He . . ." Mrs. Barrie hesitated. "He comes and goes—very busy with his work, his business. I'm sure we'll all make do until then."

"Make do," Gwen repeated, her heart sinking. *What else is there?*

3

In that hazy place between dreaming and waking, Gwen was ten again—the year before her mother died, before she'd been withdrawn from school to care for Marion.

"You must learn to boil eggs, Gwendolyn," her domestic science teacher insisted.

"But I know how to boil eggs. I was born knowing."

A ruler slap across her fingers. "Insolent girl!"

Gwen winced. She wasn't being insolent. She knew how to boil eggs, to scramble eggs, to poach eggs, to fry and flip them. She knew those things as instinctively as she knew how to toast and butter bread or make tea or brew coffee or cobble together a meal from whatever was left in the sparse larder from the day before.

She'd been doing all those things ever since her mother began coughing so hard her body shook, staining her handkerchief in blood, unable to stand. Ever since Marion was born. Mother contracting consumption and Marion entering the world—a screaming infant in constant need of comfort, demanding endless bottles of milk, desperate to burp, continually in need of diaper changes—merged as one and the same in Gwen's mind. Didn't Teacher know that?

The scene changed, and Marion, now six, and Gwen, eleven, stood at their mother's open grave as Father, still unsteady from his bout of drinking the night before, cast a clod of dirt upon the closed lid of the casket. He handed a clod to Marion, who dutifully threw it atop the lowered casket, creating a loud thud. He held one out to Gwen, but Gwen refused to accept it, which embarrassed Father, making him angry.

Gwen was angry too—angry with her mother for leaving them, for counting on her to grow up overnight and keep house for Father, who was just as likely to deposit his paycheck with the local liquor store as he was to bring it home, and care for Marion without so much as her guidance. She was angry with Father, who expected her to throw dirt where Mother's face should be—the only physical image she held of her mother, the last thing she could remember.

She turned to take Marion's hand and run to the carriage, but Marion was gone. Frantic, Gwen called for her little sister. She searched behind trees, calling her name over and over, tearing through the graveyard, skirting tombstones, tripping over tributes of flowers. "Marion! Marion! Where are you? Come back to me!"

"Where did you come from?" The voice—feathery, young, insolent, insistent—pulled Gwen up, up, out of the mire of dream drowning.

"Marion?" she whispered. Gwen fought sleep, struggled to open her eyes.

A tousle of flaming red hair, bright green eyes, a Cupid's bow mouth, and tiny ginger freckles appeared before her face. There, bending over her bed, stood Marion—or the image of Marion—at six. Gwen's heart triple beat.

"I said," the sprite repeated, "who are you and what are you doing in Miss Eberly's bed?"

Gwen blinked, gathering her wits, and pushed up on her elbows. "Marion's daughter. You must be Marion's daughter."

"Of course. I'm Clara. But who are you?"

"I'm your mother's sister, your aunt—Aunt Gwendolyn."

The girl scrunched her nose and looked doubtful, which made Gwen think all the more of Marion.

A male voice hissed from the hallway. "Clara! Mrs. Barrie said we're not to go in."

The little girl ignored him.

"Is that your brother?" Gwen was wide-awake now.

The sprite shrugged. "You don't look like Mother. Sisters are supposed to look like each other."

Gwen opened her mouth to respond, but the little girl continued. "Mother went away."

"I know. I'm very sorry not to see her, but I hope it means she'll get better soon and come home." Gwen hoped her tone held more promise than she felt.

"Mother sent the last governess away for making flirty eyes at Father—that's what she said. She'll send you away too, if you do that." The child crossed her arms and set her lips in a firm line.

"Clara!" the boy called again from the hallway. "That's rude."

"You might as well come in. She's awake," Clara called over her shoulder.

A head poked briefly through the doorway, then seeing Gwen still in bed, ducked his flaming face behind the doorframe. "Sorry," he said.

Gwen pulled the comforter to her chin. "Yes, do come in."

A tousle-headed, dark-haired boy of ten or so peered round the edge of the doorway again, momentarily paused, then stepped into the room. "Clara shouldn't have bothered you. Mrs. Barrie told us to give you time and space this morning."

"Thank you. That's very kind of Mrs. Barrie, but I'm glad to meet you. I take it you're—"

"Alistair." The boy dutifully came forward, extending his hand.

Gwen kept her smile to herself but met the outstretched hand. "And I'm your aunt, Gwendolyn—Aunt Gwen."

"Mother's sister, so she says." Clara cocked her head to the side as if considering whether this could be so. "Though she doesn't look a bit like her."

"Mother said she takes after her mother, but you take after her father."

"Yes, that's right. Father—your grandfather—was tall, and dark haired, like me."

"You have brown eyes," Clara accused. "Mother has green eyes, like me."

"Right again, on both counts."

"I take after Father—my father." The boy stood a bit straighter.

Gwen observed, a fleeting sadness wending its way through her heart. "Yes, you do. Very much so." She shook the momentary melancholy away. It would never do to let the children know she'd ever held feelings for their father. That might be the first thing to get her *sent away.* "Well, now if you'll both excuse me, I'll make myself presentable for the day and meet you— Where shall I meet you?"

"In the breakfast room, of course." Clara unfolded her arms.

Gwen hoped there'd be more of an explanation.

"Just down the stairs and follow the hallway to the left of the foyer." Alistair steered his sister toward the door.

"Thank you, Alistair. I'll see you both shortly."

As they trooped into the hallway and before they shut the door, Gwen heard Clara hiss, "She's not Mother. I'm not going to like her."

"She's not meant to be Mother, but at least she's . . ." Alistair's voice trailed off down the hallway before Gwen could catch his last words.

At least I'm what? Gwen sighed. She didn't know. Still, she stretched, reached for her dressing gown, and put feet to floor. Not knowing was no reason to delay.

The night before, she'd been too tired and dumbfounded at Marion's departure to think things through. With her sister in the sanatorium and Russell away on business, she assumed she was in charge of the children. She needed to gain the lay of the land from Mrs. Barrie. That might be no easy task, given the limited information the woman had received about her, but it was clear that Clara, who resented her presence, was not going to help. She wondered if she might find an ally in Alistair. It was too soon to tell.

By the time Gwen made her way into the breakfast room, the children had finished their meal and disappeared.

Mrs. Barrie was just clearing the sideboard. "Oh, you've come. I thought you might sleep in after your travels and late night."

"I had early-morning visitors." Gwen's brows rose significantly.

"Oh, I told them not to disturb you." But Mrs. Barrie didn't sound very distressed—more like *the little dears.*

"I'm sure they were curious . . . after you told them I'd arrived."

"Well, yes," Mrs. Barrie admitted. "They miss their mother terribly. I thought it might comfort them to know she had arranged for their aunt to come." She hesitated. "I believe that's what you said."

Is that a challenge? "I'm sorry my sister didn't take you into her confidence."

Mrs. Barrie stiffened.

"I'll write to Marion today. In the meantime, I hope you'll be able to help me establish a routine with Clara and Alistair."

"Really, Miss Armstrong, there's no need. The children are well cared for. I've assisted Mrs. Bennett in looking after both since they were wee bairns. If I understand correctly, you will be tutoring them in their school studies. That's quite enough. I can show you the schoolroom Mrs. Bennett set up for—for the previous governess."

Governess? Gwen couldn't decide if Mrs. Barrie was being protective of the children or of her authority. In any case, she needed to talk—at least correspond—with Marion to fully understand her wishes since the circumstances had changed. Gwen's images of reading bedtime stories to the children and her hopes of outings in the park with her niece and nephew were quickly evaporating.

Great shafts of sunlight beamed through the windows of the open and airy schoolroom. Bookcases lined one wall, overflowing with children's books and classics for young people and also holding a basic chemistry set, a sturdy microscope, an abacus, music books, and small rhythm instruments. A baby grand piano and two music stands took up an entire corner, nearly a quarter of the room. Two student desks and a teacher's desk occupied the center of the room nearest the tall windows.

Flanking the large marble fireplace were two overstuffed chairs with side tables, each holding a lamp and room enough for books. A matching sofa faced the cheerfully burning fire. A low table lay before the sofa, spread with more books and an elaborately carved chess set. The entire arrangement created the perfect spot to sit and read or hold discussions in a small group. Deeply cushioned window seats provided private nooks for solitary reading or dreaming. The layout of the room was everything Gwen could imagine. In the carefully chosen colors and textures, she saw the absolute joy of her younger sister.

Gwen smiled at Alistair and Clara, who stood uncomfortably in the doorway. "Your mother loves this room, doesn't she?"

"It's our special place," Clara defended. "Mother made it for the three of us, not you."

"Clara." Alistair frowned.

"It's all right," Gwen assured the children. "Clara's right. I'm sure your mother made it with you both in mind, and I'm sure she loves to spend time with you here, whenever she can. I do see, because of the arrangement of the desks, that she intends lessons be held here. For that reason, and because she wrote, asking me to come and teach you during the epidemic, I believe she won't mind if I join you. I think she intends for us to work here together."

Clara blinked, her stance growing not quite so rigid. Gwen hoped she was gaining ground.

"I know your mother loves you very much and wants more than anything to come home to you. She wants to keep you both well and strong for your sakes, as well as for hers, so you can be together again soon. To keep you well is why you're no longer attending school. She's arranged to have school brought to you." Gwen smiled, stretching her arms to take in the room. "That's why she created this wonderful room."

"Yes," Alistair said. "That makes sense. That's what Mother wants."

Clara looked up at him, a tiny seed of trust in her eyes.

"So, let's do your mother proud. We'll work hard and show her all you learn."

"She's not here. She won't know," Clara stubbornly insisted, but not as angrily as before.

"Because she's not here, we must write her, each and every day, and share with her what we're doing, what we're learning. So, that's the first thing we'll do this morning. We'll each write your mother a letter."

"I don't know how to write—only my name." Clara's eyes clouded.

"Then tell me, and I'll write down whatever you want to say, and you can draw her a picture. I'm sure she needs some beautiful pictures to brighten her room."

Clara lifted her chin and swiped at her eyes, brimming with moisture. She reached for her brother's hand. "Alistair can write down what I want to tell Mother."

Gwen nodded, eyebrows raised in question to Alistair, who nodded in return. "Fine. Your mother will be comforted and encouraged by your letters. We'll post them together before lunch."

Gwen was pleased when she read over Alistair's letter. His penmanship and his ability to formulate sentences and paragraphs in coherent, complete thoughts bespoke a solid early education. She looked forward to learning more of what he'd been learning, what interested him.

She smiled at Clara's picture and dictated letter. Clearly, and naturally, the little girl wanted her mother to come home. The picture she drew showed her and Alistair and a grown-up lady leaning over them in a caring, perhaps teaching, position. Gwen assumed Clara had drawn her, but Clara insisted it was Mrs. Barrie. Gwen felt a twinge of jealousy, but understood, knowing Mrs. Barrie had been the ever-present figure in the children's lives. What she didn't understand was why their father was absent from the picture.

"Don't you want to include your papa?"

"Why? Father's hardly ever here." Clara folded her picture to place in the envelope Gwen provided.

That, Gwen thought, *might be the most telling revelation of all.*

Through the next few days, while Gwen felt she was making gentle headway with the children in the classroom, she still found nightly gifts of pine cones or burrs, or sand deposited in the foot of her bedsheets—reminders that she was not fully accepted or wanted, was being encouraged to go away. Once she found the laces of her oxford shoes bound together in knots only a six-year-old might tie. She never mentioned those gifts to Mrs. Barrie or even to the children come breakfast when asked how she'd slept, which clearly confounded Clara and amused Alistair. She could see a grudging respect growing in his eyes.

But the final straw came when Gwen opened her classroom desk drawer during a midweek history lesson only to find a dead rat, eyes wide open, staring up at her.

Gwen slammed the drawer shut, but to her credit, she reassured herself, did not scream.

Clara looked up with bright eyes—the same mischievous, vindictive glint Gwen remembered occasionally seeing in Marion's eyes at that age.

"Clara, I believe you've forgotten something."

Clara's brow rose.

"You've left something in my desk. I believe it belongs to you. You may come and get it."

Clara's face reddened; her eyes opened wide.

Alistair shot his sister a glance that told Gwen he was not party to this prank.

"I—I don't know what you mean," Clara stammered.

"We both know you do. Now, come and deal with this, or shall I ask Mrs. Barrie to remove it on your behalf? I cannot imagine she will enjoy that, or that she would like to know you did such a thing."

Clara looked trapped between a wall and the sea.

Alistair stood. "I did it, Aunt Gwen. I'll take care of it."

But Gwen blocked his approach to her desk. "Exactly what is it you will take care of, Alistair?"

"Wh-what I put in your desk drawer. I'm sorry. I won't do it again. Promise."

"You'll pick it up with your bare hands?"

Alistair visibly swallowed, glancing at his sister, who shook her head from side to side. "If I need to."

Gwen stood aside. "By all means, then. Take care of it. Of course, you understand there are consequences to every action."

Alistair swallowed again. "Yes, ma'am." He opened the desk drawer and gasped, his eyes flashing to his sister, accusing.

Gwen waited.

"I—I think I'll need something to pick it up with."

"Oh?" Gwen posed innocently. "Of course. Since you put it there, you can retrieve it in the same manner."

Alistair brushed his hands distastefully down his shirt and trousers, formed his lips into a grim line, and opened the drawer again.

"Wait!" Clara stood. "Don't touch it! Use the fire tongs!"

"So, now you do know what it is?" Gwen asked quietly.

Clara looked up, eyes filled with defiance. "Yes, I did it. I found it in the back garden trash."

"And used the fire tongs to carry it all the way here. How interesting. How resourceful. How unkind."

Clara's chin trembled. She glanced at Alistair, then back to Gwen. "I'm sorry. I—I shouldn't have done it."

"Why did you?" Gwen kept her voice even.

"Because I want you to go away. You're not Mother and I don't want you here."

"Clara," Alistair admonished.

"Well, it's true. It's true for you too, but you won't say it. I want Mother to come home."

Alistair's eyes shot between his sister and Gwen.

Gwen sighed. "I want that too, Clara. You've no idea how much I want that. But getting rid of me won't bring your mother home sooner. I don't want any more of these 'gifts.' Now, take the fire tongs and dispose of the rat."

"I'll do it, Aunt Gw—"

"Clara brought it in; she'll take it out to the burn pile. Fair enough, Clara?"

Clara nodded, though clearly not expecting her aunt meant it.

"Here, wrap it in this newspaper once you've pulled it out with the tongs."

Clara's spark disappeared as she slowly walked to her aunt's desk, accepted the newspaper, and retrieved the fire tongs.

Gwen made no protest when Alistair accompanied his sister out the door carrying the newspaper-shrouded deceased. She only wondered how long this wicked little dance might go on.

4

October 23, 1918

Dear Gwen,

I'm sorry I wasn't there to meet you and that I didn't make the arrangements I promised. Truly, I didn't know if you'd come. I don't deserve your coming, much as I'd hoped for it. You're my sister and were more mother to me than the mother who birthed us. I have so much—too much—to regret where you are concerned, and I'm sorry.

I will dictate a letter to Russell and urge him to honor my promises to you immediately. As soon as strength allows, I also will write Mrs. Barrie. She can be your ally in that house. And I will write Alistair and Clara today. They are good children though I know what a little minx my daughter can be. I'll tame her lioness heart as best I can from here.

This is all the strength I have for now. Thank you, Gwen, a thousand times thank you for caring for my little ones. God bless you.

Love,
Your Marion

Gwen folded the paper and returned it to its envelope. *"God bless you." What is your relationship with God, Marion? Have you found one?* She sighed. *What is mine?* She'd been disappointed with God for so long. She couldn't remember when she'd last prayed in full faith, done more than shot desperate pleas in moments of crisis. But she knew she'd need more than her own strength now, for this venture, wherever it led, whatever it meant. *Is this a journey toward reconciliation? For both of us? It's been a long time since she was "my Marion." How I loved her, as my sister, almost as a daughter, when we were young. What must I risk to love her this time? What exactly do you regret where I'm concerned, Marion? What are you sorry for? And what do you mean that Mrs. Barrie can be an ally in this house? Do I need one?*

That night, Gwen found no pine cones in her own bed, no sand between her sheets, no prickly burrs in her cardigan or candle wax in her tooth powder. The ribbon marking her place in the book she was reading had not been moved.

The morning revealed a quiet, almost contrite Clara—so much so that Gwen wondered if the little girl was sick.

"I'm not sick," Clara pouted when Gwen asked. "I'm just being good, as Mother wrote I should." She looked up at Gwen with her deep green eyes. "Mother said you're here to help and that she wants us to trust you and not drive you away, like we . . ."

"Like you what? Or whom?"

Clara and Alistair exchanged guilty glances.

"We might have helped Miss Eberly decide to leave," Alistair confessed.

"I thought you said your mother sent her away," Gwen remembered.

"Well, she did send her away."

"For making flirty eyes at Father!" Clara interjected. "She was always leaving us to ourselves and chatting up Father whenever he was home, and it hurt Mother." Gwen saw the young lioness Marion wrote of spring in Clara's eyes. "We'll not allow anyone to hurt Mother."

"But Mother said in her letter to us that you aren't like Miss Eberly—at all. She said you won't betray her trust." Alistair surely quoted, for Gwen could hear Marion's determined voice in that, her warning voice.

"No, I won't betray your mother's trust, or yours. Can we begin again, do you think? Can you trust me?"

Alistair nodded.

"Clara?"

Clara sighed, but nodded, whispering, "Still, you're not our mother."

"I'm not trying to be—will never try to be. I'm your aunt, and for now, your teacher. Things won't always be this way. One day your mother will come home, and one day, when this epidemic is past, you'll return to school. But for now, we make the best of things. Agreed?"

Clara nodded more willingly.

"Now that we've settled that, we'll end today's lessons by writing your mother again, telling her what we've been working on. Tomorrow, we'll talk about your father. He'd surely like a letter as well." Gwen smiled. "Mrs. Barrie tells me he works with Egyptian antiquities."

"Sells them!" Alistair chimed in. "He travels to Egypt and buys wonderful old things discovered in the pyramids and sells them to collectors here in America."

Gwen remembered Russell's longtime work and fascination with Egyptian artifacts. It was one of the exotic things that had initially drawn her to him. But she frowned. "He can't be traveling to Egypt now, not with a war on."

"No," Alistair agreed, "but he still meets with dealers and buyers. He used to work with Mr. Davis, the great explorer, and he travels a great deal."

"Theodore Davis?" Gwen remembered the name from the first lecture she'd heard Russell give. Anyone interested in Egyptology and Egyptian antiquities knew the name, had followed his years of work in the Valley of the Kings. Dead now, the man had sponsored more than a dozen digs making spectacular finds. Russell had been agog over his early—and perhaps greatest—discovery in 1905, the year he'd met the wealthy man in Egypt.

She remembered reading in the papers that before the war cut off excavations in Egypt, Davis had turned in his shovel, boasting that he'd dug the Valley of the Kings through and that there was nothing left to discover. Gwen felt certain his advanced age must have had something to do with that decision. *Surely, there is always more to discover.*

"He's never here," Clara complained. "And when he is, he doesn't have time for us, or Mother."

"That's disloyal, Clara," Alistair reprimanded. "He'd be here if he could. Grown men have business to take care of—that's what Mother always says. His work is important. She says we should pray for him."

Clara looked away, not convinced. "Mrs. Barrie thinks he's a spy for the war. That's why those men come and go sometimes, but only when the moon is right."

"Clara!" Alistair warned. "We're not to speak of that."

Gwen felt her eyes widen but deemed it best not to pursue that line of discussion. She couldn't imagine Mrs. Barrie was serious or, if she were, that she would be so indiscreet—more a story to tell the children. *But who are the men Clara speaks of, and what is this coming and going when the moon is right? Is that a fairy story too?*

On the other hand, Gwen could imagine Russell as a daring and handsome spy. It sent a thrill up her spine, a thrill she'd not known in a very long time. "Well, perhaps you can draw pictures of some of those antiquities, or of the pyramids you imagine they might come from. I'm sure he'd like that."

"Clara's a great artist, aren't you, Clara?" Alistair's boast changed the subject and brightened his sister's face.

"I'm going to work with Alistair when I grow up—going to draw his discoveries."

"Are you?" Gwen was more interested than amused and glad to change the subject. It was the first time Clara had confided a dream of any kind.

"When he's digging in Egypt."

"That's right. Clara will be right beside me. Father promised that one day he would take me with him on one of his trips. I'm going to all the sites and I'm going to get to know the real archaeologists—not just the men who fund them. Father promised he'd introduce me."

"Father buys things from them—or somebody there, but Alistair's going to do the real thing, the real digging and discovering." Clara's round eyes held full sincerity and belief in her brother.

"Then that's what you both should draw. Draw your dreams. Write about them, make them as real in your minds as you possibly can. That's the first step." Gwen believed that, had at one time practiced it, though that was long ago. If she could do one thing for her niece and nephew in the wake of an absent father and a perhaps dying mother, she would try to instill the determination not only to dream but to look and walk forward in pursuit of those dreams.

Life might challenge or change their aspirations, keep them from becoming reality. But dreams meant hope, and hope, Gwen knew, was desperately needed when life around you, life and the people you've depended upon, were falling apart.

After Mrs. Barrie received a letter from Marion detailing Gwen's duties as well as her own where the children were concerned, Gwen hoped a truce could be formed with the housekeeper. Mrs. Barrie still held Gwen at arm's length, but Gwen imagined that might simply be the woman's Scottish reserve. She waited three days before approaching the housekeeper.

"An alliance, Mrs. Barrie—that's what we need where Alistair and Clara are concerned." Gwen spoke privately to the housekeeper after breakfast. "Seeing us as a united front, knowing they can count on either of us and on both of us together, can only help them feel more secure in this situation. There's no telling how long their mother might be away." *Or their father.*

"Miss Armstrong, there's been no security for these children for a frightfully long while."

"Because of my sister's illness." It was a statement, but Gwen still felt as if she didn't have a grasp on how long or how seriously Marion had been consumptive. Their mother, after all, had lasted six years.

"That, of course, unsettles them, frightens them. But—" Mrs. Barrie stopped.

"But what? What else is there?" Gwen couldn't put her finger on it, but Mrs. Barrie seemed wary of something beyond her employer's illness. "Because their father is frequently away?"

Something lit in Mrs. Barrie's eyes, but again, Gwen could not define what. "Away . . . and busy when here." The woman smoothed her hands down her aproned front, as if wanting to rid herself of whatever that busyness might be. "You're right, of course. We must do what is best for the children." Mrs. Barrie hesitated, a hesitation Gwen could not interpret, and left the room.

Gwen puzzled over their conversation all day, while she worked with Clara on her reading in the morning and, later in the afternoon, as she worked with Alistair on his first venture into algebra. She thought about it as she smiled over dinner with the children—a time of day that had grown much more comfortable—while they chattered and made plans to build a fort in the library after lessons the next day.

Late that evening, long after Mrs. Barrie had seen the children off to bed and said good night, Gwen sat alone in the schoolroom, ostensibly working on lesson plans and outlining projects she thought might interest the children as they approached Thanksgiving. Weary and unsettled, she pushed her lesson plans aside and closed her eyes.

Two weeks had passed since she'd had the children write letters and draw pictures that they'd mailed to their father in care of his lawyer—the only address Marion or Mrs. Barrie had for him. Two weeks and still no word from him, not even a postcard to his children. *Why? What is Russell involved in that keeps him from his family for weeks on end? Could he be working for the government in some way—truly a spy? Surely not. Could he be unwell?*

A door opening and closing, perhaps the front door, snapped her to attention. Rapid footsteps across the foyer tiles, more than one set, came closer then faded into the distance, along with muffled voices. *Who could be up this time of night? Day workers and supporting staff have long gone home. The household staff retired into servants' quarters hours ago. Anyway, they wouldn't use the front door.* She waited, listening, but heard nothing more. Perhaps she'd been dreaming. Weary, she couldn't be certain she hadn't.

Gwen turned off the schoolroom lamp, lit a candle from the dying embers in the fire, and walked softly to the door. The house was quiet except for the ticking of the great clock in the hall as its pendulum swung to and fro, chiming the quarter hour.

Gwen shook her head; surely, she must have been imagining things. She'd reached the bottom of the grand staircase, ready to go up, when another door opened and closed. She couldn't tell which direction it came from. Sounds tended to echo in the cavernous foyer, and she'd never been alone on the main floor this time of evening. Great houses were notorious for curious sounds in the night.

In all the time she'd spent in the home, Gwen had never ventured into Russell's domain. She'd considered the west wing and its closed doors off-limits—not because Mrs. Barrie had forbidden entry, but as a matter of respect and consideration, especially after what the children had said. After all, her work did not demand or invite exploration of the family's business, and a man's home office was his private domain—at least that's what her father had always said, though she well knew his demand for privacy afforded him time and space to drink unobserved. Besides, she'd assumed Russell's office was locked. Still, she wondered about that wing.

Alistair had said that his father kept the most valuable artifacts in display cases, under lock and key. They were never allowed to go into his museum or office unless he invited them, an occurrence so rare he couldn't remember the last time he'd been inside.

What could be the harm of looking? I'd love to see those mysterious artifacts, invited or not.

Gwen smiled at her own cloak-and-dagger imagination and her recognition that what she was really looking for was an excuse to go exploring. Teaching and getting to know her niece and nephew had become a pleasure, especially after years of caregiving for her aging and cantankerous father. Even so, being so confined to the house and grounds due to the epidemic felt, well, confining. *A little mystery doesn't come amiss. I probably can't even get in. The door is surely locked. But it can't hurt to try.*

Grinning at her own audacity, she tiptoed across the foyer and down the hallway leading to the west wing. No fire had been lit in this dark end of the house for weeks, and frugal Mrs. Barrie wasn't about to turn on the radiators there until it was "truly necessary." The chilly hallway sent goose bumps up Gwen's arms. She made her way, the candle's flame dancing, casting strange shadows and giving just enough light to count the closed doors. *What could possibly be behind all these doors? What are all these rooms used for? Guest rooms?*

Alistair said his father's museum leading to his office is the last door.

The door at the end of the hallway was larger, wider than any of the others, its very nature and location intimidating. She tried the knob, expecting it to remain steady. But it turned easily in her hand. Before she considered the consequences, she stepped inside.

Every drape was closed. Not a sliver of moonlight found its way in. Only the glow from her candle illuminated her corner of the room—a room looming far larger than Gwen had imagined. Cavernous, its ceiling high and domed, its walls covered in tapestries. Wooden shelves with glass cases lined aisles throughout the room. In the center of the room a hexagonal glass case reached two stories high, filled with artifacts she couldn't identify—artifacts not yet labeled or deliberately displayed.

Gwen shivered at the discovery, sending a trail of hot wax down her hand and an involuntary yelp from her throat. She swiped at the wax with her other hand but stood still, doing her best to process the shadows and rarities before her. *A dream. It's like a dream.* Gwen stepped deeper into the room.

Drawn to the locked glass display cases nearest, she began a slow and methodical study. She'd expected a fine but modest collection, but these were so exotic, so rare—and so many. *They should be housed in a museum. How could he have collected all this—and have purchased more to sell? He would have to have acquired them before the Great War. He can't be traveling to Egypt, not now. When we met, he'd only just begun his collection and his association with Theodore Davis. Working with Davis was his dream, but that gave him, what, eight or nine years before the war began to acquire all this? Even with his family's wealth, how did he find the income?*

Gwen's breath caught as she read the dates beneath artifacts. Her mind raced at the very idea that such mementos of the ancient past had not only been preserved but sat before her in this house in New York—out of time and place. That she could see them and, but for the glass that locked them away, might be able to touch them, to hold a piece of ancient Egypt in her hand, sent quivers through her mind.

This thrill of history, the thrill of the exotic—this is exactly what drew me to Russell. Those lectures he gave at the university about Davis's discoveries, the fire in his voice, the light in his eyes. His passion for exploration, for uncovering secrets of long ago. Does Marion share this with him? Does she appreciate this? Does she understand the importance of his work?

She ran her fingers over glass case tops, reading the inscriptions housed inside. *An oil lamp from the time of Christ, this one found in Jerusalem. A faience bowl from Egypt. Fragments of everyday objects—a comb, a cup, an ornament that might have graced a woman's hair.* She straightened to view the next display, higher on the wall—a painting of an Egyptian royal. A band of blue and green stones set in gold encircled her arm. *An armlet, perhaps worn by a princess.*

And that ignited a memory—a memory she'd pushed away each time it emerged. She'd been auditing summer classes, indulging in her own fascination with Egyptology, all the rage at the time. Russell had been invited to give a series of lectures on the recent work in Egyptian digs, those sponsored by American investors, particularly Theodore Davis and his recent discovery of the magnificent tomb of a chief officer in the Egyptian chariotry, Yuya, and his wife, Thuyu.

Photographs of the tomb alone were breathtaking, its treasures beyond comprehension. Russell had said the tomb's occupants were the grandparents of Akhenaten, known as the "heretic king" for his revolutionary beliefs. They were the great-grandparents of King Tutankhamen. Gwen had never seen or heard anything like it, and like many of the listeners in the room, she dreamed of one day traveling to Egypt to join in the adventure.

In appreciation for the photographs and Egyptian artifacts loaned by benefactors for a two-month display, the university had hosted a ball, a masquerade given in Russell's honor.

Gwen, like at least a half dozen other women, dressed as Cleopatra, queen of Egypt. Unlike other women, the role suited her. Besides being tall and slender, her raven-black hair, dark eyes, long lashes, and a slight olive cast to her skin, inherited from her father, set her apart. It was one of those rare moments in life when Gwen knew she was beautiful.

What she'd not anticipated was that Russell would come dressed as Mark Antony. When he'd asked her to dance, she saw in the eyes of other men and women that they made a striking couple, waltzing across the floor. More than that, she saw her beauty reflected in Russell's eyes, in the flash of his smile, in the quickness of his breath.

Over the days of his lectures, they'd enjoyed intellectually stimulating discussions among peers at afternoon teas—three, to be exact. Gwen had counted them, gone over them in her mind a dozen times. But as they'd danced at the ball, she sensed their relationship would lead to far more than intellectual sparring. He filled her dance card, to the chagrin of every woman there. They talked into the early hours of the morning and corresponded almost daily after he left. Within the month he'd all but pledged his life to her. Letters flew between them for weeks following, even telegrams; they exchanged locks of hair by mail.

So certain was Gwen of their relationship that she'd invited him home to Paradox to meet her father and sister before her fall teaching semester began. He was eager, saying he needed to talk privately with her father. *Surely, to ask permission for my hand. Why else? Until his eyes fell on Marion . . . Until hers fell on him.*

Despite all her determination to put that past behind her, Gwen whispered, "Where are you now, Mark Antony?"

"Here. Right here—my Cleopatra." The voice, smiling, came from the dark behind her.

Gwen jumped; her candle wavered. Even after so many years, the voice was unmistakable. She clutched the trembling candle with both hands and turned. "Russell."

"Gwen. It's been a long time."

She drew in her breath and swallowed, doing her best to gather her wits, her nerves. She was thankful she couldn't see him well, and hoped he could see her less clearly. "You've been away."

"Just back."

"How long have you been standing there?"

"Long enough. My apologies. I was curious to discover who might explore my office in the dead of night . . . and then I was charmed."

"I—I'm sorry. I couldn't sleep, and I . . . was curious. I thought I heard someone, that it might be an intruder." She knew she was stammering.

He stepped closer, into her circle of light. "You're welcome here anytime. It's good to see you, good to have you here." His smile, dazzling as ever, spoke appreciation. "You haven't changed."

She didn't know what to make of that.

"Marion wrote me that you'd come." He reached for her hand, pulling her fingers to his lips. "It means a great deal that you've come in our time of need. Thank you, Gwen."

The way he said her name sounded so personal, so warm . . . as warm as his lips on her fingers. Gwen needed to pull herself together, to step out of this too-close space. "I was glad to come, for Marion's sake." That wasn't a lie. "Alistair and Clara have eagerly awaited your return. They're wonderful children. You must be very proud."

"We should have invited you before."

She didn't know what to say to that either.

Russell went on. "I was sorry to hear of your father's passing."

Was he? Did he know it was as much relief as it was sorrow? "Thank you." That seemed sufficient. It would have to do. "It's late. You must be tired after your long trip." She meant to step around him, but he matched her step.

"I look forward to seeing more of you, and to giving you a proper tour of my little museum one day. But, please, don't mention my return to the children. Not yet."

"They're eager to see you."

"Business will keep me much occupied for a few days. I'm preparing for an extended trip abroad. I'll wait to see them until I can give them my full attention. Them, and you, of course."

Gwen was again at a loss for how to respond. She only knew that a private tour with Russell was the last thing she should look forward to. It was what she wanted, what she shouldn't want. Not trusting her voice, she moved the other way, retracing her steps as quickly as she could, offering a short "good night" over her shoulder. *No looking back. Please, God, help me. Protect me from him—from myself.*

5

Gwen both anticipated and dreaded facing Russell in daylight across the breakfast table. But when she entered the dining room the next morning, only the children were there, giving no indication that their father had returned. Remembering his intention to wait to see his children, she didn't mention his arrival either.

She waited until she found Mrs. Barrie alone in the corridor before her classes with the children and began to confide.

Mrs. Barrie shook her head, whispering, "There's no sense telling them he's home until he's ready to see them. It just upsets and confuses them."

"This is normal—for him? For them?"

Mrs. Barrie huffed. "Yes. That's all I have to say on the matter."

Gwen wouldn't press her. She'd learned enough about Mrs. Barrie to know that although there were things she heartily disapproved of in the household, she would not speak against her employer.

Gwen understood that. She'd worked under the authority of Herman Sapp for years, after all. Employment for women came with a cost, a cost that must be carefully considered, and often involved a delicate dance and a line they dared not cross. A single woman could not risk joblessness, poverty, homelessness. Gwen's position was more like the widowed Mrs. Barrie's than the older woman realized.

The first of November came before Russell engaged with his children or any of the household staff beyond Mrs. Barrie, allowing them to think he'd only just arrived.

One bright evening he joined them for dinner—a feast prepared by the cook.

"Mrs. McLearner's done it again—all of Father's favorites!" Alistair enthused when the duck à l'orange was served. "I bet you missed her cooking, didn't you, Father? Nothing like it!"

"I don't like warm beet salad"—Clara pouted—"or roasted vegetables."

"Then don't eat them, my love." Russell's magnanimous smile was directed toward his daughter, only to divert to Gwen, who looked away.

"All the more for Father!" Alistair's eager-to-please comments cut Gwen's heart. She knew what it was to crave the attention and approval of a distant father. She also saw that his fawning irritated Russell more than stroked his ego.

"I do like the pumpkin, as long as it's whipped with lots of butter." Clara toyed with the vegetables on her plate before glancing mischievously at her father. Russell smiled indulgently, then shared extra butter from his own plate.

Gwen was struck again by how much the little girl looked like her mother, and struck anew at how similar her childish ploys were. *They work on Russell just as Marion's worked on Father. He's annoyed by Alistair in the same way Father was annoyed by me. Is it because the boy looks so much like Russell? Was it because I favored Father and Marion favored Mother? Are these generational curses?*

"Will you be seeing Marion on the weekend?" Gwen could wait no longer for information about her sister. "I understand that you alone are able to visit her."

Russell's chin lifted, but he continued looking at his plate, cutting his meat. "Possibly, though I have a great deal to do before my trip. I'll be away for some time."

"You've only just come home," Alistair nearly whined. Gwen drew a breath, knowing that would irritate Russell further.

"Business, my boy—what keeps you in fine fettle and Clara in patent leather."

"Do you think I might see her? I'm very eager." Gwen clutched the napkin in her lap.

"I'm sorry. Dr. Callahan is firm that Marion rest. Should I have time to visit, at best I'll only be allowed a few minutes."

"Minutes? She must be very lonely, unable to see any of you." Gwen knew she was pushing but couldn't understand why Russell seemed to give his wife so little thought.

"I miss Mother." Clara spoke quietly, glancing up at her father, this time sincerely.

"I'm sure you do, little mite, but your mother needs her rest."

"When will she come home, Father?" Alistair set his fork down. "Will she come in time for Thanksgiving?"

"Will she?" Clara sat up straighter, hope in her eyes.

"I shouldn't think so. Too soon, much too soon. Now, no more long faces. Eat your dinner and off to bed. I've given Mrs. Barrie charge of the surprises I brought you."

Distraction. How clever. Gwen watched, willing herself not to be diverted by his charm, his handsome face. He gave the children little time and attention, but what he did give lit the room. *He's always done that, lit the room.*

"May we have them tonight?" Clara flashed her pretty green eyes at her father. "I'll eat my beets if you say so."

He laughed. "You are a little minx, my love."

"That's what Mother says!" Alistair interjected, trying so hard to join the conversation.

"Yes, eat your beets, miss, and you may have the world."

Once dinner ended, the children rose from the table. Clara kissed her father good night, receiving a half smile and a doting hug. As Alistair approached, Russell stuck out his hand, avoiding the arms that reached for him.

"Men shake hands, Alistair. I've told you that."

"Yes, Father, of course." Alistair gave his hand. The grasp looked firm, but the light in the boy's eyes fell.

He's still so young, Russell. How long has it been since you've hugged your son, patted his shoulder, given him a "well done"?

Still, it was not her place to say. She set her napkin against her plate and rose to follow the children from the room. As she passed, Russell reached for her hand, electrifying her nerves.

"Gwen, please. Wait. I'd like to speak privately with you. Will you join me in the drawing room?"

She pulled her hand away, but how could she refuse? And truly, there were things she needed to know, needed to ask him before he left again. Would he tell her more of Marion, details of her condition he might not share in front of the children? Gwen straightened. "Yes, of course."

"I'll have Mrs. Barrie bring digestifs. Brandy? Or do you prefer a sherry?"

"Chamomile tea, thank you."

His brows rose.

"I don't drink alcohol. The tea helps me sleep."

"Ah. I'd forgotten your qualms where the demon liquor is concerned." He chuckled. "As you wish, my lady. There's so much I've forgotten. You'll have to remind me."

Gwen didn't return his grin but moved toward the door. *You'd have "qualms" too, if your father had been a secret alcoholic, drinking his paycheck before putting food on the table.* It wasn't something she'd mentioned to another soul, a family shame she'd kept hidden as best she could throughout her lifetime, but his remark raised a red flag in Gwen's mind. *Hasn't Marion told you this, forbidden alcohol in the home? Doesn't she refuse drink for this very reason?* It was a pact they'd made as teens, from the time Gwen went to work, supplying their grocery bill, their shoes and dresses. *Has Marion gone back on her word? One more question in a long list to ask my sister.*

In the drawing room, Gwen took a solitary chair to one side of the fireplace, forcing a comfortable distance between them.

Russell stoked the fire before taking the seat opposite. He settled in, first gazing long at Gwen, then staring into the fire. A minute, then two passed before he spoke, turning his eyes appreciatively her way. "I'll say again, it was very good of you to come, Gwen. Though I must apologize for Marion pulling you away from your life, from your career . . . Still, I have every reason to thank her. I didn't realize how in need we've all become of a strong woman at the helm of our ship. Your being here is the perfect solution—for the children, for me."

There was much she could counter in what he'd said, but she needed answers, and alienating him, chiding him for his long absence, would not help. "At the time Marion wrote, she'd not yet been admitted to the sanatorium. How long has she been ill, Russell? Has the doctor given his prognosis? Is this confinement precautionary . . . or more than that?" Questions tumbled from her mouth as fast as she could process them.

Russell shook his head. "My wife's been sick for years, Gwen. I couldn't even tell you when her illness started—longer ago than she led me to believe. As to her prognosis, well, you of all people know where tuberculosis leads."

Gwen did know, did fear. "I don't know how far along she is. I haven't seen my sister in twelve years—twelve years! I've no idea—"

"Her health seemed fine until Clara was born. After Alistair she wanted a daughter, was determined we have a daughter. There were . . . failed attempts."

What does that mean? Did Marion lose a child? Lose children?

"Finally, Clara came. But Marion never rallied after that, never really built up her strength. That first winter, before Clara was a year old, Marion developed pneumonia. I have to think the tuberculosis set in some time after that. She wasn't strong enough to bear children. She wasn't made for that. Children were never part of the plan. She was never the same after Clara's birth, I can tell you that."

"Six years," Gwen whispered. *Mama lasted six years.*

Russell sat forward, forearms on his knees, his hands splayed. "Her life—our lives—could have been so much more."

"More than Alistair or Clara?" Gwen couldn't be hearing correctly.

He pulled a cigarette from a gold pocket case, tamping it on the metal. "Children apparently require time and attention . . . at least as far as Marion's concerned."

As any mother knows. Or father.

"We could have relegated their care to nannies—to Mrs. Barrie—but Marion insisted she wanted to 'mother' them herself. All I know is that she was no longer strong, and certainly no longer interested in taking on the world with me." He sat back.

Marion was determined to be the mother she'd been denied.

"I needed my wife beside me. I needed her to travel with me. My work, my life, is public. A partner by my side is indispensable. You remember Marion as a young woman. She was . . . electrifying."

"A bright light." *Yes, she always was. As were you. As you still light up a room.*

"A light? A goddess. You should have seen her. She made a puppet of Jacques Doucet—pioneer of haute couture—her preferred fashion designer. Those early months we traveled to France for her fittings." He shook his head. "You should have seen her in Doucet's creations—an angel of light . . . shimmering. She did the man proud." He smiled at the memory, but his smile faded. "She did me proud."

He stood, shoving hands in his pockets, and faced the fire. "I married Marion believing that together we would set the world on fire. At first, we did. Together we took Paris, Berlin, London, Cairo by storm. I could not have asked for a more social, more clever wife. Charismatic. Stunning. An asset to any man."

Marion was always stunning. Does she know her husband considered her a valuable business asset? Possibly.

"She could charm the crustiest of the old guard—the ideal hostess for a city that caters to dignitaries, old money, new money, avant-garde events . . . the ideal travel companion, ready to jump with both feet into any new venture, every adventure. We were Arthur and Guinevere." He snorted. "Our Camelot lasted all of two years. Until she decided children meant more than the life I offered . . . the world I spread at her feet." He turned to face Gwen, stepped closer. "I made a mistake all those years ago, Gwen. A mistake I've lived to regret, and I'm sorry."

Gwen's breath caught.

The door opened. Mrs. Barrie stepped inside the room, bearing a tray with tea and brandy, and placed it on the table nearest the fire. Russell stepped back.

Gwen turned to pour her tea with trembling fingers. "Thank you, Mrs. Barrie."

Mrs. Barrie straightened, eyes darting between her employer and Gwen, her mouth grim. "Will there be anything else?"

Russell shook his head once, all but waving Mrs. Barrie away. Gwen leaned toward her, searching for an anchor in the older woman's eyes, but Mrs. Barrie refused to face her.

"Good night, then." And she was gone, quietly closing the drawing room door behind her.

Gwen drew a breath. At least the spell was broken. She needed to regain her footing, establish their rightful places in this scene. "I hope you'll ask Dr. Callahan if I can see Marion."

"He's already said—"

"I understand that, but as you say, you are busy, and you mentioned you'd be traveling again soon. I could spend more time with her—not enough to tire her, but to visit, to better learn from her what she hopes me to do with Alistair and Clara beyond their classroom studies."

"I'm sure you're doing everything right. You always do. You always did." His face softened again. Once more he stepped closer.

Gwen prepared to rise, but Russell held up a hand.

"Don't go, not yet."

"I think we've said all that needs to be said."

"No. There's more. You should know that in my absence a number of deliveries will be made—antiquities—through the west wing. They'll be no bother for you or Mrs. Barrie." He smiled. "So, if you should hear footsteps or voices in the night, you needn't be alarmed, needn't 'investigate.' Which reminds me of the night I found you in my museum. I still haven't given you that private tour."

Gwen knew she needed to leave. Nothing technically improper had passed between them, but she recognized the danger signs. A lonely man, disappointed in his life, in his wife's diminished health and apparent interest . . . and now that wife's sister—a former attraction—living beneath the same roof. *And me, a lonely spinster. That's surely how Mrs. Barrie sees this. I've got to prove them both wrong. For my sake, for his, for my sister's, for Alistair and Clara.*

"I was a very foolish young man, Gwen."

Gwen stood, nearly bumping into him, knocking over her teacup. "Then take a lesson from that, Russell. Don't repeat behaviors that didn't serve you well." She walked as quickly as she dared toward the door.

"Gwen," he called after her.

"Good night, Russell."

"Wait, please." He brushed his waistcoat, suddenly all business. "I should have said this sooner. Marion wrote me of her arrangements with you. I've contacted Krueger—my accountant. I trust you're receiving the allowance that she promised. I hope it's satisfactory."

"Yes, it's most generous. Thank you." Gwen didn't turn to face him.

"You must let me know if there's anything at all you need, anything that will make your stay here more comfortable, more enjoyable. While I'm away you can contact Dr. Callahan or my lawyer, Douglas Whitfield. Dr. Callahan oversees Marion's care as our family doctor, but I've left word that he and Whitfield are to be at your disposal. You're family, Gwen . . . treasured family."

Gwen dared not respond to that, didn't know what response to give. She closed the door behind her.

6

Two days passed with no sign or word from Russell, either for the children or for Gwen. Mrs. Barrie confided that he'd been seen coming and going, meeting with business associates brought in through outside doors in the west wing, supervising the delivery of shipments that had begun in earnest. *More antiquities? Where do they all come from?*

On the third morning, Mrs. Barrie announced that Mr. Bennett had gone early, leaving word that he had business in Chicago and that as soon as the war ended, he would sail for Cairo.

"Without coming home first? He's only seen the children once."

Mrs. Barrie shrugged, helpless to answer. "He said he expects to be gone at least nine months, possibly a year or more, depending on business."

"Cairo? A year?" Gwen could not fathom it. *Marion could die in that time.*

Mrs. Barrie's lips formed a straight line, as if she was determined not to say more than was required. "This is not the first time he's absented himself for months on end, Miss Armstrong. He said to remind you that you are in charge of the household but should feel free to defer any matters you wish to Mr. Whitfield or to Dr. Callahan, as needed. He's left you their cards and said he'd given you his accountant's information—Mr. Krueger—should you need to speak with him. He will handle the household accounts as he's always done. Mr. Bennett also said he's left a key to the west wing with his business associates, so you are not to be bothered when they come and go."

Stunned, Gwen took the cards. It was as if her brief encounters with Russell had been a dream. They'd certainly not prepared her to take charge of his household for a year.

Forlornly, Alistair asked at breakfast when his father might return, but she had no clear answer. Clara seemed unfazed, used to his comings and goings. When there, she'd brazenly teased him as a coy and precocious six-year-old child could do, but his absence mattered little to her—at least it appeared to matter less than to Alistair.

Complete distraction came short days later, on November 11, when Alistair pounded on Gwen's door before breakfast.

"Do you hear the church bells ringing? Did you see the headlines, Aunt Gwen? It's over! The war's over! The armistice is signed between the Allies and Germany. It's done!"

Gwen, not finished brushing her hair, threw open her door. "Are you certain? Let me see!"

He thrust *The New York Times* into her hands. "It's true. Fighting stopped at six o'clock this morning our time—eleven o'clock in Paris. Barely an hour ago! See the headlines!"

ARMISTICE SIGNED, END OF THE WAR!
BERLIN SEIZED BY REVOLUTIONISTS;
NEW CHANCELLOR BEGS FOR ORDER;
OUSTED KAISER FLEES TO HOLLAND

"We cleaned the kaiser's clock!"

Gwen's eyes, already streaming tears she didn't realize she'd held at bay for months, raced over the front page. "The eleventh hour of the eleventh day of the eleventh month . . . praise God!" *All those children, the children I taught, longing for their loved ones—what a relief. Fathers and brothers and sons across the country, across the world, will come home!*

Only she knew they wouldn't, not all of them. That was the horror of war. She'd think on that later, wait a while, then write the young teacher who'd rented her cottage back home in Paradox to see who from their community returned, and who didn't. A prayer went up for the families who'd lost loved ones, whether they knew it yet or not. But for now, for this moment, she could only rejoice. "The war is over. It's really over!"

Even Mrs. Barrie looked as if the weight of the world had been lifted from her shoulders. "We must celebrate! If ever there was reason to rejoice, today is that day!" Her accent came thicker, stronger, than at any time since Gwen had met her. "A homecoming! Truly a homecoming for all those poor lads who've fought so bravely."

"Does that mean Father will come back now too? And Mother?" Clara asked innocently.

Mrs. Barrie clasped her hand to her heart. "No, child. I mean, I don't know. It's not the same."

Clara frowned.

Gwen leaned toward the children. "What Mrs. Barrie means is that your father didn't go to war. He's going—gone—away to Cairo on business. I think, because the war is over, he may be away a long time. Your mother will come home as soon as she's strong enough."

"When will that be?" Alistair asked, but Clara pushed in front of him.

"Why didn't he? If all the other fathers went to fight the war, why didn't Father fight?"

A good question. Many men his age volunteered. "I don't know the answer to that, Clara. Simply be glad he's safe and well and that the war is over."

"Can we go out to celebrate? Look! There're already people in the street, shouting and singing and dancing!" Alistair stood at the window, pointing.

She pushed back the curtains so they could all see. Up the long drive, beyond the iron gates, people thronged. Men in overcoats. Women in cloth coats and fur coats, some in their work clothes and others in their Sunday best. Singing. Dancing. Blowing trumpets and trombones. Shouting. Drinking, though it was only morning. How Gwen wished she could join the celebration! "No, I'm sorry, it's not prudent."

"What's *prudent*?" Clara's brow puckered.

"Wise. It's not wise. The flu epidemic, remember? We must all stay well for the sake of your mother. She'll be home as soon as she's able, and we can't risk catching anything that might hurt her. The Spanish flu would hurt her. It would hurt you!" It was the line Gwen had used each time the children begged to go out. It was what Mrs. Barrie said, what she insisted Dr. Callahan had warned, what newspapers still warned. But would Marion be coming home soon, or ever? "Let's write your mother this morning—right after breakfast. We'll celebrate with her."

"Do you think she knows the war is over?" Clara asked.

"They'll tell her, won't they?" Alistair echoed.

"Yes, I'm sure of it. The staff caring for her will tell her, as soon as she's awake this morning."

"Good." Clara spoke softly. "Mother will be glad."

"Everybody's glad!" Alistair whooped.

"Yes." Clara spoke again, words Gwen could barely hear. "Now Father can stay far away and maybe Mother won't be so sad."

7

Details of the Allies' victory and the thrill of returning troops accompanied headlines describing the continued spread of the deadly influenza.

Relief and dread mingled through Thanksgiving, the holiday passing with little fanfare. November gave way to a somber December with twice-weekly letters from Marion but still no word from Russell. Gwen was not surprised at Marion's long absence. Given all she knew of tuberculosis, she could only hope that one day Marion would be well enough to return to the children, at least for a time.

The lack of communication from their father didn't seem to worry the children, though Gwen wondered that such a thing was normal in their lives. *Is he well? Is he sick . . . or dead?* People around the world were dropping like flies from the influenza. It took them in a matter of days—sometimes in a matter of hours. She did her best to push those thoughts away.

Gwen was relieved when a postcard from Egypt came for the children in mid-December.

"He's been dying to get back there, ever since the war cut him off," Alistair declared. "I wish he'd taken me with him. He promised."

"He said when you're older," Clara reminded him. "Anyway, I don't want you to go. I don't want you to leave me, not like Mother."

"I guess I'll be grown before he makes good on that." Dejected, Alistair still peeled the Egyptian stamp from the corner of the postcard for his collection.

"He'll be gone a long while," Clara sighed, not sounding sorry in the least. "Maybe Mother will come home soon."

It was a combination of emotions Gwen couldn't untangle. But the war was over. There was every reason to be thankful, to hope—every reason except for the continuous spread of the Spanish flu. Troops returning from Europe brought not only the living but the dying and the infected, the flu spreading among them and then among their families like wildfire.

Headlines told of ravaged households, decimated neighborhoods, of the morgue overrun and private undertaking houses overburdened or closed because the pileup of bodies deposited with them surpassed their ability to embalm them or supply coffins—suddenly worth their weight in gold—let alone provide wakes, funerals, or individual burials. Corpses remained in homes for days until they could be picked up. In some neighborhoods streetcars were being used as hearses.

Doctors, pastors, service providers of all sorts were run off their feet, serving in constant danger of contracting a disease they couldn't stop, couldn't begin to stem. They, too, were dropping like flies. Word had gone out for anyone willing to provide essential nursing care to please volunteer.

After reading the headlines, Gwen could not but be grateful for the iron gates and their *Quarantine* posting that kept visitors at bay. Even the milkman and greengrocer, the butcher and iceman delivered their produce and wares outside the kitchen door, relying on Mrs. Barrie to tabulate accounts at the end of each week and have Mr. Krueger send payment by post.

Day workers on the estate were given the option of living in or losing their positions, so fearful was Mrs. Barrie of the Spanish flu being brought into the house. The slightest sore throat or chill sent workers home, not to return. If anyone in their family fell ill, they were not to return. With the staff greatly reduced, each member of the household took on more responsibilities. Meals became leaner and less formal.

Gwen didn't mind the extra chores or simpler meals, but she worried for those who were forced out of work, and for Mrs. Barrie. She'd never seen the woman look so tired. The lines in her forehead and around her mouth had deepened. Purple shadows bagged beneath her eyes.

When she finally dared to observe as much, Mrs. Barrie said, "Mr. Dornby, our gardener and the one who supplies our fireplaces, left for his sister's last night. She wrote, begging him to come. I don't imagine he'll be back. Mrs. McLearner left this morning. She received word that her daughter died last night. She's gone to care for her grandchildren. Their father's not yet returned from the war—somewhere in France he is, I think, if he's still alive. I've no idea if she'll return, but I won't allow it until this is over for good and all."

Gwen realized the older woman had carried far more of the household's burden than she'd shared. But there was something she could do about that. "Allow the children and me to take over the cooking."

Mrs. Barrie's eyebrows rose.

"No matter what you think of me, Mrs. Barrie, I know how to stretch meals. I'm good at stone soup and making thin ends meet. It won't hurt the children to learn how to lend a hand. Cooking, even a bit of work outside tidying the gardens can help relieve their boredom at being locked at home. The fresh air will do them good. That's what the papers say."

"I don't see how—"

Gwen laid a hand on the older woman's arm and was surprised when she didn't pull away. "You can't carry this load alone. I'll teach the children to make their own beds and tidy their rooms. I can teach them to wash out their clothes by hand. You know as well as I do that children need to know how to take care of themselves. It's an uncertain world—now more than ever."

Mrs. Barrie surrendered. "See what you can do. Perhaps if we all pull together, we'll get through this."

"We shall," Gwen insisted.

Later that morning, Gwen initiated a change in curriculum for her two students. "We're going to begin a study of domestic science."

"That's for girls," Alistair objected, crossing his arms.

"Domestic science, engineering, and survival training. That's for boys and for girls," Gwen corrected. "I believe learning to survive in today's world implies skills needed universally."

"Survival training. Like in the Army?" Alistair uncrossed his arms.

"How to cook, to clean, to budget funds."

Alistair rolled his eyes. "Woman's work."

"How to cook over a campfire. How to navigate by the stars. How to build a lean-to. Lots of things. Things you might need to know one day to survive. Things you'll certainly need to know if you go to Egypt to dig in the desert, Alistair. We'll make it an adventure!"

"I want to bake gingerbread and chocolate cake!" Clara declared.

Gwen smiled. "That's a fine idea. For now, we need to economize, to make whatever is in the pantry stretch. We don't know when we'll be getting more supplies."

"Is this because Mrs. McLearner's gone?"

"Partly, but also because food deliveries even to the stores have slowed, and because we need to support Mrs. Barrie, and because these are things you need to know."

"Mrs. Barrie's not sick, is she? She can't be sick! You can't send her away, not like Mother!" Clara's eyes widened.

"No, she's not sick, and no one is sending her away. But she's very tired, trying to do the work of too many people in this big house. So, we can help."

"Yes," Alistair agreed, standing. "Anything we can do for Mrs. Barrie."

She's been the one stalwart, ever-present figure in their lives. Please, God, watch over her. Keep her well, keep us all well.

Gwen made lists of activities for each day of the week, determined to do all she could to make the days lively for the children, to make helping in the house fun, and to spend as much time in the fresh air within the walled garden as they could—an activity Mrs. Barrie strongly endorsed, inspired by her bracing Scottish upbringing.

Playing recordings on the Victrola after dinner helped pass the quickly darkening days and long evenings. Gwen taught the children to dance and encouraged them to sing Christmas carols around the piano as she played. Some evenings Mrs. Barrie, content to sit at last with her knitting needles and balls of yarns, joined them at Gwen's encouragement. Occasionally she'd see the weary housekeeper mouthing the words to songs as they sang or smiling at the children's antics.

Not up to replacing Mr. Dornby's routine tasks of chopping and carrying firewood or supplying coal, they gave up the fireplaces. Mrs. Barrie turned on the steam radiators, making bedrooms so toasty warm they needed to throw open the windows. Larger rooms, like the drawing room, couldn't be kept warm enough. With its two radiators, the schoolroom became the center of the home day and night.

Two days before Christmas, a postcard came from Russell for the children.

Celebrating the season in Cairo. May return in the spring.
Merry Christmas to all.

Father

Alistair's disappointment was palpable. Clara seemed less interested. Mrs. Barrie's mouth turned grim. All Gwen could think was, what kind of father did he imagine himself to be?

8

"They're calling this Victory Christmas, in honor of the end of the war." Gwen scanned *The New York Times* over breakfast Christmas Eve morning, determined to cheer her forlorn niece and nephew. "Listen to this: *'The city's determined to welcome its conquering heroes home to great hospitality, through camps and hospitals, churches, and in the warm hospitality of ten thousand private homes'*—ten thousand! Can you imagine ten thousand families opening their homes?"

"Not us." Alistair moped over his eggs and sausages. "Mrs. Barrie won't let the butcher or the Christmas tree peddler in the door, much less a soldier."

Gwen ignored him. "They're promising a day long to be remembered by all, both in and out of uniform. Every civic organization is declaring their doors open so that no man or woman should go unfed, unhoused, or unentertained in the city."

Gwen read headline after headline, hoping to distract them from questions about their mother. "Theaters will open their doors," she summarized, "a man's uniform being his ticket to enter. A Khaki and Blue Dance will be hosted by the Warm Camp at the Seventy-first Regiment Armory this evening."

"A dance?" Clara's eyes brightened as she spread marmalade across her toast.

"Yes, it says, *'Besides the fun and the dancing, there will be three hundred pounds of chocolate fudge made by pretty girls, and ever so many pounds of iced cake, mostly made by their mothers.'"*

"Wow!" exclaimed Alistair. "Three hundred pounds of fudge would bring anybody out—everybody!"

"Made by pretty girls!" Clara emphasized. "That's what you really care about."

"Pretty girls. Bah! No, it's the fudge!"

"That's not all," Gwen continued. *"Waiting as partners for the guests will be most of the four thousand girl members of the Social Department of the War Camp. In order that there may be no partnerless soldier or sailor, each girl has written a 'home Christmas letter,' to which her name is signed. When the men in uniform arrive, each one will receive a letter to be handed to him by one of the many hostesses. Then he will seek out the writer of the letter, and she will become his partner for the first dance."*

"That's a kindness," Mrs. Barrie said, pouring a second cup of tea. "After all those poor lads have been through, it's a proper welcome home."

"How would they ever find one another in a room with four thousand girls?" Alistair gaped.

"Can we invite soldiers here for dinner? Can we give a kindness to some poor lads?" Clara asked none too innocently.

Mrs. Barrie nearly choked on her tea. "No."

"Why not? You said they're poor lads."

Gwen spoke up in reinforcement. "Mrs. Barrie's right, Clara. As much as we might want to help, we can't risk your mother's health now."

"But Mother's not here and the soldiers aren't sick, or they wouldn't be soldiers."

Gwen glanced at Mrs. Barrie. *If only that last were true.* "I'm sorry to say that many soldiers returning from the war have fallen ill. That and all the gatherings are reasons the influenza is spreading again. Mrs. Barrie and I are responsible for you and Alistair and have promised your mother we'll do everything possible to keep you well. There will come a time we can be more generous with hospitality, but not today."

"No Spanish Lady allowed in this house, sweet girl, but we'll do all we can to make this Christmas cheerful." Mrs. Barrie spoke with resolve.

"But how? We don't even have a Christmas tree."

"You'll see. Just you wait. Your Christmas dinner will be all it's ever been. I've a trick or two yet up my sleeve."

"Why don't we hold our own Khaki and Blue Dance?" Gwen grinned. "We'll dress to the nines and I'll teach you both some steps."

Clara brightened but Alistair frowned and asked, "Will there be fudge?"

"I daresay, but not three hundred pounds!" Mrs. Barrie huffed.

By the time Gwen tucked the children into bed Christmas night, she felt that she and Mrs. Barrie had done their best to give them a Christmas of sorts—not the family Christmas of their dreams, but one to remember. At least the war was over. Troops were returning home. *Perhaps 1919 will bring their parents home as well . . . both of them. And what then?*

9

Winter snows and weekday lessons gave way to spring, and spring to summer. Waves of influenza raged and receded and still Mrs. Barrie kept her sign on the front door. At Gwen's urging and Marion's written approval, Mrs. Barrie did agree to interview and hire a new cook and a housemaid. Mr. Dornby returned to double as chauffeur and gardener. It was understood that visitors were not to be invited or entertained.

But in summer, when it seemed the greatest risk had passed, when Gwen and the children felt they'd been cooped up and isolated longer than they could stand, she ordered Mr. Dornby to drive them round Central Park. Fresh air filled their lungs and sunshine warmed their skin, saturating their souls with enough hope to keep going. Whenever they slowed in traffic, if pedestrians came near, they donned their muslin masks, as they'd promised Mrs. Barrie they would do.

One late August day as they drove through the park, the muggy air lay simply too hot and close to wear masks. The breeze in their faces came as welcome refreshment until Clara spotted a group of three little girls skipping rope and singing. She cried out, "Mr. Dornby slow down! Drive closer! I want to hear their rhyme!"

"Oh, don't stop. It will be too hot," complained Alistair. "Clara, you're ditty crazy!"

Gwen smiled. "It won't hurt to hear. Clara's been hoping for a new skipping song."

Mr. Dornby slowed. The little girls, not much older than Clara, glad for the extra attention, sang out at the top of their lungs:

"I had a little bird;
His name was Enza,
I opened up the window
And in flew Enza!"

Gwen swallowed, touching the brooch at her throat before tapping Mr. Dornby on the shoulder. "Please, Mr. Dornby, drive on."

Though she believed the risk of influenza had all but passed, though she tried to put the dread of it out of her mind, the girls' words felt like a dark omen, a premonition.

October 1919 came; mercifully, the influenza did not. Gwen marked in her diary the anniversary of her first full year in New York City. Letters flew from the children to Marion, and from Gwen to Marion. When she was physically able and the doctor allowed her to write, Marion replied. Still no word came from Russell indicating his intention to return, the state of his health, or inquiries regarding his family. Gwen assumed that he kept in contact with his lawyer, his accountant, and Dr. Callahan, but what could they tell him about his wife and children?

Russell's absence was punctuated by monthly late-night deliveries made to the west wing of the mansion—deliveries both Russell and Mrs. Barrie had told Gwen she must ignore. She came to understand why the children timed the appearance of delivery trucks to the stages of the moon. Trucks came and went like clockwork on new moon nights.

Once, unmindful of the new moon rising, Gwen couldn't sleep.

She'd been thinking of Russell, wondering where he could possibly be and how much longer he intended to stay away. She'd worried what might happen if Marion didn't live until his return. She read long into the night, but even that hadn't chased her anxiety away. At last, she pulled on her dressing gown and tiptoed to the kitchen. Careful not to make a sound lest she wake Mrs. Barrie or the new cook, she heated a cup of milk for Ovaltine, hoping it might help her sleep.

She'd taken her first sip when she was startled by the gunning of what sounded like a car motor—not a delivery truck— rounding the outside of the mansion. Unmistakable sounds of doors opening and closing at the far end of the west wing followed. She tried to see who it might be from the window, but realized her view was obstructed by the angle of the wing.

Russell? Can that be you—home at last? She lifted a flashlight from the kitchen shelf, hurried up the kitchen stairs and down the long hallway to the west wing. *The children will be so glad. I'm glad!* She caught herself. *Relieved. I'm relieved.*

A light shone beneath Russell's museum door. Gwen knocked. All went quiet on the other side of the door, but there was no response. She knocked again. Before she could try the knob, the door jerked open. A burly man, several inches taller than Gwen and surely a hundred pounds of muscle heavier, filled the doorway. He was not smiling.

"I—I thought I heard Rus—Mr. Bennett. Is he here?" Gwen heard the tremor and rise in her voice but couldn't control it.

"Does it look like he's here, lass?" The man with the thick Irish brogue eyed her up and down, too slowly.

"Who are you?" Frightened as she was, Gwen felt compelled to demand, to rise to the occasion. What was this man—and the men behind him—doing in Russell's museum late at night?

"I'll ask you the same question, my pretty lady." He smirked. His eyes remained cold.

Gwen's throat crusted dry, but she summoned every stray ounce of courage. "Miss Armstrong. Mr. Bennett has left me in charge of the house in his absence."

"Did he now?" The smirk came in earnest. "Well, he left me in charge of whatever it is I'm about here, doll." He stepped closer, uncomfortably close, his breath sour with whiskey, and leered down at her. "Let me just say it's in your best interest to skedaddle. I do believe that's what 'Mr. Bennett' would say. You just ask him next time you see him."

The shuffle of footsteps behind the man came closer to the door. Without replying, Gwen lifted her chin and, with as much decorum as she could pretend, turned on her heel and forced herself to walk in measured steps down the hallway, up the stairs, and through her bedroom door, locking it behind her.

Sleep never came.

The next morning Gwen asked Mrs. Barrie if she'd heard anything unusual in the night.

Mrs. Barrie busied herself with rearranging breakfast trays on the sideboard. "Nothing that was my affair . . . or yours, Miss Armstrong." She turned to leave the room, but Gwen caught her by the sleeve.

"Mrs. Barrie, there were men—strange men in Mr. Bennett's museum. They didn't look like men delivering antiquities. They looked more—they looked like thugs."

Mrs. Barrie's eyes widened. "You saw them?"

"I asked who they were, what they were doing here."

Mrs. Barrie gasped.

"When I heard a vehicle come up the drive and the doors opening and closing in the west wing, I thought Rus—I thought Mr. Bennett had returned. But when I saw those men, I thought at first they might be burglars or— Oh, I didn't know what to think. But the man who spoke sounded as if he had Mr. Bennett's permission to be there—as if that was a job he was ordered to do."

Lines in Mrs. Barrie's forehead creased. She shook her head, her mouth a straight line. "You shouldn't have gone down there, Miss Armstrong. You've no idea what they might—"

"Who are they? What is it they're delivering so late at night?"

"It's none of your affair—or mine. It's nothing to do with us and I'm sure Mr. Bennett would say so. He did say so—he told you not to bother with them, didn't he?" Mrs. Barrie pulled her arm away, snapping, "He warned you. Best stay out of it."

In December, Gwen confided in her diary:

> *This year has been the best of times, and the worst of times. I've come to love Alistair and Clara, more than any children I've ever worked with. I'm genuinely glad to know them, to have them as part of my life. I love that they love me in return. But I came to New York believing I'd reunite with Marion—my own sister whom I've yet to see in person—and to begin a new life, a life of my own, possibly even a romantic relationship of my own. Neither of those things has happened, nor do they appear on the horizon.*

More troubling was Gwen's growing concern that something about Russell's business was not right. She couldn't imagine him doing legitimate business with such unsavory characters. Yet she hadn't dreamed those men, and she couldn't forget them. She determined that when Russell did finally appear, she would confront him, ask him who they were and why they were allowed to come and go at will, especially when he was not at home, not even in the country.

Mrs. Barrie was no help, and Gwen didn't want to worry Marion. She was loathe to contact Mr. Whitfield, Russell's attorney, in case there was something suspicious, something Russell intended to keep hidden. She couldn't help but wonder if he really was working undercover for the government and if these men were either part of that plan or part of some organized crime he was trying to bring to justice.

I want to believe the best of you, Russell. Where are you? Why don't you come home?

Despite all her misgivings, Christmas was fast approaching—her second one with the children and their second one without their mother or father. Gwen decided that for all the things she could not do, the thing she *could* do was to once again make Christmas special for Alistair and Clara.

Sharing her plan with Mrs. Barrie whisked away every bit of reserve.

"A splendid idea, Miss Armstrong. I'll do all I can to help. So many things are still in blessed short supply, but I've got a trick or two up my sleeve. I daresay that Mrs. McGinley, while an excellent cook on the whole, is a wonder with pastries. Between us we'll do Christmas Day proud."

Mrs. Barrie spared no expense or imagination as near as Gwen could tell, and thanks to her ingenuity in stockpiling sugar and other supplies, every dish traditional to the Bennett family Christmas was going to be prepared. Mrs. Barrie even allowed Gwen to include her family's favorite plum pudding in the menu—something she and the children had cobbled together in November and wrapped in cheesecloth to preserve, under the watchful and disapproving eye of Mrs. McGinley. It was a treat she and Marion had grown up with. *If only we could share it with Marion.*

"Your English plum pudding with hot custard sauce is fine, but I'll have Mrs. McGinley make my own clootie dumpling—a wee taste of home," Mrs. Barrie declared. "T'wouldn't be Christmas without it. It's been a holiday staple in the Bennett household since I joined them, oh, a good twelve years ago."

Despite all the treats and trimmings, the carols sung round the piano at night, the crafting of handmade ornaments, stringing popcorn and cranberries for the small evergreen Gwen ordered for the schoolroom, she knew the children desperately missed their mother.

Two days before Christmas, Mrs. Barrie announced that the ringing telephone had been a call from Dr. Callahan saying that Mrs. Bennett would be arriving that afternoon.

"Mother—home for Christmas!" Clara shouted. She threw her arms around Mrs. Barrie. "I'm so glad!"

"Does this mean she's well?" Alistair's eyes filled with a mixture of hope and fear to hope.

Mrs. Barrie hesitated. "No, lambs. I'm sorry to say. But he said she's stronger than when she went away, so there's that—a miracle from the good Lord Himself. There's a new surge of influenza and one of the nurses has fallen ill. He doesn't want to take a chance on that spreading to the patients, so he's sending as many home for the holidays as have a suitable place to go. He feels she'll be safer here with us, knowing how we've quarantined."

"I don't care why he's sending her home, just that she's coming." Clara breathed a huge sigh of relief.

Gwen felt her heart swell. *She loves her mother as I loved mine when she had to go away. Only Mama never returned though I prayed for her to. At least they'll have time together now.*

And I'll have this time with Marion too. I see much better now what she meant in her first letter about paying for her sins. Her life has been so lonely this long while. Besides the consumption, marriage to Russell cannot have been what she'd hoped, what she'd imagined when they ran off with the world at her feet. Is their estrangement entirely because of her illness, as Russell implied? Does it have more to do with his business? Would he travel so much if she were well? Are they not well suited? And then the question came that she'd never entirely ignored. *Would marriage to him have been any different for me?*

It was a thought she knew she should not entertain. She swallowed and turned aside, remembering that night they'd spoken in the drawing room—his words, his confidences, his eyes pleading for her understanding. Gwen drew a deep breath and ran her hands down her skirt, smoothing its fabric. She straightened her shoulders. No, it was definitely not a thought she should entertain.

10

"Mother! **MOTHER!**" Clara cried. Running down the stairs, she threw herself into her mother's arms as the gauze-masked orderly wheeled Marion through the front door held wide by Mrs. Barrie.

Gwen followed down the stairs as quickly as she could, both eager and apprehensive. Nearing the landing she stopped, shocked by her sister's altered appearance. Needing to get hold of her emotions and the muscles in her face, she stepped to the side, out of Marion's line of vision.

Masked, but sobbing, Marion enveloped her daughter in a warm embrace and kissed the top of her head. "Clara! My darling Clara! I've missed you so."

"Clara, dear, stand back, please," Mrs. Barrie urged. "We need to get your mother in out of the cold."

"Oh, Mrs. Barrie, I've known nothing but fresh air and cold since I left through this very door. That's what Dr. Callahan meant by 'taking the cure.'"

"If you want fresh, cold air, we can do that here, out in the garden, Mother, anytime you want. You don't need to go away—ever again." Alistair embraced his mother tenderly, as if she might break.

"That's right, Son, that's right! Oh, it's good to be home."

"We can take Mrs. Bennett from here," Mrs. Barrie encouraged the orderly. "There's no reason to delay."

"Yes, ma'am. I'll just set her bags inside the door." The orderly tipped his cap. "Mrs. Bennett, I wish you well and a merry Christmas with your family."

"Thank you, George. You've been so kind. Merry Christmas to you and yours."

Alistair took charge of Marion's chair. "Here, Mother, let me wheel you into the drawing room. We've heated it and laid a fire. Everything's ready!"

After more than a year of intimate family life with the children, Gwen suddenly felt very much an outsider. She hurried to help Mrs. Barrie with her sister's bags.

"You go in now, Miss Armstrong. I'm sure you'll be wanting time with your sister. I can see to these," Mrs. Barrie encouraged her, bending for the first bag.

But Gwen held back. "Yes, I—I just want to give them some time—to reunite, you know."

Mrs. Barrie looked up at Gwen, as if seeing her anew. "That's kind of you, but I think you've earned your place in this family. Go on with you now."

It was the most affirming thing Mrs. Barrie had ever said to Gwen, and it made her heart swell. She nodded. Swallowing her own fears, she followed the family into the drawing room, where Alistair had already turned his mother's chair to face the door and was helping her off with her coat and gloves.

"Gwen!" Marion removed her mask and held out her hands. "There you are! At last!"

"Marion." Gwen didn't know whether to embrace her sister or give her space, but the tugs at her heart propelled her feet forward until she carefully wrapped her fragile younger sister in her arms. "Marion." It was all she knew to say, all she could get past the thickness in her throat.

Marion held tight. When at last she allowed Gwen to pull away,

Marion swiped at tear-bright eyes and streaks on her cheeks. "Thank you. Thank you for coming, for being here."

"Wait till you see what we've made you for lunch, Mother!" Clara danced for her mother's attention. "You're going to love it!"

"What you've made?" Marion's thin brows rose.

"Well, Mrs. McGinley—but we helped. We've been doing all sorts of things!"

"We'll catch up later," Gwen whispered.

"Promise?"

"Promise." Gwen had expected to feel some reservation toward her younger sister, some leftover grudge from wrongs done in years gone by, but no. One glimpse of the fragile woman her sister had become hurled every resentment away, replacing them with pity, an inconsolable ache in her heart, and a longing for more time.

"Yes! Aunt Gwen taught Alistair and me to cook and bake when it was just us and her and Mrs. Barrie—when everybody else went away."

"Went away?" Marion's hand caught her throat.

"It was the influenza," Gwen said quickly. "I didn't tell you everything because I didn't want to worry you. There's more staff on hand now. Most left back then because they were needed at home. Mrs. Barrie knows the case for each one. But we managed, and Alistair and Clara have learned and accomplished so much. Wait till you see. You'll be so proud of them."

"I've always been proud of them." Marion's tone hinted at reprimand, perhaps because she felt proprietary of her children, perhaps because of sorrow for all she'd missed and was likely to miss.

Gwen couldn't help that, but she gave her sister's shoulder a slight squeeze. She'd do everything possible to reassure her that she was still the major figure in her children's lives, the one they longed for.

Marion mustered a smile, but paled as Clara chattered on, oblivious to everything but that her mother was home. Alistair seemed content to sit on the ottoman nearest her chair, to drink in the presence of his mother.

Neither child seemed surprised or frightened by Marion's graying, wispy hair, by her too-frail hands streaked in thin, shiny lesions, or by the change in her once creamy and clear complexion, her beautiful face now splotched with patches of raised, discolored skin—which told Gwen that the disease had progressed without their full understanding. The children, she realized, must have seen changes develop slowly, over time, so were not shocked by them now, even after more than a year. But Gwen recognized in those changes the last throes of her mother's illness. Marion might have been too little at the time to remember, but Gwen recalled each and every deteriorating sign.

She let the children chatter on until Marion's eyelids began to droop and a cough rattled her fragile chest; then she intervened.

"Your mother needs to rest, children."

"She can rest here!" Clara stood guard.

"She needs to lie down. You can see her later." Gwen rose to take charge of the chair.

"I'll wheel Mother wherever she needs to go." Alistair jumped ahead to take the handles of the chair from Gwen. "Do you want to go to the dining room, Mother, so you'll be there for lunch? Or do you want to see the garden first? We've been keeping it up with Mr. Dornby and we've been feeding the birds."

Marion reached her hand back to cover her son's. "I think your aunt is right, darling. I need to lie down, just for a little while."

"We can make a comfy bed on the sofa, here near the fire." Clara plumped the pillows.

"No, my darlings, I want to go to my bed, in my room."

"But that's up the stairs."

"I can walk . . . with help." She cast pleading eyes to Gwen, who nodded.

"I'll get Mrs. Barrie. Between us we'll help you up the stairs."

"There's no need for Mrs. Barrie. I can help Mother. I'm strong." Alistair stood firm.

"I need you to run upstairs and open the window in your mother's room, Alistair." Gwen spoke with authority, knowing her sister could not. "Make certain the radiator is giving out plenty of heat. Fresh air for the lungs is one thing, and important, but we can't have your mother freezing, now can we?"

Alistair's forehead creased, his eyes conflicted.

"Please, Alistair." Marion kissed his hand. "That's exactly what I need you to do."

"All right, Mother. I'll do anything for you."

"I know."

"I'll get Mrs. Barrie," Clara called, running out the door.

Marion heaved a sigh, sending her into another coughing fit.

"Don't try to talk, Marion. We'll get you to bed and bring luncheon upstairs—Mrs. McGinley's made one of Mrs. Barrie's Scottish potato soups—warm and hearty, just the thing, and the children have made you a special dessert. They can visit again after you've rested. They're just so excited to see you. They don't seem to understand—"

"And you must not tell them. Not yet."

Gwen hesitated. "As you wish." She understood Marion's desire to protect them, to enjoy every precious moment with them as carefree as possible. Still, she wondered just how much time there would be to prepare them for the inevitable, and whether knowing or not knowing was the greater gift.

Later that night, hours after the children had bidden their mother good night and gone to bed, Gwen heard Mrs. Barrie's footsteps on the stairs. She knew the older woman would not be up that time of night unless summoned. Marion must have pulled the bell by her bed. Gwen cinched the tie of her robe around her waist and stepped into the hallway. Mrs. Barrie was carrying a tray toward Marion's room.

"Is everything all right, Mrs. Barrie? Do you need anything?"

"Miss Armstrong," she whispered. "I think you should come. Mrs. Bennett's poorly. I've been with her for the last hour. I feel sure we should telephone the doctor, but she insists not. Perhaps she'll listen to you."

Gwen hurried down the hallway, relieving Mrs. Barrie of her tray of beef broth and hot tea. "You get some sleep. I'll sit with her. If I can convince her to let me telephone the doctor, I will. You look dead on your feet."

"That I am, but I'm also worried, miss. She's ever so much worse than when she went away. I could strangle that Dr. Callahan for sending her to that godforsaken sanatorium."

"The disease has progressed further than I'd imagined."

"Yes, and I know you've seen it before. I'm so sorry for those dear children. Their sun rises and sets in their mother."

Gwen balanced the tray on her hip and rubbed Mrs. Barrie's arm in sympathy. "Get some rest, please. We'll need you in the morning."

Mrs. Barrie nodded. "All right. Thank you, miss. Good night then. You'll call if you need me?"

"Yes, of course." Gwen turned the knob on her sister's door so the older woman would go and slipped into Marion's room.

Her sister lay small and pale in the massive bed, her eyes closed. Marion's cheeks bore red splotches of fever, and her once full head of brilliant red hair had been reduced to little more than graying strands, spread across the pillow. She opened her eyes when the door clicked closed. "Gwen."

"Mrs. Barrie prepared some broth and hot tea. She thought it might ease your cough."

"She shouldn't have woken you."

"I wasn't asleep. I told her to go on to bed. We'll need her more in the morning."

Gwen poured tea and held the cup out to her sister.

"I can't, Gwen. I can't hold it; my hands are shaking so." Marion's cough sounded like the onset of pneumonia to Gwen.

"It's chills from the fever. Let me hold it for you. Take a sip. See if it helps. Please." Supporting Marion's neck and the back of her head with one hand, Gwen held the cup to her sister's lips.

Two small sips, that's all she could manage before she lay back on the pillow, coughing brilliant red splotches into her handkerchief. Gwen set the cup aside and pulled a chair close to the bed, wiping her sister's lips with a napkin. "Do you think you could sip the broth if I hold the spoon to your lips?"

Marion shook her head. "Not now."

"Later then. We'll try later." Gwen stood to move the tray aside.

"Please don't go, Gwen."

"I'm not. I promise. I'll sit here as long as you want."

Twin tears leaked from the corners of Marion's closed eyes. "I don't deserve this, you know."

"No, of course you don't. No one does. I'm so sorry, Marion."

"I don't mean the consumption. I mean you, coming here, helping me."

"You're my sister. Of course I'll help you, all I can." Gwen would not dredge up the past. Those ghosts must rest.

"I pretended I didn't see how you loved him. I wanted so much to escape Father and Paradox, to see the world. Russell was so handsome, so charming and exciting."

"It doesn't matter now, Marion. Let it go."

Marion reached for Gwen's hand. "But it does matter. I've needed to say this for years. Let me say it now. While I can."

Gwen drew a breath to steel herself against any remnant of bitterness.

"I left you with all the care of Father, all his money and drinking troubles, everything. I knew what I was doing. Selfish. But here I am. Have you seen what it's brought me? Do you know my punishment?"

"This is a disease. A disease isn't punishment."

"I don't mean the consumption." Marion's grip tightened on Gwen's fingers.

"What do you mean? Not Russell?"

Marion released Gwen's hand.

"Because he's so often away? I know that must be terribly lonely, but—"

Marion huffed.

"Then, what? I can see he's not the attentive husband and father you wish, but look at your children, look at this beautiful home. Financial security, standing in society. Before the children came, you traveled the world—he told me. Everything you ever said you wanted. Hasn't that made up for—"

"For love? For honesty? Integrity?"

"Honesty? Integrity?" That was not what Gwen wanted to imagine, not what she wanted to hear.

"You don't know him, do you?"

"I've seen Russell all of two times since I came over a year ago. He's been away on business in the States and abroad."

"Business."

"That's what he said."

"His peculiar business. Have you seen the trucks—the deliveries?"

"Yes, but I don't understand what they are."

"No. He wouldn't have said." Marion's chest shuddered.

"You need to sleep. We'll talk more tomorrow when you've rested. We have so much to catch up on. Tomorrow is Christmas Eve. The children have prepared everything special for you."

Marion closed her eyes and turned over, her back to Gwen. "Yes, tomorrow."

Gwen woke to hear the downstairs clock chiming three—at least she believed that's what woke her. But it was the automobile lights outside Marion's window that drew her from her chair. She pulled back the curtain in time to see a truck pull round the back of the house and park behind the west wing. She couldn't see directly but heard its doors open and close. Voices, muffled, came in spurts, as if orders were fired.

She opened the window further, trying to hear. She couldn't make out more.

It was the first time she'd gotten a closer view of the trucks coming to the estate in the night, but then, her room was on the other side of the house. Gwen couldn't imagine why legitimate deliveries of any kind should be made in the dead of night, especially on Christmas Eve. But after her encounter with the thug, as she'd begun calling him in her mind, she wasn't about to go exploring.

Gwen pulled the window closed. Even Clara and Alistair knew something about them—the ones who came *when the moon is right*, the ones their mother had been warned not to cross, the ones they weren't to talk about and that Mrs. Barrie was clearly afraid of. *What does Marion know? What was she about to say?*

11

There was no tree upstairs, but Gwen and Alistair wrangled a small potted palm from the conservatory up to Marion's room. Clara insisted on making more homemade ornaments to decorate it while Alistair pulled a box from the attic containing some of the most beautiful and delicate blown-glass works of art that Gwen had ever seen.

"Your father and I bought those in Germany on our Grand Tour, just after we married. That one, with the blue and silver filigree, we found in Italy. Happy, those early days." Marion, still weary from her transition to home, directed Alistair's decorating from her bed as she stroked Clara's cheek.

"Will you be able to come downstairs tomorrow, Mother, for Christmas dinner?" Clara lay her head in her mother's lap.

"If not, my darling, will you come and eat your dinner here, with me?"

"Yes!" Clara cried.

"We'll make it a picnic," Alistair said. "We'll all come. Aunt Gwen, we can fetch a little table, can't we?"

"Certainly." They'd do whatever they could to include Marion in the festivities.

"I'm so sorry I've not been able to do any shopping this year, children." Marion combed her fingers through Clara's hair. "I'm afraid there won't be presents beneath your lovely tree."

"You're all the present we want, Mother. All we need." Alistair spoke with the seriousness and maturity of someone much older.

Whatever Marion doesn't have in her marriage, she certainly is rich in the love of her children. Gwen was glad for her sister, truly. Still, she couldn't help but wish for some of that kind of love herself. *The role of aunt is more than I had before, and I'm thankful for that. I must be content.* Gwen hoped that if she kept telling herself so, it would become true, and enough.

Christmas morning dawned bright and cold. The house filled with the tantalizing aroma of Mrs. Barrie's stuffed and slow-roasting turkey. It was the first Christmas since childhood that Gwen could remember waking to the fragrance of someone else's holiday cooking. She dressed quickly and hurried downstairs to help Mrs. Barrie in every way the older woman would allow.

"It's been quite all right," Mrs. Barrie had intoned the night before, "for you and the children to help in the kitchen as you've done. I greatly appreciated your help, and Mrs. McGinley has tolerated it better than most cooks would. But I've sent her home to her family for Christmas Day, and this year I reign supreme before the cookstove! I've been itching to do a good Scottish Christmas dinner since I came to Bennett Place."

It was all Gwen could do not to laugh. On the other hand, she could imagine no greater pleasure than seeing the housekeeper bustling about the kitchen, happily stirring her pots, singing Christmas carols in her thick brogue. She was not disappointed.

"There you are!" Mrs. Barrie sang, as Gwen entered the kitchen. "Happy Christmas, Miss Armstrong!"

"Merry Christmas, Mrs. Barrie! Something smells wonderful! I promise not to get in your way but I'm dying for a cup of tea or coffee if you've got it."

"I'm putting together a tray, coffee and tea, sugar, cream—everything. Now, I've fried tattie scones and eggs, rendered both bacon and sausage links. I've a pot of beans on the stove and a few tomatoes from the conservatory. I know not one of you will want my black pudding, so I shan't serve it."

"A Scottish Christmas feast!"

"Well, I just hope there's something here Mrs. Bennett can manage. She's not eating enough to keep a chaffinch alive. We'll carry it all upstairs. I'll send the children along when they show. She won't want to be eating alone, not today of all days."

"I'll gladly carry it up and you must join us."

"No, no. I've a baker's dozen things to do and I'd best keep at it. I want to serve our main meal at two. I think this will keep you all going until then, but it won't do Mrs. Bennett any good to have a heavy meal before settling in for the night."

"I agree. Two huge meals in a day is more than enough. I'll eat with Marion, but I want to help you today, Mrs. Barrie. I can't leave all this to you."

"I told you last night, I'm in my element. I've got my turkey in the oven and my leek and potato soup simmering, so I've a good start and I'll be most glad if you go ahead. I'm thinking . . ." She turned away to stir her simmering soup.

"You're thinking?"

Gwen could see the rise and fall of Mrs. Barrie's shoulders. "I'm thinking this will be Mrs. Bennett's last Christmas." She turned to face Gwen, clasping Gwen's hands in her own. "Spend every minute with her you're able, miss. She needs you, more than you know. You won't be sorry, and neither will the children."

Gwen's heart shuddered; she drew a ragged breath.

"I know I wasn't altogether welcoming when you first came, Miss Armstrong. I'm sorry . . . but I didn't understand the lay of the land. I thought perhaps . . ."

"Perhaps?"

"I thought perhaps you'd come with your cap set for Mr. Bennett."

"No." Though Gwen felt the heat of complex emotions rise up her neck.

"I see that now and have seen it a long while. I was wrong. You've been the world to these children, and they've needed you. They'll need you more in days to come. I love them and will be here for them as long as Mr. Bennett keeps me on, but you're their family. I'm grateful you're here, Miss Armstrong."

Gwen hardly knew what to say. Instead of words, she hugged Mrs. Barrie and held her tight. She'd never known an aunt or even a mother for many long years. She didn't imagine Mrs. Barrie to replace either of those, but she was grateful for the woman, as friend, as ally, as mentor. "Thank you, Mrs. Barrie." She blinked against a threatening tear and pulled away, half laughing out of nervousness. "Now that we've hugged, do you think we can dispense with the *Mrs.* and the *Miss*?"

Mrs. Barrie smiled. "Not while I'm in service, Miss Armstrong. Perhaps someday, when I retire . . . when pigs fly."

Gwen squeezed the older woman's arm, gave her a peck on the cheek, and took up the breakfast tray.

Marion needed a few hours' rest between breakfast and their afternoon meal. Gwen noted that her sister made a good show of pushing food around on her plate, as if eating along with the rest of them. Gwen was glad she'd convinced Mrs. Barrie to share her afternoon meal with them upstairs. It made for a brighter affair to enlarge the party, if only by one.

After the plum pudding, Alistair recited Clement C. Moore's poem, "The Night Before Christmas," and Clara sang "Away in a Manger." Gwen read the second chapter of Luke from the Bible before she and the children, along with Mrs. Barrie, sang "It Came

Upon a Midnight Clear" a cappella. Marion, having no energy to sing, closed her eyes and mouthed the words. Gwen leaned closer just in time to hear Marion whisper, "Thank You, Father, for this Christmas."

The children were just about to begin a rendition of "God Rest Ye Merry, Gentlemen" when the downstairs front doorbell rang.

Everyone froze. No one but the orderly delivering Marion had come to the front door in weeks. Mrs. Barrie still kept a quarantine sign posted on both the front gate and the front door. Only the regular delivery people entered through the back gate and left those deliveries outside the kitchen door. At least that was true of those who delivered in daylight.

"Who in the world could that be? And on Christmas Day?" Mrs. Barrie stalked disapprovingly from the room and down the stairs.

When the housekeeper didn't return, Gwen wondered if she should check on her.

She'd just reached the head of the staircase when she saw Mrs. Barrie struggling across the foyer floor with a wooden crate. "What on earth is that?" Gwen ran down the stairs to help.

"It was just sitting outside the door, along with this florist box. Not a soul to speak to and no note but addressed to the household. It looks like Christmas gifts—from Egypt, according to the wrapping. Some are for the staff, though they're addressed to some as are no longer here. I've lifted those out. Now it's not heavy, just a bit awkward with both boxes."

"Russell sent gifts!" Gwen sang, delighted for the sake of the children—and, she hoped, for Marion. "They'll have Christmas presents after all, and from their father! Here, let's take them up together."

Though Mrs. Barrie looked a little dubious, between them they carried the load up the stairs. Delivering their largesse to Marion's bedside, they found the children perched on either side of her, regaling their mother with memories of Christmases past.

"The best medicine in the world," Mrs. Barrie whispered.

"Look what Mrs. Barrie found outside the front door!" Gwen

pulled the top layer of packing from the crate and held up a wrapped gift.

"Presents!" Clara cried.

"From Father?" Alistair gaped, as if it was too good to be true.

"Let's see, shall we?" Gwen pulled the first large package from the crate and read, *"For Clara, my Egyptian princess. Merry Christmas, Father."*

Clara's eyes widened. "What is it?"

"Open it, silly, and find out!" Alistair stood, hope and expectation in his eyes.

Gwen pulled out the second package. *"For Alistair, to help with your hieroglyphics. Merry Christmas, Father."*

Alistair grabbed the package from Gwen as if it were a lifeline. He turned away from the room full of curious eyes, walking toward the window to open it alone.

"Look! It's an Egyptian princess's costume for me, and a doll, dressed just the same. Oh, it's beautiful!" Clara held up a striking dark-haired doll with kohl-painted eyes and a sumptuous gown. She pushed the richly colored stone-and-gold bracelet up her arm and twirled with her flowing costume as if in a trance. "There's even slippers—golden sandals!"

"What is it, Alistair? What do you have?" Marion asked, unable to see her son round the palm tree.

"Books, Mother. One to help me learn hieroglyphics and one on geometry." His voice came softly. Gwen knew the hieroglyphics book was just the kind of thing he would enjoy, and that the geometry would come in handy for an archaeologist in the making. *But compared to Clara's gift it must seem . . . practical.*

Alistair stepped round the palm, held up his books for all to see, and bravely smiled.

Gwen's heart ached for him.

"And here's this box, Mrs. Bennett, from the best florist in the city. Surely this is for you. Shall I open it?" Mrs. Barrie did her best to draw eyes from Alistair's flushed face.

"Please." Mrs. Bennett leaned back on her pillow, breathless.

"Ah, aren't they lovely!" Mrs. Barrie pulled two dozen long-stemmed red roses amid lush greenery, all tied in white satin ribbon, from the long florist box. "Red roses, in the dead of winter!" She laid them with the card across the coverlet on Marion's lap—a brilliant contrast to Marion's pale cheeks.

Marion struggled to sit up better and inhaled the fragrance of the roses. Gwen stuffed an extra pillow behind her back for support and sat beside her sister. "I'm so glad he remembered." Gently she squeezed Marion's arm. "That must count for something."

Marion pulled the card from the small envelope. Reading it, she paused, then set the card back among the roses.

"Shall I put them in water for you, Mrs. Bennett?" Mrs. Barrie stood at the ready.

Marion looked up, paler still, a smile pasted on her lips. "That's up to Gwen. They're for her." She pushed the massive bouquet across the coverlet to Gwen.

Mrs. Barrie's face flushed; her smiling mouth straightened.

"No, that can't be right," Gwen gasped.

"Read the card."

With trembling fingers, Gwen took the card from her sister.

For Cleopatra,
With all my thanks and love,

Russell

"It's a mistake."

Marion's eyes searched Gwen's. "Cleopatra. That was always his name for you, you know."

Gwen didn't know what to say. Mrs. Barrie turned away.

"Why is Father sending Aunt Gwen flowers? They should be for you, Mother." Alistair put his books down. Clara had stopped her twirling.

The silence became deafening, until at last Marion spoke.

"Your father appreciates that your aunt is here to be with you, since he is not." Her voice came flat, without emotion.

"He—he must not know you're home, Marion. He believes you're still at the sanatorium. He's probably sent your gifts there. We'll telephone them first thing in the morning." Gwen couldn't stop talking.

Marion placed her hand on Gwen's. "It's all right." She closed her eyes and leaned back. "It's more than all right."

But Gwen knew it wasn't. It was clear from the flat line of Mrs. Barrie's mouth, the stricken look on Clara's face, and the flash of betrayal in Alistair's eyes that it was not "all right" and could never be.

12

Three uncomfortable days passed. Gwen discreetly telephoned the sanatorium each morning and late afternoon to see if mail or packages had been delivered to Mrs. Bennett. On the third day it was reported that a fruit basket had been delivered to her room Christmas morning. Since no one was there to accept it, the fruit had already begun to turn. The accompanying note read, *"Merry Christmas, Marion. Wishing you well, Russell."*

The easy camaraderie that had developed between Gwen and Mrs. Barrie disappeared, flown like a bird abandoning its nest. Clara pouted, resisting Gwen's every suggestion of schoolwork. Alistair openly glared each time their paths crossed.

Gwen did her best to pretend she didn't notice, but the icy change cut her to the quick. She would have thrown the roses away if that could make the memory disappear, but Mrs. Barrie had taken them straightaway from Marion's room, placed them haphazardly in a somewhat ugly urn, and left them on the table in Gwen's sitting room. Gwen couldn't even dispose of them without creating a scene.

Gwen didn't need to encourage the children to spend time with their mother. They sat cross-legged on the floor of her room or lay across the foot of her bed, chatting with her every minute until Marion closed her eyes, falling into much-needed sleep. In those times Gwen motioned them from the room, reminding them that they could see their mother later. The children stalked out, not making eye contact with their aunt, determined to ignore her.

Gwen wanted to give Marion and her children all the space they needed, but by New Year's Eve she'd had enough of the frosty silent treatment. She'd done nothing to encourage Russell, whom she'd only seen twice since her arrival more than a year before, and everything to discourage him as best she knew. She didn't deserve this.

That morning, after breakfast and before the children joined their mother, Gwen determined to confront her sister, ill though she was.

"We can't go on like this, Marion. I can't. If you want me to leave, I'll go as soon as arrangements can be made, as soon as you have the help you and the children need."

"Whyever would I want you to leave?" Marion asked innocently, which took Gwen aback.

"Because of the roses. Because the children and Mrs. Barrie, and I presume you, believe I've 'set my cap' for your husband, as Mrs. Barrie said. But that's not true. I have no designs on Russell, and I won't stay and be treated as if I've betrayed you."

Marion sighed. Gwen knew that talking exhausted her sister, more each day. "I rather wish you had."

"What?"

"It would make things so much easier."

"What are you talking about?"

Marion levelled her gaze at Gwen. "I need you, Gwen. I'm dying."

"Please, don't say that. The goal in my coming here was always to help you get stronger, have longer—more time with the children, with me, and—"

"My time is in God's hands. There's nothing you or the children or Mrs. Barrie can do. You know that." She reached for Gwen's hands. "Come, sit with me."

Gwen pushed a pillow behind her sister's back and sat beside her.

"Russell doesn't love me, Gwen—hasn't for a long time. He's only waiting for me to die before he finds himself a new wife."

"Marion, you can't—"

"I want that wife to be you."

"What?" Gwen jerked back.

"I know what I'm saying. Russell will remarry. Nearly all widowed men do, and Russell most certainly will. Beyond love or passion or lust, he wants—he *needs* a social partner. He's an ambitious man. He needs a trophy on his arm. He wouldn't say it in so many words, but it's true."

Gwen couldn't deny that. Russell had said as much himself.

"Do you know what happens to the children of a first wife when a man remarries?"

Gwen shook her head. Their father had never remarried. She tried to remember children from school who'd lost parents, how that had been for them when the surviving parent remarried.

"I'll tell you. They're shipped off to boarding schools or palmed off on relatives. Sometimes, if they remain at home, they're . . . they can be very badly treated by the second wife. I don't want any of that for Clara or Alistair."

"Russell wouldn't allow that, surely."

Marion raised her eyebrows. "You see what a doting, ever-present father he is now?"

Gwen drew a deep breath. She saw clearly.

"If Russell cares for you . . . if you care for Russell . . ."

"Marion, I—"

"Listen to me. If you care for Russell, I know you will also care for my children. Until those stupid flowers came and drew a wedge between you, I saw how you love them, how they accept and love you."

"As their aunt—one they trusted not to make 'flirty eyes' at their father."

Marion half chuckled. "Clara said that, didn't she?"

"I came with no designs on your husband, Marion."

"Even if you did, I would be more relieved than upset."

Gwen shook her head again.

"I'll talk with the children, convince them there is nothing in their fears and that their father was simply thanking you, trying to include you in his Christmas remembrances."

"Is that what you believe?"

"No. I know my husband. He's laying the groundwork. And that is what I hope."

"I've no intention—I won't promise—"

"I'm not asking you to promise to marry him, Gwen. I wouldn't do that to you, not unless it's something you want. But I beg you, look after my children when I'm gone. I've done what I can to provide for their future. But whether you are part of this household or not, please, please promise me you'll stay in touch with them, watch over them, love them, protect them from Russell's negligence in every way you can. Mentor them as far as he'll allow. Promise me."

"Of course, I promise that. I love Clara and I love Alistair, Marion. They're wonderful. But I don't think they—"

"Give them time. They need you now. They'll need you more later."

That's what Mrs. Barrie said, before the roses . . .

As if Marion could read her mind, she said, "I'll talk with Mrs. Barrie. I can see she has her dander up. She's very loyal to me, but she needs to realize that her loyalty must include you."

"She loves you, very much."

"She's been my champion, almost a second mother to me—after you." Marion smiled, dropping Gwen's hands and leaning back against her pillow. "Now, let me rest until the children come."

It took time, and Marion's repeated assurances to the children, but by the end of January, Gwen felt that Alistair and even Clara were back on an even keel with her. Even Mrs. Barrie seemed to treat her as before.

Marion gained strength as the New Year progressed. By mid-February she was out of bed and resting in a chair by her open window much of the day. Dr. Callahan wanted her to return to the sanatorium, but Marion refused, determined to remain at home.

By March she was able to walk downstairs for meals and reclined on the sofa to watch the children recite in their schoolroom. When the first crocuses pushed through the snow to open in a riot of purple, yellow, and blue, Marion laughed. It was the most beautiful sound Gwen could remember hearing.

Influenza had all but petered out in the city, and the strain that endured appeared less virulent that spring. Mrs. Barrie removed her forbidding sign, somewhat the worse for wear, from the front door.

Though still terrified of the dreaded influenza for herself or her household, Marion reluctantly agreed to allow Mr. Dornby to drive Gwen and the children on brief excursions through Central Park, as long as they did not stop or speak with strangers. She and Gwen both recognized the children's need to be out and about, to see the world beyond their home's walls, even from a distance. Gwen did not mention that they'd done that and more last summer.

Russell wrote that he would sail home from Egypt in late April. He'd suffered a nasty bout of influenza himself and needed to regain his strength. Gwen thought it just as well. Marion, she believed, would better strengthen without him there, and his presence could only complicate all their relationships.

As April neared, they bundled Marion against the cold, and she progressed to short strolls in the garden. She wandered Mr. Dornby's beautifully pebbled paths among the trees, arm in arm with Gwen, or clasping Alistair or Clara's hands, contentedly strolling by the flower beds to see what new leaf or bud might have emerged in the night.

Gwen could not have been more delighted. Owing to Marion's limited health, they might never be able to explore New York together, but Gwen felt that while the calendar declared 1920, time had been turned back fifteen years, to the days when she and her sister had been all in all to one another—sharing secrets and dreams of life to come. At least, they shared dreams for Alistair and Clara. Most of their conversations centered around the children—Alistair's determination to become a real-life archaeologist and Clara's hopes of following him as his artist. Marion shared her own hopes for them—hopes that they would grow up strong and well and happy. She prayed Clara would one day be dearly loved by a good man of faith and that Alistair would find a wife to love him and share a life in Christ. She prayed they would both surrender their lives to the Lord early, knowing He was their only constant, their faithful Father and guide.

Gwen was amazed and inspired by Marion's faith and heart for God. She didn't fully understand it or know how that had come about, except that Marion attributed it to her time alone with God in the sanatorium—*patience and faith through suffering*. It certainly had not been fostered in childhood. Gwen prayed out of desperation sometimes but hadn't anything like a relationship with the Lord, or the assurance Marion expressed. Still, she cherished Marion's hopes and dreams for her children. In one way or another they became her hopes too.

When inside, Marion most often sat wrapped in blankets near an open window, taking in the fresh air as Dr. Callahan had prescribed or napping as the sun streamed through. One rare warm afternoon, she requested Mrs. Barrie serve tea in the garden.

To make it a genuine tea party, Marion asked Gwen to raid her dressing room in search of spring bonnets for themselves and Clara, even though they still needed warm coats.

Clara, beside herself in her mother's lavender bonnet, primped and preened and flamboyantly spread her white linen napkin across her lap.

"Oh, Gwen, please go to Russell's dressing room adjoining mine and find a hat for Alistair!"

"Boys—men don't wear hats to tea parties!" Alistair objected.

"But wouldn't it be fun if they did?" Marion's eyes twinkled. "Anyway, we're out of doors, so that makes it all right."

Alistair could not resist his mother's excited plea. "Oh, all right, then. Do you want me to help you look, Aunt Gwen?"

"Yes, come on, in case there are choices!" Gwen and Alistair fairly raced up the stairs.

But the doors between the dressing rooms were locked from Marion's side. "I guess that's that." Gwen willingly gave up the search.

"Father's bedroom door won't be locked, at least I think it won't, and we can get in through there."

Gwen followed Alistair, uncomfortable entering Russell's private rooms but not wanting to disappoint her sister. *A hat—such a silly little thing, but it's wonderful to see Marion laughing, suggesting anything.*

"Good! It's unlocked." Alistair turned the knob. Despite all his bravado, he walked stealthily across the room, not looking right or left, but headed for his father's dressing room.

Gwen would not have imagined that a man might possess such an extensive wardrobe or such an array of hats, shoes, or walking sticks. "It's like walking into a store!" she whispered.

Alistair stood in awe. "I've never actually been in here."

"You what? But—"

"I wasn't about to miss the chance to see when Mother suggested finding one of Father's hats."

Gwen grinned. "The apple does not fall far from the tree, nephew. Let's find that hat and get out of here." She rubbed the goosebumps stealing up her arms. The closet held the scent of Russell's cologne. She could too well imagine he might walk in any moment.

"I want that top hat."

"Top hat! That's surely your father's best silk hat. Besides, isn't that a little formal for an afternoon tea party? How about that bowler or the fedora?"

"Fedora, then," Alistair decided. "That's what the bigwig men from Tammany Hall wear, the ones that used to come to see Father from time to time."

"When was this?"

"Oh, I don't remember. Before he went away . . . before Mother went to that place that kept her so long . . . before you came. I wasn't supposed to be spying." Alistair donned the hat, checked the looking glass, and tipped it forward to a rakish angle.

"Quite dapper. You're a regular dandy. Let's get back to the tea party. Your mother and Clara are waiting."

But Gwen could not focus on the tea party, no matter how delicious Mrs. Barrie's lavender scones or how infectious Marion's or the children's laughter. The afternoon stretched beautifully before them but question after question filled Gwen's mind.

Tammany Hall . . . Haven't they a reputation for ruling with an iron fist—with a fair amount of corruption in their ranks? What business can Russell have with Tammany? What can Tammany Hall have to do with the acquiring and selling of Egyptian antiquities?

13

"Easter's coming soon—early this year, April fourth." Marion stirred sugar in her morning tea after the children had left the table.

"Mrs. Barrie said she'd have Mrs. McGinley do a lamb with mint sauce for Easter dinner," Gwen said. "I offered to bake a coconut cake, but she said that Mrs. McGinley will no longer allow us in her kitchen, and that you have your own traditions."

"Well, that's a laugh. Mrs. Barrie is the one with all the traditions. She'd turn us all into Scotsmen if she had her way. But she's a wonderful housekeeper and I rely on her implicitly. Besides, I don't really care what we eat."

"I wish you did, Marion. You could do with a little fattening up."

Marion smiled faintly at Gwen, then turned to look out the window. "I love spring, you know—new life, flowers, birds returning to nest and singing their sweet songs."

"Spring has always been your favorite season."

"Yes, it was." Marion grew quiet.

"What is it?"

Marion shifted her napkin, realigned her table silver, but didn't meet Gwen's eye. "This will be my last spring, Gwen, my last Easter Sunday. I want it to be my best—the best it can be."

"Don't say that. You're stronger, getting stronger every day. You even have color in your cheeks—very becoming—and now that it's spring, we can get out, do things, go places together . . . when we're sure it's safe." Gwen twisted the napkin in her lap, afraid if she stopped talking, Marion's words might settle in both their minds.

Marion smiled. "I'm not being morbid. I want to create wonderful memories for Alistair and Clara while I can, and memories with you. I need you to help me."

The idea cut Gwen like a too-sharp knife. But she would do anything she could for Marion, as long as she could. "What do you want me to do?"

"I want to paint boiled eggs with the children, then you hide them in the back garden so they can hunt them while I watch. I want to wake up Easter morning to the fragrance of Mrs. Barrie's hot cross buns served with a pot of steaming Earl Grey. Clara must have a new dress and Easter bonnet, and Alistair a very grown-up suit, a gentleman's suit with long trousers. You must have a new spring dress and hat. We'll dress to the nines. I want us all to go to church together."

"Church? But—"

Marion cut her off. "I'll worship and thank God for the life and time He's given me. I'll sing at the top of my lungs, sing my heart out. Well, as best I can. The house must be filled with flowers and the fragrance of Mrs. McGinley's roasting lamb and Mrs. Barrie's simnel cake." The long, impassioned speech stole Marion's breath and ended in a fit of coughing.

Gwen poured a glass of water, pressing it into Marion's hands, and gently rubbed her frail back. "Calm yourself, Marion." She swallowed the thick lump in her throat but couldn't control the floods that filled her eyes. "We'll do everything, anything you want, but . . . I don't think you should go out to church. All those people in an enclosed space . . . it's not safe, not yet. There's still influenza about."

"I knew you'd say that."

"Mrs. Barrie would insist."

"I need to take the Lord's Communion. It's been over six months since—"

"I'm sure the Lord understands, Marion. He—"

"It's for my sake, Gwen. It's my sacrifice of praise and thanksgiving. I'll see Him soon and I need to do this. It's all I have to offer Him."

"You've given Him your heart and trusted your children to Him. I see that so clearly." Still, Gwen was afraid for her sister. *She's made such strides, and now to risk it all* . . . "We'll make all the preparations, just as you've said, but please reconsider—and pray—about going to church. When the time comes, if you feel strong and are determined, I'll help you go—as long as you promise me you'll remain at home if you're not up to it. Promise?"

Marion reached across the table and squeezed her sister's hand, a fragmented smile on her lips. "I promise."

Maundy Thursday came and Marion woke with a tickling throat, a runny nose, and a slight fever. Gwen telephoned Dr. Callahan, who came before noon to check on his patient.

"It's only sniffles," Marion insisted, coughing, and quickly covered her mouth with her handkerchief. "It's nothing."

"Perhaps. A cold at the very least. But I recommend you rest in bed for a few days. Sit up as you're able. None of this going out to church as Miss Armstrong says you've determined to do. Out of the question. I'll stop by again tomorrow. In the meantime, Miss Armstrong, call me if you deem it necessary."

Marion closed her eyes and leaned back against her pillow, resignation and defeat written across her features.

After Gwen showed the doctor out, she found Marion bundled and sitting in her chair by the window, a stray tear trickling down her cheek.

"I so wanted to go, once more."

"I know, dear, but what Dr. Callahan says is for the best. You see that, don't you?"

"Please, Gwen. Telephone Reverend Sinclair and ask him to visit me, to bring me Communion. Ask him to come before Easter, if he's able. I know this is a very busy season for him, but . . . please."

"I will. I'll telephone him right away."

Mrs. Barrie bristled at the idea of bringing an outsider into the house but confessed to Gwen that at least it was better than Mrs. Bennett going out to church.

Gwen was moved by Reverend Sinclair's willingness to visit Marion early that very evening, before the Maundy Thursday Communion he would hold at church.

As much as the influenza was petering out, she'd read of continued deaths, belated funerals and memorial services. She knew that pastors, doctors, and nurses across the city, as well as coffin makers, undertakers, funeral homes, and collectors of the dead for mass burials, were still run ragged, after all this time. It was no small request to ask the reverend to add a home visit to his overburdened schedule.

Reverend Sinclair was not what Gwen had imagined. An older man, perhaps late sixties, with a thick and shining head of graying hair and weary lines etching his clear blue eyes and mouth. Gwen thought the most notable thing about him was his smile. *Kindly, benevolent—that's the look about him. When it's safe for us all to go to church again, I'd like to hear him speak.*

She and the children and Mrs. Barrie joined in the short service held in Marion's room. Clara nestled close to her mother's side.

Marion's voice came scratchy, quieter than usual. "Thank you for coming, Reverend Sinclair. I know that adding this to your duties now is a sacrifice. It means so much to me, to all of us."

"Communion is a wondrous gift from our Lord, Mrs. Bennett. I'm glad to be His hands and feet this day of all days."

Reverend Sinclair prayed and set his hand on Marion's head in blessing. For just a moment Gwen heard him sigh, thought she saw him sway, perhaps a little dizzy, then steady himself before speaking. *Poor man, he's exhausted.*

As he read passages from Luke of Jesus administering and sharing His last supper with His apostles, then broke bread and poured wine to share, Gwen sensed a holy hush in the room, a peace she'd not known before, one she didn't fully understand but didn't want to end. After the solemn service, she looked up to see great joy, peace, and contentment radiating from her sister's face.

Thank You, Lord. I don't understand all that Marion sees or feels or knows about You, but thank You, for her sake . . . and for mine, for all of us.

Gwen woke in the early dawn of Good Friday, her head pounding and fire in her throat. She'd promised to dye eggs with Marion and the children today. She'd told Mrs. McGinley that she'd take care of hard-boiling the eggs and mixing the dyes if the housekeeper would only let her in the kitchen for a half hour, but now she couldn't think of anything she'd rather do less. She pulled her feet to the floor and pushed herself upright. The room swayed. *I must be catching Marion's cold—the last thing I need, the last thing any of us need. I hope she's feeling better today.*

Gwen lay back down. *Another half hour, that's all.* She closed her eyes and fell into a fitful sleep.

When she woke, the headache had only grown more severe. Her throat burned. *I need tea . . . or honey and lemon.* Slivers of daylight slipped between the drapery panels, piercing her eyes. She looked at the clock on her mantle. *Nine thirty. Mrs. Barrie must have served breakfast. Why didn't she call me?*

Aspirin. Mrs. Barrie must have aspirin. Gwen pushed her arms through the sleeves of her robe, as if through thick sludge. Opening her bedroom door, she listened for the sound of footsteps, the distant clank of silverware or tumblers being cleared from the dining room, or the not-so-stern voice of Mrs. Barrie issuing orders, but heard nothing.

The door to Alistair's room was open but Clara's was closed.

It was Gwen's habit to check on Marion before going down to breakfast, and to empty her chamber pot, saving Mrs. Barrie the trouble. Lately, Marion would already be up, her draperies drawn open, and sitting by her window.

But when she opened her sister's door, she found the curtains closed, Marion still abed, her face turned toward the wall. A foul smell permeated the room.

"Marion?" Gwen whispered into the darkened room, uncertain if her sister was awake.

Slowly Marion turned her head toward Gwen and strained to raise a restricting hand. Her voice cracked and croaked as she whispered, "Stay away."

Nothing could have called Gwen to Marion's side quicker. She jerked open the drapes, enough to see her sister's face and the stream of vomit across her pillow. Her heart racing, Gwen poured a glass of water from the bedside carafe and lifted her sister's head to sip.

Marion tried, but the water dribbled from the corner of her mouth. Blood trickled from her nose and one eye. Simply holding her neck, Gwen could feel that fever raged beneath her sister's skin.

The ditty the girls had sung in the park last year sprang like an unwanted serpent into Gwen's mind:

I had a little bird;
His name was Enza,
I opened up the window
And in flew Enza!

"How is this possible?" How didn't matter. The dreaded evil had slithered into the garden and stolen innocence.

"Keep the children away," Marion begged.

"Yes." Gwen knew it was a promise she'd be hard-pressed to keep. "Let me change your pillow slip."

"Remember your promise."

"Yes, I'll keep them away, keep them safe."

Marion clutched Gwen's sleeve. "Your promise to watch over them, care for them, when I'm gone. Swear it."

Gwen wanted to fight the fatality in Marion's plea, but she knew it was no use. Marion could not survive this. "I promise. I'll care for them as my own, love them all their days."

"Be their mother, Gwen."

"Yes, I swear it. But fight this, Marion. They need you, far more than they need me."

Marion let go of Gwen's sleeve. "Go to them, Gwen. Leave me." She closed her eyes.

Gwen took the cloth by the washbowl, dipped it into the cool water, and cleaned her sister's face and neck as best she could, bathing her fevered brow and arms, no matter that her own head was splitting, her own throat aching. *Please, God, help us.*

From somewhere downstairs, china crashed. *Alistair. Clara.* Gwen left the cloth in the washbowl and dragged herself toward the stairs. Every footstep felt as if she wore leaden boots through sea-water. Alternately she sweated, desperate to throw off her robe, and shivered, chills racing up and down her limbs.

"Mrs. Barrie?" Gwen tried to call, but nothing more than a pant came out. She made her way down the stairs, clinging to the banister, afraid if she let go, she'd tumble to the foyer floor below.

Mrs. Barrie slumped in a chair by heaps of spilled food, milk, shattered glass and crockery. An entire pot of tea spread its dark liquid across the marble floor.

"Mrs. Barrie."

The older woman looked up, her head braced between her hands. "I dropped the tray. I'm so sorry. I don't know what's got into me. I canna—"

Gwen placed her wrist against Mrs. Barrie's forehead. "You're burning with fever." Fear gripped her heart. "Have the children been down?"

"Alistair went to fetch the broom and mop. Mrs. McGinley's taken to her bed with a raging fever. I haven't seen Clara. I was just about to call her, but I canna seem to . . . get hold. Alistair said he'd see to her."

"It's the influenza, Mrs. Barrie. I must telephone Dr. Callahan. Can you get yourself to bed?"

Gwen didn't hear her answer. She barely made it to the chair by the telephone. Lifting the receiver, calling for the operator took all the strength and focus she possessed. The clock in the hallway bonged eleven. She spoke to the operator, then to a woman who answered the telephone in the doctor's office, begging for Dr. Callahan to come. What the woman replied, Gwen couldn't say.

Before she placed the receiver in the cradle, Alistair, wailing in terror, cried from up the stairs, "Aunt Gwen, Mrs. Barrie—help! Somebody, help!"

14

That afternoon Marion fell mercifully into a coma before suffering further. She died that evening, never waking, never knowing that just down the hallway her sweet Clara, so young and full of life the day before, had gasped her last breath in a face frozen in horror, blood trickling from her eyes and nose. Gwen couldn't be certain when Mrs. McGinley passed, only that she had and not a soul was with her.

Mrs. Barrie, driven to her bed, delirious in her raging fever, knew none of it. Alistair thrashed and choked on his vomit amid fevered dreams and coughing that sounded as if he might drown. Gwen dragged herself from bed to bed, too ill to adequately nurse them, too desperate and terrified to lie down lest she pass into oblivion and they, too, die on her watch.

It was dark before Dr. Callahan arrived, explaining as he swept in with the cold evening air that he'd been out all day on calls and hadn't known of Gwen's telephone plea. He babbled on, asking questions, but Gwen's fever pulsed in her brain, her head thick with fog and her throat burning so that she couldn't speak, couldn't take in what he said or articulate her need, their need. Stumbling down the stairs to open the door had stolen her remaining strength. The cough that had subsided for moments began again in earnest, racking her chest and throat until she thought both might burst open. She summoned every reserve to point up the stairs. He misunderstood and insisted on helping her climb the staircase toward her room—a mountain she could no longer traverse. Before they reached the landing, her world began to spin, a cyclone racing faster and faster with each step until she tripped, falling, falling, until there was nothing.

Muffled voices hovered—a cultured, vaguely familiar American voice; a rich Scottish brogue, but not Mrs. Barrie's—a man's. Then echoes, as heard in the deep caverns Gwen had visited as a girl, floated in and out of her consciousness. She tried to open her eyes, to push against the deep and deepening darkness, to no avail.

At intervals came vivid dreams, stark nightmares, visions of horror, and memories she knew to be real merging, swirling, colliding in a kaleidoscope of color, a confusion of disturbing patterns played and replayed. Darkness followed once more, and quiet, until finally the voices began again. After what seemed eons and eons of time a slit of light stole through her eyes, so piercing she winced, cringed, and fell back into the deep, dark cavern.

"Miss Armstrong." The Scottish man's voice spoke near her ear, pounding in Gwen's head. She cringed again and the voice came softer. "Miss Armstrong. Can you hear me? Can you wake?"

Gwen strained to open her eyes, to focus her attention. The voice was now familiar, but she couldn't place it. The light hurt.

"Ah, there you are. That's it. Open your eyes. Did anyone ever tell you you have lovely brown eyes?"

No. Yes. I'm dreaming, dreaming.

"Miss Armstrong." This time a feminine whisper.

Gwen drew a deep breath, forced her eyes open, though it was only a slit. A cool cloth stroked her forehead, her face, her neck.

"There now, doesn't that feel good?" Mrs. Barrie's face came into view.

"Mrs. Barrie," Gwen whispered in return.

"You gave us quite a scare. But here you are now, in the land of the living, praise God."

"Marion," Gwen remembered. "And Mrs. McGinley."

"Aye, and our darling Clara, gone to Jesus."

Gwen shut her eyes tight, tears springing from those wells. "No. Dear God, please, no more."

"'*The Lord gave, and the Lord hath taken away; blessed be the name of the Lord.*'" Gwen heard the break in Mrs. Barrie's voice. She reached for her hand.

"Alistair? Please. Please say he's—"

"Alistair's sleeping in his room. He was the last to succumb, and not the worst case. The doctors—Dr. Callahan and Dr. McNeill—believe he'll make a full recovery, in time . . . as will you. The Lord's spared us for a purpose, Miss Armstrong. I don't know why, but we must thank Him."

Gwen closed her eyes. *How can I thank Him?* Her only sister was gone, and her memory of Clara's last breath was too stark, too vivid. Minutes passed while Mrs. Barrie sat in silence beside her, before the wheels in Gwen's mind took hold and she tried to push herself up from the bed.

"Hold now, where do you think you're going?"

"I must call . . . someone. An undertaker, Reverend Sinclair. Funerals."

"That's all done now. Mr. Bennett's home. He's seen to it all . . . and more." Relief mingled with disapproval in Mrs. Barrie's tone.

"Russell? Home? When?"

"A week past now."

"A week?"

"You've slept these ten days, my dear, and it's no wonder. You were so ill, so very ill we didn't know if we'd lose you too."

"And you?"

"Weary, but regaining strength day by day."

"Be careful . . . The funerals? For Marion and Clara?"

"You're not to worry. Mr. Bennett took care of them. Four days past. The day after Reverend Sinclair's."

"Reverend Sinclair?"

Mrs. Barrie sighed, shaking her head. "That dear man entered glory Easter Sunday evening. A fitting day for such a man of God, to be sure, but for all of us, a terrible loss—another terrible loss."

Gwen groaned. It was too much, too many, too close.

"We all thought we'd come to the end of it, but that Spanish Lady knows no bounds and is no respecter of persons."

It was all Gwen could take in. Her eyes, feeling as if they held weighted coins, drifted closed of their own accord.

"You sleep now, miss. There'll be plenty of time to talk later. It's getting well and strong that matters now. Mr. Bennett will be relieved to know you've woken."

Russell . . . your wife, and now your precious daughter. I'm so sorry . . . so very sorry.

Three days later Gwen put feet to floor. She needed to see that Alistair was indeed alive and recovering; to comfort him however she was able through the loss of his beloved mother and sister. How she would do that when her heart felt like lead, when she'd no idea how to comfort herself, she didn't know.

She also knew she must face Russell. She'd failed him, failed to keep his family safe. He'd long anticipated the death of his wife, but to lose his daughter, the child he doted on . . . She could not imagine how he might react.

Will he send me away? If he does, how can I fulfill my promise to Marion to watch over Alistair? How can I leave Alistair now, for his own sake, poor child? How can I leave him for mine?

Gwen found Russell in the morning room eating breakfast, coffee and newspaper in hand. When she entered the room, he looked up. His face paled as he stood. "Gwen."

"Russell. I'm sorry. I'm so very sorry."

"Sit down, Gwen. You look as if you'll pass out." He pulled out the chair nearest him, waited until she sat, and stood looking down at her. "What do you need? Coffee? Water? Brandy?"

She shook her head. "Nothing."

"You look like death warmed over." He caught himself. "Rotten choice of words." He went to the sideboard, prepared a heaping plate, and set it in front of Gwen. "Eat."

"I can't, Russell. Truly."

"Try. I won't lose you too." He looked stricken.

"I didn't—couldn't—keep them safe. I'm so very sorry." Tears she hadn't intended filled her eyes, overflowed, ran down her cheeks.

He looked away. "It's not your fault. I knew Marion could never survive influenza . . . but Clara, my beautiful Clara . . ."

Gwen reached for his hand. Whatever had or had not passed between him and her sister, the man was grieving the shock of losing his precious daughter. He held on as if her hand was a lifeline.

"Mrs. Barrie told me everything. Marion is to blame for bringing the demon to this house. If Callahan hadn't sent her home, if she hadn't insisted that ridiculous, infected preacher come—"

"No. No, it wasn't Reverend Sinclair. You mustn't think that. Marion was sick already. In fact, he may have contracted it from—"

"Don't tell me what to think."

Gwen drew her hand away.

"Mrs. Barrie knew no visitors were to be allowed in the house until the influenza passed. She's at least partly responsible."

"We all thought it had passed, and—" She stopped, before saying things she'd regret for reasons even she couldn't process.

"And what?"

"Reverend Sinclair wasn't the first visitor. There have been 'visitors' every month or sometimes more the entire time you've been gone."

Russell blinked.

"Men that come and go in the west wing in the night. They have keys to the house, to your office. I don't understand—"

"You don't need to understand that. They're not allowed anywhere inside the main part of the house. It has nothing to do with them."

"But—"

"Leave it, Gwen. My business affairs are my own."

"Alistair believes you're a spy for the government, that it all has to do with some secret mission you can't talk about." She was fishing, still trying to piece together everything that had happened and the swirl of strange dreams that never seemed far away.

"Does he?" Russell almost smiled. "A noble subterfuge."

"Are you?" She lifted her hands in confusion, frustration. "Those men—they're—they feel dangerous. And what are they delivering by the truckload?"

"You're not well, Gwen. You're imagining things." Russell folded his newspaper and laid it beside his plate. "As I said, this is none of your concern. My business affairs are separate from my private life." He paused. "What do you mean—how do you know they 'feel dangerous'?"

"I heard noises one night and went to investigate. A man, a big brute of a man all but threatened me. I can't believe you're—"

"Not all businessmen are gentlemen, Gwen. Leave it or leave my house."

Gwen felt the blood drain from her face. *Leave this house? Leave Alistair? Dear God, what do I do?* "Is that what you want? For me to leave?"

He looked away.

Her heart thudded inside her chest. "I didn't mean to overstep."

"Then don't." His face changed. His combined grief and austerity melted into a sad half smile. "And no, I don't want you to leave. I want you to stay, very much. Please."

Gwen drew a deep breath, more than willing to change the subject. "Marion insisted I promise . . . promise to watch over the children if anything—when she was no longer here . . . as if they are my own."

"And did you? Promise?"

"Yes."

"Well then. You can't leave, for Alistair or for me. He'll need looking after and some amount of maternal care, I suppose . . . at least until he returns to school."

"Returns to school? The spring semester is already underway. He needs time to mourn the loss of his mother and Clara. They were so very close. And the influenza—it may take weeks for him to regain his strength."

"And you, yours. You must take care of yourself first, Gwen." He covered her hand. "That must be your highest priority. I told you once and I will say again that you are a most valued member of this family."

Carrying a pot of fresh coffee, Mrs. Barrie gave a discreet cough from the doorway. Quickly, Gwen pulled her hand away. There'd been nothing but brotherly compassion in Russell's touch, surely, but did it appear otherwise to Mrs. Barrie?

15

Gwen felt keenly the loss of her sister and young Clara. She mourned for Alistair's loss as much as her own. That she and Alistair had missed their funerals was both relief against the sudden grief and injury beyond measure or repair. *Lack of closure. That's what they say. Nothing could truly offer that closure, but we missed the opportunity to say goodbye . . . Nothing prepared us. Why? Why, God? Why take them?*

The curse of disease and death, its cruel unfairness and indiscriminate malice, broke her spirit. By night she pounded her pillow and wept, railed against God and the universe, and cursed herself for not forgiving earlier, for not pursuing a restored relationship with her sister years sooner.

By day she summoned every reserve to remain calm and purposeful for Alistair's sake. She wrapped him in her arms, dried his tears, alternately tolerated his outbursts of anger and frustration, his frequent sullenness, his self-pity, and the questions she could not answer. She endured the flood of memories he desperately needed to share, no matter that even the good ones shredded her heart.

Gwen knew that Mrs. Barrie mourned quietly in her own way. How could she not? She'd been a devoted champion and confidante to Marion since she'd come to work and live with the newly married couple. She'd been a loving caregiver in Alistair's and Clara's lives from the moment they were born.

"I pity the child," Mrs. Barrie grieved, "for he is still a child. Eleven is a tender age and far too young to be orphaned."

"At least he has his father." Gwen tried to take and to give some comfort in that.

"Does he?" It was the most forward thing Mrs. Barrie had ever said. "Mr. Bennett hardly gives his son the time of day, let alone the needed shoulder to weep upon. I shudder to think if you were not here, Miss Armstrong, what might become of the boy. And yet . . ."

"And yet?"

"It's not my place to say . . . but be wary. Alistair needs you both, and Mr. Bennett . . . Mr. Bennett sees only to his own needs, I'm afraid, his own wants." Meaningfully, she raised her brows.

Gwen knew precisely what she meant. It was a warning for her sake and for Alistair's. And yet, there was some part of her that not only recognized Russell's forwardness but her unbidden and natural response. She had no intention of being disloyal to her sister's memory or in any way gleaning attention from Russell that Alistair deserved and needed. Even so, she couldn't help but wonder yet again what it would be like to be married to such a man—a handsome, charming, winsome man who looked at her as if the sun rose and set in her. What would it be like to have the security of marriage, to hold the intimate attention of a man she sometimes genuinely admired and sometimes admired against her will and common sense?

When a month had passed, Russell gave Gwen Marion's Bible, saying that she'd told Mrs. Barrie she wanted her sister to have it when she'd gone. He also asked her to pack up Marion's clothes. She'd swallowed the hard knot in her throat but complied. Holding her sister's Bible and gathering her sister's personal things cut her to the quick. But as she pulled ensembles, shoes and hats and silk undergarments from her sister's dressing room, she couldn't help but wonder what it would be like to dress in such fabulous gowns, to wear gloves and heels fit for a princess. She searched for Marion's jewelry, believing

Russell would want that kept separate, perhaps stored in his safe. Only there was no jewelry. *Odd. Russell must have already seen to that.*

What would it be like to be married to Russell, to not only be Alistair's aunt but his second mother as Marion hoped? She'd come to love the boy as her own. Sometimes it was difficult to remember that he wasn't.

Each time she found herself contemplating such things, she pulled herself up short, determined to keep her mind on teaching Alistair, on loving him as her nephew and seeking his highest good. She tried to push away her questions about her relationship with Russell. It was all too confusing, too complex.

As the months passed, she could almost convince herself of Russell's platonic affections until a box of flowers was delivered with an appreciative note, or he invited her for a late-night chat beside the fire in the drawing room, asking for her insights or simply her company.

There was nothing overtly intimate or improper in his overtures, and yet she felt uncertain of his motives, less certain of the speeding up of her heart. Once he invited her to see his latest Egyptian acquisitions. His eyes lit as he spoke of his time in Egypt, of his reconnection with archaeologists there after the end of the war, of his search for and discovery of rare antiquities. That light rekindled a flame in Gwen she'd thought long dead. She didn't mean to acknowledge that flame, but she couldn't deny it.

Mrs. Barrie wasn't the only one who noticed Russell's attentions to her or her response to him. Alistair watched his father and Gwen at mealtimes with troubled eyes, sometimes doing his best to hide jealous, even hostile glances.

Gwen tried to bring Alistair to his father's notice, to include him in their conversations, especially when discussions focused on archaeological digs or antiquities, subjects she knew fascinated Alistair and could surely connect the two. Inexplicably, Russell shut his son down at the least provocation, even Alistair's most innocent questions. Gwen could not understand his vexation, especially at a time when the boy needed his father more than ever.

"Why?" Gwen asked one evening when she and Russell walked in the garden, long after Alistair had gone to his room. "Why do you push him away? He loves you, looks up to you. Your work inspires all he wants to do in life. More than that, he needs you. He's lost his mother and his precious sister—his entire world."

She could see the tension in Russell's mouth, the rigid squaring of his shoulders before he answered. "You seem to forget that I, too, lost my wife and my daughter."

"I know you did, and I'm so very sorry. I didn't mean to—"

"Clara was the good—the best that came from my marriage."

"Alistair's still here. He's your son, and he needs—"

"He needs to grow up. Marion coddled the boy from the time he was born."

"He's grieving, Russell."

He turned away from her, ostensibly viewing the landscape, but she sensed there was more. "What is it? What aren't you saying?" She watched him swallow, draw a deep breath, saw the lines in his mouth and the crease across his forehead.

"His birth changed everything."

"With Marion." Gwen remembered.

"My plans, my hopes, my marriage. Everything that mattered. I've told you before she no longer had time for me. All she cared about was . . ." He stopped. "I suppose that sounds infantile to you."

You were jealous . . . of a baby.

"I admit I've never been good with children, had never intended to have them."

"Life doesn't always go as we plan."

"No." He huffed. "I'd hoped, after Clara was born, that Marion would be content in that department, that things might return to the way they were. Parents in our class, in my circle of society, don't mollycoddle their children. Nursemaids, nannies, and governesses take care of those things, freeing adults to travel, to pursue their social responsibilities." He turned to face her. "You must think that makes me an inattentive father."

That's exactly what I think, and more . . . but is there more? "Perhaps . . ."

"Yes?"

She detected a note of wistfulness if not hope in his voice. "Perhaps it simply means that you've not experienced—or explored—the genuine joy and satisfaction of a rich family life."

He stared at her as if that was a new thought. "I grew up in boarding schools most of the year. Weeks at home were spent in the company of tutors. I cannot imagine my mother or father spending days with me. They had obligations, their own interests." He paused. "I have no idea what— Do you know what a rich family life is?"

She felt the heat rise up her neck. "Not entirely . . . but I hope to . . . someday. With someone."

He didn't move but stared at her long moments. "Is that something we might explore together?"

Gwen's heart caught. "I wouldn't have thought so. You married my sister."

"And now?"

She couldn't process that, couldn't possibly answer. She began walking again. "What are your plans for Alistair?"

"Alistair should have been sent away to school years ago—a good school where he'd learn to be a man and a gentleman. He will be, in the new term."

Gwen swallowed. "I thought when you mentioned him returning to school that you meant locally—the school he attended before the epidemic."

"Local private schools were Marion's doing, not mine. I never intended the children remain at home, though I suppose I'd have given in for Clara until she was older. Finishing school for her, at the very least. None of that matters now. I'll see that Whitfield registers Alistair for the fall term."

"Then I'll be leaving, as soon as he does. It would be unthinkable for me to stay were I not caring for Alistair."

He took her hand, pulling her closer, searching her eyes. "Would it? Would it be so bad to spend your days here, with me? To see what becoming a family, as you say, might be?"

Gwen pulled her hand away and walked on, trying to make light. "Inappropriate. You know that's what it would be."

"If our relationship changed . . . might you consider—"

"Stop. Stop now."

He stepped back. "I'm sorry. You're right. It's too soon, of course. But I ask you, please, don't close your mind to—"

"Exactly. It's much too soon. It's also late. Good night, Russell." Without waiting for him to answer or accompany her, Gwen walked quickly back to the house. She was not surprised to find Mrs. Barrie watching from the veranda's open door.

Gwen waited to come down to breakfast the next morning until she believed Russell had gone for the day. She wasn't ready to answer the questions in his eyes, nor did she trust her own response.

The dining room was empty when she took her breakfast from the sideboard, but Mrs. Barrie came in shortly with hot coffee.

"Good morning, Mrs. Barrie." Gwen smiled, hoping to ease the tension growing between them since Marion's death.

"Good morning, Miss Armstrong." As Mrs. Barrie poured coffee and set the pot beside Gwen, there was nothing in the woman's tone leading her to believe a thaw was on the horizon.

"Mrs. Barrie, before you go, I'd like to talk with you, to ask your advice."

Mrs. Barrie paused; her eyebrows rose.

"I hardly know how to begin." Gwen set her napkin on the table. "I'm concerned about Alistair."

The housekeeper waited.

"It's only natural that he's grieving his mother and Clara—we all are—but I don't know what to do for him, how to help him." Gwen turned to pleading. "You've been with him since the day he was born. You know him better than anyone—now. If there's anything you can tell me that might help him, that I might do, I would be grateful."

Frost fell from Mrs. Barrie's eyes. "I'm concerned for the lad as well. More than I can say."

"Then, please, sit and talk with me. Tell me, advise me—anything."

Mrs. Barrie sat beside Gwen but didn't look her in the eye. "Might I speak freely?"

"Please—by all means."

"The lad needs his father in the worst way. The boy is eleven—growing quickly toward manhood with no one to show him the way. He's lived with women all his life."

Considering his absentee father. "I've tried explaining that to Russell—Mr. Bennett—but I'm afraid he . . . he doesn't know how to . . ."

"Or isn't inclined."

"No," Gwen admitted.

Mrs. Barrie sighed before meeting Gwen's eye. "Then it must be you. You must parent the lad if his own father won't."

"I'm not his mother, Mrs. Barrie. I love Alistair with all my heart, but I don't want to confuse him further."

"He's afraid that you'll marry his father and push him aside."

"Did he say that?"

"He doesn't have to say what's written all over his face, what's leaping like tadpoles from his eyes."

"No. I see that."

"Do you intend to marry Mr. Bennett?"

"I've no intentions beyond seeing to Alistair's welfare as long as I'm allowed to do so. Beyond loving my nephew. I promised my sister that I would."

"Then do what's best for Alistair."

"And what is that? Please tell me."

"Take him away for a time. Get him out of this house where he's watched those he loved most die before his eyes. Give him fresh air and sunshine and a new adventure. Give him space from his father, who is so deep in his own version of self-pity and preoccupation that he cannot see what his son needs, let alone provide it."

Gwen sat back. "I have no authority to do that . . . and where would I take him?"

"Mrs. Bennett, before she became too ill, would take the children to the seaside each summer for a month. Mr. Bennett rarely joined them. Sometimes I'd go along to help her—especially after she became weaker—but before that she went alone with the children. It was their greatest bonding time. They'd come back suntanned and freckle-faced and full of laughter. It was a tonic for their souls."

"A tonic for their souls . . . yes. That's what he needs . . . we both need." Gwen straightened. "Do you think Mr. Bennett would allow it?"

"I don't see why not. He did before. I think he'd appreciate seeing less of Alistair now. The way he looks at the child—I don't mean to speak poorly of him. He's grieving in his own way, I suppose, but he looks at Alistair as if he resents him."

He does. He always has. If you only knew . . . Perhaps you do.

"I think it would do them both a world of good to be apart for a time," Mrs. Barrie went on. "It would allow Alistair to have all the love and attention and affirmation you can give him. He needs to run in the waves, to fill his lungs with sea air. He needs to laugh. And so do you."

I can't remember when I last laughed.

"And it might allow Mr. Bennett's passions, or what he believes are his passions, to cool for a bit. It might give you both time to clear your heads and consider if you want a—a relationship in the future."

"Space to breathe."

"Aye."

"Thank you. Thank you, Mrs. Barrie. You're a true friend."

"I hope I didn't speak too plainly, miss."

Gwen shook her head. "I asked you to. I needed you to, and I hope you always will."

Mrs. Barrie nodded, but Gwen saw it was not without some reservation.

Gwen wrote Russell a note, suggesting that she and Alistair repeat the vacation that he'd taken in the past with his mother and sister. She slipped it under his museum door in the afternoon, knowing he'd be out that evening and leaving the next day for Chicago.

She waited all night on pins and needles for his answer, which came the next day in the form of a note at the breakfast table.

Dear Gwen,

Yes, a trip to the seaside might do you both a world of good.

I'll have Whitfield arrange for your train tickets and rent a cottage for the two of you.

Take charge, my dear Cleopatra. Adventures await.

Enjoy your summer. I look forward to the autumn.

Fondly,
Russell

She hadn't expected it to be so easy, and she didn't know what Russell meant by *"adventures await"* or *"I look forward to the autumn."* Nor did she quite know how she felt about his easy dismissal of her for the entire summer. *I should be glad . . . thrilled, relieved. Shouldn't I?*

PART TWO

16

SUMMER 1920

Gwen and Alistair boarded the train early on a late-June morning.

Despite the comfortable first-class accommodations, for most of the train ride Alistair sat quietly, staring out the window, watching the miles go by. He'd been loath to leave Mrs. Barrie, and though she'd genuinely encouraged him, she was clearly sorry to see him go.

Gwen had half expected that Russell would insist Mrs. Barrie accompany them, but he had not. He'd made certain Gwen was supplied with sufficient funds that they might eat out every meal or do anything in the world that struck their fancy, but he'd not offered a third ticket.

If Marion could manage alone with two children, certainly I can manage with one. She hadn't realized how much she'd come to depend on Mrs. Barrie, or how comfortable that arrangement was. The idea of keeping Alistair entertained every day while supplying food and clean clothing hadn't quite entered her mind before, but it did as she watched him watching nothing.

"Off to the seaside, you and your son?" A lady across the aisle, wrangling a baby and a toddler, struck up a conversation.

"Oh, he's not—" Gwen decided it best not to explain. "Sea Isle

City. We're looking forward to some cool breezes. The city's begun to swelter."

"Sea Isle City? Oh, you'll have a good time. They've done the town proud since the storm."

"The storm?"

"You don't know? A great nor'easter this February. Nine inches of rain in twenty-four hours. Winds you'd not believe—storefronts smashed in, Ocean Pier crushed, the band pavilion nothing but kindling. You wouldn't be traveling by train then—washed out the railroad bed. We got to the mainland by rowboats!"

"And now?"

"Oh, as I say, they've done the town proud. Boy Scouts from St. Joe's Church did a right good job with their cleanup round town. The builders have been going at it tooth and nail. They're ready for the summer crowd. Got to gather their nuts while they may."

Gwen nodded and did her best to smile. She hoped the woman was right. How could seaside cottages sustain such abuse and be repaired in time for an influx of visitors?

When Gwen and Alistair stepped from the train, the town was abuzz with tourists decked out in their casual summer whites, the merriest sign of life Gwen had seen in two years.

Alistair, now nearly as tall as Gwen, crooked his arm. The gentlemanly offer took Gwen by surprise—enough that she didn't respond right away. Color heightened in Alistair's cheek. Gwen realized her mistake and quickly took his arm.

"Miss Armstrong?" A burly, suntanned man with a smart mustache tipped his hat to Gwen.

"Yes?"

"How do you do? I'm Cecil Cassa. Mr. Whitfield asked me to introduce you to Sea Isle City and escort you and Master—*Mister* Bennett, now I see—to your cottage."

"Mr. Cassa." Alistair took the man's hand and shook it. "It's good to see you again."

"And you, son. It's been a long spell since you and your—since you've been here." The man's forehead creased. "I was real sorry to hear about your mother and sister. A terrible loss."

The smile left Alistair's face. He dropped his hand. "Thank you."

A regretful glance passed between Mr. Cassa and Gwen. She lifted her chin as if to say they'd best get on.

"Let me see to collecting your bags and we'll be on our way. My carriage is just there." He pointed to a carriage and two black mares standing across the street.

Gwen sat with Alistair as Mr. Cassa drove, giving his guided tour. He pointed out the boardwalk, and just on its west side, a large, three-story building. "Excursion House. It's filled to the hilt most times, always something lively going on. Dances, movies in its theater, roller skating—even boxing matches on occasion. You'll want to get in on their basketball games, Alistair. I'd wager with your height you could sink a basket or two." He turned and winked.

"As long as there's ice cream." Alistair brooked no argument.

"Ha! Ice cream! You'll find the best at Ocean Pier Theater—ice cream, fishing, dancing. Sea Isle City won't disappoint. But if you're looking for fudge, go to—"

"Anna Pauline Candies on the boardwalk! Genesee Cream Fudge!" Alistair's enthusiasm surprised Gwen. "I remember."

"Best there is!" Mr. Cassa winked again.

"I'm glad to hear there are so many things to see and do. We heard there'd been a terrible storm last winter, that it had done a great deal of damage."

"Oh, terrible. But we depend on the tourist trade, so folks got up and at it right away. Fishing's our main industry, mind you, selling locally and to buyers from Philadelphia and New York, but, no, we couldn't get by without our tourist trade." He pulled to a stop along the curb in front of a two-story house, larger than the home Gwen had grown up in, but small compared to Bennett Place. "Ah, here we are. Let's get you settled."

"I thought we were staying in a cottage."

Mr. Cassa laughed, lifted their heaviest trunk from his car, and started up the walkway. "This is the cottage, ma'am—one of the best. Not the one Mr. Bennett rented in years gone by. That was too badly damaged by the storm, but you'll find this just as comfortable and freshly painted."

"I'm glad it's not the same one," Alistair said quietly, staring.

"Are you?" Gwen wrapped her arm around his shoulder, used to his sudden changes in mood. "Then I am too. Let's get settled, shall we? Then we can explore." She smiled and together they climbed the steps.

Mr. Whitfield had thought of everything, including a telephone. The cupboards and icebox were all well supplied. There were chairs and umbrellas on the porch overlooking the sea, and everything one could need to enjoy time on the beach, from sandcastle building to badminton.

"I don't think we'll need to go shopping for a month!" Gwen declared, overwhelmed by such largesse.

"That's Father's doing. He always had Mr. Whitfield make sure Mother had everything we wanted. She liked that." Alistair sobered again at the mention of his mother.

That's the first positive thing he's said about his father since . . . Yes, it was very generous of Russell. "There's one thing I don't see."

"What?" Alistair looked as if he couldn't imagine what that might be.

"Do you know how to ride a bicycle?"

Alistair almost grinned. "I'll say I do! Do you?"

Gwen laughed. "I'll say I do too! That was my mode of transportation back in Paradox. We never owned an automobile and never had need to travel more than a few miles."

"There's a place to rent bicycles on the boardwalk—or there was."

"Let's go tomorrow, once we've settled in. I'm dying for a walk along the beach. I've never actually put my feet in the ocean."

"In all your life?" Alistair gaped.

"In all my life. You'll have to introduce me to the ocean—and to seaside life."

Alistair mocked a bow. "'Twill be my pleasure, my lady."

They both laughed.

17

The last week of June passed quickly. Gwen had imagined she'd regained her health back in New York, but she'd never felt quite like this—stronger, sun-kissed, eager for each new morning. She saw the change in Alistair too.

Bicycling the promenade against sea breezes each morning strengthened their legs. Afternoons she spent wading along the shore or reading beneath an umbrella while Alistair swam laps under the watchful eye of the lifeguard. She didn't own a bathing costume and refused to buy one. *Those one-piece affairs are hideous, belted or not. I'd sink to the bottom wearing that heavy thing. No, I'll not be caught dead in that.*

Early evenings they often spent in town so Alistair could play basketball, or they might take in a film. Twice they tried roller skating. Gwen found skating freeing, a reminder of ice skating on the local pond while growing up in Paradox. Alistair, having never tried before, ended up on the floor more often than not. She decided a different activity might do more for his confidence.

"Ice cream," Alistair announced. "We should end each day with a cone of ice cream. It's the perfect close."

"The perfect close to a lovely day," Gwen agreed, "but perhaps not every day."

"Well, it was a good try." He grinned.

Gwen laughed. "A very good try." *Do you have any idea how good it is to see you smile?*

In July they tried fishing, which Alistair took to with gusto, proud to be photographed with his catch. Gwen was not thrilled about baiting her hook. She insisted Alistair take care of that, which he gallantly did.

July 18 brought great excitement when an airplane swooped over houses and landed on the beach. Everyone ran to help, believing the pilot's engine must be in trouble.

But Alistair returned to Gwen. "It's not engine trouble at all! He's here to collect paying passengers. Can we go?"

"What? Ride in one of those—in the sky?"

"Yes!"

"No!"

"Aunt Gwen, it's the chance of a lifetime. The pilot said he flew from Princeton to Wildwood in one hour, thirty-five minutes! Can you imagine? Don't you think we might give it a try? It's for a good cause. They're raising money for the Princeton Club," Alistair all but begged.

But Gwen stood her ground. *I've no idea what the Princeton Club is, but I've lost your mother and your sister. I'll not have you—or me—falling out of a sky machine!*

Alistair sulked for a week. Gwen tried to make it up to him by going twice to see Mary Pickford's latest film, *Suds*, at Ocean Pier Theater, but it was little consolation.

August brought hotter days, and land breezes with pesky no-see-ums and deerflies with their nasty bites. Many of those days they stayed indoors, thankful for a screened back porch. Gwen encouraged Alistair to help with the cooking. They experimented with a recipe book they found in the bookcase. Equally delighted and disappointed in their creations, they found working on projects together a pleasure.

A storm broke the heat at last, casting a great lightning display across the ocean.

"Magnificent, thrilling—the forces of nature. Don't you think?" Gwen stood by the window, watching the wind raise tumultuous waves made visible by flashes of lightning across the water. A crash of thunder exploded like cannon fire through the heavens, rattling the windowpanes.

"I especially like it at night. Something I could never imagine by day."

"Exactly," Gwen agreed.

They stood together on the front porch, watching the last of the storm play out. In the darkness Alistair reached for Gwen's hand. She felt a bond form, an understanding. They'd survived another storm the last months—more fierce than the one they'd just witnessed. And after the storm, a calm. They'd forged a new connection through weeks spent exploring and discovering and enjoying time together at the seashore, one Gwen could not have imagined before they came.

No wonder Marion loved this time away with her children. Far away from tensions and expectations, everything in the city and everyone.

A second storm came the next night—less explosive, but producing a deluge of rain. Gwen had just slipped into bed when a pounding came at the front door.

Alistair was up in moments, standing sleepy-eyed in his doorway. "Who is it?"

Gwen cinched her robe tight around her waist as she met him in the hallway. "I don't know. I can't imagine."

The pounding came again.

Alistair picked up his baseball bat.

Please, God, don't let us need that. Gwen walked to the door, pulled back the curtain, and peered through the window, but couldn't discern who it was.

The pounding came once more. "Gwen! For pity's sake, open the door! It's pouring out here!"

"Russell!" Gwen gasped, unlocking the door.

"Father?" Alistair dropped his bat.

Russell stomped on the mat, rainwater pouring from his hat and coat and apparently useless umbrella.

"What are you doing here?" Gwen jumped back from the torrent of water before rushing for towels.

"Not exactly the open-arm welcome I hoped for."

"It's the middle of the night! You scared us half to death!"

"Barely ten o'clock."

Gwen mopped the floor as Russell peeled off his dripping coat, holding it out to Alistair. "We weren't expecting you, or anyone at this hour." She stood, still shaken.

"I see I should have telephoned first." He was miffed, and possibly a little drunk.

"That would have been most kind." Gwen glanced at him quickly before taking the sopping towels to the kitchen sink.

He followed her, too closely. "My apologies, Gwen. This is not the visit I'd planned."

"Visit?" She swallowed. "You don't mean to stay here, do you—tonight?"

"It is my house," he reminded her, stepping closer, the faint stink of whiskey on his breath. "I'm accustomed to visiting my house and my family in the summer."

"When your wife was alive."

"She means it's not appropriate, Father. She's not Mother." Alistair spoke grimly from the doorway.

Russell turned, focusing on Alistair for the first time.

Surprised to see your son? The thought did not comfort Gwen.

"That's not your affair, young man. Go back to bed."

"Aunt Gwen?" Alistair looked as if he would defend Gwen, die for Gwen, despite his father's order.

"It's all right, Alistair." She faced Russell. "The guest room is made up. It's upstairs, first door on the right. You can sleep there. If you're hungry, there's leftover chicken in the icebox, cake in the pantry. Help yourself." She wiped her hands on the tea towel. "Good night, Russell." She ushered Alistair from the kitchen toward his bedroom.

"What's he doing here?" Alistair whispered as they walked.

She shook her head. She'd no idea, but after smelling the alcohol on his breath, she knew she would lock her door.

Russell slept late the next morning. Gwen made certain she and Alistair went for their normal early-morning bike ride, but neither spoke as freely as they'd done before. They stopped at their favorite spot to take in the view, just as they'd done every morning.

"Do you think he'll stay?" Alistair kept his eyes on the horizon, just above the waves.

"I don't think so. I didn't expect him to come at all."

"You're sure?" Alistair's hostility, gone for weeks, shone through.

"Of course I'm sure. But we won't know his intentions until we ask him." She softened. "He is your father, Alistair. It's possible he wants to spend time with you."

Alistair raised his brows as if to say neither of them believed that.

And truly, Gwen didn't. *If he'd come with fatherly intentions, he wouldn't have come intoxicated. Prohibition doesn't seem to make much difference to him.*

"I don't want to stay here if he's staying."

"We've had a wonderful time, haven't we?"

"By ourselves."

The apple doesn't fall far from the tree, does it? Gwen didn't know how to navigate their male jealousies, if that's what it was.

"Has Father said anything to you about my returning to school? Because I don't want to. I want you to go on tutoring me. You will, won't you, Aunt Gwen? We could even do it here, in Sea Isle. We don't have to go back to New York."

Gwen moistened her lips and looked out to sea, wishing he'd not asked her, not today of all days. "Your father thinks going away to school will be the best thing for you, that you'll make good friends there, develop keen interests, and—"

"I don't want to go away. I told Mother that."

"Your mother expected to send you away to school?"

Alistair kicked a shell off the boardwalk. "She said that was their plan once I turned twelve, to send me to boarding school. She made it sound like a grand adventure. But I don't want to go so far away." He looked at her, eyes troubled. "You're all I have left of Mother and Clara, Aunt Gwen. I don't want things to change more than they have."

Gwen sighed, taking Alistair's chin in her hand. "No one ever does. I don't want to leave you either. Change is hard, but don't close your mind to the idea of school. It might be that grand adventure after all." *Don't close your mind—weren't those the words Russell said to me?*

Alistair set his jaw, swung his leg over his bike and pedaled fast away. Gwen did not try to keep up with him.

By the time they returned to the house, Russell had washed and shaved. They found him in his business suit, sitting at the kitchen table drinking black coffee and reading the newspaper. He stood as they entered the room. "Gwen, Alistair, I must apologize for my late-night arrival, and not in the best of condition." He looked so contrite Gwen felt a little sorry for him, for his shame, though she was aware of Alistair's stiff posture beside her.

"You found the coffee. Would you like some breakfast? I'm going to make banana pancakes and eggs this morning."

"Banana pancakes—that sounds splendid! I could eat a horse—or a stack of pancakes, if you please."

It was his smile, genuine and open, that did Gwen in. She smiled in return and pulled an apron from the hook.

Alistair turned on his heel and left the room. The front screen door slammed.

"So, how's he been these weeks? He looks as if he's built up—a little height, a bit of muscle definition. That's an improvement."

"Yes, we've been riding bikes every morning and he often spends afternoons swimming laps or rowing or playing basketball with boys in town."

Russell nodded. "Good. And his mental state? Still wallowing in his grief? Any improvement there?"

Gwen drew a deep breath. "Yes, a great deal, actually. He's just been taken off guard by your arrival." She sliced and chunked bananas, then measured flour, mixed in cinnamon, milk, eggs, oil, vanilla, and whisked the pancake batter, folding in the bananas.

"I was in Atlantic City on business and thought, being this close, that I'd pop down . . . see how you're doing—both of you. Is everything all right? Everything to your liking?"

"Everything's wonderful. It's been a splendid vacation for both of us. Fresh air and sunshine—"

"Does wonders. You're suntanned and rosy . . . beautiful, Gwen . . . my Cleopatra."

"Please don't call me that." She greased the griddle with more force than necessary.

"Why not? It's fitting."

"That was a long time ago."

"Like yesterday in my mind." He rose to stand behind her.

Gwen almost slammed the griddle onto the stovetop. "What business do you have in Atlantic City?" She lit the gas.

"You know I'm involved in imports. Atlantic City is a port."

"You said your antiquities come through New York." She poured the batter into four even circles across the griddle, refusing to face him.

"For the most part, they do. Why the interrogation? You know I don't allow my business to intrude on family life."

"I'm simply trying to understand your motivation for coming."

"Am I not welcome?"

"Your staying in the house here is not appropriate . . . and it's not wise."

"Because you're afraid people will talk, or because you find me irresistible?" She heard the smile in his voice and knew she shouldn't, mustn't turn to face him. She didn't answer. "Well, you needn't worry. I'll abscond by nightfall. I thought I might take you to lunch—Alistair as well—at one of the hotels in Cape May. Those grand old Victorians are something to see. How does that sound?"

"Unexpected." She flipped the pancakes.

He laughed. "I'm full of surprises. Such as . . ."

"Such as?"

"I've been thinking about Alistair's schooling."

She turned to face him. "So has he, and he doesn't want to—"

"I've been thinking that if you'll agree to stay, I could see my way to enrolling him within a day's distance—a private boarding school, of course. He could come home occasional weekends, if the headmaster allows."

"You don't think I can tutor him?" She held her breath.

"You're likely the best teacher he will ever have, but I do think the boy needs the influence of men in his life. He needs to gain some worldly wisdom, prepare to take his place in society."

She couldn't disagree with that. *Though what he needs more is his father.*

"But he'll still need supervision when at home," Russell added.

"And Mrs. Barrie?" She turned to plate the pancakes and pour a second round of batter onto the griddle.

"What about her? She's my housekeeper. I don't know how I'd manage without her. But she's getting on in years, rather too old to keep up with a boy his age, don't you think?"

"Possibly." *That's fair.*

"You could explore New York in your free time. That's what Marion originally had in mind for you, she said."

"She did."

"And perhaps, if you're willing, you could help in my work on occasion."

"What does that mean?" She wouldn't face him again. She needed to think clearly.

"It can mean whatever you're comfortable with. Helping me catalog imported artifacts from Egypt, create displays in my home museum. I bring clients there. Sometimes I entertain business associates—dinner parties, theater evenings, though I've fallen down on that in recent years. It would help immeasurably if you could entertain the wives while I talk business with their husbands."

Isn't that what a wife does? She flipped the pancakes.

"What do you say?"

"I need to think about it."

"All right, though time is of the essence. Whitfield needs to know whether to cancel Alistair's boarding school reservation in Connecticut."

"You've already enrolled him?" *Where in Connecticut? How far away?*

"Pending an examination. If he's going to apply closer to home, he should do it. There will surely be an entrance exam there too. Whitfield said schools are near capacity now that the influenza has passed."

She plated the second round of pancakes. "I'll let you know by the end of the week. Is that sufficient?"

"If it takes that long." He stepped close enough that she could feel his breath on her neck.

Dear God, please help me. I'm both attracted to this man and afraid of that attraction.

The front screen door opened. Gwen stepped away from the stove. "If you want to help, crack the eggs in this." She pushed a bowl into Russell's hands.

"Cook together?" He smiled. "What could be more domestic?"

Mercifully, the telephone rang, a thing so rare Gwen jumped.

"I'll get it." Russell quickly followed the ring, closing the kitchen door behind him.

Alistair appeared the moment Russell left. "Is he staying?"

"He wants to take us to Cape May for lunch. He'll leave before nightfall. Make an effort, Alistair, please, for both your sakes. He's your father. He's trying to do better by you."

Whatever news the telephone call brought changed Russell's demeanor. "I'm sorry to say I won't be able to make good on our plans for today." He looked Alistair in the eye, briefly. "I'd hoped we'd all have a day together. But business calls. I'll see you both at home soon." He turned to Gwen. "You'll telephone your answer by the end of the week? I need to inform Whitfield."

"Yes, yes, of course."

"Very well." He picked up his hat and umbrella. "Alistair, mind your aunt."

"Yes, sir." It was the most respectful thing he'd said to his father during the entire visit.

18

It wasn't difficult for Gwen to decide to stay in New York. She knew Alistair needed her, even if their time together was less and sporadic, and she needed her nephew. Russell was more than pleased when she telephoned to say she would stay. She couldn't deny the bit of pleasure that shot up her spine.

The summer had been so lovely that the last days of August grew bittersweet. In contrast, Sea Isle's much-photographed highlight of the season came on Wednesday, August 25, when the boardwalk was awash with 150 children and proud mothers out for the annual Baby Parade.

"I don't think I've ever seen so many children in one place, not even in school!" Gwen gasped.

"They do this every year. It's organized by the Women's Civic Club. Mother loved it. She paraded Clara and me time and again, hoping we'd win some kind of ribbon."

Yes, I can believe that of Marion. "She was so proud of you both, her beautiful children."

"Clara was, wasn't she? Beautiful, I mean." Alistair grew somber.

"Yes. Yes, she was." Gwen rested her hand on Alistair's shoulder, which had grown nearly equal in height to her own over the summer.

"We never did win. Mother always took us for ice cream afterward, a consolation prize. We liked the ice cream, but I think the consolation was for her."

Gwen smiled. "How about we go for ice cream now? I won't even make you march in the Baby Parade."

Alistair huffed. "It's only for kids one to twelve. I'm nearly twelve. I won't do it."

Gwen laughed, but Alistair did not.

"I want to leave now, Aunt Gwen."

This parade was a bad idea; it brings back too many memories. Such a dance, grief. One I still don't know the steps to, even after losing my parents, my sister . . . my niece. The heart of the day had gone for Gwen too. They walked back to the cottage without speaking.

Over lunch, Alistair asked, "It's almost time to go home, isn't it?"

"Yes." Gwen set down her fork. "I thought we'd stay until Monday. The rental is only until September first. School will begin the day after Labor Day. We'll need time to get you fitted for your uniform, and there's the entrance exam. Your father said they're willing to hold your place until September third."

Alistair sighed. "I don't want to go to that school, but I guess it's better than being sent far away."

"Yes." She reached for his hand. "Think of it that way. You'll be home most weekends if we can arrange it."

"I'm grateful you'll be there, Aunt Gwen. I hope you never leave."

Gwen smiled. "I can't imagine my life without you now. I'll never take the place of your mother, Alistair. I'll never try. But I love you and want the very best for you. Never doubt that."

"I don't." He gave a half smile. "I just worry that Father might try to force you to be something to him—more than you want. I don't trust him. I can't say why, exactly. But you shouldn't either."

"That's nothing for you to worry about. I'm a grown woman. I have rights. I can look out for myself." Gwen lifted her chin in bravado.

Alistair grinned. "Well, you do have the vote now."

Gwen forced a laugh. "Ha! Just! And about time!"

Alistair aced the entrance exam. Gwen had known he would. He'd come far in his studies in the last year, despite his season of illness and grief. He started the school year in fine form—healthy and strong. Gwen believed all would go well.

He would not be allowed to come home until mid-October. Neither Alistair nor Gwen was prepared for that, but the school's letter explained it was in students' best interest to participate fully in their studies and to join in the life of the school.

Gwen found the time heavy on her hands. Initially, she made excursions into the heart of the city—museums, shopping, even took in a matinee. But she missed teaching, missed Alistair. She wrote him twice weekly—would have written every day except she knew he'd be teased about that by the boys at school.

When Russell wasn't traveling, he breakfasted early and spent his days in his office or museum or out and about on business. Rarely was he home in the evenings. Days went by when Gwen never saw him. On the rare occasions their paths crossed, he was polite, if distant and preoccupied. He didn't ask for her help with his work. By the end of the second week, Gwen wondered if he would, even began to hope he might.

Perhaps I misread his intentions. Maybe his overtures weren't what they seemed. Maybe that was just his grief and loneliness talking. But I can't just wander these halls all day. I see Marion and Clara everywhere I go. I miss Alistair. I need something to do.

The third week Russell was home more, at least in the evenings for dinner. Gwen found she enjoyed their talks about his work, his correspondence with collectors, news of the ongoing digs in Egypt, where Russell hoped to spend more time.

He asked her to join him for after-dinner coffee in the drawing room, where they talked about their day, about books Gwen had read or was reading, about the theaters in New York and what was playing, the story behind those productions. Sharing time in the evenings became a habit, one they both enjoyed.

Gwen was relieved when one night, just as Mrs. Barrie brought coffee to the drawing room, Russell asked if she might help him with something.

"You'd like me to help with the cataloging—or the displays in your museum?"

"Not that, at least not yet. I have a more pressing difficulty." He waited until Mrs. Barrie set down the tray. "I'm to entertain some very important clients and their wives next week—Monday evening, the twenty-seventh. Dinner and the theater. We've tickets for the opening night of *Don't Tell* at the Nora Bayes Theatre. Don't ask me what it's about—no idea." He frowned.

"Yes?"

Mrs. Barrie poured the coffee.

"Embarrassing, really. Two of my clients' wives have proposed I accompany their daughters for the evening. That's not something I want to do, and how can I select one over the other? That would be disastrous for my business. Every society matron seems intent on setting me up with her marriageable daughters or nieces. Suddenly, I'm the most available, desirable widower."

"That's quite a dilemma." Gwen was amused but not sympathetic.

"Will you accompany me? Save me from the dragons?"

Mrs. Barrie set the coffeepot down, glancing at Gwen.

"I don't know. That might give a wrong impression. And I don't think I'd be very good company in high society, Russell."

"You'll be perfect. I'll introduce you as my sister-in-law, could even mention that you tutored my children throughout the influenza, cared for your sister in her final illness. Family. That should squelch any speculations and might show that I'm not in need of company and not ready for their romantic attachments."

Gwen looked to Mrs. Barrie, hoping for reassurance, or a bit of direction. "I've nothing to wear for such an outing."

"That's a little thing—easily arranged. Please. I wouldn't ask, but there is no one else who won't believe I have designs on them."

"Well . . ." Gwen couldn't think what to say.

"You did say you'd help me in my work. This is what I need most right now."

Mrs. Barrie quietly left the room.

"Well, yes, I did say that, but I more imagined working in your mu—"

"I swear on my life, I'll prove the perfect gentleman. Your honor will be in no way impugned."

Gwen nearly laughed at his formal speech. *How can I refuse? I did say I'd help. That was the agreement for Alistair to go to school closer to home.* "All right. I suppose."

"Excellent! Thank you, Gwen. This means the world to me."

Gwen's uncertainty over her decision warred with her common sense. She could almost imagine she was simply doing her brother-in-law a favor until the day a large box arrived from a leading New York designer, accompanied by a beribboned three-foot florist box.

She hesitated before untying the ribbon from the florist's box, reminded of the gift Russell had sent at Christmas—and the horrible moment they all realized he'd sent roses to her and not to his wife. She lifted the lid and stared at the beautiful pink roses. No one had ever sent her pink roses—her favorite. *How did he know?* The card simply read, *With all my thanks, Russell.*

The evening gown, boxed and wrapped carefully in layers of tissue, made her gasp. A dusty-lavender silk gown, with shimmering overlay, gossamer and dewdrops against a liquid sky. She lifted the fabric and inhaled. Never had she seen or felt anything so smooth, so fine. *It must have cost a fortune. What have I done? What will Alistair say? Or Mrs. Barrie?*

Mrs. Barrie's reaction was clear the evening of the event when she met Gwen on the stairs. Her hand clutching her throat, she said, "You fair take my breath away, Miss Armstrong." She gazed at Gwen with admiration, then a tinge of worry, and whispered, "Take care."

Gwen reached for her hand, as if for a lifeline.

Mrs. Barrie pressed it. "Mr. Bennett is waiting in the drawing room."

Gwen drew a deep breath and kept going, uncertain if she felt she was on her way to a lovely evening or a huge mistake.

If there was any clamoring doubt in her mind about her appearance, Russell squelched that when she entered the room. He stood, mesmerized. "Regal. You look regal."

"That's a bit of an overstatement."

"No, it isn't. Every inch a queen."

She saw he meant it but still her nerves jangled. "I'm afraid I won't know what to say to these women."

"It doesn't matter what you say." He smiled, his most charming smile. "Their husbands will be as dazzled as I am. They'll all be pea green with envy. You'll make an instant enemy of every woman there."

"That's not comforting." Gwen twisted her gloves in her hands.

"Then let me reassure you. You're more articulate, more compassionate, and kinder than any woman I've ever known. Simply be yourself. By the end of the evening even the most jealous and hardened among them will melt under your spell."

Gwen couldn't help but smile.

"One thing's lacking."

Gwen looked down at her dress, checked that she held both gloves. She couldn't imagine what she might have forgotten.

Russell pulled a slim box from his coat pocket. "This is for this evening. A perfect complement to your eyes and your gown." He opened the box and lifted the most exquisite amethyst pendant from its silk lining, placing it in her hand. "An original, from the cache of a pharaoh's queen."

"It's extraordinary—but I can't possibly accept—"

"Don't fret, Gwen. It's a loan for tonight. Remember I said this is a business event. I'm trying to encourage collectors. When their wives see you wearing this, and how beautiful you are, they'll want one like it, copy though it may be. That means their husbands will come knocking at my door, ready to buy."

"A copy? I thought you dealt only in antiquities."

"Yes, well, the war put a delay on new finds for quite some time, though there's no telling what might be discovered any day now. Meanwhile, Egyptology is all the rage in New York and around the country. Most don't expect to own a piece of Egypt but are thrilled to wear something that looks like it."

He took the pendant from her. "May I?"

She turned, lifting her hair. He placed the delicate silver chain around her neck. A shiver raced down her spine as he clasped it behind her.

He turned her to face him, and his eyes lit. "Exquisite."

Gwen stood apart from him, catching her breath, her head swimming.

He lifted a fur stole she'd not seen before from the chair behind him and held it open for her. "Shall we?"

She couldn't find words. *It's a loan. It's all a loan, just for tonight . . . for business. Remember that. Remember.*

There was a moment during the play when Gwen forgot the other men and women of their society, forgot to feel nervous or an imposter or be concerned what others thought or might say, when she laughed with abandon at the comedy performed on the stage. She glanced at Russell, who laughed with her. It felt good, and rich. She felt alive for the first time in a long while, and glad to share the moment.

The late-night dinner at Barbetta's opulent Italian restaurant was another thing. She tried to keep up, to appear poised and witty and charming amid the fine china, the plethora of silver, and the clinking of crystal. The law of Prohibition didn't seem to keep the wine or champagne from flowing through their exclusive party, though Gwen placed her hand over her glass each time the waiter drew near.

To his credit, Russell took only one glass, discreetly winking at Gwen and whispering, "For business's sake."

He'd been correct. Women eyed her with envy, speaking up or down to her in tones she knew lacked sincerity. Still, she tried to make polite conversation, though she didn't know the people they gossiped about or the designers they compared. One woman in particular watched her throughout the evening, though the lady made no effort to speak to Gwen alone. Gwen didn't know her name but saw that her escort was a man of some standing, a man Russell took special care to speak with.

By midnight Gwen was exhausted. Her smile was frozen, and her feet ached in the unfamiliar heels. She waited only for the too-glittering evening to end.

On the way home she never realized she'd fallen asleep on Russell's shoulder until the car came to a stop and he gently roused her.

"If you were a child, I would carry you upstairs to your room," he whispered, "but as you're a lady you may prefer I do not."

Gwen lifted her weary head, embarrassed, and sat up. "Forgive me. I'm so sorry."

"Don't be. You were wonderful tonight. I was very proud of you, Gwen. The belle of the ball."

Gwen wasn't sure what to do with that. She'd not felt a belle since the early days of her relationship with Russell, years before. "I don't think so. But I do think I could sleep for a week."

He chuckled. "Then do so. You've earned it."

19

Russell began spending more evenings at home, regularly inviting Gwen to join him in the drawing room. The after-dinner meetings became a habit Gwen grew comfortable with. She even found herself looking forward to their talks, to sharing whatever of his day he was inclined to share, and to his companionship.

Sometimes he'd challenge her to a game of chess. She was good at chess and mentally stimulated by the good-natured sparring the game inspired. As evenings grew cooler, he pulled the chess table between them where they sat before the fire. Mrs. Barrie served coffee or hot cocoa upon request.

As time passed, Gwen found herself thinking more and more of Russell throughout the day, anticipating their congenial evenings together. Mrs. Barrie's warning about him now seemed overly cautious to Gwen. He'd not pressured her, had not hinted at anything romantic or in any way inappropriate . . . and yet she found herself once again imagining what life as his wife might be. Each time those thoughts arose, she squelched them, but in no time found them reappearing in her mind.

Always fastidious, she now took special care in her appearance. She even thought of following the new style and bobbing her hair as so many women in his circle of society had done. Russell overheard her discussing the idea with Mrs. Barrie one morning at breakfast, asking if she could recommend a hair stylist.

"Please don't," he said.

"I beg your pardon?"

"Please don't cut your hair." His color rose, a thing Gwen found surprising and most attractive.

She forced a gentle laugh. "It's only hair, and I'm feeling a little bit old-fashioned, out of step."

"Your hair . . . is magnificent as it is." He seemed to become aware of Mrs. Barrie's raised eyebrows though the woman turned quickly away, careful not to intrude in the conversation. "It's not a bad thing to be out of step." He picked up his newspaper and quickly left the table.

Gwen searched Mrs. Barrie's eyes, hoping for some sign she approved, but found only a crease in her forehead. Gwen looked away, not wanting her pleasure at Russell's remark to be sullied.

Alistair's completion of midterm exams in the middle of October meant that at long last he could come home for the weekend. Gwen and Mrs. Barrie made a list of all his favorite foods. It felt good to conspire over his return, to eagerly anticipate all that the brief but precious holiday might hold. They not only made certain his room was ready but added touches here and there that might reflect his maturing—a more manly lamp for his bedside table, a new Sunday suit for cooler weather that Gwen had ordered from Russell's tailor based on Alistair's school uniform measurements, and a winter coat cut similarly to his father's. Gwen couldn't resist creating a bouquet of the last of the season's roses, knowing how Alistair loved beauty, how he'd enjoyed the garden's multicolored roses in particular.

She'd have gone to the train station to meet him personally if Russell hadn't persuaded her not to.

"He's a young man now, Gwen, at least I hope he's trying to be. Dornby will meet him. Let him come to you." Russell clearly meant what he said, but his eyes held understanding. "Let him grow up."

Gwen determined to try, but she could hardly wait to see her strong and capable young nephew. It was hard not to think of him and Russell and herself as a family, a real family. She cautioned her heart at such a thought, knew there was much repair work to be done between father and son, but she could hope, and she did.

From the moment Mr. Dornby left the drive to meet Alistair at the station, Gwen took up residence by the front window. She might have agreed to wait at home, but she would swoop the boy into her arms the minute he crossed the threshold.

"You're like a child waiting for Christmas morning," Mrs. Barrie good-naturedly scolded.

"And you're like his doting grandmother!" The words came out of Gwen's mouth before she realized what she was saying. Both women laughed, delighted with their pleasure.

The clock ticked on. The half hour came. The hour came and went.

"Where are they?" Gwen paced up and down the drawing room carpet. Mrs. Barrie had gone back to her duties, but Gwen refused to leave her window facing the drive.

At last, the car passed the iron gates. The boy who stepped from the car seemed taller than when he went away, and slightly thinner—stretched out. His school uniform did not pull quite so taut across his shoulders as it had. His pants looked like what the boys at school used to call "high waders." Gwen smiled. *He's definitely growing.* Proper or not, she'd meet him at the door.

Alistair walked in first, followed by Mr. Dornby with his bag.

"Alistair!" Gwen strode to him with open arms.

"Aunt Gwen!" He wrapped his arms around his aunt and held her close.

She stepped back, holding him at arm's length. "Let me look at you." He'd lost a bit of his bulk, but that was to be expected if he spent most hours in studies. His face had thinned just a little, his cheekbones grown more prominent. *The face of a boy no longer, but a young man. Aren't they feeding you enough?* She wouldn't make a fuss, at least not in front of Mr. Dornby.

Instead, she bravely smiled and said, "It's so good to have you home, Alistair."

"I'm glad to be home. More than I can say."

"Let's get you settled. Your father will be home for dinner, and Mrs. Barrie's dying to see you . . . though you might like to rest or wash up before dinner after your long journey."

"Yes, I'd like to lie down a little. I'm pretty tired—and thirsty. There wasn't much to drink on the train."

"Yes, of course. There's a carafe of cold water by your bed. I'll bring you some fresh apple cider as well."

She watched him climb the stairs. *He's never tired. Was he up late nights studying for his exams? Is he ill? Have they been working him to exhaustion?*

Alistair didn't come downstairs until time for dinner. He shook his father's hand.

"Welcome home, Alistair."

"Thank you, sir. I'm sorry I slept the afternoon away." He apologized to Gwen, already seated at the table.

"I'm just glad you got some rest." Gwen smiled, hiding her worry. "You looked as if you needed it."

"Can't think why, but I did."

"Haven't been sleeping well at school?" Russell asked, more critical than concerned, Gwen thought.

"I have, actually. I just seem to be more tired than usual."

"Likely a more rigorous schedule than you're used to at home, or in the summer for that matter."

"Maybe." Alistair seemed uncertain.

"How do you think you did on your midterms?" Russell's question sounded authoritarian rather than fatherly.

"Pretty well, I think. The mathematics portion was harder than I'd imagined."

"Not harder than you prepared for, I trust."

Alistair looked at his plate. "No, sir."

"Well, let's eat up," Gwen encouraged. "You're here now and we need to fatten you up a bit. Mrs. Barrie and Mrs. LaMott, our new cook, have outdone themselves. They've special menus for every meal while you're here—all your favorites."

"That sounds good. I'm starving!"

Gwen forced a smile.

Mrs. Barrie made certain to serve the table that night. "It's so good to have you home, Alistair," she whispered as she offered the platter of roast beef.

"You've no idea how glad I am for this meal. It looks great!" He heaped his plate.

"I'll tell Mrs. LaMott. She'll be so pleased." Mrs. Barrie affectionately squeezed Alistair's shoulder. She paused, seemed about to say something, but passed by, eyeing him curiously. Gwen made a note to talk with her later, to ask what she noticed.

"So, tell us, how are your studies going? What clubs have you joined? Those are important connections to make." Russell spoke without looking at his son.

"Studies are okay, I guess."

"Okay? You guess?" Russell raised his eyebrows and frowned. "I thought the entrance exam proved you were capable."

"It did, but . . . things are just harder than I expected. It's hard to concentrate sometimes."

"Because you're living in a dormitory, sharing a room with another boy?" Gwen asked, certain there must be a simple explanation.

"I don't think that's it. Brayden is a brick, a good fellow, and studious. We get along, better than anyone there I could imagine."

"Then what is the problem?" Russell set down his knife and fork. "Are you moping? Not applying yourself?"

"Russell," Gwen cautioned, laying her hand on his arm.

Alistair looked up, caught the intimacy between them, and frowned, searching Gwen's eyes. She removed her hand.

"I asked you a question, Alistair," Russell reminded him.

"I'm doing the best I can. I just— I don't know what it is. I'm doing pretty well in history and all the language arts, but mathematics . . ." He shook his head. "I just can't seem to get it, can't keep up. Some days are better than others."

"Then I suggest you take yourself in hand and buckle down. Your academic career will be your making—or your failing."

"Yes, sir." Alistair visibly gulped and drained his glass of water.

After dinner, Alistair sat back in his chair, sated. "That was the best meal I've eaten since I left home."

"Is the food there terrible, or not enough?" Gwen asked. He'd eaten two platefuls, more than she'd ever known him to eat.

"Gwen," Russell reprimanded. "It's a school."

"The food's all right. Everybody gets the same. It's just I'm always hungry."

"Growing. It's perfectly natural." Russell stood. "Gwen and I spend our evenings in the drawing room. We've set up a chess game. Would you like to join us?"

Alistair looked uncomfortable, glancing between them. Gwen wished Russell hadn't made their evenings sound so intimate, but in truth, that's what they were.

"It's been a long day. I think I'll get to bed early tonight."

"As you wish." Russell sounded formal, and relieved. "We'll see you in the morning." He held out his hand to Gwen, something he'd never done. It appeared proprietary, even to her. "Gwen? Shall we?"

She didn't take his hand, but leaned forward, toward Alistair across the table. "Tomorrow, then. Is there anything you need? Anything you want for tonight?"

"I'm fine. Thanks."

Gwen nodded. She didn't want to leave the table. She wanted to stay and talk with Alistair, learn everything she could about his studies, his new interests, his life at school. But Russell stood, waiting, so she rose and followed him. At the doorway she turned to smile at Alistair, to wish him good night, but he sat alone, staring at his plate.

20

"He's lost weight," Mrs. Barrie observed, when Gwen cornered her the next morning. "They must be starving the lad."

"You don't think it's a growth spurt? That's what Russell said. He said he was the same way at that age—shooting up inches within a few months. That would slim anybody down."

Mrs. Barrie shook her head. "I canna say for certain, but it seems unnatural to me—and in so short a time. He doesn't seem quite himself—preoccupied, and a bit down. That's not like Alistair, certainly not since the two of you were away in the summer."

Gwen sighed. "I agree, but I don't know what to think. Russell says we mustn't coddle him. He thinks he's being childish, vying for my attention. I'm wondering if it's more to do with grief. Everything is so different for him here, with Marion and Clara gone."

Mrs. Barrie straightened and eyed Gwen significantly. "I'm more wondering if Mr. Bennett's worried that attention to Alistair might be holding you back from him. There's more than the young that need to grow up."

The point of Mrs. Barrie's observation sank into Gwen's heart. *How can I help one without alienating the other? Can time sort things out? That's what Russell said—give it time. Am I acting like a fussy mother hen?* Gwen didn't have answers or authority to pursue them. In the end, she determined to wait until Alistair's next visit to push the subject further, hoping he would improve in every way and that her concerns were needless.

Two evenings after Alistair returned to school, as Gwen and Russell sat before their chessboard, deep into their game, Russell posed a question. "I need to go to Chicago on business next month—over Thanksgiving and into early December. I'll be meeting with some important clients there. There'll be occasions for entertaining them and their wives—dinners, theaters, clubs. Very much like what we did last month.

"I'd like you to join me, help me entertain and host them. You'll need a complete wardrobe, anything you want—it's a business expense. What do you say?" He smiled and she felt her insides melt, her pulse quicken.

"It sounds wonderful, but I don't think . . ."

"Don't think what? We don't have to make it all business. I can take time. We can see the sights, take in a show or two on our own."

"It's not that . . . It's not appropriate for me to travel alone with you, Russell."

"You're concerned what people might say."

"Yes. For you, and for me. Besides, I expect Alistair will come home again after his finals, and I need to be here. It will be Thanksgiving, after all."

"You don't need to be here for Alistair, not every time he comes. He's not in need of a nursemaid."

"I don't consider myself his nursemaid, but I am his aunt, and the reason I'm living here is to supervise him, watch over him. That's what you said. That was our agreement." She shook her head once and set her jaw, her insides trembling beneath his frown. "In any case, I can't travel alone with you."

"You agreed to help me in my business. I believed I could count on you."

"Traveling with you is not something I agreed to. I'm sorry."

The evening turned frosty, enough that Russell excused himself even before Mrs. Barrie delivered their after-dinner coffee.

Only Gwen's place was set in the dining room the next evening.

"Russell's not here?" Gwen asked Mrs. Barrie.

"Mr. Bennett said he'd be dining out with clients most of the week and not to expect him home until late in the evenings."

Gwen knew enough to realize his absence was pointed. She wasn't sure what repercussions there might be from her refusal to accompany him to Chicago, but knew she'd made the right decision . . . At least she hoped she had.

Their paths crossed intermittently over the next month before his train left for Chicago. He informed her that when he returned, he'd be hosting dinner parties and business meetings for New York clientele on a regular basis, particularly through the Christmas season and into the New Year.

It was a statement, in no way an invitation to join him. Gwen didn't know what he expected of her, a thing that both irritated and concerned her.

The night before leaving, he once again invited her to a chess game in the drawing room. Gwen wondered what the real game might be.

He moved his castle once she'd left open space, keeping his eyes on the board. "I'm sorry you won't be going with me. I'm afraid I took that news rather badly. I don't take no easily."

"I'm aware." Her heart thrummed.

He looked up, holding her eyes in his. "We could set the world on fire together, Gwen, you and I. You're capable, smart, beautiful. Any man would be proud to have you on his arm, to claim you as his own. I, most of all."

"That's what you said about Marion. I'm not your wife, Russell." Her mind blistered in defense of her sister but her heart raced at his compliments.

"You could be. Think what that might mean. Dinners, theater, the best circles, the most beautiful clothes—jewels, whatever you—"

"Those things are wonderful, but not what matters most to me."

"We could travel the world. You've always wanted to go to Europe, to Egypt. Now that the war is over, it's possible—see the pyramids, visit every archaeological dig your heart desires. I've got connections across the continent."

"That's the desire of Alistair's heart as well."

"Alistair." He said the name without emotion.

"Your son."

Russell looked away.

Gwen reached for his hand. "I understand what you're offering me, Russell, and of course, it's fabulous, beyond anyone's wildest dreams. But it's too soon. It's too soon after Marion's death for you to be looking for a replacement wife. It's too soon after my sister's death for me to consider stepping into her rightful place, and it's too soon for Alistair, who's lost his mother and his sister. They were everything to him. He loves me as his aunt, but he'd see me as an interloper into your affections, as a rival to their memory. That's not fair to any of us."

"Alistair. Always first. The children held Marion back. And now you." He pushed her hand away.

Gwen saw options for her life slipping away, options she wasn't sure she might not want in time. "I didn't say never. I said it's too soon."

"You mean to give me hope?"

"No. Yes. I don't know." She put her fingers to her temples. "You're pressing me."

"I don't mean to." He exhaled. "I love you, Gwen. I hope you know that."

Her breath caught. She couldn't formulate thoughts, let alone words. *What does love mean to you?*

"Take time. Take all the time you need. Only, I beg you, don't let Alistair replace me. I can't go through that again."

I understand you were hurt; you're still hurting. What I want is all of us together, a family. Could we ever be that? Are you capable? Is Alistair?

Gwen breathed a sigh of relief when Mr. Dornby drove Russell to the station. It was as if the entire house sighed in relief.

Gwen asked Mrs. Barrie if she'd take luncheon with her in the dining room, a thing the housekeeper was unaccustomed to.

"I'm not comfortable sitting to eat here," Mrs. Barrie said, placing her napkin across her lap. "I canna imagine what Mr. Bennett might say."

"He's not here and I don't care. I hate playing lady of the manor and eating alone, no matter how delicious the chicken salad."

Mrs. Barrie smiled. "I thought you might be about practicing for the future these days."

Gwen nearly choked, but drew a breath and composed herself. "He asked me. Sort of."

"To wed?"

Gwen nodded. "I think so."

"And what did you say, if you don't mind my asking?"

"It's too soon—too soon after Marion and Clara's passing. But he thinks my reticence is because I put Alistair above him."

"And he doesn't like that."

"No." Gwen closed her eyes, but she was desperate for confession, for advice, for someone to care. "I'm terribly attracted to him. Why wouldn't I be? He's handsome, and well-mannered. Masculine, exciting . . . charming, when he wants to be. He makes me feel beautiful and wanted. If I married him, I'd never worry about finances or a home or security again."

"He offers all you've ever wanted."

What I once wanted. But that was years ago . . . I don't know if I could trust him again with my heart. Gwen shook her head slowly. "I don't think I know what I want. I don't know if I love him, or if I want to." She looked up. "Is that so bad?"

"You're wise not to be swept into the heat of the moment. For all you've lived here these two years, you hardly know the man, at least as a suitor, a potential husband. Taking time is prudent."

"And there's Alistair to consider."

"Yes."

"I know my heart for Alistair . . . much more than I do for Russell. And I promised Marion I'd care for her son, watch over him." Gwen leaned toward Mrs. Barrie and lowered her voice, though there was not another soul in the room. "I'm afraid if I refuse Russell that in time he'll send me away, that I'll lose my connection to Alistair. For Marion's sake, for the sake of my promise, I can't do that."

"And for your sake? For Alistair's?"

"In truth I think I'm Alistair's greatest advocate where his father is concerned. I love him, almost as if he were my own son."

"He loves you. I see it in his eyes, in his demeanor. He trusts you."

"He did. I hope he still does. You should have seen the way he looked at me when he was here last, when Russell said we spend our evenings together."

"I did see, at least before he left."

"I can't help but wonder if that's why he's decided not to come home for Thanksgiving. He wrote that he needs to remain at school, to study for his examinations."

"The lad's lonely and confused, and I don't know . . . Something's not quite right, something beyond his grieving. I took his uniform in at the waist while he was here. Perhaps we can fatten him up a bit when he comes again. I'm glad he'll be home through Christmas."

"Me too." Gwen reached for Mrs. Barrie's hand, glad to have a friend and coconspirator. "When Alistair was here in October, we talked about Christmas. He doesn't want to celebrate this year. It doesn't feel right to him, without his mother and Clara."

Mrs. Barrie sighed. "I understand. What does Mr. Bennett say?"

"I mentioned it to him last night. I don't believe he cares. He's so consumed with his business clients and business dinners and business meetings. I just mention it now so you can plan ahead, keeping things as normal as possible through the holidays."

As she cleared away the luncheon plates, Mrs. Barrie spoke up. "I should tell you that Mr. Bennett is expecting to entertain clients on a grand scale for dinners and business meetings when he returns."

"He mentioned that to me too."

"He said you'd want to be excused from some of those dinners."

"Are they all business clients, then?"

"I suppose they are. Of sorts. From New York and Atlantic City."

"Antiquity collectors?"

"I'm sure I couldn't say." But Mrs. Barrie looked troubled and that troubled Gwen.

21

Gwen insisted the staff spend Thanksgiving and the following day with their families. Russell was in Chicago, after all, and Alistair remained at school. Mrs. Barrie spent the day resting in her rooms. Gwen could see no point in sitting by herself to feast on a giant turkey, and just as Alistair had said of Christmas, celebrating felt disrespectful to the memory of the dear ones they'd lost.

Conversely, in preparation for Alistair's December tenth homecoming, Mrs. Barrie and Gwen pulled out all the stops to plan every dish and sweet and beverage the young man might enjoy. They might not be celebrating as in years past, but at least traditional foods might bring some sort of comfort, a warm welcome and the feeling that not everything had changed. He'd have to return to school in January for a second semester, but until then they intended to spoil him as much as he—or Russell—allowed.

This time, with Russell gone, Gwen rode with Mr. Dornby to the train station to meet her nephew. She'd have stood on the platform if she wasn't afraid Mr. Dornby would suffer apoplexy. "If you catch cold or anything at all should happen to you, Miss Armstrong, Mr. Bennett would have my head—and send me packing. He'll not like that I've driven you to the station as it is."

"Then it's our secret, and I promise I'll wait in the car if you'll go to meet Alistair."

"That I will, and not to worry." He smiled. "I'll bring the young gentleman to you myself."

Gwen sat on pins and needles. *This will be almost like our time at the Jersey Shore—just the two of us, and Mrs. Barrie from time to time.*

The December cold seeped deep into her bones. A dusting of snow in the night had coated gardens and streets and houses, giving everything an otherworldly, gingerbread-and-fairy-tale cast. *A perfect homecoming for Alistair!*

Gwen imagined a bonfire in the garden that evening. Mr. Dornby had already laid the wood. Mrs. Barrie was on board to bring hot cider, chips, and Nathan's hot dogs for a roast that evening. *We'll pop corn over the fire and talk until the cold drives us in. We'll listen to the radio. I'll teach Alistair more dance steps, so he'll be ready to ask a girl to their spring ball. He'll see. He'll love it! I will love it!*

Minutes passed. Gwen looked at her watch. *What can be taking them so long? The train should have been here ages ago.*

The young man Mr. Dornby finally brought to the car looked more like a weary waif than a young gentleman. Though Alistair was just as tall as when she last saw him, the coat Gwen had bought him at the start of school looked like it was made for a larger man, and the trousers Mrs. Barrie had altered in October bagged on him. Gray patches formed dark circles beneath his eyes. He smiled when he saw Gwen, but the smile did not reach his blue eyes and there was no sparkle there.

"Aunt Gwen."

"Alistair." She poured all the warmth she could into her smile as he sank into the seat beside her. She took his hands. They felt rough and dry, his skin cracked. "Alistair, your knuckles. They're bleeding." She took out her handkerchief and dabbed at the spots of blood.

"Oh, that. It's been happening some—weather, I guess."

"Where are your gloves?"

"Not sure. Guess I left them at school."

He slumped enough to lay his head atop the back seat. She wanted to draw it to her shoulder, but she sat quietly, holding his hand.

Once home, Mr. Dornby carried his bag, setting it by the staircase. Even he glanced at Alistair, concerned.

"Have you eaten?" Gwen asked.

"Lunch on the train, but I'm starving."

"Mrs. Barrie will be delighted to hear that." Gwen was delighted too. *If he has an appetite, it can't be all bad.*

"I'll go to the kitchen, Aunt Gwen. I want to see Mrs. Barrie and I'd like to sit at the table there, like we used to for that bit of time."

"Sounds perfect." Gwen was glad for an informal start to the weekend. "I'm sure Mr. Dornby's up for a good meal as well. Won't you join us, Mr. Dornby?"

"Well, now, a right celebration. Don't mind if I do!"

Mrs. Barrie threw all protocol to the wind and wrapped her arms around Alistair, giving him a great bear hug. "It's good to have you home, lad!"

"It's good to be home!" Alistair's shoulders shook with emotion. He pulled away after a time and swiped his sleeve across his eyes. "Don't know what's got into me."

Mrs. Barrie and Gwen exchanged a glance. Nothing more was said as they all gathered round the kitchen table. Mrs. LaMott set about heaping a plate of her best for Alistair—roast chicken, whipped potatoes, gravy, green beans, cranberry sauce. Alistair wolfed his meal, asked for seconds, plus two pieces of her prizewinning chocolate cake.

At last he sat back, rubbing his stomach. "I should be stuffed, but I could eat this good food forever. There's nothing like it at school. Thank you, Mrs. LaMott. Thank you, Mrs. Barrie."

Mrs. LaMott raised her eyebrows, set her fists on her hips, and laughed. "Well, it's good to have a real man's appetite round here at last!"

Alistair grinned, a first glimpse of the boy Gwen knew. But then he rose suddenly from the table, his forehead creased. "Excuse me, please." He made a mad dash out of the kitchen.

Mrs. Barrie stared after him. "Whatever is the matter?"

Mr. Dornby raised a cautionary hand. "Best let him go."

Gwen cocked her head in question.

Mr. Dornby's color rose. "Was like that at the station. It's why we took so long." He shrugged. "Weak bladder, I reckon."

Now all the women's color rose.

Alistair slept late the next morning. Gwen knew if he'd been home, Russell would have been much annoyed. He was big on punctuality, especially where Alistair was concerned. But Gwen knew the boy needed sleep. He'd looked exhausted and moved slower from the moment he'd arrived, as if achy in his muscles and joints.

She couldn't account for Alistair's insatiable thirst—cup after cup of hot cider as they'd huddled round the bonfire the night before. He'd topped it off with two cups of cocoa and a glass of water before going to bed. If she drank all that, she'd be up half the night. *Something's off. I don't know what.*

By the time Gwen searched for Alistair he'd disappeared, presumably for a walk in the gardens. She saw Mrs. Barrie in deep conversation with Tilley, the housemaid, outside Alistair's bedroom door. Tilley appeared flushed with embarrassment. Mrs. Barrie looked flustered, something Gwen had rarely seen.

When Tilley headed down the stairs with a load of sheets in her arms, Gwen asked if everything was okay.

"I don't know. I simply don't know what to think."

"What's the matter?"

"It's Alistair." She kept her voice low. "He's wet the bed. He's not done that since he was a toddler. He was the easiest of the two to train, and that's saying something for a boy."

"Well, he did drink an awful lot of cider—and then cocoa—last night. Do you think that—"

"He would have woken up, wouldn't he, if he knew he needed

to use the loo? No, he's never done this. Something's the matter. I brought morning tea up early, like I did when he was a boy—just as a treat, mind you—and he was sound asleep."

"He was very tired."

"Yes, but he was restless and moaning in his sleep."

"Dreaming?"

Mrs. Barrie shook her head. "I think he was in a bit of pain."

"Pain?"

"Aye, but when I asked him how he felt this morning, he said he was fine, and sounded ashamed, even annoyed that I'd asked him. Alistair's not one to be irritable—not normally, not unless something's bothering him. He's not himself, I tell you."

"I agree. I've asked him, but he refuses to say anything bad has happened at school. Perhaps I should ask Russell to call the school or if he'll allow me to do so."

"You might wish to call Dr. Callahan."

"Without consulting Russell?"

"He left you in charge of Alistair, didn't he? He expects you to care for his son, doesn't he?"

"Yes. Yes, of course. It's just . . . he thinks Alistair's all right, that he's sulking, craving sympathy and attention—and going through a growth spurt."

"A great lad of twelve would not wet the bed for attention."

"You're right, of course. I'll telephone."

"Doctor runs office hours on Saturdays, but he'll be closed tomorrow. It might be best to take him directly there. If you telephone, he might want you to make an appointment, turn you away, and this morning may be your best chance."

My best chance to do this before Russell returns. That's what you mean.

It didn't take much convincing for Alistair to agree to see Dr. Callahan, just a hearty meal—too late for breakfast, almost time for luncheon.

"I'm sorry," the receptionist said once they'd arrived at the doctor's office. "Dr. Callahan is on rounds at the hospital this morning, and Dr. McNeill is booked until the end of the day."

Gwen's heart dropped. "Will Dr. Callahan be here this afternoon?"

"No, I'm sorry, he won't. He has house calls this afternoon and his schedule is fully booked. But if it's urgent and you're willing to wait, perhaps Dr. McNeill can see you near the end of the day."

"Dr. McNeill?" *What if Russell doesn't approve of Alistair seeing a doctor other than Dr. Callahan?*

"Yes, Dr. McNeill joined the practice this spring. Patients who've seen him have been very pleased." The woman lowered her voice. "He's younger, a veteran from Scotland," she whispered, "but very kind and quite capable. Still, it will be a long wait."

Alistair nudged his aunt. "I'd like to see him . . . please."

That's all it took for Gwen. "Yes, thank you. We'll wait."

"Very well. Take a seat. I'll put you on the list." She tapped her pencil on her desk. "You might wish to get a bite to eat at the shop down the block. He's taken on extras today and won't be done until nearly five o'clock."

Gwen appreciated the woman's concern, but she wasn't hungry. Alistair, on the other hand, grabbed Gwen's hand, ready to find the café.

Hours later Gwen wished they'd at least brought something to read. During luncheon and throughout the afternoon, Alistair excused himself three times, and not until his leg jiggled with urgency. Gwen tried not to notice.

Finally, at a quarter to five, they were ushered into Dr. McNeill's office, a room lined with barrister cases of medical books, a wall filled with diplomas and citations, and a massive desk facing chairs for consultation.

Dr. McNeill introduced himself and indicated the chairs for Gwen and Alistair. He resumed the seat behind his desk. Gwen hadn't known what to expect, but when the man kindly smiled and spoke in a Scottish brogue so strong she had to listen carefully to understand, her first thought was that Mrs. Barrie would heartily approve.

"Well now, young man, what seems to be the problem?"

Alistair didn't speak at first. Gwen nudged him, believing it important that he describe his symptoms. Only he could know what he truly felt.

"I'm not sure anything is, but I'm tired—not just at night, but all the time, like I can't get my breath, like I've been running a mile. For some reason I can't concentrate like I know I should." He looked down, self-consciously. "Not so good for my examinations. Maybe it's just that I'm not sleeping enough. I'm always hungry . . . and thirsty."

"Are you now? You don't look as if you've overeaten." Dr. McNeill's brow creased in concentration. He glanced from Alistair to Gwen, as if looking for confirmation.

But Gwen was momentarily distracted by the doctor's eyes. *Green as a spring lawn—greener than Marion's were . . . and filled with light.* She blinked. "Yes, he's ravenous, and always thirsty. It may only be a growth spurt—he's grown taller—but he's lost a bit of weight since going away to school, in just these two months. With all he's eating, I can't understand it."

"Ach. School away is quite the change from home, is it?"

Alistair shrugged.

"Fevers?"

"None that I can tell," Gwen broke in.

"Might there be something worrying you?"

Alistair shrugged again. "Just . . . just feeling like this. I feel sick to my stomach sometimes."

"Any other symptoms?"

Alistair glanced at Gwen, colored, and looked away, shaking his head.

"Might you feel grand and suddenly low at times?"

"Yes," Alistair confessed.

Dr. McNeill sat back, frowning. "Mother, I need to examine your son, possibly run a test or two to get to the bottom of this. If you'll be so kind as to wait here, we'll see what we can figure out between us, eh, lad?"

"Yes, of course." She hadn't told him she was not Alistair's mother. It was natural the doctor assumed that. Would her lack of formal guardianship make a difference to the care Alistair received, change the doctor's willingness to treat him?

"She's not my mother. She's my aunt, Aunt Gwen."

Well, that's done. "Alistair's mother was my late sister. I'm charged with Alistair's care while his father's away on business."

"I see. Well, Mrs. . . ."

"Miss Armstrong."

"Miss Armstrong." He smiled, and Gwen thought his eyes might have grown a bit brighter. "We'll see what we can discover. Nurse will show Alistair to the examining room." He nodded Alistair toward the door. "I'll return shortly."

Twenty agonizing minutes passed before the door opened and Dr. McNeill returned, not smiling. "Alistair's getting dressed. He'll join you in the lobby."

Heart thumping, Gwen watched the man walk behind his desk and take a seat. He rubbed his eyes. For the first time Gwen saw worry lines there, as if the doctor hadn't slept.

Doctors had been overworked and in short supply throughout the influenza epidemic and ever since. She knew that and pitied him, but her nerves had grown to nearly a fever pitch while waiting. "What's wrong with him, Dr. McNeill? He's not himself."

"Which is why I'm wanting to speak with you privately, Miss Armstrong. Alistair mentioned his appetite, his thirst, his inability to concentrate, fatigue, a general achiness, malaise. You mentioned his weight loss. What do you think of his emotional state? He's not said, but is there anything troubling him at school? At home?"

"I don't know about school—he won't say. But his mother and sister died suddenly this spring from influenza. Alistair himself was sick with it—we all were."

"I remember."

"Do you?"

"Yes, I'm sorry to say I'd forgotten until you mentioned your relationship to Alistair. I accompanied Dr. Callahan on his rounds. Your family was one of my first cases in this country. I'm so very sorry. Terrible losses for all of you."

"Thank you. It's been very hard." Gwen drew a needed breath. "For Alistair especially. His mother and sister were his world. But he made such progress over the summer before he went away to school. He was strong and fit."

"Do you think he's fairly treated at school—by his teachers and headmaster?"

"I have no way of knowing. He says he is, but he's just not the same. I didn't want to say this in front of him, but he's emotional in ways he wasn't before. Like what you said—feeling grand one minute and low the next. He's often irritable and sometimes close to tears. None of that's like Alistair, not at all."

"What does his father say?"

Gwen wished he hadn't asked that. Russell's viewpoint might diminish the doctor's objectivity.

"Miss Armstrong?"

"His father's away and hasn't seen him this trip home from school, but I know what he'll say. He thinks there's nothing wrong with Alistair, that he's sulking, acting out, wallowing in his grief, and vying for my attention."

"Ach." Dr. McNeill sat back in his chair.

"I don't believe that. And there's something else, something terribly embarrassing for Alistair, that he might not have told you . . . Last night, he soiled the bed. I don't know if it's related or not, but I know Alistair would never do that intentionally."

"I agree. He mentioned that."

"He did?" Gwen could hardly believe it. Alistair had seemed so embarrassed, so ashamed.

"Aye. Apparently, it's happened at school, which as you can imagine is terrible for a lad his age. He said the others teased him, and lads can be cruel at that age. Not a stunt he'd pull for attention."

"What's wrong with him, Doctor?"

Dr. McNeill leaned forward and clasped his hands on his desk. "I've an idea, but as I said, I need to run some tests. If it's what I think it may be, I'll need to consult with Dr. Callahan. I'll be able to do that Monday morning. Might you come back then?"

"Alistair's home from school for the holidays, so I'm sure we can. Is there anything we should do in the meantime?"

"I recommend keeping him home, letting him take things easy, not overeating, and cut down on the sweets, at least until we know what we're dealing with. Encourage him to drink plenty of water."

"Keep him home? We'd planned to go to the theater tomorrow night . . ."

Dr. McNeill's eyebrows rose.

"I mean, do you mean I should keep him home all the time? Is that necessary?"

"Necessary?" He hesitated. "His frequent need to visit the lavatory might prove a difficulty for him, then there's a fair amount of sickness about. Enclosed, packed spaces such as theaters might not be the best. You don't want the lad coming down with anything more, especially not until we know what we're dealing with."

"No, of course not." Gwen frowned in concentration. *Anything more? What we're dealing with? What is it you're not saying?*

"Good." Dr. McNeill rose and forced a smile. "I'll see you Monday, Miss Armstrong. In the meantime, take good care of the lad, let him rest as much as possible, and try not to worry."

Gwen forced a smile in return, knowing she'd do nothing but worry.

PART THREE

22

DECEMBER 1919

Malcolm McNeill was glad he'd not seen Alistair Bennett until late that afternoon. He was able to test the lad's urine sample right away. He hoped it was not what he suspected, but he'd seen a number of cases before coming to America and he'd never been wrong in his suspected diagnosis, not yet. *Please, Lord, let this be a first time.*

He doffed his jacket and headed for the small lab in the back of the building. With no Benedict's solution on hand, he'd have to mix his own. Hoping Dr. Callahan stocked everything he needed, he began pulling chemicals from the supply closet and setting them on the table: sodium carbonate, sodium citrate, and copper(II) sulfate pentahydrate. He knew the mixture by heart. He'd created it for tests in Scotland, and more during the war.

Good. Everything's here. Scrubbing thoroughly, he pushed his hands through a clean lab coat, set up the equipment he needed—enough for two tests, just to make certain—and mixed the solution. Setting it aside, he lit a burner to low heat beneath a pan of water. As the water gently boiled, he dropped five milliliters of Benedict's solution into each clean test tube and, with a clamp, held it in the water until it boiled without overflowing. He added eight drops of Alistair's urine to the solution, then returned the tubes to their water baths, allowing the mixture to heat to a slow boil again for three to four minutes. Now the agony of waiting and watching began, though it didn't take long. The heart of a father in him didn't want to look for the color changes. The mind of a scientist and the responsibility of a doctor in him knew he must.

Blue would indicate no sugar in the urine; green meant a low concentration of glucose; yellow, a bit more; orange, more yet. If it turned brick red, there could be no doubt.

Each time he'd performed this test, his heart railed against the cruelty of what a red or brown color meant for the child, the man, the woman—any who suffered from this dreaded disease for which there was no explanation, and no cure. It was not contagious, did not spread from germs. It struck personally and indiscriminately. Sometimes it seemed genetic, with more than one person in a family developing it, especially at an early age.

But he'd seen more cases develop, especially among young people, since the influenza. He couldn't prove it, had read no reports in medical journals touting studies or connections between the two. He based his suspicions on the anecdotal experiences of his own patients and those of other doctors. There were too many cases to ignore—including that of his own daughter, God rest her sweet soul.

He watched the color changes in both test tubes. For Alistair, there was no doubt.

Malcolm rubbed his eyes. He felt desperately tired, and not only because he'd been up since four that morning, making necessary house calls before he'd ever come to the office for scheduled appointments.

He recorded his findings in Alistair's file before pouring his tests and remaining samples down the drain. He sterilized all the instruments and carefully put them away, leaving the room spotless, as if it had never borne witness.

Malcolm knew Dr. Callahan refused to see patients on a Sunday unless life and death hung in the balance. Now that Malcolm had been brought into the practice, the good doctor relied on him to see those desperate cases unless they concerned any of their oldest or wealthiest clients.

Malcolm assumed the Bennett family ranked among the practice's wealthier clients, if not among its older ones. Still, there was nothing Dr. Callahan could do to change the diagnosis or offer a cure, and he needed the doctor in a receptive mood to hear and approve his proposed method of treatment. Discussing Alistair's case first thing Monday morning was his best bet.

In the meantime, Malcolm would go to church on Sunday, just as he always did, and pray to the God he loved and trusted for wisdom, for clarity, for skill in the work He'd given him to do. Daily he prayed for each of his patients by name, laying their cases before the Great Physician, seeking the restoration of mind and body that only He could give. But he found much peace in offering those prayers in church as well. The serene beauty of the sanctuary calmed him, called him to lay down his stethoscope and notebook, to be still, to remember that God was sovereign, eternal, and all knowing.

Helping people was what Malcolm did. Numbering their days was God's business. Though sometimes it was hard for Malcolm to remember that.

He'd not been able to save many of the sick and wounded men he'd tended in Egypt during the war. He'd not been able to save his own wee daughter from this horrid wasting disease or his precious wife from the deadly influenza when they were home in Scotland, near starving, while he'd served over two thousand miles south in the land of the pyramids. Those were the grievous losses he laid at the foot of the cross each night, as he begged God to heal his heart or bring him home, then found himself taking up again at dawn.

This morning, Malcolm sang the old hymns, especially the carols of Christmas, with gusto in his strong baritone. Momentarily, they lifted and filled his heart, because he believed in the God he sang those praises to. He listened, like one starving, to the pastor's sermon, hoping to gain strength to walk out the door and make his rounds for one more week. And he prayed for Alistair Bennett. He prayed for the aunt who clearly loved him, and he prayed for the father who held no understanding of all his son was going through with his health, or apparently with his grief.

Tomorrow I'll talk with Dr. Callahan. If I can convince him of Dr. Allen's treatment, radical though it may be, perhaps the boy will have a chance. Isn't one chance in a million better than none? Malcolm believed it to be so. He had to believe it.

"Diabetes mellitus. A death sentence." Dr. Callahan shook his head after reading Alistair's chart and the details of Malcolm's experiment.

"I hope not." Malcolm spoke with measured calm.

Dr. Callahan registered surprise at his colleague's statement. "There is no cure. Surely you know that."

"No cure *yet*, Doctor," Malcolm acknowledged, "but a great deal of research is being done."

"Research . . ." Dr. Callahan removed his glasses and rubbed his eyes, weary before the day began. "Research means little in a case like this, where time is of the essence. I give the boy a few months, possibly a year, depending on how fast the disease progresses. Has anyone else in the family been diagnosed with diabetes . . . possibly hereditary? I suppose you did ask."

"I will ask. I didn't want to frighten the boy or his aunt before knowing the results of the test. I'll meet with them today."

"Bennett. A pity. That family's been through hell this year already. First the mother, the daughter, now the son. There were others in the house that developed influenza as well, as I recall."

"Yes, staff members, and the aunt. The aunt survived. It was she brought the lad in. He's home from school for the holidays."

"Not much of a Christmas present, is it? So, the aunt is still there. I wonder if she's his legal guardian. Bennett, the father, travels a great deal for business. I don't like delivering a diagnosis like this without the father being present."

"She seems very devoted to the boy and said he's in her charge while his father's away. I believe she'll be willing to do anything she can to help him, to preserve the young man's life."

"There's little she can do other than to make him comfortable, allow him to enjoy the time he has left as he's able."

"But if through a strict regimen that time could be prolonged, a cure might—"

"You're not talking about a starvation diet, surely?"

"It's called that, but Dr. Allen has demonstrated success in prolonging life—"

"Frederick Allen is a quack! His starvation diet is cruel beyond belief. Absolutely not. I'd not subject anyone, let alone a boy of twelve, to such tomfoolery."

I'd have tried anything to keep my Sheenagh alive as long as possible. "The diet can help prevent his blood sugar from rising. He'd not feel so sick. And is it not cruel to withhold possibilities, hope for—"

"False hope. There's no evidence that a cure can come within this young man's lifetime. I realize you have a personal and vested interest in the curing of this disease. I understand that. Yet, hard as this truth might be, Doctor, we cannot lie. We must lay the facts before them. Speak with the aunt privately. I'd like to be with you when you meet with her."

"Of course, Doctor. As you wish." Malcolm tried to keep his tone respectful.

"Not that I question your diagnosis, Dr. McNeill. The results of the test are clear. I simply feel I owe it to the family to remain a presence. Mrs. Bennett was my patient for several years—tuberculosis, though it was influenza and pneumonia that took her in the end. What time is your appointment?"

"I'll check the chart and let you know."

"Very well." Dr. Callahan hesitated. "Break the news gently as you can. I'll be there for moral support."

"I understand, sir."

Alistair was Malcolm's fifth appointment of the day. He did his best to give full attention to each of his earlier patients, but his mind was on Alistair. He felt for the lad, knowing he'd be anxious to know his diagnosis. Ethically he agreed with Dr. Callahan. It was best to talk privately with the aunt, to prepare her and the lad's father ahead of time. If she wanted him to deliver the diagnosis to Alistair, he would do so, assuming she had the authority to make that decision. Otherwise, he would need to consult the father.

It was ten thirty when the receptionist brought him Alistair's chart and ushered Miss Armstrong into his office. He stood and invited her to take a chair.

The striking woman across the desk from him moistened her lips, maintained a half smile, nervously blinked more often than was necessary. He pitied her. He'd pity her more once he'd delivered the diagnosis.

"Dr. Callahan, being the family's longtime physician, would like to join us. We'll take a moment until he arrives. How is Alistair today?"

"Anxious. Sitting in the waiting room. The receptionist asked me in alone. Should he not be here as well?"

"Yes, I'm sure he is anxious, but for now, it's best he wait there."

"Do you wish to examine him again?"

"Not today—at least not yet. Today we need to speak with you. Perhaps we'll need to speak with Alistair's father as well."

"His father? Why?" The woman fidgeted, almost winced.

"Might I ask, have you been appointed Alistair's legal guardian, Miss Armstrong?"

"There's nothing on paper, if that's what you mean."

"I see."

"Before she died, his mother—my sister—asked me to care for Alistair as my own as long as I live. I vowed I would do that."

He nodded. "And his father?"

"Is away on business but has given me supervision of Alistair."

"Does he know you've brought Alistair here?"

"No. If he needs to know, of course I will tell him. I'm hoping you have a pill or a procedure or something that will help Alistair so he can get better over the next weeks and return to school in January. He has a rigorous academic schedule, and I know his father is concerned that he keeps up with that, maintains his standing."

"I see." Malcolm nodded. "Would Mr. Bennett consider having Alistair tutored at home?"

"Home? He's adamant about not doing that. He believes boarding school an important experience for a young man." The woman's twist of mouth said she might think differently.

"You don't agree?"

She blinked again, lifting her shoulders in surrender. "He may be right. I only know Alistair is struggling. I tutored Alistair—both of my sister's children during the epidemic. They did well and learned a great deal until—" She stopped, looked down.

"I remember the young lass. I'm so very sorry."

She took a moment to compose herself. "I believe that education, however it is pursued, is lifelong learning, Dr. McNeill—the reward of natural curiosity and enthusiasm for life."

"I could not agree more." *She'll surely be the boy's strongest advocate.*

A knock came at the door, and Dr. Callahan entered. "Good morning. Ah, Miss Armstrong, it's good to see you again. You look fully recovered from the last time I saw you."

"Yes, Doctor, thank you. I'm very well, only concerned for my nephew, and growing more concerned by the minute. Were the tests you ran not conclusive?"

Dr. Callahan exchanged a glance with Malcolm, nodding in his direction, and took the chair beside Miss Armstrong.

Malcolm felt both pairs of eyes on him. He cleared his throat. "I'm sorry to say that Alistair's test results were positive . . ."

Hope sprang in her eyes. "Positive?"

"For juvenile diabetes."

"I've heard the name, but I don't know what—"

"More commonly called the wasting disease."

Astonishment dawned on the woman's face, then concern. "What does that mean?"

Malcolm swallowed, drew a breath. "Juvenile diabetes, diabetes mellitus—*diabetes* from the Greek word for *sieve*. You know of Alistair's incessant thirst and urination. His body acts like a sieve. *Mellitus* is Latin for *honey* or *sweet*, as the urine of a patient with diabetes mellitus is sweet."

The woman narrowed her eyes in concentration. "I still don't understand."

"The body is normally able to process food so it turns to sugars," Malcolm explained, "which we need to function, to use for energy. In those with diabetes, this process has broken down. The pancreas does not function correctly, so the body is unable to metabolize glucose—sugar. We know of no way to fix that, to restore the pancreas to a healthy state. The overload of sugars is sent to the kidneys, which explains his constant thirst and frequent urination. I'm sorry to say that at this time there is no cure, but—"

"He should not have sugar? Is that the problem?"

"Not entirely." Malcolm leaned forward. "His pancreas cannot—"

Dr. Callahan cut him off. "The important thing is to keep him comfortable, and on an even keel in the time he has left."

Concern changed to alarm in the woman's eyes. "What do you mean *the time he has left*?"

"Alistair has a few months, possibly a year, depending on how fast the disease progresses." Dr. Callahan set his hand on her arm. "I'm so very sorry, Miss Armstrong. I know this will come as a terrible blow to the boy's father."

The woman paled. "A year? To live?"

"However, there's a great deal of research being done now," Malcolm said quickly. "There's every reason to hope that before long—"

"We mustn't give false hope," Dr. Callahan cautioned. "There is no cure. I believe Dr. McNeill will agree with me that the prescribed course of action is to make Alistair's life as normal and pleasant as possible for as long as he's able to enjoy it."

"Wait. Stop! You're telling me there's nothing to be done? He's walking around. He's on his feet. It's not like the influenza. He's not bedridden. There's no raging fever!" Her voice rose with each phrase until it broke.

"No."

"There must be something you can do—something I can do. Please," she begged. "I'll do anything."

"I'm very sorry, Miss Armstrong." Dr. Callahan leaned compassionately toward her. "I know this is difficult. There is really nothing anyone can do, except, as I say, to make his life as pleasant as possible. Fresh air and moderate exercise may be helpful to keep his spirits up and to keep his glucose in a more moderate zone, but nothing too strenuous." Dr. Callahan shook his head. "News like this is never easy. Never easy to give, never easy to receive. Do you have questions?"

Miss Armstrong sat as if in a stupor. She shook her head, but Malcolm knew it didn't mean she had no questions, only that she could not believe or absorb all Dr. Callahan had said.

"Would you like me to talk with Mr. Bennett, Miss Armstrong? I imagine he'll want to know the details of our tests." Dr. Callahan waited.

"Miss Armstrong?" Malcolm prodded gently. He knew the impossible weight of this diagnosis.

"How did he get it?"

"We don't know," Malcolm answered. "There's a possibility that it may be genetic—hereditary. Do you know of anyone in the family who has suffered in this way—now or in the past?"

Miss Armstrong shook her head again, slowly. "I don't know anything about Russell's family—Mr. Bennett's. No one in my family—my sister's family—that I've ever heard of."

"We've seen an increase in these diagnoses since the influenza."

"Influenza caused this?"

"There's no proof of that, Dr. McNeill. Pure speculation. Anecdotal at best."

Malcolm felt his temper rising. *Anecdotal, yes, but too many cases to dismiss. And I cannot pretend there's no hope.* "I would be remiss if I didn't tell you that a great deal of research is being done in the field and there is real hope that in the near future—"

"Dr. McNeill, there is no cure."

"You are correct, of course, Dr. Callahan. There is no cure—at this time. But if we can help keep Alistair alive long enough, there may be help." He drew a deep breath and plunged ahead. "Dr. Frederick Allen has developed a radical and somewhat controversial treatment that cannot cure but may prolong—"

"Starvation is not a cure."

"No, but—"

"Enough, Doctor. We've already spoken of this." Dr. Callahan stood, taking Miss Armstrong's hand. "I apologize for Dr. McNeill's outburst, Miss Armstrong. The man he references advocates nothing more than a starvation diet. It is cruel, and it is cruel to give false hope, to prevent a patient or his family from preparing for the inevitable and from making the most of the time left. I advise letting the boy eat what he wants, do what he wants and is able to do. He'll suffer in the end regardless."

"What does that mean? How will he suffer?"

"His food will do him no good, Miss Armstrong. His body won't turn it into the energy he needs. His blood sugar will— Let me say simply that he will eventually slip into a coma until the end." Dr.

Callahan released her hand. "I understand this is a great deal to absorb. You will need time to do that, time to arrange for the care he needs. As questions arise, feel free to telephone for guidance or to make an appointment. For now, if you're ready, if you have no further questions, I'll walk you out."

But she didn't rise. "I was even worried about bringing him here . . . what his father would say." She spoke as if waking slowly from a dream.

"Withdraw him from school. His ability to concentrate will only diminish as his blood sugars increase. He won't be able to control his need to urinate."

She shook her head slowly. "His father—"

"Will he return soon?"

"Tomorrow."

"Have Mr. Bennett call me, or better yet, come in. I'll speak with him. I recommend you do not share this diagnosis with the boy until his father returns and is there to help him through it." Dr. Callahan reached for her arm and helped her stand.

Pale, eyes glistening with unshed tears, she looked at Malcolm, as if grasping for a lifeline, but he had none to offer—none Dr. Callahan would allow. He nodded to her once and watched as Dr. Callahan led her out.

23

Before rejoining Alistair in the waiting room, Gwen asked the receptionist where she could be excused. In the lavatory, Gwen locked the door, leaned against the counter, and gritted her teeth. *No. No! Please, God! This is so unfair! Why did You spare him from influenza only to put him through this? Why make him suffer the loss of his mother and sister only to suffer more?* She beat her fist on the marble countertop, willing to break her hand if it could in any way spare Alistair. *Can't the doctors be wrong? Please, let them be wrong.*

A knock came at the door.

Gwen swiped at her tears. "I'll be out in a minute." She inhaled a ragged breath, feeling as if she were choking, as if her clothes were too tight to breathe. *I can't let Alistair see me like this. I can't tell him he's dying. I won't. No, dear God, please, no. It's impossible . . . simply impossible. There's got to be something that can be done.*

Gwen splashed water against her red-rimmed eyes and dried them, then resolutely pinched color into her pale cheeks. Drawing one deep and shuddering breath, she squared her shoulders and walked out the door.

During the drive home, Alistair fired questions. "What did he say is wrong with me? Why did he talk to you and not to me? Why even have me come if he wasn't going to see me? If there's nothing wrong with me, Father's not going to like this . . . but, Aunt Gwen, there is something. I know it."

Gwen's head was splitting. *How am I to answer any of this?* In the end, she stalled. "Give them time. Doctors don't know everything. Sometimes it takes time to figure things out." *There has to be a better answer. There must be.*

"How much time?"

"I don't know." *All the time we have.*

"Well, what now?"

"Dr. Callahan suggests staying at home for now, taking it easy."

"For how long?"

"Going forward. I can tutor you, so you won't fall behind. We'll send for your books . . . after Christmas."

Alistair stared at her. "Father won't like that. He'll never allow it."

Gwen looked straight ahead. "I'll talk with him."

"You'd go against Father for me?"

She wasn't sure if he was incredulous or sarcastic. "Yes." *I'll fight death and hell for you.* "He'll be home from his trip tomorrow. I'll speak with him then."

Alistair leaned back against the seat. Gwen watched him from the corner of her eye. Despite the summer tan he'd achieved in their months at Sea Isle City, he now looked pale, wan, a bit gray. *How does a malfunctioning pancreas make you feel? What can I do to help you?*

"Are you tired?"

"A little. Mostly hungry . . . and thirsty."

"We'll be home soon. Mrs. Barrie will have lunch waiting."

"Good," he sighed. "I'm starved."

Truer words were never spoken. Gwen closed her eyes.

Gwen was not able to face Mrs. Barrie's questions either, not yet. She excused herself from luncheon, claiming she suffered a splitting headache, and no, she did not want Tilley to bring a tray to her room.

Gwen knew Mrs. Barrie searched her face and Alistair's expression. She forced a half smile, determined that neither Mrs. Barrie nor anyone else would read in her eyes what she'd learned that morning.

I've got to remain steady for Alistair's sake. Something can still happen. God will intervene. He must! A cure will be found—Dr. McNeill said so. Please, God, please! It was all she could do not to slam her bedroom door and throw herself onto her bed, screaming.

But she didn't. She sat by the window and looked out on the bare-limbed garden, dusted in snow. *Can this be Alistair's last Christmas? The last winter he'll watch snow fall, or sit by bonfires at night? What about his dreams—the digs, his father's promise to take him to Egypt? A year . . . or less. How can it be?* She didn't catch the tears that streamed down her face or stop the white knuckling of her hands as she gripped the arms of the chair, not until Tilley came in with the tray she'd said she didn't want and set it beside her.

"Are you ill, Miss Armstrong? Is there something I can do for you, or get for you?" The young maid looked genuinely concerned.

"What? No, no thank you, Tilley. My head hurts, that's all. I need . . . a nap. Please let Mrs. Barrie know that I don't wish to be disturbed. Please close the door on your way out."

"Yes, miss." Tilley tiptoed away.

If Gwen could have hidden in her room for a year, it wouldn't have been long enough. But three hours was all she allowed herself.

I must talk with Russell. I don't understand his grieving process for his daughter or even for Marion—if he grieves for her at all. But what will this do to him, so fast on the heels of those losses? He's never been close to Alistair. Will this diagnosis bring him to his senses? Will it draw them closer or drive them further apart? She couldn't guess.

A knock came softly at her bedroom door in the late afternoon, waking Gwen from a desperately needed nap.

"Yes?" she responded unwillingly.

Mrs. Barrie opened the door and spoke into the darkened room. "Mr. Whitfield telephoned, Miss Armstrong. He's received a concerned phone call from Alistair's school about his examinations and needs to speak with you."

"Oh," Gwen groaned. "I can imagine. Is he still on the line?"

"He requests that you telephone him at your earliest convenience."

"Thank you." Gwen put her feet to the floor, pushing hair from her eyes. The door had not closed.

"Might I ask," Mrs. Barrie spoke quietly, "did the doctor say what we might do to help Alistair?"

Gwen closed her eyes against the question. She couldn't look at Mrs. Barrie and withhold information. *She didn't ask his diagnosis; that's good.* "We're to keep him home and let him rest for now. Plenty of fluids—water—moderate exercise, let him determine what he wants to eat, what he wants to do."

"I see. Did he say—"

"Dr. Callahan will speak with Mr. Bennett when he returns." *That's the truth. Not all of it, but the truth.*

"Yes, of course." Mrs. Barrie stepped back to the door. "Well, we'll do just as the doctor says and hope that our lad feels right as rain soon enough." But her worried tone did not fool Gwen.

Unable to sleep, Gwen sat in the schoolroom late that night, staring into the fire. *A year ago, Clara and Alistair and I were here, happy in our "one-room schoolhouse." Clara's love of art, Alistair's passion for archaeology and all things Egyptian. Our mutual love of literature, our joy in experiments exploring the natural world. Marion came home for Christmas. It was perfect—nearly. All things we took for granted, things we assumed might go on forever. How naive.*

Lights played across the wall. Gwen turned toward the window, surprised to see automobile lights headed toward the house so late at night. *Dr. Callahan found he was wrong and is coming to make amends. There's nothing wrong with Alistair that rest won't heal. Or there is, but a cure for diabetes mellitus has been discovered. Either way. Either way, God, let it be so.*

She ran to the foyer and threw open the front door. The car slowed to a halt. She couldn't see through the dark until Russell reached the first step. Her heart fell.

"I wasn't expecting a welcoming committee this time of night"—she heard the smile in his voice—"but I'm pleased just the same."

"Russell." Her voice fell flat and breathless at the same time.

"Not who you were expecting?" He removed his hat, stepping into the foyer.

"I thought— We didn't expect you until tomorrow."

"I needed to get back. I'm expecting important guests tomorrow night. I'm glad you're up. I'll need your help, and Mrs. Barrie's—all hands on deck. I trust she's hired servers for Friday evening and some-one to help Mrs. LaMott?" He unbuttoned his coat. Gwen took it. "I know we agreed not to celebrate Christmas this year, but the house should be decorated. They'll expect it. You could help Mrs. Barrie—"

"Russell, we need to talk—"

"These are serious collectors—top-notch. I must insist, Gwen—not about the decorating. Mrs. Barrie can hire help. But with the entertaining. No, that's not what I meant to say. I'm asking you. I need your help. Please."

He searched her face and frowned. "What is it? Is everything all right? You look—I don't know . . ."

"It's Alistair."

Russell blew out a breath, exasperated and relieved at once. "What's the boy done now? Failed chemistry? Sabotaged his exams?"

Gwen's head spun. "He's sick."

"Not influenza again?" He looked panic-stricken.

"No."

"Contagious? Hospitalized?"

"No, nothing like that. It's not contagious. He's home—here, asleep."

"Is he making excuses for a poor exam performance? He's barely hanging onto his spot now, slacking off."

"Please, Russell, listen. You don't understand—"

"I know my son better than you do." He clasped her arms. "He's playing you like a violin. I will not allow him to use you like this. You look done in. You're exhausted."

She pushed him away, throwing his coat to the nearest chair. "I am done in. I am exhausted, but not because Alistair's 'playing me.' Listen to me. You have to know."

"Know what?"

"Alistair's very sick."

"So you said."

"It's not what I said, it's what Dr. Callahan and Dr. McNeill said."

"You took him to Callahan? Knowing I told you—"

"Yes, on Saturday. Dr. McNeill ran tests. He told me to keep Alistair resting at home until the results came in. I saw him today."

"And?" Russell was clearly not in the mood for discussion.

"Alistair has diabetes mellitus—juvenile diabetes."

"Juvenile . . . whatever. So, he'll grow out of it."

"No, he won't." She lowered her voice. "He'll die."

Russell stared at her, as if not hearing, not comprehending her words.

She stepped closer, in pity, and rested her hand on his arm. "There is no cure. That's what they said."

A crease formed between Russell's eyes, as if he was trying to read her, to understand her.

"Dr. Callahan wants you to call him. He can explain the results of the test they ran, what it all means."

Russell stepped away. "I don't know what that is. How did he get it?"

"No one knows. It could be hereditary. It could be because of the influenza." She shrugged.

"How long?"

"We don't know when he got it. His pancreas isn't working right—Dr. Callahan can explain it better than I can."

"I meant how long does he have?"

Gwen drew a breath from deep inside. "A few months. A year at most."

Russell pushed long fingers through his hair. "I can't do this."

Her heart broke for him. *To lose your wife, your daughter, and now your only son in so short a time . . . As impossible as it is for me, as it will be for Mrs. Barrie, it is insurmountable for you.*

"I am so sorry, Russell. Alistair doesn't know yet. He only—"

"Horace Greenwood and his wife, Alexandra, will be here tomorrow night at eight. Henri Gainsbourg, Stephen Scarpello, Mr. and Mrs. Anthony Rosenberg . . . They'll all be here to view my museum, my acquisitions, potentially to buy, and if all goes to their liking, to hire me to negotiate major acquisitions for them in Cairo. The most noted collectors of our time will—"

"Did you hear me? Do you hear yourself?"

"I heard you, Gwen. You said nothing can be done—there is no cure for this, whatever it is, however he got it." He stood across the foyer from her, his voice low. "I will telephone Callahan the day after they leave. I cannot risk these meetings falling through. More is at stake than you realize."

"I realize your son is dying."

"That won't happen tomorrow. You said so yourself. I'll deal with Callahan when our guests leave. I can't help Alistair now. I need your help. I don't ask much of you, Gwen, but I'm asking this."

She opened her mouth to speak, then closed it, afraid of what she might say.

"It's late and I've a great deal to do. I'll see you tomorrow. Good night." He walked quickly down the hall to his office. She heard the door close.

Gwen stared after him in disbelief, trying to comprehend his reaction, or lack of reaction, to his son's—his only child's—diagnosis. *Is this grief? Denial? Utter selfishness?* She didn't know.

24

Russell had eaten and gone before Gwen or Alistair appeared for breakfast but not before he'd left a detailed list for Mrs. Barrie to oversee—including what he expected of Gwen.

"It seems we're all in for a veritable whirlwind these next days—beginning with this evening." Mrs. Barrie shook her head. "I hardly know how we'll manage, but manage we shall."

"What does Father want me to do?" Alistair looked at Mrs. Barrie.

"You're not on the list, count your lucky stars."

"Guess I'm supposed to lay low, then—be invisible. Nothing new." Alistair smirked. But Gwen could see he felt the omission. "Does Father even know I'm here?"

Gwen swallowed. "I saw him briefly last night and told him."

"What did he say about me not returning to school? Is he angry?"

"We didn't talk about that, not yet. When this hullabaloo is over, he'll talk with Dr. Callahan. He'll learn more then. We'll all learn more."

Both Mrs. Barrie and Alistair eyed Gwen warily.

They know I'm holding back. For your sake, my dear nephew . . . for your sake. "Perhaps by then you'll feel better . . . or Dr. Callahan will have new information." *Dr. Callahan said it was wrong to give false hope. But how can hope of any kind be false?* "Let's see my list, Mrs. Barrie. It sounds as if time is of the essence."

The next two days, Gwen found herself positioned as "lady of the Christmas manor," a role she resented, yet one that at any other time she might have thrilled to. She was introduced as Alistair's aunt, sister of Russell's late wife, who had come to help in their time of need.

Gwen wasn't at all certain the company bought that notion. Mrs. Rosenberg, in particular, cast Gwen pointed looks. She didn't actually say *gold digger*, but the aura hung low in the air amid fragrances of evergreen trees and expensive perfumes.

While Gwen regretted the time stolen from Alistair, she knew that the only way to get Russell's full attention and support for his son was to first appease his business obligations, and no doubt his ego. It was upside down and wrong, but she would do it. She put to good use her grammar school skills of playacting. What she'd learned of high-society guests the one summer evening she'd helped Russell entertain his associates at theater and dinner came in helpful too. The candlelight dinners served were as lavish as the five-star restaurant they'd eaten at then. *At least I know which fork to use.*

Alexandra Greenwood was a beautiful but quiet woman, a fashionable dresser, with little inclination to join the conversation. It was all Gwen could do to draw her out.

Mrs. Rosenberg—Eugenia—was a woman from another era. Regal, exacting . . . Gwen wouldn't have been surprised to see her lift a lorgnette to her gray and piercing eyes if it wouldn't interfere with her upturned nose. Mr. Rosenberg—Henry—was overtly friendly toward Gwen, which didn't help Russell's cause with Eugenia.

But Russell was devilishly handsome and charming, able to draw out Alexandra despite the woman's reticence. For all her concern over Alistair, and Russell's lack of urgency in the matter, Gwen found herself returning Russell's smiles and yielding to his generous and friendly demeanor. She watched with curiosity as he wooed Eugenia Rosenberg to a more receptive mood. They'd have much to talk over after the affair, as long as the visit ended well for Russell's business.

She couldn't understand Russell's underlying anxiety about the investors. *Why is he so concerned about these transactions? Is he not as solvent as he projects? He spends money as if it were wastewater. The grocery bill for this affair alone could feed a family of five for more than a year. Is it really the money, or the prestige, or does it have more to do with his desire to return to Cairo, to further his business there?*

That thought gave Gwen pause. *Last time he spent months and months in Egypt. If he goes for so long again, he could be gone when Alistair . . .* She couldn't think of that now.

Instead, Gwen continued to lift her shoulders and paste on her smile. She would do it for Russell, trusting that entertaining his guests would later buy his ear when it came to his son.

Finally, on the last day of the illustrious visit, Gwen was excused from joining the group in their trip to the Metropolitan Museum of Art to view the Davis Collection, including open-mouthed storage jars containing the embalming cache of the obscure king named Tutankhamen—a collection Gwen had already viewed twice. Russell was eager to show the exhibition and to exploit his relationship to his late mentor, the generous sponsor Theodore Davis, who believed those jars proved he'd discovered the tomb of the young king. By the time Davis had discontinued digging, he believed the tomb had yielded its treasures and there were no more to be found, at least no more of significance.

Gwen knew Russell wasn't certain of that. He'd told her that he'd met with Howard Carter when he was last in Luxor to purchase antiquities from Muhammad Mohassib's shop—artifacts he confided might have been stolen from digs with poor security supervision, including Davis's own, which made determining their provenance impossible.

"Once Davis gave up his concessions to the Valley of the Kings, wealthy Lord Carnarvon, of England, received concessions to dig there." Russell's eyes had lit as he'd told her, "Carter was leading the work on Carnarvon's behalf until the Great War interrupted. He began digging again in 1917, convinced there was still much to find."

Gwen had previously been glad of that notion, remembering Alistair's determination to join those digs once he grew up. It had been easy to imagine his dreams coming to pass, especially with Russell's connections. Now she knew that would not happen, could not happen. The realization was overwhelming, heartbreaking.

Relieved of her duties, she donned her everyday clothes and went in search of Alistair.

Mrs. Barrie met her in the hallway. "He's in the garden. I was just about to take him his coat. He grumbled that he didn't need it, but he must be freezing out there."

"I'll take it to him. I want to speak with him anyway." Gwen reached for the coat, but Mrs. Barrie seemed reluctant to let it go.

"He nearly bit poor Mrs. LaMott's head off when she asked him how he could eat enough for three grown men and still be skinny as a stick. I know she shouldn't have put it like that, but you should have heard him—most disrespectful."

"I'm so sorry. Mrs. LaMott doesn't deserve that."

"The point is, it's not like him. He's elated one minute and angry the next. I'd think there was something worrying him, but he's certainly not gone off his appetite. He's ravenous, if anything."

Gwen rubbed her hand across her forehead.

"What do you know, Miss Armstrong? What are you not telling me?"

The crease in Mrs. Barrie's brow, the lines by her eyes and around her mouth reminded Gwen that this beautiful Scottish woman she relied upon for so much, the one person who was truly as much in Alistair's corner as she, who was more like a grandmother to Alistair than any other, deserved to know.

Gwen looked up and down the hallway to make certain no one was within hearing. "Give the coat to Tilley to take to Alistair, then meet me in the schoolroom."

Mrs. Barrie's eyes widened, but she nodded and quickly walked away.

Gwen waited until Mrs. Barrie appeared in the schoolroom doorway. "Please, close the door and join me." They sat side by side on the sofa before the fire. Gwen reached for the older woman's hand. She'd wished someone had held her hand when she first received the news. "Dr. Callahan and a new doctor, Dr. McNeill, ran a urine test for Alistair the first day we went to see him. They said it showed that sugar, which is what digested food normally becomes for fuel, isn't being processed by his body—something about the pancreas not working as it should. They called it diabetes mellitus—juvenile diabetes. Both doctors said there's no cure."

"What does that mean, there is no cure?"

Gwen drew a deep breath. "It means Alistair has a year or less."

Mrs. Barrie pulled back her hand. "A year or less . . . to live?" Her voice rose in alarm.

"I begged them for a treatment—anything at all we can do . . . but there's nothing. They said there's nothing."

Mrs. Barrie's face reflected the tornado of feelings that had ripped through Gwen. "That canna be right. No, I don't believe it. I canna believe it."

Gwen reached over and rubbed the woman's arm, wanting to comfort her, knowing there was none to give.

"Does he know? Is that why he's so short-tempered, poor lad?"

Gwen shook her head. "No, he doesn't know. Dr. Callahan was firm about not telling him, at least until he has a chance to speak with Russell. He wants Russell to be there for him."

Mrs. Barrie huffed. "I canna imagine . . ."

"Neither can I." Gwen sighed. "Alistair will need us in the days ahead."

"Did the doctor say what we can do for him?"

"Dr. Callahan said to make Alistair's life as pleasant as possible. Moderate exercise and good nutrition might help for a time, but let him eat what he wants, do what he wants as long as he's able. The anger—the mood swings, up and down, are all part of it, as his sugar levels rise and fall, I guess. They said it's all because his pancreas isn't functioning. They know of no way to fix that."

"And Dr. McNeill agreed?"

"He said the same . . . well, nearly. He started to say something about some other doctor and a diet, but Dr. Callahan said it was nothing but quackery and cruelty and cut him off."

"I'd like to know what Dr. McNeill had to say. I know him, at least I've met him."

"How?"

"Well, he was here, wasn't he, when we all suffered so from the influenza?"

"Yes. He said we were among his first patients."

"Aye. I remember him coming to see you and Alistair and he was very good, very kind. If he saw me while I was in the throes of it, I wouldn't remember. He's from Scotland, a widower."

Gwen smiled sadly. "Someone from home."

"Aye, and I see him at church . . . a fine, rich baritone. But he's younger than Dr. Callahan. He served during the Great War, treating so many kinds of illnesses."

"You think he might know of more progressive treatments, more recent?"

"That I canna know or be saying. I just . . . want something more for our lad."

Gwen agreed.

Mrs. Barrie, uncharacteristically, sat back against the sofa, the wind knocked out of her. "There have been things in these last years that have tested my faith—Mrs. Bennett's tuberculosis, the war, the influenza, and wee Clara's death. But this . . . when we all thought we'd put the worst behind us."

"I'm afraid I have little faith left." Gwen kept her voice even though anger simmered beneath.

Mrs. Barrie eyed her sadly. "Then I'm sorriest of all for you, Miss Armstrong. You're going to need it as you never have."

25

The Saturday before Christmas, Malcolm spent the morning making hospital rounds and the afternoon at the office, relieving Dr. Callahan of patients. By six thirty he'd finished, hung up his medical coat, donned his jacket, and said "good night and good Lord's Day tomorrow" to the receptionist.

It had been a challenging week, made harder by delivering Alistair Bennett's deadly diagnosis. A lad—a very fine lad, by all accounts—ready to step into the prime of his life who would not live to see it.

Malcolm could not get his earlier meeting with Alistair, the later sad exchange with his aunt, or Dr. Callahan's stubborn refusal to credit one feeble ray of hope from his mind. He'd asked Dr. Callahan if he'd seen Mr. Bennett, but the doctor had received no call. Malcolm couldn't understand that. Surely the lad's aunt would have relayed the urgency.

He spent Saturday night tossing and turning, struggling with himself and with the Lord, uncertain if his acquiescence to silence was because he feared crossing Dr. Callahan or if he was being censored by God for reasons only He knew.

You've brought me to these shores, Father, I've no doubt, for good purpose. You've aligned me with Dr. Callahan, whom I know is a caring doctor of integrity, one who's done much good in his time. Much good, but is he too set in his time, not looking to the world of new possibilities?

If I speak to Miss Armstrong, or to Mr. Bennett, go against Dr. Callahan's injunction, he'll not trust me, perhaps even revoke the partnership he's planned on extending.

Still, Lord, I believe in Dr. Allen's work—for the time it might buy for the cure to come. I know the research being done, at least some of it. There is reason to hope, slim though it seems now. I'd have tried it with my own bonnie wee Sheenagh if I'd known of it then. If I'd been home from the war when she was diagnosed, if Fenella had agreed—and I'd surely have persuaded her. I'd have tried anything to keep my darling daughter alive as long as possible.

Weary beyond words, Malcolm stood as the candles for the fourth week of Advent were lit the following morning. He took in the evergreen boughs beneath the stained glass windows, the way the sun poured through the colors and helped to warm the great room. Beautiful in ways he craved, but that morning the colors jarred him. He'd not slept. As if by rote he followed the line of worshippers and knelt at the altar rail for Holy Communion. *Is this sin, Lord, taking Your supper with my heart in such turmoil?*

He took it anyway, begging the Lord for forgiveness, for direction, for peace in his soul. Malcolm rose to join congregants returning to their seats.

Making his way down the aisle, he saw a young lad whisper to the older woman beside him, motioning in Malcolm's direction. Then they both nodded to Malcolm, the woman half smiling, the lad's face a muddle of concern. Malcolm automatically nodded in return. His mind was so consumed with his thoughts that who they were didn't register until he'd returned to his pew.

Alistair. Alistair Bennett, and the Scottish housekeeper from your home, lad. Of course . . . the woman heartbroken for Mrs. Bennett and her daughter, who was so concerned for you and your aunt despite her own influenza. What is her name? She said she'd been with the family since its beginning. Where is your aunt, lad? Your father? Is this a sign, Lord?

Malcolm had every intention of telephoning the Bennett residence first thing Monday morning. He'd made his decision by the time he returned from church the day before and had come to work a half hour early to do just that, never expecting an urgent Caesarean section to derail his plans.

The woman was waiting on the clinic's steps in full-blown labor, her baby breech, when he'd arrived. Neither Dr. Callahan nor the nurse or receptionist had yet made an appearance. It was not a surgery he'd performed often, but there'd been no time to move the mother to the hospital.

By the time Malcolm had got the woman on the table, scrubbed, and donned his mask and gown, Nurse Cummings had arrived.

"Thank You, Lord!" It was all Malcolm could say aloud, but he prayed silently through the entire operation.

An hour later the woman was stitched and settled. Though sleepy, she held her newborn daughter in her arms. Malcolm felt he'd been dragged through a waterwheel backward.

"Well done, Dr. McNeill." Dr. Callahan clapped him on the back when he came out of surgery. "A near Christmas miracle. Not something we do in the office every day, eh?" The older doctor looked too pleased by far.

"I hope not. Let's not be about setting a precedent." Malcolm tried to make light, but seeing the wee bairn, so fragile and premature, had undone him. All he could think of was the day he'd held his new daughter, his bonnie wee Sheenagh, in his arms after her beautiful mother delivered her. *My darling Fenella . . . I miss you both.*

It was nearly ten o'clock by the time Malcolm was prepared to resume office duties. He checked the receptionist's appointment schedule to see which patients Dr. Callahan had seen in his stead and who was next.

"I see Mr. Bennett was here."

"Yes, Doctor, an hour or so ago. Dr. Callahan saw him."

Malcolm's heart fell. That had been his only reasonable opportunity to meet directly with Russell Bennett, to supplement what Dr. Callahan might say. He was certain Dr. Callahan had delivered the terrible diagnosis with compassion. He was equally certain he wouldn't have shared details of ongoing research or Dr. Allen's recommended treatment.

He took up his next patient's medical chart, placing one foot in front of the other.

Six thirty came before Malcolm knew it. A busier day he couldn't remember. Twice more he'd checked on the baby and new mother. The second time the father was there, having been called in from work. Malcolm forced his own loss to the back of his mind and did his best to smile, to offer congratulations, to concentrate on the joy of the young family. For all the sickness, disease, and death he faced on a regular basis, it was good to see the beginning of life, to be part of that.

Weary as he was, Malcolm didn't like disorder and refused to leave before his notes were completed and his charts filed. Dr. Callahan had gone home, as had the nurse and receptionist. It was seven o'clock as he sat at his desk. Again he thought of Alistair Bennett, the lad who'd not live to manhood, barring a miracle.

I am the God of miracles.

The thought came so strong to Malcolm's mind that he looked about the room half expecting to see the embodiment of the voice. His heart quickened. There was no one there.

Holy Spirit, be my guide, Malcolm prayed.

The determination had barely filled his mind, penetrated his heart, before his hand reached for the telephone. He'd make the call he'd come in so early to make that morning, before he'd met the woman in labor, before everything had derailed him from his purpose. He still had the number somewhere on his desk. *There, under the phone, waiting.*

Still praying, he dialed the operator and gave the number. The phone rang once, twice, three times before a woman with a strong Scottish accent answered, "Good evening, Bennett Place."

"Good evening . . . Mrs. Barrie?" Hearing her voice Malcolm recalled her name. It never hurt to have a trusted and longtime housekeeper on your side, the one woman also in charge of the cook.

"Yes, yes, it is. May I ask who's calling?"

"Malcolm McNeill—Dr. McNeill."

"Ach, I remember you, Dr. McNeill. Alistair and I saw you in church on Sunday." Her lowered voice made him think she knew Alistair's diagnosis.

"I've seen you there before as well, Mrs. Barrie, but I didn't realize Alistair attended. It was good to see him."

"It was his first time."

Does that mean he knows? "He's looking for comfort, for faith, then."

Her voice dropped to a whisper. "He doesn't know, Doctor, about—you know. He's confused over feeling so poorly."

"His father hasn't told him?" Malcolm knew he shouldn't be talking to Mr. Bennett's housekeeper about Alistair's diagnosis, but he'd seen the bond between the woman and Alistair not only at church but when the influenza had ravaged the household. The one family member he'd never seen was the father.

"No. I don't know how they will tell him. It's—it's impossible."

He heard the break in her voice. *Holy Spirit, give me words.* "Mrs. Barrie, I'd like to speak with Mr. Bennett, or Miss Armstrong. Whoever is responsible for Alistair's daily care."

"Do you have some hope to offer?" He heard the pleading in her voice.

"I'd like to suggest a program that may be considered somewhat radical. It's a difficult regimen, a restrictive diet for the most part. My hope is that by severely regulating Alistair's food intake, we might prolong his life." He sealed his lips and waited, knowing he could so easily get carried away in presenting this silken thread of hope. "Mrs.

Barrie, I believe a cure will be found. There's intense research going on now—very hopeful research—but Alistair needs to stay alive long enough for that cure to be discovered."

He heard her breathing, hesitating on the line. Then she said, "Miss Armstrong said that Dr. Callahan thinks the regimen cruel. He called it a starvation diet."

"It is difficult. I canna deny that, but . . . perhaps I can give Mr. Bennett a book that explains the regimen, so he can consider—"

"Something to explain. That might help."

"I'll send my copy round by post first thing tomorrow. Once Mr. Bennett's read it, I'd like to discuss it with him. I must urge, time is of the essence. I canna stress more clearly, Mrs. Barrie, that without intervention Alistair will die—sooner rather than later."

"Send it to me, Dr. McNeill, at this address. I'll make certain Miss Armstrong gets it. I think it best she reads it first . . . and not to be presumptuous, but I want to read it as well. I know Miss Armstrong would agree. If she believes it something that might help Alistair, perhaps she'll wish to meet with you. We'll do anything—try anything to keep our boy alive."

Thank You, Lord.

Mrs. Barrie went on. "Perhaps it's best if the meeting is private."

"You don't think Mr. Bennett should—"

"Not yet. May God forgive me if I'm doing wrong, but I say meet with Miss Armstrong first. She's the lad's strongest advocate and the one most likely to find the ear of Mr. Bennett."

"I understand." He didn't, but he trusted this fellow Scot. *What other choice is there?* He prayed they were fast readers.

Mrs. Barrie usually collected mail from the front door and distributed it to the household. Twice the next day she made certain she was in the foyer twenty minutes before postal delivery was expected.

The package addressed to Mrs. Barrie arrived in the afternoon mail. She could hardly wait for a free moment to open it in her room, to begin reading whatever Dr. McNeill had to offer for Alistair's sake.

She'd not yet mentioned the doctor's offering to Miss Armstrong. She wanted to make certain she understood all that would be required in this "starvation diet." *Anything, Lord. I'll do anything for that dear boy.*

She stayed up late that night reading case studies and making lists of recipes and menus from the slim volume, *The Starvation Treatment of Diabetes*, by a Dr. Lewis Webb Hill and dietician Sarah Eckman, all based on Dr. Frederick Allen's starvation diet. The regimen was preposterous. The plan advocated two days of normal eating for observation, then one or two or more days on nothing but black coffee with an ounce of whiskey, or bouillon, if preferred, every two hours from 7 a.m. to 7 p.m.—however long it took for the patient to become sugar-free. Daily urine samples were to be tested for sugar content. Once the patient tested sugar-free, small quantities of vegetables could be added. Daily testing continued, and assuming the patient's sugar did not increase, small amounts of protein and fat could be added, then gradually raised. A careful recording of the effects of raised carbohydrates compared with the effects of protein should be made and studied to determine the more troublesome of the two. The diet included no refined sugar. Carbohydrates of any kind were severely restricted. Vegetables must be boiled three times to reduce the number of carbohydrates they contained.

"A typical breakfast could later be bacon and eggs," she murmured, *"or simply canned asparagus, coffee, and clear soup."* She read on. When she came to the supper menu detailing lettuce, raw tomato, and cauliflower, she closed her eyes.

Twice she threw the book to her bed, disgusted with the idea of starving the child she loved.

When, as a young woman back in Scotland, she'd miscarried her babe, she'd known mothers everywhere risked the same time and again to bear children. She'd have risked life and limb to bear a live child of her own and had planned to do just that, as soon as she became pregnant again. But when her husband succumbed to pneumonia the second winter of their marriage, that opportunity was denied. Broken-hearted as she was, she'd not railed against God. She'd accepted his death as a natural part of life. He'd been a miner, after all, and if the pneumonia hadn't gotten him, the black lung or the tumbling of the mountain's walls or the demon drink might have.

She'd gone to church, she'd prayed, and the prayer that remained in her heart all those years came from Job's words: *"The Lord gave, and the Lord hath taken away; blessed be the name of the Lord."* She'd meant it then. She'd meant it when Mrs. Bennett and even dear Clara died.

She tried to surrender now, trusting Alistair to God's care. But if there was something she could do, some way God was leading her to help the lad, she'd risk life and limb again—and Mr. Bennett's wrath—to do it.

He'll do nothing to help his son, God forgive him. He did little enough to help his wife or daughter, so consumed with business he was . . . and still is, perhaps more so. But Miss Armstrong, that's another thing. She's the one, if anyone will stand up to the man.

She took up the book again.

26

Gwen was more than a little surprised when a weary but agitated Mrs. Barrie followed her to her room after breakfast and pressed the slim volume into her hands.

"You need to read this, Miss Armstrong—right away if you can. Dr. McNeill said time is of the essence."

"Dr. McNeill? You spoke with him?"

"On the telephone," Mrs. Barrie confessed, squaring her shoulders. "We canna let the lad perish without doing what we can, harsh though it seems."

Gwen frowned, flipping through the pages. "This is the diet Dr. Callahan said was quackery—and cruel."

"Aye. It is cruel. But isn't it crueler not to tell Alistair of this and let him choose?"

Gwen looked away. That was why she'd disagreed with Russell about not telling Alistair his diagnosis. She'd want to know, to choose to fight for her life with every ounce of her being. She understood Russell didn't want more anxiety for Alistair or chaos in his household when he believed the outcome was inevitable. But why was she hesitating to offer that truth, and now this choice, to Alistair?

Because I know Russell won't go against Dr. Callahan's recommendation. Because going along is an easy way of saying, "There was nothing anyone could have done. It was God's will . . ." When I don't know what he believes about God. When, God forgive me, he wants Alistair to disappear.

The thought quickened Gwen's pulse. She was angry with Russell, but she shouldn't judge him so. She saw his actions—or lack thereof—but didn't know his heart or what he truly believed. He'd conveniently blamed the church for the deaths of Marion and Clara, taking no responsibility for his absence or lack of relationship with either of them or with Alistair. *I can't blame him for their deaths. I can't blame him for Alistair's diabetes. But does he fear risking his reputation by doing something unpopular—radical, as Dr. McNeill said?*

Mrs. Barrie spoke into Gwen's hesitation. "I believe we can do this, here at home, if Alistair is willing and if his father doesn't object. He wouldn't be able to eat at table or even in the kitchen—that would be torture with all Mrs. LaMott's wonderful cooking. More likely in his room or the schoolroom, or in the garden when the weather is fine."

"Not alone. That would be beyond cruel."

Mrs. Barrie lifted her hands. "One of us could be with him, do our best to make his meager meals cheerful. You could play the gramophone—or read to him."

"There are no other options, I suppose." Gwen resented that truth.

"Apparently some doctors advocate fasting altogether for extended periods of time as a way of reducing the sugar in the urine. But I canna see that going on for long." Mrs. Barrie leaned closer. "Please, Miss Armstrong, read it, and let's talk. Dr. McNeill is eager to meet with you to discuss details or answer any questions you might have. He's willing to meet with Mr. Bennett as well. I cautioned him to meet with you first . . . if you think it wise to proceed."

"And you do—think it wise?"

"What choice do we have?"

"Dr. Callahan said he'll die anyway . . . You know that."

"Aye. But perhaps not so soon. If we don't do all we can, what then?"

Gwen nodded, echoing Mrs. Barrie's brogue. "Aye."

It was just past midnight in the early hours of Friday morning, Christmas Eve, when Gwen closed *The Starvation Treatment of Diabetes*.

How Mrs. Barrie believed they'd be able to keep Alistair to such a restrictive, paltry diet when he was constantly ravenous now, she could not imagine. The holidays presented all manner of landmines in that way.

She needed to talk with Dr. McNeill, needed to know everything he knew about current research and exactly how real the prospects for a diabetes cure might be. She wouldn't put Alistair through misery for a pie-in-the-sky imagining. But if the hope—the prospect for a cure was real . . .

After breakfast, Gwen waited until Russell had gone for the day, until Mr. Dornby was in the garden. Mrs. Barrie distracted Alistair in the school room with a request to help her sort board games he might consider too babyish to keep on the shelf.

Quietly, Gwen opened the door to Russell's museum and made her way through to his office. His telephone was the only truly private line in the house. Sitting at his desk, she pulled Dr. Callahan's office telephone number from her pocket and placed the call.

"Yes, good morning, may I speak with Dr. McNeill?"

"He's seeing patients now, but I can take a message or direct you to Dr. Callahan. May I ask who's calling and if this is an emergency?"

"Miss Armstrong. I need to speak with Dr. McNeill directly. I'm returning his call. The doctor's expecting me momentarily. I can wait on the line." It wasn't true, but Gwen felt it would expedite matters and keep Dr. Callahan from the conversation.

"I can have him return your call."

"It is a matter of some urgency. He said to wait on the line."

Momentary silence on the other end of the line made it clear this was not a normal practice. "I'm sorry, but—"

"Please." Gwen assumed her most authoritarian voice. "I don't have time to wait for his return call. I must speak with him now."

"Very well, Miss Armstrong. Let me see what I can do. Please hold the line."

Gwen felt her pulse quicken. She hoped Dr. Callahan was nowhere nearby. Dr. McNeill had gone out on a limb, professionally speaking, to share his recommendation. Why he willingly risked alienating his supervisor, she did not know. She had to believe . . . she didn't know what, but she would find out.

Minutes mounted. While she waited, she ran her fingers over the telephone's cord and idly mulled over the items on Russell's desk . . . a letter opener with a replica of a pharaoh's head, a pen-and-ink set that looked as if it came from a line of Victorian royalty, a stack of letters waiting to be answered beneath an Egyptian paperweight.

What is taking so long? She pushed back from the desk. Beneath sat a wastepaper basket. A crumpled sheet of paper lay on the floor. *Not a very good pitcher, are you, Russell?* She picked up the crumpled sheet to toss it in the trash, but the note was written in large letters in blood-red ink. Curious, she smoothed the paper and narrowed her eyes to decipher the almost illegible writing.

Pay up. Stay off the docks. Remember Meehan. Merry Christmas,
W. B.

A tribute? A threat?

Meehan? Wasn't that the name of the Irish dock mobster—the leader of the White Hand Gang—murdered this spring? And W. B.? Who—

"Miss Armstrong?" The familiar Scottish brogue came on the line.

Her heart leapt—whether because of his voice or because of what she'd just read, just remembered, she wasn't certain. She didn't hear the click of the receptionist's line and knew the woman had not hung up. *Focus. Focus.*

"Dr. McNeill, I'm returning your call." Distracted, she stumbled on. "Yes, I do think the treatment needs further explanation. I realize there is some urgency."

"Yes, of course." He sounded slightly wary, but relieved. "Miss O'Brien, I believe you're still on the line? Could you check my schedule for the remainder of the day and see if I have any openings? Write a note of available times and bring it to me straightaway, please."

There was a slight gasp on the line and a faint, "Yes, Doctor." The essential click followed.

Gwen half smiled as she again crumpled the note in her hand. *He's no fool, and well aware of his eavesdropping receptionist.*

"Miss Armstrong, when and where would you like to meet?"

Saturday was Christmas Day, a day the Bennett household would not be formally celebrating this year. Gwen spent the day with Alistair in the schoolroom and drawing room, playing board games before the fire, listening to carols on the gramophone and to the president's speech on the radio . . . the urgency and finality of Alistair's condition constantly warring with the note she'd found in Russell's office for supremacy in her mind.

Russell, moody, joined them for meals and in the evening for a game of chess, hardly looking Alistair in the eye. It had been all Gwen could do to keep from probing him. *What is your relationship with the Irish mobsters at the docks? What have you gotten yourself into?* Regardless, she knew this was not the time to approach him about a radical treatment for Alistair. She needed to learn more from Dr. McNeill before championing the protocol.

Mrs. Barrie and Alistair attended church Sunday morning, returning to the house at luncheon. Though Gwen wasn't ready to make peace with God herself, she was glad for the apparent comfort going to church gave Alistair. Gwen waited until the middle of the afternoon to go for her Sunday walk. A few minutes ahead of the scheduled midafternoon meeting, she met Mrs. Barrie at a small English tea shop not far from the house, a place Russell and his Irish friends—or enemies—would not frequent. In anticipation of Dr. McNeill's arrival, they ordered a pot of tea and half a dozen scones with lemon curd and raspberry jam.

The tea and scones had just been delivered to the corner table when Dr. McNeill breezed in, rubbing his hands against the cold, and bearing the fragrance of brisk December air on his wool tweed jacket. Mrs. Barrie could not have smiled wider.

Gwen saw that her trusted friend trusted the man. *He's a fellow Scot . . . but is that enough to entrust Alistair's life to him? Mrs. Barrie's not easily influenced. But what does she know of him?*

Gwen meant to reserve judgment, to ask necessary questions, to share her concerns but remain objective. But the man's piercing green eyes, his hair, brown and brushed in wild waves from the wind, and his brilliant smile made her momentarily forget.

"Mrs. Barrie, Miss Armstrong, happy Boxing Day." He nodded, reaching for their hands one after the other. "Thank you for meeting with me."

As if we are doing him the favor.

"You've read the book. Both of you?"

"We have, and happy Christmas and Boxing Day to you, Doctor. We're eager to know more for sake of our lad," Mrs. Barrie began, then, her coloring high, apologized. "Forgive me, Miss Armstrong. You should speak."

Gwen touched the arm of her ally, for that's how she thought of her. "We both want to know more, Dr. McNeill. We appreciate that you've taken your private time and—and taken it upon yourself to share this information. It makes me realize you must firmly believe in Dr. Allen's work . . ."

"I do, Miss Armstrong. Of course, it is not a cure, but I do believe a cure will be forthcoming. If Alistair's life can be prolonged to take advantage of that cure—"

"But how likely do you believe it that a cure will come in

time—even if we do everything the book says? I mean—it is starvation. The book firmly states that."

"Aye. It will be hard for Alistair to keep to the diet and hard for those who administer and regulate it."

"Police it."

He nodded again. "But essential. Any deviation forfeits hope. Keeping his blood sugar on an even keel will make him feel better, not so sick or unstable."

Gwen swallowed. "There can be no exceptions to the diet, can there?"

"None. That's why it's impossible to administer the program at home." He looked at Mrs. Barrie. "Even when regulated by the most careful and well-meaning of caregivers."

"What do you mean impossible?" Mrs. Barrie frowned for the first time.

"I mean"—he leaned forward, extending his hands to explain—"that inevitably those who love him will either give in to his pleas or demands for more food or will, in their well-meaning pity, offer him foods that ultimately harm him and shorten his life."

"I think we can be trusted on both those counts, Doctor," Mrs. Barrie all but huffed. "We can begin by gradually lowering the amount of carbohydrates in his food."

"That will not be enough. I know you're capable and sincere, Mrs. Barrie. I do not doubt either of you. I'm simply explaining what is best for Alistair."

"And what is that, Doctor, if we don't keep him at home?" Gwen wondered. "I certainly don't want to send him to an institution. He needs to be with us, who love him and will do everything we can to care for him."

"If you love him, send him to Dr. Allen's Physiatric Institute in New Jersey. Place him under Dr. Allen's care where every mouthful is regulated and testing is performed every day. It's his best chance at keeping his metabolism under control."

"Alone? Far from home? To an uncertain end?" Gwen shook her head. "He needs us. We need him."

"I understand that. It's a very big step, for each of you. At the very least, I encourage you to take Alistair there for evaluation, see the institute for yourselves, train under Dr. Allen, then decide." He sat back. "You say you love him, and I believe you. Do what's best for him."

Conflicted, Gwen glanced at Mrs. Barrie, who'd drawn back, reserved. "We need to think about this. In any case, it's not up to me. It will be up to his father."

"And what about Alistair? What do you think he will choose, given the choice?"

Gwen drew in her breath. *What indeed?* "I don't yet know if his father will give him that choice."

"Alistair is twelve, a lad on the edge of manhood." Dr. McNeill tilted his head. "He knows his diagnosis, his prognosis—doesn't he?"

Gwen exchanged a troubled glance with Mrs. Barrie. "His father hasn't told him."

Dr. McNeill's eyes widened in disbelief. His neck reddened and his face flushed. "Not telling him gives him no chance at all. No chance to fight this wicked disease with everything he's got. Every single day—every meal matters. Do you know the rate of suicide among patients with no hope?"

Gwen gasped.

"I'm sorry, Miss Armstrong, Mrs. Barrie. I didna mean to speak so forcefully. It's a subject near and dear to my heart. Alistair needs to know. Now."

"Those decisions are not ours to make."

Dr. McNeill stared, disbelieving, from one woman to the other. At last he stood, taking up his hat. "You'll have to excuse me. I thought you were ready to proceed. I see I was mistaken."

"Dr. McNeill, please. You don't understand. I can't—" Gwen saw her train of tentative hope leaving the station.

"No, Miss Armstrong. I don't understand. I don't understand why

Alistair's not been told. I don't understand why his father is not looking into every possible— I'd have done anything in this world to keep my—" The doctor's eyes brightened with what looked like unshed tears. "I'm begging your pardon. If you change your minds, you know where to reach me."

Before Gwen could say more, he was gone.

27

At home, Gwen found Russell alone in his museum, examining the exotic armlet she'd admired the night she'd first explored the room . . . the night Russell had called her Cleopatra for the first time in many years. He looked up as she entered, repositioning the band of blue and green stones set in gold amongst his display of Egyptian jewelry.

"Exquisite, isn't it?" He smiled as he closed the display door, looking more at peace than she'd seen him in days. Working in his museum did that for him, steadied him. "I'm delivering it personally to Gainsbourg in Chicago this week. He's paid handsomely—an anniversary gift for his wife. He wants letters of provenance, of course."

"Yes, it's beautiful." She was sorry to see it go, and more than a little surprised that he could gather documentary provenance, based on what he'd said about the uncertain origin of many of the artifacts he'd purchased. Still, that wasn't why she'd wanted to see him. "You're leaving again? So soon?"

"A short trip. You'll miss me?" he teased.

"Russell, have you spoken with Alistair? Have you told him his diagnosis?"

Russell's brows rose. "Not yet. I see no reason to hurry. It will only distress him."

"He has a right to know. He should have some say in how he—"

"Spends the rest of his life?"

Gwen felt heat rush to her neck. "Yes. And how he fights for it."

"Callahan said there's nothing to be done. How would he fight for it?"

Gwen chose her words carefully. She would not implicate Dr. McNeill unless Russell seemed favorable to the treatment. "Mrs. Barrie and I have been doing some reading. We've learned more about the diet Dr. Allen prescribes."

"The quack?"

"He's not a quack. He's had a great deal of success in helping patients live past their life expectancy."

"Callahan said that only means starvation—a slower, more painful death. I wouldn't have thought you'd subject Alistair to that."

"It can also mean making him more comfortable by keeping his sugar levels lower and steadier. It's the rise in blood sugar that wreaks so much havoc."

Russell locked the cabinet door. "Callahan said he might have a few months, a year at the outside. I don't see the point."

Gwen felt the knot in her stomach tighten. "There's research being done, hope for a cure. If we can just keep him alive long enough to—"

"You want to nursemaid him." It was a statement—not a happy one.

"I'll do everything I can."

"I need you, Gwen. You don't know what a difference your presence made to my negotiations with—"

"Russell, we're talking about Alistair's life! Besides that, I promised Marion—"

"Oh, yes, I know how my late wife wields power beyond the grave." He smirked, all but fumed.

"Russell . . . he's your son."

"But that doesn't matter to you, does it, Father?"

Gwen whirled to find Alistair standing in the doorway. "Alistair!"

"I'm dying?"

"This is not how we planned to tell you." Russell spoke with little emotion, moving closer to Gwen. "Eavesdropping—"

"Eavesdropping is the only way I learned. You'll be glad, won't you? A few months or a year—it can't go by fast enough for you, can it, Father? Then you'll be rid of your entire family. You can start over, replace Mother with Aunt Gwen. No Clara, no me to get in the way of your business plans."

"Alistair, that's not true." Gwen reached for him, but he jerked away.

"Open your eyes, Aunt Gwen! Or is this why you've stayed? Not because you made a promise to Mother. Not because you care for me. You're just biding your time, ready to step into Mother's place, is that it? Is that all it ever was?" Anger and hurt wrestled in his features.

"Apologize to your aunt," Russell ordered.

"Why should I? What does it matter if I'm going to die?" Alistair looked as if he'd explode or cry or both.

"Please, Alistair." Gwen went to take him in her arms, but he stormed from the room.

"Let him go, Gwen."

Horrified, Gwen turned on Russell. "I didn't know he was there."

"Neither did I. He's got to deal with this on his own."

"He's twelve! Russell, I want your permission to speak to him about Dr. Allen's treatment, to try it if he's willing."

"It won't change anything, Gwen. You'll just be putting you both through torture."

"He should have the choice. He should be given the choice. I need to give him that."

Russell stared at her for a long moment. He walked closer.

"What he said isn't true. I didn't stay to lure you to me." But she didn't sound convincing, not even to herself.

"I know. I know. Come here. It was a cruel thing to say after all you've done." He pulled her into his arms. "None of this is your fault."

"If you want to comfort me, then please, let me help him. Let me try." She pleaded with everything in her.

"You won't let this go, will you?"

"No. I can't, and if I don't do this—everything I can to help him—I'll regret it all my life."

"That sounds like a threat."

"It's the truth. I'll never get beyond it if I don't help him."

Russell sighed deeply. "All right. Do what you want. Take charge of his care. Is that better?"

"It needs to be legal. You're away so often, I need to know I can make decisions about his care when you're not here—in case of emergency. Please, Russell."

"All right, all right." He nestled her closer. "I'll have Whitfield draw up the papers. But I beg you not to let Alistair come between us. Don't let your love for him drive a wedge between you and me, please. I fear that's what he'll do."

There is no "us," Russell. Gwen wasn't sure whether that was true, but she knew this was not the time to voice her confusion. "Thank you. Thank you, Russell." She let him hold her. It was the sealing of the deal.

Mrs. Barrie watched through the window as Alistair stormed into the back garden, knocking over plant pots, pounding his fist bloody on the stone table. He'd not taken his coat. The frigid winter wind whipped his shirt and hair; he didn't seem to notice.

Mrs. Barrie closed her eyes against the torment. *She must have told him, or perhaps his father did. Dear God in heaven, help him. Help him. Show me how to help the dear lad.*

She no longer cared enough about keeping her longtime position to worry about obtaining Mr. Bennett's approval. Her place or not, she'd tell Alistair about Dr. McNeill's book, let him read it for himself. *He's an intelligent lad. He'll do what he can. And if he won't, I'll convince him. I'll not lose this precious soul too.*

She grabbed her shawl from the hook by the kitchen door and a blanket from the cupboard. In less than half a minute she was out the door, making a beeline for the boy she'd helped bring into this world, the one she'd helped raise more than any other on earth.

"Alistair." She said his name, holding the blanket open.

He turned at her voice and without a word stumbled to her arms, letting her enfold him, rock him back and forth, no matter that he stood a head taller.

"My dear, dear lad," she crooned, her voice breaking.

She felt his body shudder, heave, tremble, and shudder again. She'd hold him as long as he allowed, let him cry the tears he'd long needed to shed for the pure sake of not feeling well, and now for the horrific news delivered.

He gulped, pulled out his handkerchief, and wiped his nose, his eyes, heaved a great sigh. He didn't lift his head, but whispered, "They said I'm going to die."

She tightened her grip on his shoulders.

"He doesn't care. He'd as soon see me go so he can get on with his business and his life with Aunt Gwen."

"Hush now, I don't believe that."

Alistair pulled away. "Don't pretend, Mrs. Barrie. And don't lie to me."

That cut like a knife in her heart. "I'd never lie to you, Alistair. You know better than that." Still, she couldn't pretend that she didn't see, didn't recognize his father for who he was. "I don't understand your father, I'll say that, but I know your aunt loves you, is fighting for you."

"It didn't look that way."

"She is, and I'll tell you this: She and I have met with Dr. McNeill to see what we can do. We'll not give you up."

"You knew?" He stepped back in disbelief. "And you didn't tell me? Mrs. Barrie?"

"I've known only a short while. It was your father's place to tell you. Dr. Callahan insisted."

"But he didn't. I only know because I overheard him and Aunt Gwen talking."

"Eavesdropping?" She gave a sympathetic smile. "Well, in this case I don't blame you. You've a right to know, and you've a right to know what can be done."

"Father said nothing can be done. I don't even know what's wrong with me."

"Dr. McNeill said it is something called juvenile diabetes. There is no cure—not yet, but he said there is a treatment that can prolong your life. It's a difficult treatment, but he's confident that a cure will be found soon. He said researchers are working day and night to find it. We just need more time."

Alistair furrowed his brow. "I don't know what juvenile—"

"It's a disease where your body fights against itself." Gwen's voice startled them both. Alistair's mouth turned rigid. "I can explain it all to you, but just as Mrs. Barrie said, there is hope for a cure, as long as you can stay alive long enough to take advantage of it."

"How can that happen?" Skepticism and defiance warred in his eyes.

"Through a special diet."

"Aye. It's all written down in a book—a diet made up by another doctor." Mrs. Barrie wrung her hands.

"Dr. Frederick Allen." Gwen stepped closer, despite Alistair now warily eyeing them both. "He's done a great deal of research and has found a way to prolong life. It is considered radical, extreme, but it has worked so far for a number of his patients. Mrs. Barrie and I have read all we can and talked with Dr. McNeill. We needed to learn what we could do before we told you, and we needed your father's permission."

"His permission? Will he give it?"

"He just did." Gwen smiled. "He's placed you in my care, said I could pursue this, if you're willing. It's a rigorous program."

Alistair's eyes shifted uncertainly.

"At least let us explain. We love you, more than anything. We want to keep you with us."

Alistair's eyes filled again. It was clear he wanted to believe his aunt, and clear he was afraid to.

Mrs. Barrie took his hand. "Let's go inside where it's warm. I'll make us a cup of tea and we'll tell you everything—won't we, Miss Armstrong?"

"Yes," Gwen affirmed, "absolutely everything."

28

When the envelope, marked *Personal,* arrived in the post from Miss Armstrong, Malcolm was more than a little surprised. Reading that they'd told Alistair everything and that he'd fully agreed to the diet prescribed by Dr. Allen elated him. Realizing that they intended to administer the diet at home alarmed him. *They'll not be able to keep at it. Not keeping at it will mean misery and no help for Alistair. Barring a miracle, he'll die. I've told them this. Did they not understand? Not wish to understand?*

Malcolm replied to Miss Armstrong that he wished them all success, that he was available at all times, day or night, should they need him, and that if they should wish to contact Dr. Allen, he would reach out to the doctor as well. He urged her to do so. He could do no more than that.

It was a mercy Mr. Bennett traveled extensively over the next two months. Mrs. Barrie could not imagine catering to her employer's whims and demands while dealing with Alistair's needs on the new regimen. Nor could she remember feeling so hopeless as she did that winter, not even when Mrs. Bennett's tuberculosis had raged and she'd been sent to the sanatorium.

She, Mrs. LaMott, and Gwen had turned Bennett Place inside out and upside down working to incorporate Dr. Allen's starvation diet, daily urine testing, and a strict but gentle exercise program into Alistair's life. Gwen tutored him, making lessons as interesting as she could, but Mrs. Barrie saw that the lad's interest quickly waned, his energy flagged, and it wasn't long before he lost the ability to concentrate. His thirst was insatiable, but water, coffee, or tea were the only liquids allowed. The miniscule amount of food he received each day made her heart ache. She saw him starving before her eyes, and more often than she would like to admit was forced to look away. His moods swung wildly. There were times he became so despondent, so moody and withdrawn that she feared for his life, though she'd never say that aloud.

I can see those effects of his blood sugar rising and falling as sure as I see the mercury move up and down in that thermometer Mr. Dornsby set up in the back garden.

"I'm thankful you're here, Miss Armstrong," she confided over a late-night cup of tea in the kitchen. "I don't know that I could carry on with this regimen alone, no matter that I love the lad as I love my life."

Gwen nodded. "It's certainly harder than I imagined, and I'd known it would be difficult."

"Treats, favorite foods, were always a great motivator for him—and for Clara—from the time they were wee bairns. Now, it feels as if I'm cloaking love in cruelty to withhold those gifts. And I've so few ideas what else might encourage or comfort him."

"I hate seeing him so exhausted all the time. I can't help but compare him to the way he was last summer in Sea Isle—so beautifully tanned and strong and energetic." Gwen set her cup in the saucer, too loudly. "The worry is that even with all we're doing, he's no better."

"Well, he wouldn't be, would he? We're keeping him alive but that's only a stemming of the tide. I don't know how long his body can keep going like this."

"We're not giving up," Gwen insisted.

"No, of course not, but why is he wasting so quickly? Is there something we're not doing that we should be doing? Should we be giving him some kind of tonic? There must be something more we can do."

29

Winter's snow and frigid temperatures gave way to spring winds, to carpets of crocuses, then beds of daffodils and tulips. Lilacs and roses bloomed in gardens across the city.

During those months, as Malcolm prayed daily for his many patients, he thought often of Alistair Bennett. He knew Dr. Callahan was in touch with the family as their longtime physician. Periodically, he checked Alistair's chart. It did not appear that the boy had been back to the office or that any home visits had been made. *What can that mean? Are they having success with the diet? Is he dying?*

In late May, as he entered the office after making hospital rounds, the receptionist stopped Malcolm, handing him a file and a phone number. "Miss Armstrong wants you to call her, Dr. McNeill."

Malcolm's heart went to this throat. *Please, Lord, not yet. Don't take him yet.* He picked up the phone, gave the operator the number, and waited.

"Bennett Place. Mrs. Barrie speaking."

"Mrs. Barrie, it's Dr. McNeill. I'm returning Miss Armstrong's call."

"Dr. McNeill, thank you for calling so quickly."

"How is Alistair, Mrs. Barrie?" He knew he should wait and talk with Miss Armstrong, but his rapport with this Scotswoman came so easily.

"Not well, Doctor. We're doing everything we can according to Dr. Allen's diet, but he's not feeling well and certainly doesn't act himself. The diet seemed to be working at first, but now . . . We just don't know if there's more can be done, and I think— Well, you need to speak with Miss Armstrong. I'll get her straightaway. Please hold the line."

He sensed the frustration, the helplessness in her voice—qualities he understood well in dealing with this disease.

"Dr. McNeill? Gwen Armstrong. Doctor, Alistair needs help. We need help."

Though relieved that at last he'd be allowed to help, he could not quite account for the lift in his heart or the quickening in his pulse upon hearing her voice. He tried to separate that from whatever he might say professionally.

"We've been following the diet religiously. At first it seemed to make a great deal of difference, at least in some ways, but now . . . I don't know if we're doing something wrong. He's lost more weight. His hair has begun to fall out. He's tired all the time."

"Given his diagnosis, those symptoms are not surprising, Miss Armstrong. Do you want me to examine him?"

"I want to know about Dr. Allen and his institute. Do you think he'd be willing to see Alistair?"

"I've not met Dr. Allen in person and canna speak for him, but we've had regular correspondence. I believe if I ask him, he'll examine Alistair. Before he'd take him as a patient, I feel certain he'd want to admit Alistair to the institute."

"You mean live there."

"Yes—if he believes he can help Alistair and if there is room. The institute has been taking children for some time but only officially opened last month. I understand they're full, that staffing and resources are already stretched thin. Dr. Allen won't admit him unless he has staff to care for him properly; you can be assured of that."

There was silence on the other end of the line.

"It's for Alistair's good, Miss Armstrong." *How can I convince her?*

"All right. I'll need to get his father's permission, but I don't think that will be a problem. Is there something we need to do to encourage Dr. Allen to take him? Money should not be a deterrent."

"I'll phone him today, ask your questions, and make the appointment for as soon as Dr. Allen can see him."

He heard her ragged breath through the phone. "We'll do anything, Doctor. Anything to save him."

Malcolm's heart clutched. "I understand, Miss Armstrong." They weren't idle words. "I'll call as soon as I know anything."

30

Gwen had felt certain Russell would agree to let Alistair go to Dr. Allen's Physiatric Institute, that he might even be relieved. But he was more obstinate than she'd expected.

"I don't see the point in sending him there, putting him through that, when it won't change the outcome."

"We don't know that."

"We do."

"Dr. Allen's treatment won't change the eventual outcome unless a cure is found; that's true. But he may buy time for Alistair and that buys us all hope."

Russell's mouth turned grim, exasperation in his breath. "Gwen, I don't have time to take him there. You know I have to leave for Atlantic City tomorrow."

Why? What is there that is so important?

"I'm worried about you. You're too taken up with Alistair's illness, too emotionally involved. I don't want—"

She stepped close, taking his face in her hands. "You do want me to be happy, don't you?"

His tension faded, if only slightly. "You know I do."

"Then let me do this. I can handle everything. You don't have to be involved. Let me know I've tried everything on God's green earth that I can to save him. It's the only way I'll have peace."

He wrapped her in his arms and pulled her head to his shoulder. "I suppose it's the only way we'll have peace between us."

"Yes," she whispered. *Please. Please say yes.*

He snorted in resignation. "Do what you want. It might be better that he's there when—"

"Please don't say that."

He stopped, stroked her hair, planted a kiss on the top of her head, her cheek, lifted her face to his. "I love you, Gwen. I'll do anything for you; you know that."

"This. This is all I'm asking." But she didn't stop him from taking a kiss she wasn't certain she meant to give.

Gwen and Mrs. Barrie helped Alistair pack a trunk filled with clothing, books, writing paper—anything he wanted minus food—in the hope that Dr. Allen would admit him.

Dr. McNeill had been as good as his word. He'd arranged through the institute's secretary for Dr. Allen to examine Alistair the following afternoon. There was no promise of admittance, but Gwen knew Dr. McNeill would push for that. What Gwen hadn't expected was that Dr. McNeill insisted on driving them.

"That's very good of him," Mrs. Barrie approved, refolding Alistair's last cardigan and placing it atop the growing pile on his bed.

"I don't understand it really. I'm sure he has patients of his own to see. Why he'd take the time, I can't imagine."

"Maybe he's interested in more than me." Alistair wiggled his thin eyebrows at Gwen, much to her astonishment. It was the first bit of lightheartedness she'd seen in her nephew in months, and she couldn't help but grin. She'd grown used to the changes in Alistair's appearance, but looked at him now with new eyes, eyes that might see what Dr. Allen would see. His face looked longer, older, to Gwen. His cheekbones and chin formed sharp angles, and his forehead rose high for one so young, mostly because his hairline receded unnaturally. No matter how many times Mrs. Barrie had taken in his trousers, they hung loose, and his neck and chest had grown so thin it looked as if all muscle had wasted away. Gwen's grin faded as she felt a catch in her heart.

Mrs. Barrie smiled. "It may be that the man has more than you on his mind, young man, but I think it also has to do with—" She stopped mid-sentence.

"With what?"

"With—with the fact that he's a kind and caring doctor, and very eager to see a cure for this diabetes. He seems very informed of the research being done." Mrs. Barrie looked away and busied herself with refolding shirts that didn't need refolding.

Gwen had hoped to pursue Mrs. Barrie's halted observation, but she found no time alone with the housekeeper before Dr. McNeill arrived, ready to stow Alistair's case in his car and be off.

Alistair lingered behind with Mrs. Barrie. Gwen could see they were praying, hands clasped together. Mrs. Barrie wrapped him in her arms. He clung just as tightly to her and kissed her cheek. Gwen sent up a silent prayer to the God she both pleaded with and railed against. *Don't let this be their last meeting. Please, God. Please.*

Dr. McNeill and Alistair rode in the front seat of Dr. McNeill's Model T. Gwen insisted on sitting in the back. She wanted Alistair to talk with Dr. McNeill, ask anything he wished, feel comfortable in his presence. If this was going to work, she realized that Dr. McNeill would be Alistair's greatest ally with Dr. Allen, though she still didn't know why he cared so much. He couldn't possibly invest this much time in every patient.

It didn't take long for Alistair to warm to Dr. McNeill. The young doctor questioned Alistair about his interests, drew him out, encouraged him to think about things that mattered to him.

"Egypt—especially the pyramids—fascinate me."

"Do they now? They're fascinating, to be sure."

"As long as I can remember I've wanted to study archaeology, maybe one day discover an ancient tomb—some long-forgotten pharaoh. My father worked with Theodore Davis for a time. I want to work with Howard Carter and Lord Carnarvon. Mr. Carter believes there are more tombs to discover in the Valley of the Kings. I'd love to be part of such a dig."

"I wouldn't be surprised. I'd hoped to visit the pyramids during the war, but it wasn't to be."

"You were in Egypt?"

"Aye, but hundreds of miles north, nearer Cairo, for the most part. Disappointed I was to miss seeing them, at first, but it turned out to be providential. It was there that I met Chaplain Chambers when I needed spiritual guidance the most. I don't know how I'd made it through the war without him." There was a long pause. Gwen thought he might say more.

"I don't expect I'll ever get to Egypt now, but thanks for asking me, Doctor. It's just a dream. I wonder if there's any point. If there's no hope of me getting well . . . why think about things I'll never be able to do? I won't even grow up."

"You don't know that. I urge you to think positively, to believe, and to hope, most of all to pray."

"I do pray."

Gwen was surprised by the intensity of Alistair's declaration.

"Mrs. Barrie's been helping me. Before her I never knew much more than that God exists—is just there."

"That's true for a great many people. It's the place to begin."

"That's what Mrs. Barrie said. I've been going to church with her. She prays with me at night—is helping me learn to pray. She says believing in God is a choice we make and that I should talk to God like my best friend, but with more respect, and know that He listens—like a loving father, she said."

"Aye. A wise woman, Mrs. Barrie. You're close, I take it."

"She's been there all my life—even when Mother was sick for so long."

Gwen heard the emotion in Alistair's voice.

"Like your nanna—your grandmother, she is."

Perceptive.

"Yeah, I guess so. I never knew either of my grandmothers, or grandfathers. It was always just Mother and Clara, until . . . until Aunt Gwen came."

"And your father?"

"Not around much." Alistair shrugged. "He's all I know about fathers. It makes it hard to believe God cares."

"Ach, but He does. More than you can imagine. More than I can imagine, and I have a fair imagination." He winked. "You're fortunate to have a woman like Mrs. Barrie in your life, and your aunt."

"I know."

Gwen barely heard Alistair's response. *No wonder. It's hard to think of your life as fortunate in any way, isn't it? How can you think of God as a loving Father if your own father barely gives you the time of day?* The thought startled Gwen. *Am I thinking of Alistair and his father, or of myself, and my own father?*

"Keep faith, Alistair. This journey is only part of your story, a story God's long known."

"Mrs. Barrie says our times are in God's hands."

"Indeed, they are."

"Then why doesn't He do something about this? Why didn't He keep Mother and Clara from dying? Why doesn't He stop this disease, or show us a cure?"

Dr. McNeill nodded. "Why doesn't He stop wars? Or influenza? Or poverty? Or all suffering? Those are questions I've asked, questions most of us ask. Much like those a man in the Bible once asked, ready to argue his case before the Lord."

"Somebody argued with God? Who?"

Dr. McNeill chuckled. "Many of us—perhaps most of us argue with God from time to time. In this case, it was a man named Job. He was a good man, a faithful father and husband, good to those he was responsible for, well-thought-of in the community. He loved God with all his heart and was obedient in every way he knew. But one day he was tested and tried beyond endurance. In a short span of time, he lost his children, his home, his livelihood and possessions, and then he lost his health. His own wife told him to curse God and die."

"Did he?"

"No. He tried arguing his innocence, but it wasn't about his guilt or innocence. It wasn't that God wasn't able to intervene either. He could have, but He allowed Job to suffer, to be tested and tried. There are things in this world we don't understand, and never will, this side of heaven. To say that suffering makes us grow, makes us stronger in our characters, is true. To say that through the comfort we receive from God we are able to help others who suffer similarly is true. But it is not God's will that we suffer forever."

"When will it stop?"

"Ach, when there is no sin. Our world's filled with sin and has been since the first act of disobedience. That's when our relationship with God was broken. I imagine Mrs. Barrie's told you that."

"Sort of."

"And did she say how that relationship can be restored?"

"Through Christ, through what He did for us by giving His life."

"Aye, He died to pay the penalty for sin. He took our sins on His shoulders—the sins of the entire world for all time—and sacrificed Himself so that we don't have to. He paid our ransom from sin and death. We need only repent of our sins and believe Him, believe that He died for us and was raised from the dead."

"I believe that . . . at least I'm trying to. It's not always easy."

"I understand that. But you keep thinking on it, keep praying. The stronger your faith, the greater your peace, and you will need your faith and your peace in the days to come. One day, just like Job, you'll be healed. We don't know if that will be in this life or the next, but the promise is sure because of what Jesus did."

"I want to believe that."

"Then choose to believe. The road ahead will be hard, lad, there's no doubt. Just mind that you're not walking it alone. God is with you. Our Lord Jesus is with you. The Holy Spirit will guide you and never let you go. And for the physical arms and shoulders you need to hold you up, you've got your aunt here, and Mrs. Barrie, and you've got me. I promise."

Gwen swiped tears that filled her eyes. She'd never heard faith presented like that. *Who is this man and how does he know these things?*

The hour's ride to the institute flew by.

The Physiatric Institute was a bustling place. Nurses walked quickly up and down hallways. Music came from a common room down one corridor and sounds of a radio program from some other place in the building.

Gwen and Alistair waited in the lobby while Dr. McNeill met with Dr. Allen in his office. It didn't take long. Dr. Allen, a grim-faced man whose frown indicated an unlikely bedside manner, strode rapidly through the lobby toward them, Dr. McNeill in his wake.

"Dr. McNeill is quite your champion, young man." Dr. Allen crossed his arms, observing Alistair.

Alistair offered his hand. "I know, and I'm glad of that, Dr. Allen, but I'm able to speak for myself if you'll permit me. I promise to follow your regimen exactly. We've already been doing it for months—well, as best we can, but maybe there's something we're not doing right. I very much want to be admitted to your institute, if you'll have me, sir."

Gwen's brows went up at her nephew's speech. *He must have rehearsed that ahead.*

Dr. Allen uncrossed his arms, accepting Alistair's handshake, which Gwen knew did not hold the grip it once had. "As I've explained to Dr. McNeill, I would very much like to help you, Alistair, but we have room for only twenty patients. We're at capacity now."

"Please reconsider, Doctor," Gwen pleaded. "We'll gladly pay whatever—"

"It's not a question of payment, Miss Armstrong, it's a question of available rooms—beds, staffing."

"I slept in a closet once when I was little, Doctor. That was just for fun, but I can do it again." Alistair gave a lopsided grin before he sobered. "I'll wash dishes or clean floors, when I'm up to it. I want to live."

Gwen swallowed the lump in her throat. All along she'd been orchestrating Alistair's diet, his exercise, his life. *How little credit I've given him—how little freedom to set his own course.*

Dr. McNeill gave Alistair a gentle clap on the back. "As you can see, Doctor, the lad's quite determined."

Dr. Allen nodded. "Dr. McNeill, Miss Armstrong, wait here. Come with me, Alistair. I'll examine you and we can talk. But I promise nothing."

Gwen's heart plummeted to her feet. She felt Dr. McNeill's supportive hand at her back.

"We understand, Doctor. Thank you. Miss Armstrong and I will wait here." He ushered her back to her seat. "Have faith," he whispered.

"My faith is small," she replied, staring after her nephew and Dr. Allen as they walked down the hallway.

"Ach, Miss Armstrong, you're going to need it like you never have."

"That's what Mrs. Barrie said."

"She's helped Alistair find his; perhaps she'll help you."

Gwen sighed. "I can't see him die."

Dr. McNeill sat quietly for a time before he spoke. "It's hard to surrender those we love, whether in life or in death."

"I don't want to surrender. I want to fight this."

"You're not strong enough, Miss Armstrong. It's a disease that Alistair carries within his body. Only God can fight this battle."

She stared straight ahead. *All this God talk is well and good, but I want results.* "You don't believe that. If you did, we wouldn't be here."

He looked at her for a long while, his eyes changing, but what that meant, what he was thinking, she couldn't tell. Finally, he stood, walked to the window, and looked out. "You're wrong. That's exactly why I'm here."

Forty-five minutes later, Dr. Allen and Alistair returned—Dr. Allen with measured steps and perpetual frown; Alistair, paler yet, and walking a bit slower than usual, but grinning like the Cheshire cat.

Gwen stood, her heart thumping.

"Dr. Allen says I can stay." Alistair's smile widened more.

"Thank you, Dr. Allen. Thank you!" Gwen felt she could kiss him.

Dr. McNeill pumped his hand. "Yes, thank you, Doctor. You won't be sorry."

"I don't believe I will, especially if he washes dishes." Dr. Allen's frown temporarily diminished.

Gwen smiled uncertainly and looked at Alistair, who winked at her. *You've come into your own. You'll be all right here . . . won't you?*

"You understand, Miss Armstrong, there will be papers to sign. You've been administering the diet the best you can, I understand, but here every gram of food will be weighed; every drop of liquid will be measured; blood glucose levels and urine will be tested daily. There is a strict regimen for sleeping, waking, moderate exercise, activities, and time for socialization. You are free to write letters, as is Alistair, when he wishes to do so. Visitation days are Sunday afternoons but must be scheduled through my staff. Anything brought into the building—absolutely everything—must be seen and approved by my staff. Absolutely no outside food or drink may be brought in under any circumstances. There can be no exceptions."

"I understand, Dr. Allen."

"As I've explained to Alistair, we do our best to maintain a cheerful atmosphere. Radio, gramophone playing, scrapbooking, reading, walking for those who are up to it in good weather—are all common activities among our patients. Every nurse is a trained dietician, all graduates of the Domestic Science School in Framingham, Massachusetts. Our dieticians work hard to create appetizing meals. Portions are small, and ingredients naturally limited."

Gwen listened, uncertain if the information was more for her or for Alistair until Dr. Allen pulled her aside, motioning Dr. McNeill to see to Alistair.

"Miss Armstrong, I caution you in writing letters to Alistair. He will need to hear from you, certainly, but I urge you to keep your letters positive and on an even keel. Emotional stability is vital in maintaining steady glucose levels. We know that even slight emotional changes can upset the body's metabolic balance. Remember our goal—to keep Alistair's blood sugar at a moderate and consistent level, as close to that of a person who has no diabetes as possible."

Gwen nodded, thinking how the roller coaster of emotions for the last year—and even now where his father was concerned—must have done Alistair harm. She grimaced for her part in that. "I understand, Doctor. You'll keep me informed of any changes, and anytime Alistair needs me to come?"

Dr. Allen appeared to soften, his mouth momentarily losing its grim line. "There will be changes, Miss Armstrong. You must expect that—weight loss, weakness, growing fatigue, continual thinning of hair and changes in the skin. If we can keep him from vomiting, from slipping into a coma, we may be able to prolong his life until a cure is found. I cannot make him happy here. I can do my best to keep him alive."

Gwen felt her body lose its resiliency.

"Dr. McNeill can keep you abreast of the research being done. He's well acquainted with some of those doing the work."

"Thank you, Doctor. Thank you." Gwen's words came out measured as she counted the cost.

"I'll let you say your goodbyes, and a nurse will get Alistair settled."

Dr. Allen's caution against emotional upset and the harm it could do Alistair rolled through her mind as she hugged him, fighting tears while feeling the bones in his spine with her hands, the lightness of his weight against her chest.

Alistair was the brave one, waving goodbye as he walked down the hallway with Dr. Allen.

31

Though deliveries and outgoing shipments from the back of Bennett Place continued through the summer of 1921, Russell was rarely there. He traveled incessantly. At times Gwen wondered if he was all but running away. The note she'd found from the White Hand Gang plagued her, inspiring weeks of scouring newspapers for any mention of the gang. She finally believed she'd connected enough dots to identify "W. B." as Wild Bill Lovett—a notorious character who'd evidently taken over the White Hand Gang once Meehan was murdered in cold blood. If that was true, Russell could not afford to have anything to do with the man or his "turf"—the docks. But concern over his unpredictable reaction when he'd learned she'd been in his office without permission prevented her from speaking.

When home, he entertained lavishly, sometimes insisting Gwen help, sometimes excluding her altogether. He frequently appeared stressed. She worried for him, sometimes prayed for him, and wondered what dark avenues his business traveled. At the same time, she was relieved that he seemed too preoccupied to pressure her into a relationship more binding than she could commit to.

It seemed to Gwen during that time that Alistair grew a little stronger and more stable, making her believe she'd made the right decision in sending him to Dr. Allen.

Summer turned to autumn, and though terribly thin, Alistair seemed to be holding his own.

Visits to the Physiatric Institute were allowed only on Sunday afternoons. Gwen hated asking Mr. Dornby to drive her on his one day off, and Russell, when home, sometimes took the car on those days. Not once did he ask to see Alistair, nor did he ask about her visits. He didn't even inquire as to how or whether she went to see him. His lack of interest hurt. His lack of interference was a relief.

If Dr. McNeill was going to visit Alistair or consult with Dr. Allen, which he frequently did, he offered to drive Gwen and Mrs. Barrie after church. It only made sense for Gwen to accompany Mrs. Barrie to church, where they would meet the doctor and go from there. Gwen insisted her attendance was only a matter of making things convenient, but in truth she found comfort in the rhythm of hymns and Scripture reading at church, and in the sermon. She needed comfort these days, especially as she saw Alistair's body wasting, the hair on his head growing thinner and gradually disappearing.

In good weather, Mrs. Barrie packed a lunch of cold meat sandwiches and boiled eggs for their drive, perhaps a slice of ginger cake or cookies. Dr. McNeill knew of a lovely park on the way where they could stop to eat, a place to fortify themselves before affixing smiles to their faces for Alistair's benefit.

Gwen found those times a comfort, a reassurance that she was not alone but among friends who shared her journey into whatever lay ahead.

On one such day, Dr. McNeill encouraged, "You must call me Malcolm, Miss Armstrong, Mrs. Barrie, since we enjoy one another's company on a regular basis." The man's smile across the picnic blanket lit his eyes and Gwen's heart.

"Then I'm Gwen."

"And, I suppose, since we're becoming altogether informal, you may both call me Cora." Mrs. Barrie looked pointedly at Gwen, her brows raised, and said, "When we're in this relaxed company, that is. At Bennett Place I'm still Mrs. Barrie, and you, my dear, are Miss Armstrong."

"Yes, ma'am," Gwen replied with all seriousness, then smiled. There was a great deal she wondered about Malcolm McNeill but was hesitant to ask. She was glad when Mrs. Barrie opened the discussion.

"Do you miss our homeland, Malcolm? You came from Inverness, I think you said."

"Aye, Inverness, born and bred. I miss it sometimes, but not always." He set his sandwich down. "When I'm weary or when I've not been able to help a patient as I'd like, that's when the shadows come."

"I canna imagine that happens often—that there's a patient you canna help."

Malcolm smiled. "I wish that were so. More often than I'd like. Medicine is not a perfect science."

Gwen was curious. "What do you miss most? Your home? Your family? Your town?"

Malcolm grew serious. "I've no family there now . . . no home."

No family? No home? Nothing and no one? How can that be?

"What I miss most, I suppose, are the Highlands—the rugged, untamed beauty of those magnificent fells and dales and the heather running riot in full bloom."

"Ah, I hear a bit of Robert Burns in those longings. I know them too," Mrs. Barrie confided with a sigh.

Malcolm smiled. "That you would. *'Wherever I wander, wherever I rove, the hills of the Highlands forever I love.'*"

Mrs. Barrie nodded and joined him for the chorus: *"'My heart's in the Highlands, my heart is not here, my heart's in the Highlands, a-chasing the deer; a-chasing the wild-deer, and following the roe, my heart's in the Highlands wherever I go.'"*

Gwen applauded. Malcolm and Mrs. Barrie gave a mock bow, but neither could hide the bright unshed tears of longing in their eyes.

Gwen could not imagine what it was to long for a place, a home, but something in her ached to know, to hold in her heart what Malcolm and Mrs. Barrie held in theirs.

In September, Alistair wrote:

Dear Aunt Gwen,

You mustn't worry about me. I'm holding my own, that's what Dr. Allen said yesterday. That's not true of everybody, I'm sorry to say. There's lots worse off than me.

I miss you and Mrs. Barrie, but I've made friends here. There's a boy about my age named Eddie. He's pretty weak and not always in the best of moods, but he knows a lot about the war and he's wild about carrier pigeons. Did you know they were real heroes in the war—sending and bringing messages? Because of one named Cher Ami, two hundred men were saved.

Eddie and a girl here, Elizabeth Hughes, are great bird-watchers. They have binoculars and watch the birds on the institute's grounds for hours at a time, recording their migratory paths—forever talking about the different kinds of birds and their habits, their characteristics, things I never knew.

Elizabeth convinced Dr. Allen to let Eddie keep a canary. They named it Ami in honor of that brave carrier pigeon. It even sings. Clara would have liked a bird like that. I think about Clara a lot, and Mother. I wonder if Mother's time in the sanatorium was like it is here. I hope she made friends there, so she wasn't too lonely.

We play games sometimes—board games or mostly just talking games. Our favorite is to imagine what we'd eat if we could eat anything in the world. I always vote first for roast turkey with stuffing and gravy and cranberry sauce, and two helpings of Mrs. LaMott's whipped potatoes and Mrs. Barrie's clootie dumpling. I hate to think I can never have those foods again—not even at Thanksgiving or Christmas.

I miss you, Aunt Gwen. Tell Mrs. Barrie I miss her too.

Love,
Alistair

Gwen shared the letter with Mrs. Barrie, and railed, "They're children! Children should be dreaming, *What will I be when I grow up?* Not *What would I eat if I could?*"

"It's because they canna think of anything they desire more than food." Wearily, Mrs. Barrie set the letter down. "And because they never expect to grow up."

Gwen renewed her determination to keep Alistair looking forward. She committed part of each day to searching for news she might share, desperate to keep his mind active, his focus on things outside the institute.

She researched anything she could learn of ongoing digs in Egypt. She tracked down the address for the Cairo Museum, names and addresses of curators there and in other museums. She wrote, saying she was writing on behalf of Russell Bennett, their business associate, and for the interests of his ill son.

The one letter she received claimed no knowledge of a business associate by that name but answered her questions just the same and wished the boy well.

Gwen didn't know what to think. *Is the person new that he doesn't know Russell . . . or is there another explanation?* She shoved the thought away. She'd not entertain uncertainties about Russell and his business. Not now.

She wrote to those who'd obtained concessions not only near Luxor in the Valley of the Kings on the west bank of the Nile, but in places farther north, like Amarna, on the east bank of the Nile. Most important of all were the names and mailing addresses she tracked down of those in charge of the digs.

By writing from one individual to another, she eventually reached the archaeologists directly responsible for supervising the digs, the very position Alistair had long dreamed of. Those discoveries were pure gold. She hoped her tidbits would keep Alistair interested, his spirits high, and motivate him to keep going with his diet and regimen, as challenging and discouraging as it was day by day.

The archaeologist mainly responsible for supervising the dig of the House of Ranefer in Amarna, A. G. K. Hayter, was wonderful about writing back. He kept a meticulous notebook, including his own sketches, of the work being done. He included a couple of those sketches in his response to Gwen's plea for anything that might entice her nephew to hang on to life. She was not, she'd assured him, an idle curiosity seeker, but one determined to keep her loved one alive until a cure for diabetes was found.

She also wrote to Howard Carter, the man digging in the Valley of the Kings, the very place Alistair and Clara had dreamed of going one day—Alistair to dig and Clara to sketch his magnificent finds. Sadly, Carter was not quick to respond.

She made it a point to meet and speak with Carr Van Anda, managing editor at the *New York Times*. Van Anda was known for his stories of adventure, science, and his passion for hieroglyphics. If anyone in American journalism was going to be on the cutting edge of archaeological achievements—or medical breakthroughs—it would be him.

Gwen wrote every bit of news to Alistair. When she visited him, she gave him the letters, maps she'd traced, and books, so that he might see them, hold them, become inspired by the stamps from exotic places, and continue to dream his dreams. She even encouraged him that one day they might travel the world together, that she had long dreamed of going to faraway places too.

Am I giving him false hope or keeping him alive? Do I even believe a cure will be found? Gwen didn't know, but if anything she could do might save him, prolong his life, she would do it.

Despite her determination, it was hard to see the children around

Alistair growing thinner, more lethargic week by week. They were all wretchedly hungry, starved, waiting, hoping for a cure. She didn't want Alistair focusing on his decline but knew she didn't have the power to stop it.

Surrender. Malcolm keeps speaking to me of surrendering Alistair to God's care, but how can I? I don't know that He'll intervene for him any more than He intervened for Marion or Clara, or for my own mother.

By mid-October she noticed a change. Alistair's letters were less enthusiastic, shorter, not as frequent. Sometimes he combined a letter to Gwen and Mrs. Barrie, and sometimes included Malcolm too. Writing letters required energy he did not possess.

Dr. Allen assured her that it was encouraging Alistair had lived this long, that he was adhering to the diet, that the research going on worldwide was very promising indeed. "There is every reason to hope as long as we can keep Alistair's metabolism steady."

Hope is that elusive thing with feathers. Hope comes and goes with a will of its own.

In late October, Russell remained at home for two long weeks. Throughout the fall he'd often been away, traveling to Chicago, to Atlantic City, to Philadelphia, and places unknown and undisclosed to Gwen. There didn't seem to be a pattern to his travels; it wasn't a circuit, but he treated each trip as if it were urgent. He no longer spoke of returning to Egypt and rarely spoke of acquiring or delivering antiquities, came home with nothing visible, and gave no clues about his work. He never returned refreshed or energized, but increasingly on edge.

While Gwen didn't crave Russell's advances, she was lonely, anxious. When he was home, she tried to make herself agreeable. Sometimes that came as a natural response to his friendliness and flirtation, in those rare moments when he relaxed. Sometimes he was so on edge that she trod carefully, as if on eggshells. He'd agreed to make sizable and regular donations to the Physiatric Institute per her request. She couldn't risk him pulling his funding. She didn't know what effect that might have on Alistair's ability to remain under Dr. Allen's care.

The evenings he was home, he and Gwen shared dinner in the dining room and later drinks—he brandy and she tea—in the drawing room.

"What do you say to a game of chess?" Gwen teased on one of those occasions. "It's been a long while. Are you up to the challenge?"

Russell continued staring into blank space.

"Russell?"

"Hmm? I'm sorry, what did you say?"

"Chess. Are you up to a game of chess? I've gotten quite good at it, you know. I'll be hard to beat."

He smiled. "I imagine so. Yes, I accept the challenge." He set up the board and magnanimously gave her the first move.

They were deep into the game, Russell clearly winning, when a pounding came at the front door, so loud they could hear it in the drawing room with the door closed. Gwen looked up in alarm.

Russell tensed. "Go upstairs. Now, and lock your door."

"Why? What is it?"

He rose, pulling her by the arm into the foyer, pushing her toward the stairs. Mrs. Barrie met them in the hallway, about to answer the door. "I'll get it, Mrs. Barrie. Go upstairs with Gwen. Now, please."

Both women stared at him, stunned.

"Do as I say!"

The pounding came again. Frightened, Gwen pulled a wide-eyed Mrs. Barrie along beside her and up the stairs.

Russell stood at the bottom of the stairs, watching, until they'd rounded the corner.

"He said to go to my room and lock the door," Gwen whispered to Mrs. Barrie, "but I need to see who it is, what they want."

"If Mr. Bennett says go to your room, I think we'd best do it, Gwen, and hurry."

Gwen was nearly as surprised that Mrs. Barrie had broken her own rule by using her Christian name as she was by the pounding on the front door. Mrs. Barrie looked frightened indeed, and that was enough to make Gwen comply, despite her curiosity and her concern for Russell.

They closed her bedroom door and locked it, just as the pounding stopped and shouting began.

"Who can it be? What do they want?" Gwen had never seen Russell look so frightened.

"I don't know, but I'm afraid Mr. Bennett has gotten himself into something dangerous."

Gwen searched Mrs. Barrie's face. "What do you know? What do you know that I don't?"

"I don't know anything for sure and certain. I just . . ."

"Just what?"

"What do you suppose all those trucks deliver? What do you suppose that trailing of cars takes away?"

"Antiquities. He said they deliver antiquity shipments."

A crash belowstairs made both women jump.

Mrs. Barrie's brows raised, her eyes skeptical.

She's right. That makes no sense. There would never be that many deliveries of legitimate antiquities . . . unless he's dealing in estate sales. But is it something illegal? Something to do with the threat to stay off the docks?

When she'd first come to Bennett Place, deliveries had arrived once a month at most. Now trucks came and went every two weeks or ten days, sometimes more often. Cars—long black touring cars—came more frequently. Russell had said they were business clients. He always had those clients go directly to his office through the west wing entrance, never through the front door.

More shouting and another crash downstairs made Gwen's heart jump. She reached for Mrs. Barrie, who'd switched off the lamp by the bed, whispering, "It's best if they think no one else is here."

"Russell!" Gwen trembled. *What's happening to you?*

More shouting, and another, quieter voice—Russell's, surely—though they couldn't make out the words of either. A blast came and the shattering of glass—*a gunshot?*

The front door slammed and in less than a minute the motor of a car roared to life.

Gwen fumbled for the lock on her door in the dark. "Turn on the light!" She yanked open her door and flew to the top of the stairs. In the foyer below, shards of broken Ming Dynasty vases littered the marble floor, the floor-to-ceiling mirror framed in gold gilt shattered into a thousand pieces. Russell was not there.

Gwen hurried to the bottom of the stairs, Mrs. Barrie stumbling on her heels. Tilley and Mrs. LaMott peeked through the hallway door.

"What's happened? Who were those men?" Tilley looked white as a ghost.

"Both of you, back to your rooms now," Mrs. Barrie ordered. "We'll take care of this. Go!"

The women scurried back, terror in their eyes.

The drawing room door stood ajar. Bile rose in Gwen's throat for fear of what she might find as she pushed it open. "Russell!"

Russell lay face down across the carpet. Gently, Gwen and Mrs. Barrie rolled him to his back. He moaned, eyes closed. Blood trickled from the corner of his mouth, his cheek and one eye already swelling, but she didn't see a gunshot wound.

"Call Malcolm, Cora—call him now," Gwen pleaded. "Have Tilley bring cold water and a cloth."

Mrs. Barrie hurried to do as she was told.

Gwen called after her, "Lock the front door!"

Slowly, Russell began coming round. He opened one eye, but winced, as though the light hurt him. The other eye was swollen shut. "I'm all right," he slurred.

"Not by half, you're not. Who were those men, Russell? What did they want?"

He closed his good eye. She couldn't tell if he'd slipped back into oblivion or was refusing to answer. But he did not speak again.

Gwen gently bathed Russell's cheek, his mouth and eye with the water Tilley brought. His face was already beginning to look like a map of mountains, craters, and dark lakes.

When the bell rang, Mrs. Barrie ushered Malcolm through the foyer's broken china, mirror glass, and porcelain. Gwen heard their feet crunch on the pieces and Malcolm's urgency. "What's happened here? Is Gwen all right?"

Malcolm's here now. He'll put things right. It was a desperate thought. Whatever was going on that had brought Russell to this couldn't be put right by Malcolm's presence. Still, the moment he came through the drawing room door and their eyes connected, Gwen released her breath.

Kneeling, Malcolm ran his hands over Russell's shoulders, his arms and legs and torso. "No limbs broken, but I'll wager there's a cracked rib or two. Concussed. Let's get him to the sofa."

As Malcolm lifted Russell from beneath his armpits, it was all Gwen and Mrs. Barrie could do to lift his legs. Russell groaned and cursed beneath his breath as they stretched him out, causing Gwen more shame than concern.

"It's all right, Russell, Dr. McNeill's here."

Russell groaned again. "I don't need a doctor. Tell him to go away."

Mrs. Barrie huffed, making Malcolm smile.

"It looks as if you do, Mr. Bennett. When you're able, you'll need to sit up. I should wrap those ribs for you. We'll excuse the ladies for that procedure."

It took a few minutes, but Russell sat up with Malcolm's help. Gwen helped him release Russell from his suit jacket and tie. She winced at the sight of cuts and bruises already forming around his neck.

The women waited in the hallway as Dr. McNeill worked. Mrs. Barrie shook her head at the mess strewn across the floor. "I'll get a broom and dustpan. Tilley can help me clear this up."

"Do you think we should wait? The police might need to see what those men did."

"I'm not thinking Mr. Bennett will be wanting to call the police on this. He didn't even want the doctor here."

Gwen sat down on a hallway chair with a thud. Whether she liked it or not, Russell was involved in something dangerous, so dangerous and surely illegal that he dared not involve the police. *What have you done, Russell?*

Twenty minutes later, she was still waiting in the hallway alone when Malcolm came out of the drawing room, quietly closing the door behind him.

Gwen stood to meet him. "Thank you for coming. I didn't know who else to call."

"You can always call me, Gwen, day or night." He reached for her hand, concern written across his features. "Are you truly all right? What happened here?"

Helpless to give him answers, she shook her head. "I don't know. Some men banged on the door. They didn't ring the bell, just kept pounding. Russell said he'd deal with it and ordered Mrs. Barrie and me up the stairs to my room. He must have let them in. For a time, the banging stopped, and then we heard shouting and crashes—the vases in the hallway. Then more shouting and finally a gunshot and a shattering of glass—the mirror, I think, but I so feared they'd killed him."

He squeezed her hand.

"We heard the front door slam, and a car roar off. We hurried downstairs as fast as we could. That's when we found him."

"This is not good, Gwen, not at all. Did you see the men? Could you read the license plate?"

"No. Nothing. It was too dark, and we were in my room."

"Have you telephoned the police? Why aren't they here yet?"

Gwen hesitated, looked away.

"Gwen?" He leaned closer.

"Mrs. Barrie thinks Russell won't want that."

"They nearly killed him! It should be reported."

Gwen shook her head, uncertain.

"What if they come back? What then?"

"I—I don't know."

Malcolm stepped back, observing her—clinically, she knew. "What is he wrapped up in, Gwen? These men, whoever they are, are not playing games."

"I don't know. Truly—I don't know. He deals in antiquities; that's what he's said. That's all he's told me."

She wasn't at all sure Malcolm believed her. At that moment Mrs. Barrie returned with cups of tea for Gwen and the doctor. "Extra sugar, to settle your nerves. We canna thank you enough for coming so quickly, Doctor—Malcolm."

Malcolm swallowed the tea in long gulps before speaking. He set the cup on the tray Mrs. Barrie held. "I should report this to the police."

Gwen felt Mrs. Barrie straighten beside her.

"Mr. Bennett won't want that."

"I'm not concerned with what Mr. Bennett wants. I'm far more concerned for the two of you, and for any others in the household." He looked from woman to woman, then walked across the foyer and lifted the telephone receiver in the hallway. He clicked for the operator.

"Put it down."

Gwen, Mrs. Barrie, and Malcolm turned as one toward the drawing room door where Russell stood unsteady, leaning against the doorjamb for support.

"You shouldn't be up." Malcolm's voice was flat.

"Put it down." It was not a request.

"This should be reported. It's possible those ruffians could return. Your body can't stand a repeat performance, and you must not risk the safety of these ladies."

Russell winced, drawing his arm across his rib cage.

"You need to lie down. Those ribs won't mend with you on your feet. I'll help you up the stairs."

"I don't want your help. I want you to leave. Now, Doctor."

"Russell!" Gwen couldn't believe his rudeness, not after all Malcolm had done.

"If you're not concerned for yourself, think of the women."

"I am thinking of the women. The police won't help—not for this."

Gwen stared at Russell. It was as if he were talking in code, a code Malcolm looked as if he understood.

"No?" Malcolm hesitated but replaced the receiver in its cradle. "I see."

"Well, I don't. What do you mean they won't help? Why not?" Gwen's fear had turned to exasperation.

Mrs. Barrie stepped toward Malcolm and took his arm. "I think it best we do as Mr. Bennett says, Doctor. I'll make certain he gets a good lie down, and we'll lock the doors. There's no need to worry. I'll see you out."

The concern in Malcolm's eyes did not diminish, but a surge of fury and distrust of Russell bled through. "Call me if you need me." Malcolm addressed Russell, but his eyes settled on Gwen again.

"Thank you for coming, Malcolm" was all she could say.

He allowed Mrs. Barrie to lead him toward the door. Gwen saw that she whispered something to him, but she couldn't hear what.

"Gwen." Russell looked as if he might faint.

She rushed to him and ducked beneath his arm, bearing his weight. "Can you climb the stairs?"

"With your help." He groaned again.

Mrs. Barrie was there in a minute and bore up his other side. Together and slowly, they climbed the stairs, one at a time.

When they finally got him to bed, Gwen pulled off his shoes and socks and found his nightclothes. She turned away as Mrs. Barrie helped him change clothes. Once he was beneath the covers, Gwen went to his side. "Who were they? Why did they do this?"

Russell closed his eyes. "Not tonight, Gwen. They won't be back. They've got what they want."

Gwen looked to Mrs. Barrie, who warily, wearily shook her head and left the room.

"Let me sleep."

Gwen wanted to argue. She wanted answers, but she knew she'd get nowhere that night. She turned down the lamp and walked to the door, wondering if he'd actually sleep after all that had happened. She didn't expect to.

Just before she closed the door, Russell spoke.

"Who is that man?"

"What man?"

"The doctor. You called him Malcolm."

Gwen knew his question was not idle. "A friend," she said, and closed the door.

32

Gwen wondered if Russell's booting Malcolm from the house would be the end of their friendship, even wondered if it meant there would be no more trips together to see Alistair.

Russell kept himself locked in his rooms until he was able to come down the stairs to his office under his own power. He allowed Mrs. Barrie to bring him food, and Mr. Dornby came and went for instructions and errands. He didn't ask to see Gwen, and though she worried about him, she was not eager to have him grill her about her relationship with Malcolm. She'd seen jealousy and that proprietary nature she despised in his eyes.

She did, however, want answers, and she believed Mrs. Barrie could give them. Convincing her to do so was another thing.

Mrs. Barrie had avoided Gwen for the better part of the week following Russell's beating, until Sunday, when they walked to church together.

"What do you know about Russell's business that I don't? And why is he afraid to call the police for help? Why did he let them get away with it?" Gwen kept up with the older woman, who always set a brisk pace in her walks.

Mrs. Barrie didn't slow and didn't answer.

"You might as well tell me because I won't stop asking. If I have to go snooping, I will."

Mrs. Barrie stopped short and looked at Gwen. "I wouldn't advise that. You've seen what those 'business associates' are capable of."

"Then tell me. I've a right to know."

Exasperated, Mrs. Barrie nearly snorted. "It's not that I know anything. I'm guessing, but I don't believe I'm far off."

"What, then?"

Mrs. Barrie looked at Gwen as if she were a child needing a much-too-simple explanation. "What do you think is in those trucks coming and going at all hours?"

"Russell said antiquities."

Mrs. Barrie raised her brows.

"I know, that doesn't make sense—not such a quantity. Where are they coming from and where are they going?"

"They wouldn't need to come under cover of darkness for anything legal."

Gwen had wondered about that herself.

"Have you not read the papers?" Mrs. Barrie went on. "Think about the timing of when it all began."

"It began before I ever arrived—I've no idea when. Alistair and Clara said it had been going on awhile."

"Prohibition started in January of last year. Everyone knew for a year or more that it was coming. The rich men—men who could afford it—filled their wine cellars. Those who wanted to make a great deal of money filled warehouses with whiskey so they could sell on the black market. All that's needed is a clientele and a safe-enough place with plenty of room to store it, and legitimate reasons for coming and going . . . and in some cases 'police protection.' From what I've read in the papers, whiskey's brought in on ships through the docks. Mr. Bennett already imported a great deal for his 'legitimate' business."

"Docks . . ." *New York, Philadelphia, Atlantic City. Stay off the docks—that's what the note said.* "All those rooms in the west wing."

"And a full cellar beneath."

"Russell said they're filled with artifacts, some he's been storing for years, waiting until he finds the perfect buyer, and some awaiting space for restoration and display at the Met." Gwen closed her eyes. *How foolish I've been.* "That's why he's afraid of having the police come."

"He did start with artifacts, before the war. He imported all sorts, but even then, I—I don't know. Something didn't seem quite right. The quantity . . . something. But since the war, the rough men he's entertained, the times he's not invited you to join his dinner parties at the house, so many of the same men from Tammany Hall time and again . . . and I don't know where all . . ."

Gwen blinked. "So the police are in on it."

"That would be my guess. Some, at any rate. Perhaps Mr. Bennett double-crossed someone involved or 'forgot' to pay them, and now he's paid the price."

Gwen remembered the note in Russell's office, and she remembered the look on Malcolm's face. "Do you think Malcolm suspects that?"

"He's worried for you, and . . ."

"And what?"

"Might even wonder if you're privy to it, part of it."

"He can't think that!"

"Why wouldn't he? You've been living in the house with the man for three years, and we both went along with not calling the police, even though he's honor bound as a doctor to do so. We put him in a terrible position."

"This can't go on. If we can't trust the police—"

"There are surely those we can; we simply don't know which ones. But if Mr. Bennett is arrested, what will that mean for Alistair? Would his funds be frozen? Would the institute still be allowed to care for the lad? Would they make him leave?"

"It's what's keeping him alive . . . for now." Gwen dared not venture into Russell's activities or what they might bring into Alistair's future. That future was tenuous at best, short and fatal at worst. Holding onto sanity and hope in the moment was hard enough, a daily gauntlet to run. Of all the people she trusted outside Mrs.

Barrie, she trusted Malcolm. Of all the people she dared not turn to now, for his sake and theirs, Malcolm stood at the top of that list.

Malcolm was not in church that Sunday, or the next. Gwen didn't know what to think but could not let another Sunday go by without seeing Alistair.

"We'll see if Mr. Dornby will drive us," she said to Mrs. Barrie on the way home.

"He's gone to visit his sister in Brooklyn and won't return until evening. That's what Mrs. LaMott said."

Gwen groaned. "This is impossible. I need to learn to drive."

"Drive? You think Mr. Bennett will allow you to drive the Bentley? Not likely."

"Alistair's going to think we don't want to come, that we can't be bothered."

Mrs. Barrie shook her head in frustration. "This won't do; it simply won't do."

Despite Gwen's lapse in visits, Alistair's spirits did not become of critical concern until November, when he wrote:

Dear Aunt Gwen,

Yesterday, my friend Eddie was so hungry he ate Ami's birdseed. Dr. Allen said it threw his metabolism into shock, and he died—Eddie, I mean. One of the nurses set Ami free, but I think Eddie is the one who's truly free.

Please, Aunt Gwen. I don't think I can do this anymore. I want to come home.

Alistair

33

Gwen knew she had no right to keep Alistair's letter from his father or Mrs. Barrie. She had no heart to deny Alistair's plea, and yet she feared what bringing him home might mean. She'd have liked to ask Malcolm, but she hadn't seen or heard from him for weeks. She needed Mrs. Barrie's perspective.

Stopping the housekeeper in the hallway after luncheon, Gwen showed her the letter, then said, "We can't keep his metabolism as steady as Dr. Allen has. What if we bring him home and he goes into shock, like this boy Eddie?"

"We canna know God's timing for Alistair any more than we can know His timing for ourselves."

Gwen didn't want to think about God's timing. She wanted to keep Alistair safe. "I'm afraid that if we don't bring him home, he'll sink faster, thinking we don't want him here. But I'm afraid that if we bring him home, he'll die because we're not doing enough."

"He'll not think we don't want him. He won't think that. It's just . . . if we bring him home with the . . . the unrest in the house, what then? What about what Dr. Allen said about upsets?"

"They can cause serious fluctuations in his sugar levels, creating havoc."

"Aye, what then?"

"Russell did say those men won't be back, that they got whatever they wanted."

"For now." Mrs. Barrie sighed.

That evening, over tea and brandy in the drawing room, Gwen showed Alistair's letter to Russell.

Russell crumpled the letter in a ball and threw it toward the fire, wincing—surely from his unhealed ribs.

Gwen felt for him but was horrified at his blatant dismissal of Alistair's letter. She stood to pick it up, smoothing out the paper, slipping it into her pocket. She didn't want to lose one word that Alistair had written.

"How can you do it?" Russell asked.

"What?"

"How can you keep him in a place that starves children to the point they eat birdseed and die? Once this gets out, everyone who knows I've allowed him to go there will throw it in my face."

Gwen felt heat spread from her neck to her face, from her torso to her fingertips. "It's not like that, not for him, and it's got nothing to do with what other people think. They don't know. They don't understand."

"It's a starvation diet. Callahan said—"

"Dr. Callahan's recommendation would have seen Alistair in his grave by now."

"Is that worse than this?"

Gwen turned away from him, faced the fire. "I want to keep him alive. There's work being done to find a cure." Her words sounded feeble, even to her. *What work? What progress? How close is the cure? How much time does Alistair have?*

"I've placed him in your care, Gwen . . . It's your decision, but

I think you should bring him home. Let him spend his last days in his own bed."

"Is that what you want?"

"I never wanted any of this." He swallowed the last of his brandy in one gulp. "You know I never wanted children, and I certainly don't want to see my son sick or watch him dying or starving. But bringing him home seems the only humane thing to do."

Gwen didn't know whether to be relieved or frightened, but she wanted Alistair home, with her, where she could see him, talk with him day by day, help him in any way she could. *Home in time for Christmas—a Christmas as precious as Marion and Clara's last one turned out to be.*

"But I won't have you worn to a frazzle looking after him. Hire a nurse."

"That's not necessary. I can—"

"No. That is my one condition. I'm going to need you to help with entertaining during December. Clients are coming from Chicago. I have people from New York expecting a dinner party. I can't afford to let them down. I need you to play the dazzling hostess again. You're very good at it." He smiled his most charming smile, one Gwen might have melted under if something less important, less life-and-death had been at stake. She closed her eyes.

"I trust that's not asking too much." He waited, testily.

"No, no, of course not. It's just with Alistair—"

"He can be here, Gwen, but our lives must go on. I have obligations. I can't pretend my business doesn't exist because my personal life is falling apart, and neither can you. There's more at stake than—" He stopped, pushed long fingers through his hair. "We're adults. We need to act like it, guard our emotions. I need you by my side."

He's afraid. Afraid of those thugs returning? Of worse? "Yes, of course, I'll help."

He reached for her hand. "We'll get through this, all of this, together."

She forced a half smile. *At what cost?*

Gwen called Malcolm at his office the next morning, only to learn that he was out of town and not expected to return for another week. The receptionist offered Dr. Callahan's services if she needed to make an appointment.

"No, thank you. It's all right." Gwen hung up the phone, perturbed. *Why didn't he tell us he'd be away so long? I'd feel better if I could talk with him about bringing Alistair home, though I know he'll not think it's the right thing to do. He won't understand. But he's not family. Why do I put so much store in what he says, what he thinks?*

Gwen dialed the institute's number and asked for Dr. Allen. She told him of Alistair's letter and of his father's wish for Alistair to return home.

"I cannot urge you strongly enough to leave Alistair here, under my care, Miss Armstrong. I realize Eddie's death has been traumatic for all our patients, but I also believe it underscores how crucial it is that patients strictly adhere to this program. Any deviation and you see what can happen. There was nothing to be done for Eddie."

"I realize that, Doctor, but Alistair has grown despondent. You said yourself that changes in temperament—subtle emotional changes—can cause metabolic upset."

"As can changes in situation, climate, so many things. You'll remember that Alistair initially improved here, where life is regulated and kept on an even keel. You've been pleased with his care, I trust."

"Yes, Dr. Allen, I have, but he wants to come home. I can't deny his plea. We love him and we need him with us."

"That very love will be his undoing, Miss Armstrong. How long before, from sympathy or pity, you break his diet and send him into a diabetic coma?"

Gwen's heart throbbed and her head pounded. It was the very thing that terrified her. Still, Russell had spoken, and he was Alistair's father. There was nothing else she could do. That's what she told herself. That's what she wanted to believe.

"A cure is coming," Dr. Allen went on. "We know that. We need more time. Alistair needs all the time we can give him. You won't be able to do at home what we can do here. Please reconsider, for his sake. Talk with Dr. McNeill. He'd advise the same."

"Mr. Bennett said we should hire a nurse."

"A nurse not trained at my facility will not be able to keep to the regimen."

Gwen couldn't argue with him. She knew he was right. She knew, too, that Alistair needed to come home, and not die away from those who loved him. "We'll pick Alistair up on Saturday, Dr. Allen. Please make certain he's ready."

Gwen hung up the phone. *Burning bridges. Never a good idea.* But she'd run out of good ideas.

34

Sitting as a guest amid a gathering of the Journal Club of the University of Toronto Department of Physiology in mid-November, Malcolm leaned forward to hear Dr. John Macleod, a fellow Scot, describe the work Dr. Frederick Banting and Charles Best had done over the summer. Their research and experiments regarding pancreatic extracts and their potential for treating pancreatic diabetes teetered on the breakthrough Alistair and millions of other children around the world desperately needed.

As Dr. Macleod spoke, Malcolm's mouth went dry, and his heart beat wildly, a raging bird trapped inside a cage. He could barely steady his pen to write the notes he needed. The man most responsible, Banting, was clearly not the public speaker meant to beat the drum, but Malcolm didn't blame him. He understood that, after all, as he himself was giddy enough to be rendered tongue-tied.

Though he'd have given much to have stayed and shadowed Dr. Banting and Mr. Best, Malcolm was forced to return to his patients in New York after two weeks. Dr. Callahan was overwhelmed, swamped with flu cases. It was not the Spanish flu, but with that Spanish Lady claiming so many in recent memory, no one knew where it might lead.

Still, Malcolm had time to establish a strong relationship with

Dr. Macleod, chair of physiology at the university. Malcolm was sure to hear through him of any further breakthroughs. He'd even shared with Macleod the details of Alistair Bennett's case and discussed the important work of Dr. Allen. They were stories all too familiar to Dr. Macleod, making Malcolm realize that the doctor received hundreds of similar letters, phone calls, and in-person pleas from doctors and frantic parents everywhere. It was grueling pressure to work under. Dr. Macleod assured him that Dr. Banting, driven and dedicated, worked frantically to discover the needed cure.

Malcolm had not shared his trip with either Mrs. Barrie or Gwen, unwilling to get their hopes up, though his were flying high. He'd have much to share with Alistair upon his return.

Malcolm learned in early December that Banting and his team had injected a diabetic dog with his extract. So began a serious test of longevity. *Waiting. Waiting. That's the next thing. Each day that dog lives is a day hope grows stronger.*

Between travel and Sunday emergencies, Malcolm had not been to church or seen Gwen or Mrs. Barrie since he'd treated Russell Bennett for his beating. He hated thinking of the fear in Gwen's eyes that night and what might be going on in that household. *What does Gwen know? Whether or not she knows, what danger is she in? And what is her relationship to that man?* Malcolm feared for both women, but he could no longer deny his growing concern, even affection for Gwen Armstrong. He'd not expected to find himself attracted to another woman after losing his wife, the love of his young life. But he smiled to recognize the symptoms—a palpitating heart in her presence, a lightening of his soul when she spoke, a keen desire to protect her, body and soul.

He prayed daily for everyone in that house, though he found it harder to commend Bennett to God's care. *Whatever the man's involved in, Lord, protect those who are innocent. Thank You, Father, that Alistair's not there.*

He assumed that Gwen and Mrs. Barrie made the trip to see Alistair each week, despite his lack of availability. Because Dr. Allen had been eager for news Malcolm would bring from Toronto, the two men scheduled an evening meeting the second week of December. It was a weeknight after office hours—not a visiting day—but Malcolm hoped Dr. Allen would permit him to see Alistair while there. He'd bring Gwen and Mrs. Barrie on Sunday, but he couldn't wait to tell Alistair of the promising work Dr. Banting and his team were doing.

He pulled into the institute's parking lot and hurried in, braving the frigid December wind, smiling into the woolen muffler wound round his neck.

No one sat at the front desk. Being after hours, he wasn't surprised. Since he was a few minutes early and Dr. Allen was not in his office, Malcolm pulled off his hat and muffler, taking the opportunity to nip down to Alistair's room. He wouldn't stay long, wouldn't tire the lad, but could think of no better gift to give him this Christmas season than hope.

"May I help you?" A nurse stopped him in the hallway, just outside Alistair's doorway.

"Good evening, Nurse Pritchard. Do you remember me, Dr. McNeill?"

"Yes, Doctor, of course I do. Merry Christmas season."

"And to you, Nurse Pritchard. I'm here to see Dr. Allen, but he's not back to his office yet so I thought I'd take a moment to visit my young friend, Alistair Bennett. I've got some good news for him."

"Oh, has no one told you, Dr. McNeill? Alistair's no longer with us." She smiled, a thing Malcolm could not reconcile with her words.

"No longer—" He felt the blood drain from his head but forced himself to stand still. "When? What happened?"

"His aunt and father took him home last Saturday. Dr. Allen was none too pleased, I daresay."

"Took him home—alive, then?"

"Oh, yes, very much alive, for now." She tsked. "I don't know what they were thinking. Dr. Allen did his best to stop them."

Malcolm's emotions roller coasted through his brain. *Why, Gwen, why? We're so close to a cure—surely.*

"There's Dr. Allen now. He can tell you more. Good night, Doctor."

"Good night, Nurse." Malcolm's words were automatic, rote.

Dr. Allen filled in the blanks for Malcolm—Eddie's death and how it had affected Alistair, his aunt's overreaction to Alistair's letter, the father's insistence, including his threat to withdraw funding and discredit the Institute. "I all but begged them not to remove the boy for his sake, but of course, they were free to do as they wished. It was an unpleasant ending. I hold little hope they'll be able to keep to the diet at home."

Malcolm nodded. *Dear God in heaven, help them. Help Alistair.*

It was all Malcolm could do to keep his eyes on the road driving home. He voiced loudly multiple versions of conversations he'd have with Gwen were she there, none of them calm, none of them complimentary. *If she cannot deal with the letter of a frightened lad, how will she handle his pleas for food—food that will send him into a coma?* He'd not felt such anger since he'd learned of his daughter's death. *Foolish. Ungrateful. Unwise.*

His head throbbed. It might not be his place to speak his piece to Gwendolyn Armstrong—at least Russell Bennett would see it that way—but Malcolm determined to do just that.

35

By mid-December, Bennett Place had been professionally decorated from top to bottom and extra servants hired for the upcoming holiday events, with caterers coming and going in addition to Mrs. LaMott's steady supply of the finest fare. The entryway to the mansion looked like an invitation to a Victorian Christmas. No expense or work was spared.

Gwen could only think, *If this is Alistair's last Christmas, I'm glad it's a beautiful one. There's so little to bring him joy.*

The first dinner party was a boisterous affair for Russell's New York contacts. She couldn't look at them without replaying Mrs. Barrie's observations through her mind. *Are these men bootleggers? I can't imagine them prowling the docks of New York. Are they the brains behind the brawn? Do their wives know? Why are you doing this, Russell?*

But Russell gave nothing away, played the charming host, and showcased Gwen in ways meant to flatter her—ways that now made her most uncomfortable.

A pretend world . . . a fairy tale . . . or a nightmare, one I can't wake up from.

They'd just sat down to dinner in the formal dining room—twenty-four guests, even numbers of men and women extravagantly made up and dressed. Given the disparity in the ages between the men and the young and beautiful women on their arms, Gwen didn't believe for a moment that all were wives. Cranberry-orange roast duckling was served after the oysters Rockefeller. They were perhaps halfway through the course when a newly hired footman bent low to murmur a message in Gwen's ear.

Surprised, she excused herself from the guests closest to her. At the far end of the table, Russell's brow furrowed, though he kept the smile pasted on his lips. Gwen left her seat quietly, the train of her wine-colored gown whispering behind.

She didn't believe she'd even be missed after the second glass of wine was served, but she'd make quick work of whoever waited in the drawing room, insisting on an audience. She closed the door to the room behind her.

"Malcolm!" Her heart skipped a beat.

"Gwen." If she didn't know better, she'd have said he was angry, but as he took in her face, her form, her hair, his eyes widened in admiration.

Self-conscious, she tried to make light. "I only dress like— A dinner party."

"It's very becoming. You're lovely."

It was said so simply, so sincerely, that she felt a blush of appreciation run through her skin. "Thank you. It's good to see you, Malcolm." *Why did you disappear?*

He nodded. "And you." A crease formed between his eyes. "I went to see Alistair. Dr. Allen said you've brought him here."

"Yes." Her pulse picked up. "He needed to come home."

"He needs to remain under Dr. Allen's care." It sounded like an accusation.

"He asked to come home. He lost a friend—"

"Yes, Dr. Allen told me. People die, Gwen. Children with diabetes die. You don't want Alistair to be among them if you can help it."

Gwen felt heat rush over her body. "I can't stop it. He needs to be home, with people who love him and care for him, if these are his last days. Not in a clinical institution."

"If he remains under Dr. Allen's care, he may not die—not before a cure—"

"You talk of a cure as if you know it's coming. But there's no such thing—not now, and maybe never. Have you seen him? No, of course not. The last few weeks you've disappeared, apparently frightened off by Russell's rotten visitors."

His mouth dropped open.

Gwen kept going. "Well, I'm not disappearing and I'm not running out on him. We can do here what Dr. Allen has been doing—maybe not as well, but Cora and I have learned a great deal from him and the nurses there. We can do this—and we will."

"I did not run out on Alistair—or you. I was in Toronto, attending lectures. There's been a breakthrough—every reason to hope that in the near future there will be a pancreatic extract that—"

"That cures?" Hope swelled in Gwen's chest.

"That can lower blood glucose, bring it to normal levels. Just this month they've injected a diabetic dog and so far—"

"A dog?"

"Yes, they need to make certain it's safe and that it works as expected before a human trial."

"You're saying they don't know if it will keep the dog alive."

"Not yet, but there's every reason—"

"And then what? A human guinea pig?"

"There will be human trials, eventually," he conceded. "When they're confident it works on the dogs, and when they're confident it's safe."

"You want me to leave him with Dr. Allen in the far-off hope that—"

"You were willing before, strong before. You hoped, had faith. What changed?"

Gwen crossed her arms. "His father thinks this slow and painful death is cruel, as does Dr. Callahan." She didn't want to admit there were others who'd questioned Russell, implying he was heartless to leave his son with Dr. Allen—men and their wives whose good will

Russell sought. She also wouldn't admit that she missed Alistair sorely, or that Alistair was afraid to stay there, to die far from home.

"The father who never visited his son." The words came out flat.

"That's not fair. You can't know what Russell's been through, what we've all been through." *Why am I taking up for him?*

Malcolm stared at her in silence. The longer he stared, waiting for her to explain or defend herself or see his point of view, the more she knew there was no defense, no magnanimous reason. *Yes, Russell told me to bring him home, but I wanted him with me. Selfish. Yes, I'm selfish. I could have told him no—told them both no—but I hadn't the strength.* The words that came out belied that truth. "The decision is out of my hands. Now, if you'll excuse me, I must get back to our guests."

"I'd like to see Alistair, if I may. Perhaps Mrs. Barrie could accompany me . . . or simply tell me the way to his room. I needn't keep you."

"I don't know. I don't know what Russell would say . . . I think you should leave now."

Malcolm looked away, looked as if he were about to speak, but didn't. He picked up his hat. She knew she'd betrayed his friendship, his trust, his best advice and kindness long and unselfishly given. "Of course, Miss Armstrong, attend to your guests."

Gwen bristled, but at that moment, Mrs. Barrie entered with a tray. "I thought you might like a cup of tea, Doctor." She smiled, the welcoming, kindhearted smile indicative of their friendship. Gwen felt suddenly jealous of their easy camaraderie. She felt out of sorts, self-conscious in the opulence of her surroundings, in the extravagance of her gown, of the divide that stretched between them.

"That's very kind of you, Mrs. Barrie. I was hoping to see Alistair."

"Certainly! I know the lad would be ever so glad for your visit." She turned to Gwen. "I'll take Dr. McNeill up to see him, if you like."

"I need to get back to the dinner."

"So you said." Malcolm stood rigid.

"The main course is nearly done." Mrs. Barrie looked quizzically between the two of them. "Mr. Bennett asked me to see if everything is all right."

Gwen's breath tightened in her chest. "I'll say good night, then."

Malcolm bowed his head once. "Good night, Miss Armstrong. Call if you should need me, if Alistair needs me."

Gwen felt her heart give way, felt it crumble, then harden, as she walked past Malcolm and Mrs. Barrie, to return to the long table surrounded by people she didn't know or care to know.

36

Christmas Eve came. Mrs. Barrie could not see Alistair spending the blessed day in his room, but he was no longer able to safely navigate the stairs. She knew that Mr. Bennett would expect Gwen to spend the day with him in the drawing room, before one of the several magnificent trees in the mansion, replete with crackling fire and carols on the radio or gramophone.

"It's intolerable, thinking of our lad shut away alone like that. Mind you, he rarely complains. I don't think he has the strength." Mrs. Barrie plunked the silver service on the dining room sideboard, harder than was warranted.

"I'm with him every moment I can be," Gwen defended, sipping her morning coffee. "He absolutely refused we hire another nurse after he sent the first one away. He said he won't have someone staring at him all the time." She closed her eyes. "Russell agreed, as long as I don't spend every waking moment with him, which I would, if only—" Gwen shook her head in despair.

She always looks guilty and torn when talking about Alistair. Mrs. Barrie turned to press the younger woman's arm. "I know, but you canna be all in all to him. You canna take the place of his father and friends. No one can."

Gwen shrugged her shoulders helplessly. "What, then?"

"Dr. McNeill made a suggestion when he was here."

"Oh, what was that?" Gwen bristled at the doctor's name though it was apparent she wanted to know.

"He suggested we move Alistair to a room on the main floor so he can see the comings and goings and doings in the house. Especially with all this Christmas fanfare, it would be something to distract him from pain and worry. Even seeing Tilley about her business day by day would be something, rather than sitting upstairs alone."

Gwen stared at her. "I hadn't thought of that."

"Nor had I. It was Malcolm's suggestion. He cares very much for the lad."

Gwen looked away.

"Did you and the doctor have a falling out?" Mrs. Barrie had wanted to know ever since the doctor left the night of the dinner party.

"I don't know what you mean."

"You've been as chilly as first frost each time I mention him, ever since he returned from his trip."

"He disapproves of bringing Alistair home. He thinks he should have stayed with Dr. Allen."

Mrs. Barrie sighed. *He's likely right, though it does precious little good to say that now.* "It comes from a good heart, a knowing heart."

"I'm not judging his heart, and he shouldn't be judging mine."

"It's not your heart he's questioning."

"I didn't expect that from you, Mrs. Barrie. He doesn't understand what it is to need a seriously ill child at home. He can't."

"Oh, I think he can. Do you not know that he lost his own wee daughter to this juvenile diabetes? He's walked the walk you fear. He knows its torment."

"What?"

"Back in Scotland, during the war—while he was conscripted to serve and away doctoring soldiers in Egypt—she died. He lost his daughter to the diabetes and his wife to the Spanish flu. The man knows a thing or two about suffering beyond what he sees each day in his practice."

"I had no idea. He never said."

"Did you give him a chance to say? Did you ask him why he's so passionate about finding a cure for this horrid disease?"

"No—I—I didn't." Gwen turned away. Mrs. Barrie knew she'd hit the mark.

"Well, I think his suggestion to bring Alistair downstairs is a good one. What about the schoolroom? There's more than enough to keep him quietly occupied there when his energy allows, and it's bright and cheerful."

"Yes, that's an excellent idea. I'm sorry I didn't think of it. I'm sorry I didn't ask Malcolm . . . I don't know, ask him . . ." She drew a breath. "I'll ask Russell as soon as I see him."

"As for Malcolm, it's not too late. As for Mr. Bennett, why not take the move upon yourself?"

"Do you think he'll say no?"

"Don't you? He's not likely to be fond of the idea of his guests getting a gander at his son as he is now."

"No. He's not." Gwen turned toward the window. Mrs. Barrie knew she was considering.

"The piano is there, the Victrola, paints—no, perhaps not paints. I believe Dr. Allen forbade that after the one child ate— Well, one cannot be tempted to eat what isn't there."

"Right. No paints . . . We could keep his door closed and someone with him when guests are in the house."

"Aye."

"Russell is busy with clients until this evening."

"What better time? Shall I ask Mr. Dornby to help?"

Gwen bit her lip but finally nodded. "In for a penny . . ."

"In for a pound," Mrs. Barrie finished, smiling in approval.

The move was accomplished in half a day. Mr. Dornby and the hired footman carried Alistair's wheeled chair downstairs, then formed a seat with their linked arms and carried him. Mrs. Barrie imagined he weighed less than the chair, but two made the transfer safer than one. Tilley carried clothes and bedding.

Light sprang in Alistair's eyes as the men carried him downstairs. "Look at that tree! And all the ornaments. We never had such a big tree or so many ornaments and lights before!"

"They're only rented, not to keep." Mrs. Barrie spoke disapprovingly of what she considered a lavish deception but was pleased to see Alistair's pleasure just the same. "Quite the extravagance this year, but festive, I'll give you that."

"Wheel me around all the rooms, please. I want to see them!"

Mr. Dornby was glad to do the honors, though Mrs. Barrie saw the horror and pity in his eyes when he looked on Alistair's wasted form. While Alistair enthused over the dining room decorations, Mr. Dornby whispered to Mrs. Barrie, "A shame. A crying shame for that poor boy. You let me know if there's anything at all I can do, Mrs. Barrie. I'm your man, and the missus feels the same—day or night, you call on us."

Mrs. Barrie nodded, close to tears at his sympathy.

By the time they'd toured the house and reached the schoolroom, Alistair was spent. His bed had been set up where Gwen's desk once stood, and he gladly took to it. The smaller desks once used by Alistair and Clara were gone. The room remained cheerful in its natural light, made cozier by the crackling fire, but having been closed off for months, it was not decorated like the rest of the house.

"What this room needs is a Christmas tree," Mr. Dornby, purveyor of Christmas cheer, announced, hands on his hips.

"You're right," Mrs. Barrie agreed.

"What about the family ornaments? Would you like those on a tree in this room, Alistair?" Gwen chimed in, clearly eager to please the boy.

"Sure," Alistair responded quietly, closing his eyes.

Mrs. Barrie put her finger to her lips and nodded toward the open door. Gwen pulled the duvet up to Alistair's chin. He was asleep or pretended to be. She was never quite certain.

Outside the schoolroom, Mrs. Barrie pulled the door closed.

Mr. Dornby frowned. "He don't seem too excited about that tree idea, does he?"

"He's tired, worn through. That tour of the house was the most he's done at once for a time," Gwen said.

"Perhaps it's not enough—all this inactivity," Mrs. Barrie mused.

"He's not up to much," Gwen defended.

"No, but I'm wondering if we've kept him inactive upstairs too long. Remember how Dr. Allen encourages moderate exercise? At any rate, I think making the room cheerful is a good idea. Something to brighten his days, and so he doesn't feel so excluded from everything."

"I'll be off to the Christmas tree lot, then, if it's okay by you, Miss Armstrong. I'll bring the tallest one can fit in that schoolroom if I may."

"Thank you, Mr. Dornby, that's a fine idea. Mrs. Barrie and I can find the ornaments and lights."

By nightfall the room was transformed. Alistair slept through all the activity, a particular sorrow to Mrs. Barrie.

"I hoped he'd want to help decorate the tree from his chair. I don't suppose he's up to that."

"Maybe not," Gwen whispered, "but we mustn't give up. I think you may be right that we've kept him idle too long. I can work on that."

"We can work on that," corrected Mrs. Barrie.

Dinner had been served. Alistair was still fast asleep. Mrs. Barrie hated to wake him, to rouse him from what may be a pleasant sleep simply to deny him a decent meal. But he needed to eat something. No food could be worse than too much food—or the wrong food. Either extreme might prove fatal. The weight of each decision sometimes felt too much to bear.

Determined to keep her tears at bay, she set her mouth in a grim line and prepared the prescribed tray of one slice of cold boiled ham, one slice of bread, two tablespoons of peas, three lettuce leaves, six stalks of celery—each four and one half inches long—butter, and tea. "A veritable feast compared to where we started, I suppose." She shook her head. "So little on a night meant to celebrate so much." She made what felt like a long journey to Alistair's room.

At least his new room was cheerful with a steady fire in the grate and the beautiful tree. Several of the shining ornaments caught the light from the dancing flames. She turned on the electric tree lights, hoping they'd bring a smile when he woke. She was glad for anything that brought her dear lad a bit of cheer.

"Alistair," she urged, setting the tray on the table beside his bed. "Time for dinner, my dear boy."

He didn't open his eyes, but she could see he was breathing by the slight rise and fall of his chest. She never knew in these moments if he didn't hear or if it just seemed too much trouble. She massaged his shoulders, and propped a pillow behind him, doing her best to wake him gently. He was so thin now that she imagined every handling of his body pained him.

"Leave it, Mrs. Barrie." His voice came raspy, and he still hadn't opened his eyes.

"And you not eat what I've brought? I should say not." She pretended to huff. "I'll just feed you as I did when you were a bairn if that's the way it's to be." She tried to tease, to make light, but she knew that sometimes it was simply too much for him to lift the spoon to his mouth.

Once he began swallowing, she could see the awakened desire for food. That may have been the worst of all.

"Rest now," she said, gently stroking his arm, when he'd eaten his small allotment. She didn't need to say it twice. His eyes closed involuntarily.

A half hour later she delivered the evening's tea tray and brandy to Gwen and Mr. Bennett in the drawing room, where they listened to carols on the radio. She'd returned to the kitchen for her own pot of tea, about to retire for the evening when a knock came at the back kitchen door.

"Dr. McNeill! What a lovely surprise. Happy Christmas!"

"Happy Christmas, Mrs. Barrie."

"Do come in, out of the snow, and let me fetch you a cup of tea."

"Thank you kindly, but I won't stay. I just wanted to leave you with a little something for Alistair."

"Step in out of the cold, won't you? Why didn't you come to the front door?" As soon as the words left her mouth, she knew.

"I don't think . . . The drawing room drapes have not been drawn. It looked a family scene, and I don't mean to intrude." His face flushed.

Gwen and Mr. Bennett together . . . I suppose it does look that way, poor smitten man.

"You'd never be intruding, Malcolm, but I confess I'm that glad to see you. It's been too long. Please, come in. I know Alistair would love your visit, if we wake him. He sleeps more now."

"Aye, I'm not surprised."

"We've moved him, just today, downstairs. I'm sorry we didn't do it from the first when bringing him home."

"Is he able to keep to the diet?" Concern filled the doctor's eyes.

"Yes, so far that's going as well as can be expected. He's just so tired, but Miss Armstrong and I were discussing today that he may need to be more active."

"As much as he can tolerate is best."

"Aye. I'll see to it." Mrs. Barrie grew conscious of footsteps beyond the door.

As if sensing her discomfort, the doctor pressed a cheerily wrapped gift into Mrs. Barrie's hands. "You may wish to give it to him privately." He tipped his hat, about to turn. Then he stopped, not looking her in the eye. "Is she happy—Miss Armstrong?"

How can I answer that? "She's worried for Alistair. I don't think she knows if she's made the right decision. She thinks his welfare depends on her, and yet . . . As for happy, well, it's hard to say."

He nodded. "Hard for any of us to say. Good night and God bless you, Mrs. Barrie."

"Good night and God go with you, Malcolm." She closed the door against the night's cold, warmed by his brief visit yet sad that even she trod softly in the house she called home.

She carried Malcolm's gift, heavy for its size, to Alistair's room, where the tree lights still shone and firelight burned low. "Alistair, lad, are you awake?" she whispered, but there was no response, only even breathing.

She placed the gift on the bed beside his pillow, the card facing him, then tiptoed from the room. Closing the door, she whispered, "Happy Christmas, dear Alistair. The moment you wake this blessed Christmas morning, you'll see you've not been forgotten."

Alistair opened his eyes the minute he heard Mrs. Barrie close his door. Before she'd come in, he'd been lying quietly, staring at the fire, remembering the last Christmas he'd shared with his mother and Clara, with Mrs. Barrie and Aunt Gwen, his father in faraway Egypt as the influenza raged. So much had happened since then.

He supposed that by next Christmas he'd be gone. *Father and Aunt Gwen will marry. Mrs. Barrie will be kept on. The house can't run without her.*

It made him glad to think of Mrs. Barrie, steady and stalwart as ever. Thinking of his aunt married to his father made him glad she'd be there—sad in one way and relieved in another. He wouldn't be there to see it, or to be excluded from their lives as he surely would be.

When Mrs. Barrie entered the room, he hadn't wanted her to see he'd been crying, so he'd kept his head turned away, nearly covered by the duvet. He'd mastered even breathing at the institute, pretending sleep when he didn't want to talk to someone. It was like slipping into his own private room where no one else could go.

He turned over to see what she'd set on his bed. His heart quickened at the sight of the box wrapped in white tissue paper, tied with red ribbon. *A present!*

She'd barely gone from the room before he tore open the wrapping paper and lifted the lid of the wooden box. Nestled inside was a wooden stable and inside that several small figures wrapped in cloth, each bound with a bit of twine. Alistair struggled to sit up in bed, unwrapping each of the hand-carved figures until his bed was transformed into the hills of Bethlehem, replete with sheep and shepherds, a donkey, three kings, Mary, Joseph, a trio of angels, and the babe lovingly wrapped in swaddling cloths, lying in a manger.

How should it be set up? Alistair didn't know, but gritting his teeth, he wrestled himself into his wheeled chair. As soon as he caught his breath, he began arranging the pieces on the table nearest the fire where he could best see them from his bed.

In all of Bennett Place's hundreds of lavish Christmas decorations and streams of tinsel there was not one nativity scene. *Until now.* Alistair smiled. He'd been so taken with opening the gift and arranging the scene that he'd not even read the card.

He wheeled himself back to his bed and tore open the envelope.

Dear Alistair,

I hope this nativity will be a glad reminder of our Savior's great love for you.

Jesus came as a helpless babe in need of care, just as we all are.

In manhood He showed us how to live a victorious life, a Kingdom life—a life that begins by His grace now and moves through eternity.

He gave His life to cover the cost of our sins. By His resurrection, He broke those chains of sin and death that bind, opening a door to life we've never known. He gave us His victory, restoring relationship with our heavenly Father.

All we need to accept His freely given gift is to realize we can't do this on our own, confess our failures to God, and trust in Him. That is the substance of faith. Think of that, Alistair—nothing more or less is required. It's available to you and to me, to all of us, and it's only the beginning. Knowing Him, walking with Him, changes everything. He loves you with everlasting love, my friend, and will never leave or forsake you.

My heart and prayers are with you daily, Alistair.

Wishing you a happy Christmas and a blessed New Year,

Your friend,
Malcolm McNeill

The nativity, the card—they were the best gifts Alistair could imagine, the best he'd ever received. He'd gone to church with Mrs. Barrie in times past, but he'd never been sure how it all fit together.

In the stillness of that Christmas Eve, alone in his room, Alistair gave his life to the One determined to save him, the only One who could.

37

New York opened 1922 with opulent parties, parades, and great flair. Russell, fully healed and determined to show the world confidence, bravado, and charm, attended several events, insisting Gwen accompany him far more than she wanted. He traveled incessantly within the States, but Gwen continued her refusal to join him on such trips, much to his growing displeasure.

Ever since Christmas, Gwen had noticed a change in Alistair, one she could neither define nor understand. He was not despondent, but he seemed in a state she could only call tranquil.

"It's called peace," Mrs. Barrie assured her, smiling.

"Does that mean he's given up?"

"It means he trusts the One who will never let him down—not now, not ever."

"Is this more about God?" Gwen recognized the look on Mrs. Barrie's face. It was that serene, quiet, confident knowing that Malcolm wore, the look she remembered seeing when the three of them had spent Sunday afternoon picnics together—once upon a time in what felt like long ago. It was a serenity, a peace she could not relate to.

"It's about knowing God. It's about surrendering one's life and will to Him, trusting Him, knowing He knows best."

"I don't trust God. He's not cured Alistair. He let Marion and Clara die. He let my mother die when I needed her most."

Mrs. Barrie didn't say anything, which was just as well. Gwen had no intention of listening. She wanted to rant. She wanted to pound her fist on the table and scream, *Why don't You heal him if You're so almighty?* But she clamped her lips together.

"You canna control the outcome of Alistair's life, or your own, or anything, really. You can fight all you want, my dear, but in the end, what good will it do? Certainly, it does Alistair no good . . . and it harms you."

It was as if Mrs. Barrie could read her mind, which infuriated Gwen further. She knew Mrs. Barrie meant well, but she did not want to hear any more. From childhood she'd had to work hard, plow ahead through sheer force of will to make things come right. Why should this be different? And yet it was. No matter how hard she tried—testing urine daily, measuring every ounce of liquid, weighing every gram of Alistair's food, working beside him to encourage frequent movement—she could not change what needed to change. She'd never give up. Still, even she knew she might break in the process.

She hadn't returned to church with Mrs. Barrie since Alistair had come home. He'd asked to be taken twice, but Gwen would not allow it, though she knew her denial hurt him. "The slightest cold or infection could be your undoing, Alistair. We can't risk it. I won't risk it."

It was a legitimate concern, but she also wanted to avoid Malcolm. After her shameful performance the night of the December dinner party, she dreaded seeing him, couldn't face him. Knowing that he'd lost his own daughter to this horrible disease gave credibility to his urgent pleas, his near-desperate demands. Part of her wanted to reach out to him, to comfort him. He'd urged the treatment he believed best for Alistair, what he would have done for his own child. But Alistair wasn't his child. The decision for his treatment was hers to make.

No, she wouldn't go to church, wouldn't see him.

But she missed the little peace she'd found in her time singing hymns, listening to the Scripture reading, absorbing and challenging the sermon by turns and discussing its details with Malcolm and Mrs. Barrie. She wouldn't admit it; she couldn't. It would be tantamount to giving in, to surrendering, as Mrs. Barrie said. It would mean she'd failed. It would spell defeat. Gwen had no intention of being beaten.

In late January, Mrs. Barrie handed Gwen a short newspaper clipping taken from the Canadian newspaper *Toronto Star*. "May Cure Diabetes" was the headline. The article mentioned research that Professor J. R. Macleod had been doing for several months at the Toronto university. A thirteen-year-old boy had been injected with a serum as a last resort. The results were encouraging enough that the treatments would continue daily. It was the first human experiment of a cure for diabetes.

The only words Gwen could focus on were *as a last resort.* So certain was she that this would mean one more dashed hope that she didn't ask how Mrs. Barrie had gotten hold of the clipping. She was more concerned with sticking to the program she knew, doing her best to keep Alistair alive as long as possible, and keeping Russell from interfering. She gave the clipping back to Mrs. Barrie without a word.

Gwen should not have been surprised when Russell declared he would host an extravagant Valentine's Day party to be held the Friday before the holiday. The devastation and deprivation of the war lay behind, and Gwen saw New York exploding in a passion for escapism from those dark years. Economic boom and widespread prosperity, affordable availability of automobiles and electricity, combined with the people's war against Prohibition fueled the frenzy. The upbeat tempo of jazz; the wild new dance, the Charleston; women's right to vote and their newfound freedom from corsets and the brazen introduction of flappers—it all exuded a revelry she'd never seen.

She understood. Sometimes she felt the fever—like cabin fever—pulse in her own veins. A desperate need to escape, to fly free.

Planning, organizing, and being fitted for yet another stunning evening gown took more time from Alistair than she wished. She'd grown suspicious of Russell's design. *How hard will he work to draw me away from his son and closer to himself? Is that what this is about, or is it truly for business? What does "business" even mean now?*

On the outside, Russell's plan appeared to be working. Ever the congenial hostess, Gwen did her best to make him proud, hoping that would keep him even-keeled where his son was concerned. He'd speculated more than once about sending Alistair to a sanatorium for Gwen's sake if she wasn't willing to hire another nurse. She knew Alistair would continue to refuse a nurse at home. She couldn't allow Russell to think she was in any way overburdened or not willing to stand by his side in the entertainments he hosted or attended. She didn't want to know the truth or details of his business—she dared not take that in now, think it through. Her sole focus was Alistair, keeping him alive, making sure he survived.

The night of the party, she stopped in Alistair's room before the festivities, making certain he lacked nothing. "I hope you'll enjoy the music tonight. Your father's hired a band."

"There'll be dancing?"

"Yes, and music of all sorts. He's opened the ballroom, but you should be able to hear the music from here. I can leave the door ajar a bit if you'd like. We just won't mention that to anyone else." She smiled, hoping he would think it their little secret. She'd always presented the locking of his door when guests came as a protection so he wouldn't be disturbed, though it was Russell's order. He didn't want guests to see his emaciated son and judge him a cruel father.

"I'd like that." Alistair smiled. "I'm feeling better this evening. If I could, I'd like to dance with you, Aunt Gwen. You're beautiful in your red dress. You look like a queen."

Gwen laughed. "Thank you, kind Sir Alistair. You make me feel like a queen." She kissed his forehead good night. After closing the door, she opened it just a crack and stuck her hand through to give a queenly wave. From his bed he inclined his head in a mock bow.

The evening was resplendent in long buffet tables groaning with lavish culinary delights—everything from exotic appetizers to glistening, glazed roasted fowl to an entire table filled with tiers of colorful pastries and nut-studded dates. It looked in all parts like a fairy tale come to life, but it turned Gwen's stomach, knowing there was not one morsel on those tables admissible for Alistair. She drew a deep breath. She couldn't think about that now but affixed a smile to her face, determined to play the role required of her.

Red hearts and white lights dangled from the band's orchestra balcony and every crystal chandelier. The band's performance rocked the walls as dance partners swept the floor to top songs—"Look for the Silver Lining," "Crazy Blues," "I Ain't Got Nobody," and "Lena from Palesteena."

Gwen had only just mastered the Charleston and shimmy, but her foxtrot was perfect. She hoped the band would include a waltz or two. She felt more sure of herself in its graceful *one, two, three* count.

Russell was the magnanimous host and perfect dance partner—accomplished, suave, handsome, debonair. Every woman he tangoed or two-stepped with found herself picture framed in his arms. In acknowledgment of his guests, he changed dance partners frequently and expected Gwen to do the same.

An odd moment came as she danced with a man she'd met at another of Russell's entertainments, a New York client to whom he significantly catered. Russell partnered his wife for the same dance and made a point of holding her at arm's length, admiring the band of blue and green stones on her bare upper arm before he twirled her to begin their foxtrot. She laughed, delighted with her jewelry and the man apparently responsible for it.

As the couples danced closer, Gwen ventured a glance at the woman's arm. The armlet didn't flash or shine but appeared quite old, heavy, and very familiar—a museum piece, she was certain. It wasn't until their second turn around the floor that Gwen remembered. *The armlet in the Cleopatra display . . . the one you showed me when I first came to Bennett Place. The one you said you sold to—to whom? Gainsbourg. The one you hand delivered to him in Chicago.*

What is it doing on Madeline Ingraham's arm now?

Gwen squinted, trying to focus. *Gainsbourg would never have sold it. It was a huge investment, and an anniversary gift for his wife. If this isn't the original . . . a reproduction? Does Madeline realize it's costume jewelry? She doesn't act like it.*

Frowning in concentration, she looked from the armlet to Russell. He caught her eye with a warning flash and subtle shake of his head. Stunned, she quickstepped when she should have slowed, causing her partner to stumble. "I'm so sorry, Mr. Ingraham. I don't know what's become of my timing." Slightly inebriated, the man was gracious enough. They made it to the end of the dance.

Later, across the punch bowl, Gwen admired Madeline's armlet.

"Yes, lovely, isn't it? Well, perhaps not by today's standards, but it's ancient, an original from Egyptian royalty, the only one in the world. Worth a fortune if the price is anything to go by," the woman confided, more than a little tipsy, pulling the armlet to dangle as a bracelet before Gwen. "Exquisite in its way."

"Original?"

"Oh, yes, Mr. Bennett brought it from Egypt himself and sold it to my husband. An investment, really, but Robbie said I could wear it tonight. I promised not to let anything happen to it." She leaned forward and stage-whispered, "At least it's insured!" The woman laughed.

It was nearly eleven thirty. Gwen was spent, her feet were killing her, and her head hurt. She didn't know what to think of the armlet or, even more, of Russell's clear warning. She'd all but turned a blind eye toward Russell's acquisition of alcohol that flowed freely at his dinners and parties, despite Prohibition, but how could he account for two identical "original" and one-of-a-kind armlets?

She excused herself, ostensibly for the powder room, but headed toward Alistair's room, intending to give herself time and space, and to close his door. He'd surely be asleep by now, and she didn't want the conversations or inebriated roaming guests to disturb him.

She reached the wide-open door of his room only to find Blanche Eustace, intoxicated heiress and flapper extraordinaire, the so-called wife of another of Russell's favorite clients, sitting on the edge of Alistair's bed, waving a French éclair from a plate full of delectable pastries under his nose.

"Just one bite. It can't possibly hurt, you poor, starving boy. They really should feed you."

Alistair's eyes widened. Before Gwen's aching head could take in just what was happening, before she could believe her eyes, Alistair shoved the éclair in his mouth.

Terror ripped through Gwen.

"No! Alistair, no!" She stumbled across the room in her heels. Shoving Blanche and her plate aside, she wrestled Alistair for the food. Though weak, he desperately fought her off, his mouth making as short work as possible of the mouthful he'd obtained. She pushed him back against the pillow, forcing open his mouth. With her finger she swiped out every bit she could. "Don't swallow it!"

Tears of rage, of desperation, hunger, and humiliation, sprang from Alistair's eyes. "Leave me alone!"

The woman on the floor screamed in fury and pain. "My wrist! Idiot woman! You broke my wrist!"

Gwen ignored her. "Alistair, think what you're doing. Please, please stop."

How much he'd actually swallowed, she couldn't tell. *How quickly will this take effect? Will he fall into a coma now? In a few hours? Dear God, please, God! Help him.*

Gwen hardly realized her own tears in the midst of Alistair's or the histrionics of the injured woman now on the floor amid a squashed sea of party pastries.

Blanche's ranting and raving brought a maid, who fetched Russell and Dr. Callahan—a guest Russell had expressly invited to talk sense into Gwen and one Gwen had studiously avoided all evening—from the ballroom.

At the sight of Blanche, still loudly bemoaning her insult more than her injury, Russell lifted her up, consoled her, and asked Dr. Callahan to tend to her injuries first. He shot Gwen and Alistair furious glances as he escorted her from the room.

Dr. Callahan's frown tarried on Alistair until Russell called him from the hallway. "As soon as I tend to Mrs. Eustace, I'll be back." The doctor's words were directed to Gwen but the concern in his eyes fixed on Alistair.

Once she'd removed as much of the éclair as was left, Gwen gave Alistair water to drink. He gulped it greedily until it ran down the sides of his mouth. She wiped his cheek and chin with the bedsheet and swiped the remainder of her tears with the back of her hand. "I'm sorry. I'm so very sorry it's this way, Alistair. But that éclair is deadly. You've got to remember that."

He didn't speak, but she saw him gulp, close his eyes, as if shutting her out.

"I love you. I only want what's best for you."

"To keep me alive." He spoke quietly, bitterly. "But I'm not living, Aunt Gwen."

"Yes, you are. We just have to keep going. They're working on a cure." But the assertion again sounded hollow.

She sat with him, neither of them speaking more until Dr. Callahan returned. The doctor brought in his bag and set it on the floor by Alistair's bed. He cast a withering glance Gwen's way but said to Alistair, "Now let's take a look at you, young man." He checked the pupils of Alistair's eyes, felt the glands in his neck, checked his pulse.

"I didn't mean to eat it. I couldn't help it."

Dr. Callahan nodded, pity in his eyes. "Let's take a listen." He pulled out his stethoscope, opened Alistair's pajama top, and pressing the scope to his frail chest, listened for a few moments. He stood, nodding.

"Dr. Callahan, we don't know how much Alistair ate—it was a French éclair. But it will raise his glucose—shoot it up. Is there anything we can do to bring it down quickly?"

Dr. Callahan wouldn't look at Gwen, didn't answer her directly. "Your mouth will likely feel very dry. Drink as much water as you can, Alistair. It will help to flush the kidneys. Beyond that . . . I recommend resting for the next couple of days. You may find yourself extra tired, sleepy, needing to urinate more frequently. If your vision becomes blurred, if you have headaches, be sure to lie down." He looked at Alistair's emaciated legs. "Are you still able to walk?"

"Sometimes, if it's not far." Alistair said it apologetically, as if he'd been slacking off.

"That's very good, Alistair." He gave a gentle reassuring pat to Alistair's arm. "Miss Armstrong, you will see me out." It was not so much a request as an order.

Gwen picked up the remnants of the pastries smashed into the carpet and took them with her.

Three feet beyond Alistair's closed door, the doctor turned on her. "You're killing the boy with this ridiculous starvation diet."

"He's alive, Dr. Callahan, beyond the few months to a year you gave him."

"He's suffering to no avail."

Gwen's heart beat furiously. How to explain? What could she say that made any sense? She remembered Mrs. Barrie's clipping. "Have you seen the Toronto paper? They've discovered a treatment for diabetes. Doctors there just tried it on a human patient. I've got to keep Alistair alive so—"

"For all we know that could be a snake oil cure—no cure at all. It's an experiment." He lengthened each syllable of his last word. "I cannot believe Russell Bennett sanctions such cruelty to his son. Is this the work of Dr. McNeill and his passion for Allen's work? If he's—"

"It has nothing to do with Dr. McNeill. Alistair was a patient at Dr. Allen's institute for months, at my discretion and with Russell's permission. It was my decision to bring him home and treat him with the same program here, as nearly as we can—a decision Dr. McNeill did not approve."

"Is Dr. McNeill—"

"Neither Alistair nor I have seen Dr. McNeill since last year. He has nothing to do with Alistair's care now and neither do you. I think it's time you checked on your other patient again, don't you, Dr. Callahan? She claimed her wrist is broken." Gwen's fury and fear warred within her, but she squared her shoulders and raised her chin. She'd no idea how much influence, how much power Dr. Callahan might wield over Russell. *He can't defer to this man. We can't give up now.*

Dr. Callahan's mouth turned grim. He shifted his medical bag and gave a stiff nod. "I'll say good evening, Miss Armstrong," he said, emphasizing the *Miss*. He stopped partway down the hall and spoke over his shoulder. "Call if Alistair needs me, if he begins vomiting, though at that point there's little can be done."

Horrified, Gwen waited until he'd turned the corner at the end of the hallway before returning to Alistair's room. Alistair lay staring at the ceiling.

"Alistair."

"I want to be alone."

"I'd like to sit with you, at least for a while, if I may."

"I need to be alone."

Gwen racked her brain, trying to remember all that Dr. Allen had said about possible effects and the timing of those things should his blood sugar stay too high too long. She closed her eyes. She didn't want to leave him. She wanted to stay and watch him sleep, watch him breathe, make certain he lived through the night.

"Is there anything I can get you? I can fill your water carafe."

"No."

Alistair was thirteen years old now, a young man. So much had been taken from him in life; she couldn't steal his last vestige of pride. She couldn't tell him how to think or what to do. She couldn't control him any more than she could control the diabetes. Those decisions were uniquely his.

"Yes. All right. Ring the bell if you need me."

"I won't."

You won't ring the bell, or you won't need me? Both thoughts cut like a knife through Gwen's heart. She went to kiss his forehead, but he turned his face away. "I'll see you in the morning, then." *Please, God, let it be so.*

He didn't respond.

She walked out, her heart weighted, and closed the door.

On the other side of the door stood Mrs. Barrie, waiting. She linked her arm in Gwen's and walked her down the hallway and into another corridor. "I heard what happened, at least one version. Is he all right?"

Gwen shook her head, very near tears. "I don't know. That stupid woman gave him an éclair—from a plate full of pastries. I don't know how much he ate, or if he ate. But he fought me for it. He's starving, Cora—he's starving, and I literally pulled food from his mouth."

Mrs. Barrie's arms encircled her, rubbing her back, as Gwen cried bitter tears.

38

On Saturday, Russell was reportedly too angry with Gwen and too busy shutting down the rumor mill among his guests and clients to speak with her. Gwen counted that information from Mrs. Barrie a blessing but knew that eventually the other shoe would drop.

She worried what that might mean for her status in the household—her presence—but of greater importance was her need to repair her relationship with Alistair.

Should I act as if nothing happened, as if everything is the same? Should I ask his forgiveness? Is he irritable because of what happened? Is his blood sugar level making him more so? Gwen didn't have the answers to any of those questions. She only knew that given the same circumstances as the night of the party, she would make the same brutal choice.

Heavy on her mind was Dr. Allen's motto, engraved on the brass paperweight on his desk at the institute: *The less food, the more life.* It had become her mantra for Alistair. So far, it had worked. He was still alive, months after Dr. Callahan had predicted him dead and gone. Each day brought them closer to whatever possibility of cure there might be. That's what Malcolm had said. That's what she held on to, despite her acting as if she didn't believe—her only self-protection mechanism.

But would he make it? Would she? Sometimes she feared she might crack.

When she stopped in Alistair's room Saturday morning, he was still sleeping. She needed to know his sleep was not a coma.

Mrs. Barrie brought his tea and breakfast. When she set the tray on the side table, he stirred. Gwen sighed in relief.

But he gagged on breakfast, sending Mrs. Barrie and Gwen scrambling for towels, a basin, water.

"I'm okay. I'm okay," he sputtered, swiping at his mouth.

Dr. Callahan said once you start vomiting, there may be little that can be done. Gwen felt the bile rise in her own throat. "Relax, Alistair. Breathe. Breathe deeply, slowly." It was all she could think to say.

He closed his eyes, nodding, and breathed slowly, evenly. After a few moments he reached for Gwen's hand. "I think I'm okay now."

"Praise God!" Mrs. Barrie heaved a sigh.

Gwen breathed in unison, not realizing she'd been holding her breath. She sat on the edge of Alistair's bed, still holding his hand.

"I don't think I want to eat anything now. Maybe that will help bring my glucose level down."

Gwen gently squeezed his hand. He squeezed back.

Mrs. Barrie took his water carafe away to wash and fill, saying, "I'll be back in two shakes of a lamb's tail."

The click of her heels faded down the hallway.

"I've been thinking, Aunt Gwen."

"Yes?"

"I don't know how much longer I can hang on. You need to let me go."

Fear gripped Gwen's heart.

"You need to surrender me to God. Whatever He does is best for me. I trust that. You need to trust Him too."

Trusting, relying on anyone else, even God, goes against everything in me. Gwen shuddered. "I can't let you go. You're all that's left to me."

"If you love me, you'll do as I ask. You'll try. Promise me."

Tears streamed down Gwen's face, much as she didn't want them to. "How? How can I possibly do that?"

"Talk to Mrs. Barrie. Talk to Malcolm. Pray—talk to God. He's not afraid of your anger or your tears. There's a verse in Psalms—Malcolm showed me when I was at the institute—where it says God collects our tears in a bottle. He counts them precious." Alistair wiped her cheek with the corner of his sheet and smiled.

Gwen couldn't see anything to smile about. She couldn't imagine surrendering Alistair or talking to Malcolm after their last encounter. She couldn't imagine going to Mrs. Barrie for more talk about God when she'd so rudely pushed her friend away.

The conversation stopped when Mrs. Barrie entered the room with water and a vase of fresh flowers dripping red hearts left over from the ball. The irony of bleeding hearts was too great for Gwen.

Gwen checked on Alistair throughout the day, but he slept through most of it. Still, there was no more vomiting, and for that she was immensely relieved.

She thought of Alistair's wishes. She'd do anything to please him, but she couldn't fake trust. That needed to be real. *Surrender. How can I surrender when I'm this afraid? This angry?*

She tried reading the Bible Russell had given her, the one that had belonged to Marion. But she hardly knew where to begin. She'd heard people say to start by reading the Gospel of John, but the closest thing she found to expressing her feelings was in Psalms, the book Alistair had mentioned.

She remembered the pastor at church talking about crying out to the Lord in anguish. He'd called it *lament* and said the Psalms were filled with lament—he'd particularly read Psalm 77, by a man named Asaph. It had taken Gwen by surprise; she'd never known it was okay to rant and rave before God. She'd always believed that if she cried out in her anguish, God would punish her, or worse yet, might pull the rug from under Alistair. It's what her own father had done, promising to bring home his paycheck for food and the mortgage, then using it to buy drink and locking himself away in his home office. Could a heavenly Father be any different?

She looked through Marion's Bible until she found Psalm 77. It began, *"I cried unto God with my voice, even unto God with my voice; and he gave ear unto me."*

Do You hear me, God?

She felt kinship with Asaph when she read, *"My soul refused to be comforted."*

I feel a stubborn resistance to comfort. It feels false, untrue, a trick. "I am so troubled that I cannot speak." Exactly. That's exactly how I feel. "Hath God forgotten to be gracious? Hath he in anger shut up his tender mercies?" Have You shut up Your mercies—Your compassion? What is the answer, Lord? Tell me!

Gwen kept reading.

"I will remember the years of the right hand of the most High. I will remember the works of the Lord: surely I will remember thy wonders of old. I will meditate also of all thy work, and talk of thy doings."

Gwen stopped. She didn't want to meditate on God's works of the past. She wanted Him to heal Alistair now, today.

She closed the Bible.

Gwen had hoped Russell would not be dining at home Saturday evening, but he was, and called for Gwen to join him. It was not a casual invitation.

There was no conversation over dinner. When Russell asked her to join him in the drawing room, she knew it would not be for a quiet game of chess. He closed the door.

Once they were seated on opposite sides of the fire, he stared at her. "I've spent the better part of last night and today in an attempt to salvage the disaster you created last night."

"I'm sorry for the upset."

"Upset? Is that what you call it?" Tendons in his neck visibly strained. "You knocked a guest, a very important guest, to the floor, with dire consequences!"

"She claimed her wrist was broken. Was it?" Gwen held her breath.

"A sprain, but you humiliated her."

"She could have killed Alistair. I was intent on saving your son's life." She would not be cowed.

Russell closed his eyes, swore under his breath. "He's dying, Gwen. Don't you get that? Don't you see?"

Tears sprang to her eyes. "Of course I see. I'm trying to keep him alive."

"Word has spread that I'm keeping my son cruelly locked in a room where I allow my 'kept woman' to starve him to death."

"They don't understand—and besides, I'm not a 'kept woman.' That's ridiculous and insulting to us both."

"Aren't you? A kept woman?"

Gwen felt her skin prickle. Heat rose up her chest, flushing her neck and face and arms. "How dare you! I came to care for your family—*your family*—while you were off traipsing the world! And now I'm caring for your ill son."

"You're killing him, and I've stood by and let you. Blanche imagines you're trying to get rid of him under the guise of protecting him, that we're waiting until he's out of the way so we can start fresh, unencumbered."

"That's a vile thing to say! You know that if we can only keep him alive until—"

"A cure, yes, I know. The almighty apple-pie-in-the-sky cure. Dr. Callahan thinks you're demented and I should send you away."

Gwen's heart raced. *What will become of Alistair?* "Is that what you want?"

"What I want is for you to give up this insanity. It's killing Alistair. It's dragging you down with him. It's ruining my reputation and endangering everything I've built." Russell snorted. "What I wanted was for you to be the dazzling woman you were on the dance floor last night, the impeccable hostess you are capable of being. I wanted you to marry me, Gwen, but what I need in you is a partner, not a liability."

For all the times Gwen had wondered if she might indeed wish to marry Russell someday, she suddenly found clarity. "A partner in crime?"

He bristled and swore.

"How is it that Madeline Ingraham wore the armlet last night—identical in every way to the one you sold to Mr. Gainsbourg in Chicago? Both owners declare them originals, straight from the tombs of Egyptian royalty. How is that possible?"

He grimaced. She could imagine his teeth grinding, but she wouldn't stop.

"And while we're speaking of crime, where does all the liquor come from—New York's docks, Atlantic City? And where before that? Who are the thugs that have invaded your house, that beat you up? What do you have to do with the White Hand Gang? Who is W. B.?" Gwen knew the answers to most of those questions, but she needed to force Russell's confession before "Wild Bill" of the White Hand Gang put a bullet through his head. Perhaps she could yet save him from himself and save Alistair in the process.

"How do you know—" Russell momentarily paled before fury took over, but she refused to stop.

"Where do the delivery trucks and well-heeled cars go once they've taken their booty from your locked rooms and cellar—all during this era of Prohibition? You're going to get yourself arrested or killed!"

"My business is none—"

"Yes, none of my business, I know. If you treated your son with a quarter of the concern you treat your business, he'd—"

"I can't deal with another dying soul!" Fists clenched, Russell pushed from his chair in desperation.

"Then let me. Leave his care to me. If I fail, I fail. But I'm not willing to give up on him like your Dr. Callahan."

Russell glared at her. She visualized steam shooting from his nostrils. He walked to the fire, picked up the poker, hefted it in his hand, and savagely poked the burning logs. Flares of embers shot high. "You're not as compliant as your sister was."

"No." Gwen squared her shoulders. *Compliance did not serve Marion well. She did not gain the respect she deserved from you.*

Two long minutes passed. Neither spoke as Russell continued staring into the fire. Finally, he walked to the sideboard and poured himself a glass of brandy—double the size of his usual. "I'll postpone dinner parties. We need time for this to blow over, to wait until someone else's societal faux pas takes over the rumor mill."

Gwen inwardly sighed in relief.

"It's best if I'm out of sight for a few months. There are things I can do in Egypt. By the time I return, someone else will headline the gossip."

"Egypt? If you go away now, I don't know if Alistair—"

He cut her off. "I leave on Monday. You can take care of things until I get back, I presume . . . you and Mrs. Barrie. Ignore the comings and goings of my clients. They know what to do."

"When will you—"

"I don't know when I'll be back. May, at the earliest. Possibly later."

Questions ripe with accusations and fear of repercussions ran rampant in Gwen's mind, but she knew better than to ask. *Leave it alone.* "And Alistair?"

Russell downed his brandy in two long gulps and headed for the door. "Do as you wish." He hesitated, his hand on the door. "By the time I return, things should be settled."

39

Malcolm boarded the train to Washington, DC, in May. Professor Macleod of Toronto was slated to present a paper to the Association of American Physicians—his official announcement of the discovery of insulin, a miracle in the treatment of diabetes.

Doctors flocked to the presentation from far and wide, desperate to witness the climactic moment, desperate to learn everything they could on behalf of their dying patients.

Even as Professor Macleod spoke, Malcolm begged God that Alistair might hold on to life long enough to receive the crucial injections. The miracle had not come in time for his precious Sheenagh. That was an ache in his heart that would never dim, never leave. But if he could help Alistair, and other children he'd yet to treat, he would praise his Maker.

After the professor's presentation, the room went crazy. The standing applause was deafening. Malcolm wasn't the only doctor shedding tears of relief and gratitude and surely of remembrance.

Headlines raced around the globe. Just as quickly doctors everywhere begged for supplies of insulin for their dying patients. There was next to none to be had. Mass production on a grand scale was required to supply enough insulin for those desperately in need, but how that could happen, Malcolm had no idea.

In late May, Malcolm drove to Rochester, New York, to meet with Dr. John Williams, who treated twenty-two-year-old James Havens. James had been diagnosed with diabetes seven long years before. In 1919, when his metabolism became dangerously unstable, Havens spent over a month with Dr. Allen at his institute. Since that time, despite the stabilizing of the starvation diet, he'd continued to decline. He now weighed a mere seventy-three and a half pounds.

"Not much more than a skeleton," Dr. Williams told Malcolm. "Before insulin he cried most of the time. I'd estimated him a week to live."

"Please, Doctor, tell me everything." Malcolm held his breath.

"Dr. Banting of Toronto gave me the insulin. It didn't seem to make much difference at first, but once Banting tripled the dose, James began showing signs of improvement. I can't say yet what will be long-term, but Banting's promised to keep me supplied for James, as long as it doesn't get to the papers. You understand that, don't you, Dr. McNeill? You can't say a word."

Malcolm nodded, knowing the importance of keeping James alive, but he wanted to shout this news from the housetops. Most of all, he wanted to get insulin for Alistair. The lad was fading week by week according to Mrs. Barrie.

Dr. Williams had no insulin to spare. Malcolm determined to go to the source. If he could get a steady supply or convince Dr. Banting to take Alistair under his care in Toronto, he felt sure the lad's life could be saved.

He wrote Dr. Banting before the end of May. He telegraphed Dr. Banting in early June. He telephoned in mid-June. When none of those brought the response he craved, he drove to Toronto in July. According to Mrs. Barrie, Alistair was still hanging on. Now that a treatment was available, Malcolm would not take no for an answer.

"Admit the lad to your care, Dr. Banting, I beg you. I'll bring him myself. He's held on this long." Malcolm had not obtained permission from Gwen or from Russell Bennett, but if the doctor granted his request, he'd convince them to let him bring Alistair. He was sure

Mrs. Barrie would help him persuade Gwen, and Gwen was the neck that turned Bennett's head.

Dr. Banting, as a professional courtesy and favor to Professor Macleod, allowed Malcolm to join him as he walked his rounds. The diabetic clinic for Toronto General was not yet open, so Dr. Banting had his private patients rent rooms about a half mile from his office. Most were in the Athelma Apartments, so he could walk from room to room, floor to floor and see them one after another. There Malcolm saw the state of things. Skeletal children with gaunt, hollow cheeks, dark shadows beneath sunken and lifeless eyes, distended stomachs, and little to no hair. Even Alistair had not reached this point, according to Mrs. Barrie.

"There are problems beyond discovery," Dr. Banting confided. "We've not found a consistent means of establishing purity or a stable potency. It's impossible to know precisely the required dosage for each patient. You must understand that I've only taken the direst cases—cases where the patient would surely die soon without intervention."

"Human experiments," Malcolm whispered.

Dr. Banting did not deny it. "I'm deluged with hundreds of pleas from doctors and parents and patients themselves begging to come here, to be treated with insulin, declaring it a matter of life and death. I understand. I do not have insulin now to keep my patients alive. I cannot take more. Perhaps in September, write to me again. Things may be different then. I can't promise."

Malcolm saw and understood. He drove home with warring discouragement and elation in his mind. September seemed impossibly far away given Alistair's reportedly deteriorating condition. He was going off weekly reports from Mrs. Barrie at church; he'd not actually seen Alistair for months, not been invited to the home, not had a word in person with Gwen, and Dr. Callahan had renewed his warning to stay away.

After meeting with Dr. Williams and now Dr. Banting, Malcolm knew that the insulin produced was as little and rare and unlikely to be obtained as discovering a cache of gold doubloons in the middle of New York. It might be a long time before it could be made commercially available. The small initial supply would not be doled out to individual patients living in homes across the country. It would most likely be given first to notable, vetted doctors. Dr. Frederick Allen was a likely candidate. If only Malcolm could convince Gwen to return Alistair to the Physiatric Institute, he might have a chance of getting some of that early supply. *Lord, if this is Your will, provide the opening, I pray.*

Alone in his room the night of his return to New York, Malcolm wrote another letter to Alistair, not unlike the many letters of encouragement and spiritual counsel he'd written to the lad since Christmas, the ones he'd given to Mrs. Barrie to hand deliver. He wasn't certain mail posted from him would be passed along to Alistair, and Mrs. Barrie was glad to foster the relationship, taking Malcolm's letters and gifts, and bringing him Alistair's letters in return.

Despite his great hope for insulin's work, Malcolm promised nothing in the way of a cure for diabetes but encouraged Alistair to hold on. Above all, he pointed the lad to the Great Physician, the one who loved him with everlasting love and would care for him eternally. He encouraged him to spend time with the Lord and to pursue, as he was able, his interest in the gifts and passions God had given him. He finished every letter with the admonition to remember, *God has a plan and purpose for your life, Alistair. Never doubt that.*

Folding the letter and placing it in its envelope, he sank to his knees and commended Alistair and each one of his patients to the care of Almighty God, the prayer he prayed each night.

The first Sunday in August, Malcolm looked for Mrs. Barrie, whom he'd come to sit with each week, eager for her report of Alistair and hoping to exchange letters. He was surprised to see Gwen beside her. He'd not seen Gwen since December, more than seven months before. He'd never say it to a lady, but she looked tired and worn, and that concerned him.

He wasn't certain he'd be welcome to join them. He tried to catch Mrs. Barrie's eye, knowing she could warn him either way, but Gwen looked up first.

"Dr. McNeill." Her eyes grew wide.

"Miss Armstrong." Malcolm gave a slight bow.

"Ah, Malcolm." Mrs. Barrie smiled. "Won't you join us?"

Malcolm looked to Gwen. "If I may?"

Gwen looked a bit flustered. "Yes, of course, please do." She moved farther down the pew.

Malcolm wondered if Mrs. Barrie had sat on the inside of the pew by design, forcing Malcolm to sit beside Gwen. But he had little time to contemplate that as the service began.

There were not enough hymnbooks in the pew for every participant to have their own. Mrs. Barrie offered to share with the woman to her right. Malcolm could only offer to share with Gwen, which flustered them both. The more he tried to hold the book and give her space, the more often it seemed their hands brushed. He hadn't meant for that to happen, and felt an electric current shoot up his arm each time it did, no matter that her hand was gloved.

Whatever the pastor said in that service was a mystery to Malcolm. He couldn't keep his mind on anything but the nearness of Gwen. He ran a mental scourge, reminding himself that she'd all but ousted him from her home, ignored his medical advice, no longer sought his services for Alistair, and was in some kind of relationship with Russell Bennett—a relationship he didn't understand. He should be miffed; he should be pitied; he should be angry; he was mightily attracted to the woman—the argument in his head ran on and on.

Why are you here, Gwen? Has something happened to Alistair? Please, God, not that. Have you realized your need for God? Been willing to surrender to Him? Please, God.

When the last hymn was sung, the last prayer said, and the benediction given, Malcolm drew a breath and turned to Gwen. "It's good to see you, Miss Armstrong." He held out his hand.

Gwen ignored his hand or perhaps didn't see it. "It's good to see you too, Malcolm."

Malcolm. She said my name—my Christian name. "It's been a long while. Too long."

She looked at Mrs. Barrie, perhaps for reinforcement, then back to Malcolm. "I owe you an apology."

"No, you do not owe me anything—"

"I was unforgivably rude to you and I'm sorry. It's no excuse for my behavior, but I didn't understand why you insisted, why you felt so passionate about returning Alistair to Dr. Allen's care. I was foolish and arrogant." She looked at her hands, then deeply into Malcolm's eyes. "I didn't realize you understood—that you'd lost your daughter to diabetes. That was horrible, surely. I'm so sorry. I'm so very sorry. I hope we can be friends again."

"Of course. I'd like that very much." Malcolm's heart lifted while his eyes filled. "I accept your apology. There was no way you could have known." Over Gwen's shoulder, he saw Mrs. Barrie smile.

"Malcolm," Mrs. Barrie said, "I've told Gwen about the letters you and Alistair exchange. Well, not I, really. Alistair told her."

"They've been a great help to him, a great encouragement. He told me so. He said they've kept him going. I don't know how to thank you."

"It's been my pleasure, a gift to me as well as to him. Alistair's a fine lad, and a great heart for the Lord."

"I know that now. I didn't always. He's teaching me."

"Is he now? I'm glad for you both. What greater purpose could he have than to share the love of Christ with the one he loves best?" Malcolm smiled, sending Gwen every bit of sincerity and encouragement he could.

Gwen blushed. "He means the world to me."

"I know he does."

Mrs. Barrie interrupted. "Do you have time to stop for a cup of tea, Dr. McNeill? We'll need to be getting home to Alistair soon, but I think we've a bit of catching up to do. I'm eager to hear about your trip to Toronto, and I think Miss Armstrong—Gwen—is too."

Malcolm couldn't be more pleased—or hopeful.

Over tea in the very shop where he'd first met the women together, Malcolm shared all that he'd learned in Washington, in New York, and in Toronto.

"So, you're saying there's no real hope for Alistair to get this insulin?" Gwen's face paled.

"Not yet, I canna lie. But it will be available in time. There's a company here in the US, the Eli Lilly company, working on its production."

"We're running out of time. Alistair can barely sit up in bed, propped by pillows."

Mrs. Barrie covered Gwen's trembling hand with her own and asked, "Is there anything we can do to get Alistair on some kind of list or move him up on a list to receive it?"

Malcolm pushed back from the table. "I wish there were. I begged Dr. Banting to take Alistair as one of his patients in Toronto, but he—"

"You what?" Gwen pulled away from Mrs. Barrie's hand in shock.

"I only wanted to see if he'd be willing to—"

"You had no right." Gwen's eyes flashed.

Malcolm was dumbfounded. The woman had just apologized to him, acknowledged that she now knew how he'd suffered the loss of his own daughter—that he wanted the very best for Alistair. "I had no intention of kidnapping the lad, if that's what you're thinking. I was only trying to see what help there might be to save his life. Toronto is where the insulin is. It's the first and right now the only place to get it."

Mrs. Barrie intervened. "Do you hear yourselves, the two of you? You both want the best for Alistair. You both want him to stay alive long enough to get the insulin. Think how you can work together, not at odds with one another." Her eyes met Malcolm's, but he knew her words were equally directed to Gwen.

"I don't want him going to Toronto. He'd not survive the trip, he's so weak." Gwen wound the napkin in her lap. "He needs to be home, to have the insulin delivered." She looked up at Malcolm. "You could inject him. You could administer the correct dosage."

"Dr. Banting won't send it directly to me. He'll send his earliest supply to doctors treating multiple patients, like Dr. Allen. I think, if you can get Dr. Allen to take Alistair back, there's a chance—"

"No. Alistair's too weak to go. He needs to be home with us. We're able to keep him to the diet. Dr. Allen can do no more than that."

"You've done a remarkable thing, keeping Alistair this well this long. I only mean that his best chance of getting insulin is through Dr. Allen, and I know he has enough patients of his own that he'll treat those at his institute first."

"You said this Dr. Williams received insulin from Dr. Banting to treat the Havens young man. You said James is the son of a vice president of Eastman Kodak. That means he's wealthy. Money is no object where Alistair is concerned. His father can afford—"

"I never said money is the reason Dr. Banting treated him. I don't know why Dr. Banting made that decision. I only know that Dr. Allen is far more likely to receive insulin than a doctor in a small private practice or than individuals at home."

Gwen stood. "Thank you, Dr. McNeill. I'll take my chances. If money talks, I can convince this Dr. Banting."

Malcolm rose too. "I don't see how, Miss Armstrong. Time is of the essence. You know that. You're making a mistake."

Gwen's color shot up her neck. "I disagree. Let's leave it at that." She reached out to shake his hand.

He didn't want to let it go but had no alternative.

"Are you coming, Mrs. Barrie?"

Mrs. Barrie didn't look up but felt the teapot. "Oh, I think I'll stay and have another cuppa. It's still hot. You don't mind, do you?" She smiled.

"Of course not. I'll see you at home."

Malcolm felt a stiff breeze blow through the door as Gwen walked out. He stared after her, dismally conscious of his failure to convince her, and of what that might mean for Alistair.

"Sit down, Malcolm, and take some sugar in your tea. You need it for shock."

"I didna handle that well."

"You handled it just fine. She's afraid and that's put a bee in her bonnet. She'll get over it."

"But will it be in time for Alistair?"

"I don't know. But God knows, and He's not done working."

"How is Alistair, really?"

"Not well. It's as she said: He's in bed all the time now, barely able to sit up enough to eat what little we give the poor lad. He's not given up, but he's not afraid to go either. Your letters mean the world to him. I read his Bible to him each day, and she reads him all manner of things to do with digging up bones in Egypt. His eyes light at those things, and the lad finds ways to connect what she reads to Bible stories in ways I never imagined. He's a clever clogs."

"She said Alistair is teaching her to know God. Is it working?"

Mrs. Barrie shook her head as she poured them both cups of tea with two sugars. "Traveling the Nile past all those showy pagan idols is a slow and cumbersome path to reach the Lamb of God, but she'll get there in time. The great Father is not done with her yet, just as He's not done with any of us. You mind that."

40

Gwen had no intention of sending Alistair away but every intention of getting the insulin he desperately needed. Russell, who without explanation had not returned from Egypt until early August, had given her cart blanche where his son and his checkbook were concerned. She'd taken full charge of the former but had rarely taken advantage of the latter. That, she determined, was about to change.

Since returning to the US, he'd spent little time at home and none with Alistair, despite bringing lavish gifts for him and Gwen from Egypt. Gwen was grateful for the British books of historic digs in Egypt and the many maps he'd brought Alistair from Cairo at her behest. They gave her fascinating things to read to her nephew and to talk about, to dream about. But she was glad Russell was away now. She felt no compunction to ask his permission for what she was about to do.

After his trip to Egypt had defused his temper over the Valentine affair, he'd left a key to his museum and office in Mrs. Barrie's care, to be used only in case of emergency—fire, for instance.

Well, this is an emergency if ever there was one, and it's an emergency Mrs. Barrie best know nothing about. Directly home from the tea shop, Gwen tiptoed into the housekeeper's sitting room. She found Mrs. Barrie's house keys in her desk drawer, including, she trusted, ones to Russell's museum and office. She slipped the ring into her pocket.

With any luck, she'd get it back in place before Mrs. Barrie returned. Gwen imagined the housekeeper and Malcolm were having a good long natter about her poor behavior. But she couldn't afford to care.

Making certain neither Tilley nor Mr. Dornby was within hearing, she made her way to the west wing, unlocked the museum door with the key marked *M*, and slipped inside. It was light enough once she pulled open one of the drapes just a bit.

She hadn't been in the museum in months. At any other time, she'd be curious as to exactly what Russell displayed. Since his most recent trip to Egypt, he'd had clients in to peruse his acquisitions, but this time he'd not told her about them, not invited her to see. He was cordial, but his ardor toward her had clearly cooled. She wasn't sorry.

It took some time, but she finally found the key to fit Russell's office door. Inside was completely dark. There were no windows. She'd not realized that when she'd been in once before. She must have left the door open that time. She spread her fingers across the wall beside the door but found no light switch. She stumbled across the room toward the desk and fumbled for the lamp pull.

Flooded with light, the room looked sterile and smelled of old wax. Nothing out of place, and not a sound could be heard from outside or anywhere inside the house. *The room is soundproof. Why?* Unaccountably, chills raced up her arms.

Focus, Gwen, focus. Get in. Get out. All she needed was letterhead and envelopes. She'd use her own pen in her own room to write Dr. Banting, but she needed the authoritative, ostentatious letterhead of a man who could pay any amount for his dying son's care.

She crossed the room to the gigantic desk. Nothing sat atop the desk but the polished gold pen and inkwell set, the heavy gold Egyptian paperweight she'd seen before, and a lethal-looking letter opener. *No pictures. Nothing else.*

Gwen prayed the desk was not locked. It was. *What to do? Where would he keep a key?* She searched every available pot or trinket on the shelves behind the desk, everywhere she could imagine a man might hide a key. Flummoxed, she sat in his desk chair and looked over the room. *Does he keep the only key in his pocket? No, if he lost it, what then? Where? Somewhere convenient, easily accessible, but out of sight.* She ran her fingers beneath the desk chair, beneath the middle of the desk, along the legs.

Wait. A crack in the wood? She ran her fingers over the inside leg again. It wasn't visible in the dim light but there was what felt like a hairline slit in the wood. She pressed it and it popped open. *Bingo.*

She pulled the key from its hiding place. It fit perfectly.

Pulling open the middle drawer, she found pens, pencils, a ledger. She opened the top right desk drawer. *A pistol, a very big pistol. What are you doing with this, Russell?*

She picked it up, remembering the night the thugs came to beat out of him whatever it was they'd wanted. *Money, a guarantee to stay off the docks of New York and off their turf? Did you get this for protection? Have you ever fired it, used it on anyone?* Gwen set it carefully on the desk, not knowing if it was loaded.

She glanced through papers shoved into the drawer. *No letterhead stationery. What's this?* She pulled out a sheaf of papers: bills of lading, photographs and sketches of Egyptian purchases, each page stamped with a logo depicting the pyramids of Egypt. Each bill of lading listed multiple orders of specific items: bracelets, rings, other things she didn't recognize, but all sounding old.

Gwen sat back. *He's ordering reproductions of artifacts—and not just known costume jewelry as he led me to believe. Having extraordinary pieces handcrafted and selling them as if they're originals. The two armlets—identical, "one of a kind," worn by that woman from Chicago, Mrs. Gainsbourg, and by Madeline Ingraham here.* Gwen shut her eyes tight. *Russell, you fool. They paid a fortune for those. When they find out, they'll—* She dared not complete the thought, but the beating he'd received at the hands of other business associates flashed through her mind.

She shoved the papers back into the drawer and replaced the pistol. Then she pulled open the middle desk drawer and took out a long book, a ledger, marked *Egypt*. She perused page after page, column after column, year after year going back to days before the beginning of the war.

A second book lay beneath the first. The first couple of pages listed the names and contact information for pharmacies, doctors and dentists, restaurant owners, even politicians and police officials. The second section devoted entire pages to dates of purchase and pickup—begun in more recent years—and transactions with those individuals or companies. The third section listed suppliers, some within the country and some from outside. *Bootleggers.*

Russell. You're in way over your head in everything imaginable . . . all of it illegal. You're going to be found out. You're going to get caught. Her pulse throbbing and her head pounding, Gwen put everything back, careful to make it look as if it had never been disturbed. *Before it all comes crashing down, you're going to spend every penny needed to help your son, even if it bankrupts you. Dr. Banting needs money for his research, for his patients, for his production of insulin. You, my dear brother-in-law, are going to pay it.*

She found the letterhead and envelopes in the top drawer on the left-hand side of the desk. While she was at it, she may as well take extra sheets, just in case she needed to write more than once, or to more than one place.

Gwen locked the desk and returned the key to its hiding place. Opening the office door for light, she turned off the desk lamp.

As she pulled the door wider, she heard a key fit into the lock of the outside door down the hallway. Her heart jumped to her throat. *It can't be Russell. He's not due back until the end of the week.*

Footsteps, then voices came from down the hallway. "Pick that lock—no good busting it. We don't want to let on until the boss is ready to blow him out of the water. We get the proof and he's ours."

Softly she closed the door, locking it from the inside. She couldn't hear a thing outside the room, couldn't tell if someone came down the hallway, if they walked through the museum or where they'd gone. She remembered the thugs she'd met, the ones who'd threatened her, the ruffians who'd beat up Russell, and conversely, Mrs. Barrie's belief that Tammany Hall and certain police officers might be in on the profits. She also knew that federal investigators searched for incriminating evidence to prosecute those running and selling whiskey. She had no idea who the men were. And no wish to find out.

Gwen crawled beneath the desk and waited. Time passed. How much time, she had no idea.

When the call of nature came loud and clear, she crawled from beneath the desk and across the room, feeling her way. Finally she stood, quietly unlocked the door, and opened it a crack.

Footsteps hurried down the hallway. A grunt, swearing, as if they carried something heavy. The outside door opened and closed. The lock turned. Moments later a motor gunned.

Gwen opened the door wider, slipped through, locked it from the outside, and in her stocking feet scurried across the museum floor. She stopped, remembering to close the drape. Outside the museum she ran up the hallway. The door to the west wing hallway remained locked, just as she'd left it. Slipping through, she locked it again and walked quickly toward the kitchen.

She heard Mrs. Barrie's voice coming from outside Alistair's room. She'd no idea the time of day, though the light through the foyer window looked dim. She hurried through the kitchen and down the hallway to Mrs. Barrie's sitting room, slipped in, left the ring of keys in the desk. As she closed the sitting room door behind her, she met Mrs. Barrie in the hallway.

Mrs. Barrie stopped, surprised. "Were you looking for me?"

"Yes, yes, I was," Gwen answered. "I wondered what is on the menu for Alistair's supper this evening. I was going to offer to make it for him—give you an evening off."

Mrs. Barrie blinked. "That's very kind of you, Miss Armstrong, but I've just given him his evening tea."

"Oh, I see. I'm sorry I didn't speak sooner."

"I didn't see you when I returned. I thought perhaps you'd gone out."

"No, no, I was reading and lost track of the time." Gwen hid the letterhead behind her skirt, but Mrs. Barrie cocked her head, studying her.

"I see . . . By the by, Alistair was asking for you."

"Thank you, I'll see him before I go up."

"Well, if that's all then."

"Yes. Have a good evening, Mrs. Barrie. I'll see you in the morning." Gwen backed away from the housekeeper. As she turned to walk up the hallway, she switched the letterhead to her front, determined to keep a steady, unsuspecting pace.

Finally in her room, her heart still beating rapidly, she let out a long breath of relief. She didn't know who'd been in the hallway while she'd hidden in Russell's office, but it was clearly someone determined to expose him and see him taken down. *For the fake artifacts or the bootleg liquor? Thugs, police, disgruntled clients, federal investigators?* The possibilities seemed endless, and yet there was no one she could go to for help. She dared not warn Russell and admit what she'd done, what she'd discovered. She wasn't about to ask Malcolm for help or to involve Mrs. Barrie with what she'd learned or what she planned.

If what she was about to do came crashing down on her own head, so be it.

Gwen picked up her pen. Promising a fortune and forging Russell's signature in a letter to Dr. Banting might be the least of her—or Russell's—troubles.

41

After church one Sunday in late September, Malcolm was sorry to see that Gwen was not with Mrs. Barrie. He asked the older woman how Alistair was doing.

"Poorly. Hanging on—just. I don't know what else to say. It's heartbreaking, watching the lad."

Malcolm closed his eyes to gain control of his emotions. "Has Miss Armstrong reconsidered sending him to Dr. Allen?"

"No, I don't think she will send him away again. I think she may be giving up hope."

"Hope is exactly what there is, if she's not too stubborn."

"She told me she wrote to that Dr. Banting you mentioned in Toronto. She even telephoned him, begging him to take Alistair, promising him a fortune if he'd do so. He took her call, but he won't take Alistair, money or no money. He told her he's barely got enough insulin for his own patients and canna take another. She's tried to force her way—written and telephoned everywhere she can think of trying to get hold of insulin. She thinks if she can just get Alistair one good strong injection that it might—"

"It doesn't work that way. They still don't know the proper dosage. Too much can be worse than too little, and it must be consistent, continuous. Overdoses will send patients into hypoglycemic shock—doctors in Chicago and Rochester have had patients die."

Mrs. Barrie's hand flew to her mouth. "It's dangerous, then!"

Malcolm shook his head. "The proper dosage, the purity, the stability, let alone the availability—there's just so much unknown as yet. Dr. Allen is dealing with that very thing."

"Dr. Allen has insulin?"

"Aye, well, he did have. I spoke with him on Friday. He received a small supply of Eli Lilly insulin last month. On August tenth he spread that among six of his weakest patients. Because of the risk of overdosing, he injected each less than one unit. He said the results were dramatic as the patients regained strength."

"Does he have more?"

"Not yet, but he's one of the first doctors who will receive more once it's available. That's why I urged Gwen to take Alistair there."

"I don't think it's the taking him that worries her; it's the leaving him there. She doesn't want him to be alone, or to die alone, and she wants to be with him. She needs to be with him."

"Precisely how every parent feels." Malcolm snorted in frustration. "But her wants and needs canna supersede his need for life!"

"Would they let her go with him? Do you think Dr. Allen would allow her to live at the institute with Alistair?"

Malcolm considered. "He's overcrowded and understaffed as it is. They'll not be wanting to feed an extra mouth."

"Then they need help. She's cared for Alistair a long time. Perhaps she could—"

"Miss Armstrong is not a trained nurse."

"No, but she's a fast learner. I think it canna hurt to ask."

Mrs. Barrie's news of Dr. Allen and his insulin injection of patients stole Gwen's breath. She sat down hard in her chair.

"If he'd been there, he could have received the injection." Gwen leaned on the table and buried her face in her hands. *Dear God in heaven, what have I done?*

"Malcolm thinks he will get more, that it's just a matter of time. What if you took Alistair to the institute . . . and volunteered to help?"

"Volunteered?"

"Malcolm said they're overcrowded with patients but short-staffed. If you helped with the patients, did anything you could that didn't require nursing skills, might Dr. Allen allow you to live on-site there? Then you could see Alistair, be with him."

Gwen sat back. *Would he allow me to do that, especially after I took Alistair away?* She squared her shoulders. "I'll ask."

"Aye, the worst he can say is no." Mrs. Barrie seemed satisfied with her answer, but Gwen was not.

Gwen pleaded her case with Dr. Allen by telephone, not exaggerating her nursing skills but lauding her energy and commitment and willingness to donate funds. "I'll do everything Alistair needs and can help with other patients. I can clean bedpans, change sheets, wash dishes—anything you need. I just need to be with him, Dr. Allen, to watch over him."

"I'm sorry, Miss Armstrong, my answer is still no. I have no insulin at this time and no sure knowledge of when more will be forthcoming. There is nothing more I can do for Alistair. We are over—"

"Yes, I know, you're overcrowded but you're also short-staffed. I can help with that. I'm a very hard worker. I— Please, Doctor. I understand that no more insulin may come your way, but I'm willing to do anything on the chance it might. I know you're not promising to keep Alistair alive, but if he's there, he might have a chance when the insulin does come."

"I'm sorry, Miss Armstrong. I cannot help you. I wish you and Alistair well, for as long as possible. I hope with everything in me that insulin will become available soon. Goodbye."

The line clicked. The call was over, but Gwen sat with the telephone receiver in her hand.

42

Gwen worried for Alistair. She worried for Russell. She worried for everyone in the house, wondering when someone—thugs or gang members or police or police who were thugs—might break down the front door, brandishing guns or handcuffs.

It seemed hardly three nights in a row went by that traffic to and from the west wing did not. Mostly cars—expensive cars—made regular stops. Sometimes Russell was in, sequestered in the west wing and ostensibly dealing with those visitors, and sometimes he was out of town. At least that's what he told Gwen.

She'd no idea when he might come and go or how many people had keys or means of entering the house. The hallway door to the west wing was kept locked, yet how easy it would be to break through.

Even Mrs. Barrie, unruffled as she normally appeared, seemed more nervous to Gwen as each day passed.

The first Saturday of November, as Russell traveled to who knew where and Gwen and Mrs. Barrie took their supper together in the kitchen, they heard the rumbling motors of trucks driving round the back of the mansion.

Gwen set her hand on Mrs. Barrie's arm. The two listened. Truck doors slammed.

Mrs. Barrie turned off the kitchen light. Quickly they walked to the back garden window and pulled the drape aside. Three large dark trucks sat parked with their beds nearest the house, ramp tailgates pulled down and making no attempt to keep quiet.

"What can they be doing?" Gwen whispered.

"Emptying the house of all that liquor, I hope. I'd very much like to see the backside of that!"

"You think they're dry agents?"

Gwen squinted her eyes against the coming dark. The boxes they'd stacked onto handcarts and wheeled to their trucks weren't only liquor crates. In time flashlights appeared to guide their way. This didn't look like the thugs who'd threatened her, like who she imagined members of the White Hand Gang to be. "Should we call the police?"

"Mr. Bennett said whatever happens, we're not to interfere."

"But that—right there, do you see on that dolly? That's one of the display cases from Russell's museum! They're stealing! The police—we need to call the police."

"Mr. Bennett said—"

"I know what he said, but men who would do this, what else might they do? I should either challenge them or call the police."

"Don't be daft! You canna go out there and challenge them. They could be cutthroats and murderers!"

That did it for Gwen. She couldn't wait until they stormed the main part of the house. She couldn't risk Alistair or Mrs. Barrie or any of the staff being hurt. She ran for the hallway telephone, Mrs. Barrie close behind. Gwen lifted the receiver, clicked for the operator, but there was nothing. "It's dead. They've cut the line."

"Alistair. We must get to Alistair. If they burst through that door, we don't know what— The lad will be terrified."

We're terrified! "He's asleep—at least he was. I checked just before we sat down."

"Right, then, we'll lock ourselves in with him."

Mrs. Barrie sat by Alistair's bed, and Gwen kept watch near the window through a corner of the drape until the trucks roared off down the drive.

"Have they all gone, then?"

Gwen fell, exhausted, into the chair by the fire. "At last."

"The dear lad's slept through it all."

"I don't know what to think. Russell said not to interfere, but if they had his permission to take things or if they were police or dry agents, why would they have cut the line? They didn't want us calling the police, that's for certain. I can't believe Russell would've sold all that—his museum is everything to him."

"Gwen, you must take Alistair and leave."

Gwen looked up. Mrs. Barrie never called her Gwen unless she was terribly worried or laying down the law.

"It's not safe here, not for any of us—not you or Alistair, not Tilley or Mrs. LaMott, not me."

Gwen couldn't disagree, but to leave . . . "Where would we all go, especially with Alistair so sick?"

"Away from here. Away from Mr. Bennett and whatever devilment he's gotten himself into. Tilley can go home to her mother. This is no place for a young girl with all these men coming and going and carrying on. I'll give her an excellent reference.

"Mrs. LaMott can easily find a position. I know of a well-to-do family that would give their eyeteeth to have her as head cook. Perhaps you and Alistair and I could go to Sea Isle City—where you stayed that first summer after—"

"It's mostly a town for summer tourists. I've no idea what kind of medical facilities they have there in winter. I don't know anyone except people connected to Russell, which means they'd tell him we were there. He might even go there, expect to stay there with us. He did that once in the summer."

"Dr. Allen's institute, then—you and Alistair, at least. I'll do all I can there if they'll have me as well."

"He's already said no."

"He said no to you. Talk to Malcolm—ask him to intervene, to champion your plea."

"I was so rude to Malcolm—again."

"Do you think that matters now?" Mrs. Barrie raised her voice. "Swallow your pride, lass, and think of Alistair. You've no way of knowing where all this will lead."

Gwen thought of the gun in Russell's desk drawer, and the bills of lading that told more of the story than she'd ever imagined. She thought of the beating Russell had taken months before, and now this. She looked at Alistair, sleeping, still bearing the strain of pain. She leaned close to Mrs. Barrie and whispered, "I don't know if he'd be able to make that move. He's fading, Cora."

Mrs. Barrie squeezed her hand and whispered in return, "All the more reason not to delay."

43

Fear and desperation led Gwen to attend church the next day, the first Sunday in November. With no telephone line and no opportunity to have it repaired until at least Monday, church was her only hope of talking with Malcolm, to apologize for her pride and stubbornness, and to beg his help with Dr. Allen.

She needed, too, to hear whatever the pastor might say that could bring her comfort and courage to face the coming days. She had none of her own.

Tilley and Mrs. LaMott had agreed to sit at home with Alistair until they returned. Gwen didn't want him left alone now, not even for the length of a church service. Mrs. LaMott and Tilley would both leave Monday morning, before Russell was due to return.

When Gwen and Mrs. Barrie arrived at church, Malcolm wasn't there. Through the opening hymns and deep into the sermon, his accustomed seat beside Mrs. Barrie remained empty.

What the pastor spoke on, Gwen couldn't say. She'd intended to listen carefully, but her mind whirled in a tornado of fear. The one thing that did get through to her was the Scripture reading from Psalm 73—*"My flesh and my heart faileth: but God is the strength of my heart, and my portion for ever."*

Dear God, help. My flesh and my heart have failed. I have no courage, no hope left. I don't know how to help Alistair now, to be what he needs. I can't lose him, Lord. Please. Please. If You're really there, if You're listening, be my strength and portion. Be Alistair's strength and portion. Help us. Please help us.

Malcolm slipped into the pew during the final hymn. Gwen heard him whisper to Mrs. Barrie, who sat between them, "Emergency house call."

That's what doctors do: They give up everything to help in emergencies. Please see this as an emergency. Gwen wasn't certain if she was praying to God or subliminally pleading with Malcolm. Either way, she could hardly wait until the Doxology had been sung and the benediction given.

"Please, Malcolm"—she reached across Mrs. Barrie for his hand—"please let me speak with you."

Malcolm's eyes widened but he grasped her hand in return. "Aye, always."

Gwen held her breath and her emotions in check until they walked through the church door. Halfway down the outside steps, she took Malcolm's arm, a thing that startled him enough to make him tense. "Please, Malcolm, I owe you apologies—so many, too great to number. I'm so sorry for my arrogance, my rudeness."

He pressed his hand over hers. "There's no harm done. Is Alistair worse? Do you want me to come?"

Tears spilled from Gwen's eyes and she couldn't speak.

Mrs. Barrie intervened. "He's fading, Malcolm, and we're at our wits' end. She's begged Dr. Allen to take Alistair in the hope that he'll get insulin, but he's refused."

Gwen swiped at her eyes. "He says he doesn't have any more and doesn't know when he'll get it. But you were right: If he could only be there, he'd be able to get some when it does come . . . if it comes before he—" Gwen couldn't go on.

"We thought you might be able to convince Dr. Allen to take him," Mrs. Barrie went on. "Gwen's ready to go and nurse Alistair herself, to help the others there any way she can. Dr. Allen said he's overcrowded and understaffed. Surely, many hands . . ."

"I'll do anything—anything they want."

Malcolm stared at Gwen a long while. She couldn't tell whether he was trying to decide to help or to believe her intentions. "Will you let me examine him?"

"Yes, of course, although I don't think we can get him to your office. He's so weak."

"I'll come now." Malcolm hesitated. "Is his father home? Will he allow me to examine the lad?"

Gwen breathed, "He's away until tomorrow evening. Please come."

Gwen had no idea how Malcolm convinced Dr. Allen overnight to admit Alistair to his Physiatric Institute or to allow her to live on-site to care for him. She didn't question the gift. Dr. Allen would not take Mrs. Barrie as well, so she telegraphed her sister in Connecticut that she was coming for a visit, for an unspecified period of time.

With Mrs. Barrie's help, it took Gwen less than two hours Monday morning to pack everything she and Alistair might need for the foreseeable future. The last thing she needed to do was to write Russell a note.

Dear Russell,

I've taken Alistair to Dr. Allen's institute where he and I will remain as we await the next shipment of insulin. There is nothing more I can do for him here. He won't last much longer without a miracle. Insulin is the miracle we're hoping for.

If you want to see your son, you know where he is.

Please take care of yourself. You must know it is not safe here for anyone.

Gwen

She hadn't known how to sign it. *Warmly, lovingly*—no, she didn't feel those things. She was frightened for him, for what might become of him, but more frightened for Alistair and herself, for Mrs. Barrie and the rest of the staff. He'd either come looking for her to gain an explanation when he found the house empty or he'd put the pieces together. Perhaps he'd ordered the emptying of the rooms himself. She had no way of knowing.

Mostly Gwen was angry at whatever Russell had gotten himself and therefore all of them into, and at his total neglect of Alistair. *Of course it's hard to see him sick, emaciated, so weak he can barely hold his head up, but you don't desert those precious to you because they're dying.* That's what she wanted to write but did not. She knew his son was not precious to him. How that could be, she'd never fathomed.

She didn't love Russell. How she'd ever thought she might, let alone marry him, she didn't know now. *You're a coward when it comes to being there for people, Russell Bennett. Whatever business dealings you have can't be worth the selling of your soul.*

Malcolm had insisted on making arrangements to move Alistair and for that she was grateful. Just before noon an ambulance arrived, followed by Malcolm's car.

Malcolm oversaw the moving of Alistair, making certain the medics were careful, gentle. She'd seen the care and concern he felt for Alistair when he'd examined the boy on Sunday. Now, she saw the tenderness between them as Malcolm directed Alistair's transfer to the gurney. *Alistair trusts him. He has every reason to trust him. Malcolm has championed Alistair from the beginning. If only his own father would care that much.*

Once Alistair was settled in the ambulance, Gwen wrapped Mrs. Barrie in her arms and held her close. "You'll go soon, won't you? I don't think you should be here when Russell returns."

"Mr. Dornby will be taking Tilley and me to the station within the hour. Mrs. LaMott's arranged for a taxi. She's not got far to go. You're not to worry, lass."

Gwen hugged her tighter. "I don't know what we would have

done all this time without you, Mrs. Barrie. I'm going to miss you terribly."

"God go with you, Gwen, dear. Whatever happens, you know Alistair belongs to God. He'll be healed, whether now or later. You mind that. Take it to heart. You're stronger than you know. You'll be all right."

Gwen wanted to take that to heart; she wanted to believe. What she wanted most was for Alistair's suffering to end. "Come see us when you can. We'll both need you."

"Aye. Connecticut's not far away. Malcolm's promised to bring me when I can come. He's a good man, Gwen. You can trust him."

Gwen hugged her tight in return. *Trust is such a hard thing, an elusive thing.*

Malcolm opened his car door for Gwen, then followed the ambulance to the Physiatric Institute. They spoke little as they drove. Gwen wrung her gloved hands, feeling like a clock too tightly wound.

Finally, Malcolm said, "This is a good plan, Gwen. You're brave to do it."

She almost laughed. "I'm not brave. I'm terrified, and I'm desperate."

Dr. Allen was making rounds when they reached the institute. A nurse led them to Alistair's room—bright and sunny with a large window. Gwen couldn't have asked for a better room, if only Alistair could enjoy it. She knew he enjoyed very little now. He was in too much pain.

Once he was settled and asleep, a nurse directed Gwen to quarters she would share with the nursing staff. Knowing Malcolm waited for her, she simply left everything to unpack later. By the time she returned to Malcolm, Dr. Allen had finished his early rounds and joined them.

"I must again emphasize to you, Miss Armstrong, that your

presence here guarantees nothing. I have no insulin for Alistair. I can admit him but that is all."

"I understand, Dr. Allen. Thank you for letting us come. If there's even a chance that insulin will become available in the near future, it is—"

"There is no insulin. I hope I've made myself clear." Dr. Allen's expression was severe.

"Perfectly," Gwen agreed. *No insulin now, but perhaps there will be—please, God, let there be . . . before it's too late.*

"Nurse Wilkins will train you in caring for Alistair and what you can do to help with other patients. She'll work with you until you're both confident of your abilities."

"Thank you, Doctor."

Dr. Allen gave Gwen a curt nod. "Dr. McNeill, you'll join me."

"Of course, Doctor. I'll check on you and Alistair later, Gwen, before I leave." Malcolm pressed her hand, a human touch for which Gwen was most grateful.

Gwen had expected to collect and empty bedpans, to pour urine into test tubes, to hand-feed those patients too weak to feed themselves, to wash the most feeble patients and re-dress them in gowns. She was surprised when Nurse Wilkins instead told her, "The thing we need for you to do, the thing we absolutely do not have time to do, is to read to the patients—letters they receive or books or magazines, especially for those who don't receive letters. Write letters for them, engage them and keep their spirits up. Play a game of cards with those able to do that. Play the gramophone, play the piano and sing for them, take those in wheelchairs for a walk inside or out—anything to keep them from falling into despondency. These children receive only one visit per week. Some, less. Some, none."

"I can do that—gladly."

"You'll soon learn which patients are capable of what. The weather will be getting too cold soon, but for those able to go outside, fresh air would be wonderful for them."

"Yes, thank you." Gwen looked at Alistair, still sleeping soundly.

The nurse laid a compassionate hand on Gwen's arm and whispered, "You'll want to spend all the time you can with your son when he's awake, so work in the others as you're able."

Gwen's throat thickened. She nodded. She couldn't, wouldn't correct the nurse's misconception. *He's like a son to me.*

Gwen spent the rest of the afternoon getting to know the other patients. Every few minutes she'd peek in Alistair's room. For whatever time he was awake, she'd sit with him, feed him his meager meals, and talk with him.

Late that evening, to Gwen's astonishment, Malcolm stopped in. "I thought you'd gone ages ago, that I'd missed seeing you."

"I had some things to do for Dr. Allen, but I'm off home now. I just wanted to see how my favorite patient and the bonniest nurse are doing." Malcolm smiled at Alistair, who gave his first genuine smile of the day. Gwen felt her face blush in pleasure, though she was certain this late in a very long day she looked anything but pretty.

Malcolm prayed with Alistair, laying his hand on his head in blessing. Before he was even finished Alistair fell into a peaceful sleep, no sign of pain pinching his face.

Gwen followed Malcolm into the hallway to say good night. "I can't thank you enough for arranging all of this. I didn't know what to do or where to go."

"God made a way; I'm sure of that."

Gwen felt her heart drop. "I don't know if God is going to heal him."

"I don't know the answer to that either, this side of life as we know it. Whether he's healed now or in the ages of eternity, I know he's in God's loving care. Do you know that, Gwen?"

Gwen felt her breath shudder. "I want to believe it."

"Then pray like the father in Mark's gospel—the father who

pleaded with Jesus for his own suffering child: *'Help thou mine unbelief.'* He'll answer that prayer in ways you've never dreamed."

"I don't want to give up on Alistair, but I don't know how to convince him that I haven't."

"When you have?"

Gwen looked away, tears spilling from her eyes.

"Then don't. Even if he's not up to talking or reacting, continue to read to him—talk with him about the archaeological digs he's so curious about. In his letters he told me how much it means to him that you believe in him, that you take his passion seriously."

Her heart skipped a beat. *He wrote that to you?* "I'll keep on as long as he's conscious."

"And longer still. Hearing is one of the last things to go. There's more power in prayer, in faith, and in positivity, than we can possibly know." He gave her a brief hug. "Stand fast. Stand strong." He donned his hat and coat. "I'll see you tomorrow evening."

Gwen watched as Malcolm walked down the hallway and out through the front door of the institute, thanking God for this man she so little understood.

44

In between every patient she visited, Gwen walked quickly to Alistair's room to see if he might be awake. If he was, she spent every possible minute with him and sat by his side long into the evening, even after he went to sleep.

She did just as Malcolm suggested and read to him everything she discovered that might be of interest regarding archaeology, whether from old textbooks detailing former finds or news articles of current work. When she ran out of material, she read everything again.

Alistair's dream of digging in Egypt was played out in newspaper columns. As he'd become more familiar with the Bible, his dreams had taken him to Israel.

"Can you imagine what it would be like to dig up old scrolls—maybe the first recorded words of the Bible? What if I could find a psalm written by King David's own hand? Or the tablets kept inside the ark of the covenant—or the ark itself! What about the five smooth stones that slew Goliath—where are they?"

It was in those rare moments that Alistair's eyes lit, that a fire, though growing more feeble day by day, burned. Even as he slept, Gwen read and reread to him, hoping to fuel his imagination, his dreams, to keep any part of him alive.

Sometimes, even while reading aloud, she'd fall asleep in the chair by his bed. More than once, Malcolm stopped in late at night and pressed a hand to her shoulder, encouraging her to go to her room and get some sleep.

After a week of seeing him each evening not only with Alistair but visiting other patients, she grew concerned by the dark circles beneath his eyes. "Malcolm, you don't need to stop in every night. You work all day and then drive thirty miles each way. You're exhausted."

"It's quite all right. No need to worry on my account."

But she was worried, enough that the next day she spoke to Nurse Wilkins, with whom she'd become friendly, and with whom she'd seen Malcolm speaking in the hallway late the evening before.

"I understand your concern. No one can burn the candle at both ends indefinitely, but it was his decision, after all. At least that's what Dr. Allen said."

"What do you mean?"

"Working here in the evenings once he's finished at his practice. It was what convinced Dr. Allen to take your nephew, short-staffed as we are. Dr. Allen's working seven days a week; the man's exhausted and he's long needed another doctor on staff. Dr. McNeill offered to help in the evenings and on weekends if Dr. Allen would take one more patient."

Gwen's mouth dropped.

"He must care a great deal for your Alistair." Nurse Wilkins smiled a knowing smile. "But if you ask me, Alistair's not the only one he cares for."

Gwen felt herself blush.

"He doesn't light up like a Christmas tree for any of the rest of us! Don't think we haven't tried to make that happen." She winked and went on her way, leaving Gwen flustered and more pleased than she knew she had any right to be.

The week before Thanksgiving, as Gwen reread aloud an article about excavations currently taking place in the Valley of the Kings, Alistair placed his hand on her book. "Stop, please."

"You're tired."

"I need something more."

"I'm so sorry, Alistair. Dinner's not for another two hours."

He shook his head, an act that she could see was painful for him. "Psalms. That's the future I'm certain of. Will you read it to me?"

Gwen's heart caught in her throat. She wanted to argue with him, tell him to think positively, to fight. But she knew there was little point. Still, she tried to get hold of her emotions, tried to keep her voice steady. "I'll get my Bible." *Your mother's Bible.*

"Mine is here, in the drawer beside me." Alistair closed his eyes.

Gwen opened the drawer. She took the Bible she'd seen Alistair reading months before and opened it. The handwriting in the inscription was familiar:

To Alistair, friend and brother:

May the words of this Book shine a light to your feet and a lamp for your path. May its sure promises strengthen your heart and bring comfort in your darkest hours. May you find peace and promise within its pages, knowing it is a personal letter from our Father in heaven who loves you with everlasting love, now and forevermore.

Your brother in Christ Jesus,
Malcolm

A light. A lamp. Strength, comfort, peace, promise. Love. I want those things too. Can I find them here?

"Read Psalm 23 . . . please."

Gwen found the page and cleared her throat. Drawing a deep breath, she read, "'*The Lord is my shepherd.*'"

"Malcolm told me the Lord looks after us with all the care of a good shepherd, watching us day and night to protect us from predators that would do us harm."

Except diabetes. Gwen grimaced at the thought.

"It doesn't mean that nothing bad will happen, Aunt Gwen." He gave a half smile without opening his eyes. "It means He's always with us—never leaves us alone. Go on."

"'*I shall not want.*'"

"He gives us what we need."

Gwen tried to absorb that. "'*He maketh me to lie down in green pastures: he leadeth me beside the still waters.*'"

"He gives us rest in places that provide for us." Alistair opened his eyes and looked at Gwen. "He brought you into our lives when we needed you, Aunt Gwen. You and Mrs. Barrie became places of rest and refuge for Clara and me, and for Mother."

Gwen's eyes filled so she could barely see the words on the page. "'*He restoreth my soul: he leadeth me in paths of righteousness for his name's sake.*'"

"Even when I thought I couldn't go on, Malcolm showed me how I can go to Jesus. How He would take all my broken insides and restore me. He does that, not just because I need it but because of who He is—good, always and forever." Alistair closed his eyes again. Peace washed over his features.

I need my soul restored. Please, God. Gwen tried to breathe. "'*Yea, though I walk through the valley of the shadow of death—*'" It hit too close. Gwen couldn't go on.

Alistair, his eyes still closed, recited by heart, "'*I will fear no evil: for thou art with me; thy rod and thy staff they comfort me.*' I'm not afraid, Aunt Gwen. He's with me. His rod guides me, like a shepherd uses his rod to guide his sheep. His staff pulls me back from dangerous places—fear, despair, anger—things like that. I trust Him, Aunt

Gwen. I could never trust Father. Even Mother couldn't always be there. But God is—every minute. Every day. I never really knew what trust meant before."

Tears streamed down Gwen's face, so many she couldn't wipe them away fast enough. *What would it be like to truly trust someone? Depend on them? Know they'd never fail me? Anyone?* She tried to read on but failed.

Alistair continued, his eyes still closed. "'*Thou preparest a table before me in the presence of mine enemies: thou anointest my head with oil; my cup runneth over.*'" He stopped. "My enemy is this diabetes but even now God's spread a harvest before me. Not food, of course . . . He's filled me up with His Spirit. Do you know what I mean?"

"I want to," she whispered. "I'm trying."

Alistair smiled and opened his eyes, reaching across the bedcovers for Gwen's hand, forcing her to make eye contact with him. "'*Surely goodness and mercy shall follow me all the days of my life: and I will dwell in the house of the Lord for ever.*' That's the future. Mine. Yours, if you'll take it." Alistair let go of her hand and lay back.

If I'll take it. Gwen knew his talking and the intensity of his emotion had exhausted him. It was only moments before he closed his eyes and fell into a peaceful slumber, his breathing deep and even.

Gwen closed her eyes and leaned her head against the back of the chair. She'd heard the words of the twenty-third psalm recited at funerals. She'd recited them herself, paying little attention to what they meant. She was glad Alistair had found peace with God. She was glad he wasn't caught in the throes of fear or despair . . . but she was. *I need something to hold on to in this storm . . . but I'm angry—at diabetes, at the lack of insulin, at God—yes, I'm angry at You, God! How do I find this peace? Are You listening?*

Gwen sat by Alistair's bedside until she fell asleep that evening, until the now-familiar hand pressed her shoulder to waken her.

"You might want to continue this sleeping business in a more comfortable place," Malcolm chided.

She reached for his hand and wouldn't let go.

"What is it, Gwen? What's happened?"

"I need to know what Alistair knows. I need to trust God as he does. I can't."

Malcolm nodded, as if it were the most common conversation in the world. "Come with me."

Hand in hand they walked to the lobby, barely lit by a lamp at the desk, and took a seat on the sofa nearest the radiator for warmth.

"He asked me to read him Psalm 23 today—green pastures, still waters. He said his soul is restored and he's not afraid. Why can't I see what he sees? Feel what he feels?"

"Because you're in a different place. And that's perfectly understandable, Gwen. There are plenty of psalms in which David or Asaph say exactly that. They cry out in anger and fear and despair to God. But the secret is they don't stop there."

"What do they do? Tell me."

"They remember the way God has brought them, the journey He's made with them—*with* them. All the times and ways in which He's been faithful, teaching them, leading them, rescuing them, loving them with everlasting love."

That's what Alistair was saying God does as a good shepherd.

"Can you count the ways He's brought you, Gwen? Do you remember days of feeling trapped? Days of despair, of discouragement, of confusion, in which He brought you to a different place? Take time now and count them."

Gwen closed her eyes once more and gave in to remembering the things she'd been unwilling to count before. *After Mama died, I had what I needed to raise Marion, even when Father drank. When Herman Sapp continued to pressure me to marry him, when I felt there would be nothing more in my life, Marion wrote, wanting my help, opening the door to a restored relationship. I've never had children of my own, but God brought me close to Clara and Alistair. When Marion and Clara and so many died, He saved me, and He saved Alistair. When Alistair needed a doctor, we met Malcolm, and Malcolm introduced us to Dr. Allen and his treatment. Were it not for these providences, one after another, Alistair would be long dead. And even now, Malcolm is here . . . helping Alistair . . . helping me.*

Gwen opened her eyes. "Yes. I can see that—that my life is a journey, a path."

"And those things you remember—could you have orchestrated their outcomes for good? Did you make all those things happen?"

She shook her head. "Each one was its own small miracle—like the answer to a prayer I hadn't prayed."

"Ah. And have you thanked Him?"

"No. I haven't."

"Tell Him. Do it now. It's not too late." He squeezed her hands. "That, dear Gwen, is praise. At the end of lament comes confession and praise; that brings us joy."

She nodded, still uncertain it was enough.

"Peace is different. Peace comes when we surrender everything to Him—even our turmoil—ask His forgiveness for going our own stubborn way, and believe that Jesus is our Savior, our Redeemer from all that wars within us. That's the peace Alistair has found. It works every time." He smiled.

Gwen needed to sit with that, to think it through . . . alone. Finally, she stood. "Thank you, Malcolm."

"It will take time, Gwen. Take all the time you need."

Time is the one thing we don't have.

45

By Thanksgiving week, Alistair rarely woke. Each hour he slipped into deeper and deeper sleep. The first days of the week, Gwen read frantically to him—newspaper articles, psalms, poetry, anything and everything she could lay her hands on—hoping he'd hear her, stay with her.

Malcolm and Dr. Allen encouraged her to continue reading, talking, hoping he could still hear. "If he can hang on a bit longer," Dr. Allen urged, "insulin is becoming more available. Surely it can't be much longer before we receive a shipment. It simply cannot be."

But Gwen knew that three children had died within the last two weeks. There'd been no insulin for them. Why would there be now?

Thanksgiving passed. December came. Alistair took almost no food or liquid of any kind. He'd been moved into a ward with other critically ill patients. The nurses could keep a watchful eye over all of them this way rather than have them spread apart, in individual rooms.

On Friday, December 1, Nurse Wilkins brought Gwen the morning paper. "You'll want to see this. I know how you and your nephew love these Egyptian things."

Gwen took the paper. She read the *New York Times* headlines—the story of all stories for Alistair . . . if only he could hear. *Can*

He, Lord? She feared the greatest newspaper article of Alistair's life came too late, but she read the headlines aloud anyway. "*'Gem-Studded Relics In Egyptian Tomb Amaze Explorers. Art Treasures Fill 2 Sealed Antechambers, Reached Through Blocked Passages.'* Do you hear, Alistair? It's what we've dreamed of! Howard Carter and Lord Carnarvon have discovered the tomb of King Tutankhamen." She put down the paper, unable to read more just then. "You always said you thought Howard Carter would find more in the Valley of the Kings—that Theodore Davis quit too soon. You were right. You'd have stayed the course!" *You planned to join Carter in a dig one day. Oh, my dear Alistair.* It wouldn't do not to tell him everything, just in case he could hear. Gwen read the entire article aloud, swiping her tears with the back of her hand, determined to keep her voice steady. It was the one gift she could give him now.

There was no sign that he heard. Grasping his hand, Gwen laid her head across his arm. *Dear God, he's Yours . . . far more Yours than mine. I can't keep him, can't make him well. I can't force anyone to give him insulin, even if it could help now. I cannot bear to see him suffer—and it isn't about me. Please, Lord, don't let him suffer any longer.*

How long Gwen slept, she didn't know, but when she woke, she was stiff from cold. It was dark through the window. Slowly, gradually, the first streaks of light pierced the dawn. She sensed a peace she hadn't before, a relief in her soul.

Forgive me for my arrogance, Father, for thinking I know better than You what is best for him . . . or for me. You raised Jesus from the dead to life everlasting. Nothing is too hard for You. I know You can heal him. Whether now or in Your Kingdom. I'm ready to let him go to You. I surrender him to You. I trust You.

Alistair's breathing continued, a bit slower than before. Malcolm came in and checked him even before the nurses.

"I didn't know you were here," Gwen said. "I thought you'd gone home."

"I slept a few hours on Dr. Allen's office sofa. I didn't want to leave. Dr. Callahan will take my Saturday patients."

"He's not going to make it, is he?" Gwen swallowed hard.

"He's slipped into a coma. I'm sorry, Gwen." Malcolm took her in his arms.

She didn't cry, not aloud, anyway. She clung to him, keeping her cheek against his chest, thankful for the beating of his heart. "I've given him to God. He'll do what's best for Alistair. I know that now, and I'm grateful. I know He loves my boy. I know Alistair is safe."

Malcolm held her tighter. Nurses began checking vital signs among the other patients, keeping the lights of the room low.

A rush of footsteps thundered down the hallway followed by the rumbling of a trolley cart's wheels going full speed. "Lights up!" Bright light flooded the room. Dr. Allen, intense as always, stood in the doorway, casting a quick glance around the room, taking in his two dozen dying patients at once. "Start here, Nurse!"

Malcolm let go of Gwen. "What is it, Doctor? How can I help?"

"A shipment—just arrived. Prepare the syringes, Doctor. Perhaps we can save some. Be careful. Not too much. Don't overdose."

Both doctors worked frantically, Malcolm filling syringes and Dr. Allen injecting his comatose and nearly comatose patients.

Gwen stood against the wall at the head of Alistair's bed, praying. *I've given him to You, Father. Do what's best for him—whatever that is.* She meant it, but she couldn't keep her heart from hoping, from wishing, from wanting.

Alistair did not wince while receiving the injection. There was no sign of life. He was as still as before. Her heart plummeted. She touched his head—so little hair left. He didn't move. She sat again by his bed, laying her hand next to his.

The clock's ticking in the hallway had never sounded so loud. Dr. Allen had nearly made the round of injections in the room. Minutes passed. *It's too late. Too little too late.* Gwen bit her lip to keep from crying out. *Maybe it will help others, who aren't so far gone.*

Time seemed to stand still, except for that infernal clock. Then a movement caught her eye from the bed across the room—the first patient Dr. Allen had injected. *Did I see that, or did I imagine it?*

Another slight movement came two beds over. A few minutes later a sound. A faint cry. Another movement. Gradually, from one bed to the next came twitches, movements, eyes opening, a feeble request for water.

Gwen was afraid to look at Alistair, afraid of what she might not see. Something touched her finger, but it could have been that she'd simply moved it across the sheet. She swallowed, still refusing to hope, to look. Patients around the room continued to rouse, to open eyes, to blink. Malcolm stood beside her, gripped her shoulder as she forced herself to keep her eyes on others.

Resurrection! It's like watching a resurrection!

A twitch, a verifiable twitch came beside her finger. *Please, God!* Gwen turned to look.

Alistair's eyes opened. He blinked. Gwen's breath caught. He sleepily glanced her way and smiled—a half smile, a weak smile, but genuine. "Aunt Gwen," he whispered.

"Alistair! Alistair!" She'd have fallen on him if Malcolm hadn't held her up. Tears sprang from her eyes and Malcolm's and those of every nurse in the room. Gwen could have sworn they fell from brusque Dr. Allen's eyes too. And then relief and laughter, joyously restrained, spread contagious through the room.

46

Less than two hours later, Alistair ate real food—only a little, but real food. He'd barely finished when he asked, "Aunt Gwen, read me that again, please."

"Read what?"

"The *Times* article, about discovering the tomb. I didn't get it all."

"You heard that?"

"Some of it. Read it again. I might be joining Carter one day, you know . . . after all. I need to know what he's found."

Gwen laughed, kissed his forehead, and pulled out the newspaper from where it had fallen beneath the bed.

Two days later Dr. Allen had Alistair moved back to his own room, as he'd done with several of the other patients in the ward who were steadily improving.

"The supply of insulin is not guaranteed," Malcolm confided to Gwen outside Alistair's room, "but by fluctuating the dosage Dr. Allen believes he'll have enough to maintain stability. We still don't know how to gauge exactly how much insulin is needed by each patient, or how often."

"So, too little might be better than too much?" Gwen remembered that Mrs. Barrie had told her about the children in New York and Chicago who'd died.

"Aye. We've still so much to learn, but this—this is a miracle."

Gwen breathed—the first really deep breath she'd taken in days. *A miracle, indeed. Thank You, Father. Thank You!*

A second shipment of insulin arrived. Hope thrived.

As Alistair grew more alert, Gwen read aloud to him everything he wished. She scoured newspapers Malcolm brought for more on Howard Carter's discovery. She read psalms of thanksgiving and praise, more than those of lament. They prayed together, something new and wondrous for Gwen.

"It's Thanksgiving every day now, isn't it, Aunt Gwen?" Alistair smiled.

"Every given day!" *We're living in a veritable feast! As long as quality insulin is available, as long as the supply doesn't run out.*

"Do you think Dr. Allen will let us go home for Christmas?"

Gwen had not considered such a thing. "No. Not yet. We need to be here, where the supply of insulin comes." *Besides, I can't imagine returning to Bennett Place. But where else would we go?*

"Have you heard anything from Father?" She heard the uncertainty in his voice, not unlike the uncertainty she felt. *Where is he?*

"No, I haven't. I should call Mr. Whitfield, tell him how well you're doing. He'll want to know, and perhaps he knows where your father is and can get word to him."

"I don't know if he'll care."

Gwen wanted to refute that, but she couldn't lie to him. "Malcolm has promised we'll spend Christmas together, right here."

"Aye, we will!" Malcolm appeared in the doorway, smiling.

"Come in! We were just talking about you."

"So I heard. I'm brazenly guilty of eavesdropping. But I've

word of another Christmas surprise, one even better than me being here."

"I'm not sure there is anything better." Gwen said the words aloud before she thought, then felt heat rush up her neck.

Malcolm beamed, taking her hand and pressing it to his chest. "I'll take that to heart."

"What's the surprise?" Alistair brought them down to earth.

"I've a letter here from Mrs. Barrie. I told her about Alistair's improvement. She's coming for Christmas, can't wait to spend it with her lad."

"Mrs. Barrie!" Alistair crowed. "I can't wait to see her!"

Gwen laughed with all the joy her heart could hold. *Life. Future. Christmas. Family! Thank You! Thank You!*

Christmas Day at the institute came without feasting in the usual sense. Gwen knew, however, that egg on toast was the first and best and fullest meal Alistair had enjoyed in ages. To watch him eat was a gift from heaven itself.

Mrs. Barrie peppered him with questions about his plans. "So you're still on about going to Egypt and digging amongst those pyramids, are you?"

"More than ever! Aunt Gwen and I've been making up stories about the adventures we're going to have. You should come too, Mrs. Barrie."

Mrs. Barrie laughed. "I think I'll keep the home fires burning while you're away. You'll need a soft place to land upon your return!"

Gwen caught the gleam in her friend's eye and wondered what she was thinking. *She'd not say such a thing lightly.*

When Alistair finally fell asleep, Gwen led Mrs. Barrie to the institute's kitchen for a proper meal and a pot of tea. She needed to update the older woman on what little she knew about Bennett Place. "I spoke with Mr. Whitfield two weeks ago to let him know how well Alistair is doing, and so he could let Russell know when they're in touch. He said that he believes Bennett Place will be sold. That's all I know. He couldn't, or wouldn't, tell me more."

"Aye, I spoke with him yesterday when I arrived in New York."

"You did?"

"I never mentioned it before, but for several years Mr. Whitfield has managed some small investments for me."

Gwen's brows shot up.

Mrs. Barrie shrugged. "Mr. Bennett paid a generous wage and I'd very little need, so it seemed prudent to invest, a saving toward my retirement years."

"I hope he's done well by you."

"Oh, he has. I think Mr. Whitfield's an honest, if severe, man. He's the soul of discretion, as well he should be, but now things have come out into the open."

"Things?"

Mrs. Barrie pulled a newspaper clipping from her purse. "I don't suppose you've seen this?"

Gwen read the headline: *"Millionaire Sought in Fraud and Smuggling Scandal."*

"Over the years, in addition to antiquities he bought in Egypt, he's stolen and smuggled rare artifacts, then had very good reproductions made here and pawned them off as originals. Even for the legitimate ones, he was supposed to have a special license from the antiquities department and did not. Once he got wind the authorities were on to him and closing in, he had the house and museum cleared out and all those rooms full of things distributed far and wide to hide them."

"That was when we—"

"Aye! That was the day we thought the world and all would end for us." Mrs. Barrie shook her head in disbelief. "Even now, it's hard to fathom how he could do such a thing, knowing we were in the house—us and his own son. All that besides his importing and distribution of bootleg whiskey. The dry agents have raided the house, as well—whatever was left after Mr. Bennett's 'clients' finished fishing out their share. Mr. Whitfield said the house now looks as if it's been ransacked by hoodlums, top to bottom."

"That beautiful house."

"Well, it was. It's being sold. It turns out there's not only a double mortgage on the estate, but Mr. Bennett ran up a vast number of gambling debts during his travels besides. Not that that will bother him much now. I reckon he'll be gone a long while."

"Prison, then?" Gwen couldn't get the idea through her head. *At least Marion didn't live to see this.*

"Aye, well, it would be if they catch him, but I figure that to be unlikely. Mr. Whitfield said he's gone to Egypt."

"Egypt?"

"Aye, for good and all, Mr. Whitfield believes, and likely to reinvent himself there. He didn't say it directly, but I got the impression Mr. Bennett had money offshore somewhere—one of those Swiss bank accounts, maybe—so I assume he'll be all right. I can't imagine he was short of funds—and then, to go and leave all those debts here." She shook her head. "I doubt they'll ever catch him, clever as he is."

"He left us without money, and knowing we all might be in danger." Gwen could not process that.

Mrs. Barrie shrugged. "Giving the benefit of doubt, perhaps he thought we'd be safest not knowing his plans . . . at least that's as Mr. Whitfield's painted the picture. I told Mr. Whitfield I'd be with you and Alistair here for Christmas. He asked me to have you telephone him after the holiday. He wants to speak with you about the lad."

"Alistair." Gwen hadn't thought beyond the moment, beyond Alistair's recovery. She'd given Russell very little thought since coming to the institute, but now, with him permanently out of the country and all the money gone . . . "What does this mean for Alistair? I was left in charge of medical decisions for him . . . but . . . what now?"

"Mr. Whitfield will be wanting to explain things himself, but he did say that Mr. Bennett's relinquished guardianship to you."

"Legally? Legal guardianship?"

"Aye, if you'll have it."

"Then I can adopt him."

"Aye." Mrs. Barrie smiled. "That, too."

Gwen's heart warmed, as if the sun rose within her chest.

"Have you thought what you'll do when you leave here, Gwen?"

"No. That's been the least of my concerns . . . until now." Her head swam. "I'll need to get a job—a teaching job to support us . . . when Alistair is a bit stronger, before the new school year starts. I have some savings, and I still own my house in Paradox, but I can't return there, not with Herman Sapp the principal of the local high school. Perhaps I can sell it."

"Well, I've been giving it a great deal of thought." Mrs. Barrie straightened her shoulders. "I've saved enough to buy a house—not a grand house, but a wee cottage."

"I thought you'd moved in with your sister."

"We tried that, but we're both rather too old and set in our ways to make it a cheerful plan long-term. No, I was thinking—wondering, that is, if you and Alistair might like to come live with me."

"The three of us, live together?" Gwen had never imagined such a thing.

"Aye, for now." Mrs. Barrie smiled. "We could see how it goes, if we get on comfortably . . . if you want to, that is. We can choose a place together."

Gwen looked at her friend, more aunt, more mentor than she'd ever known. "I'd love that. I know Alistair would, if he's allowed to stay with me. I can't believe you'd offer."

"Well, we'd share the cooking and such, help one another—like family."

"Of course, and I've saved too—as well as the rent I receive—so I'll pay you rent. That should help with the mortgage."

"There'll be no mortgage. I'm too much of a Scot for that. I'll buy what I've saved for, but I wouldn't turn away help with the cost of things."

Gwen reached for her hand. "You're a gift, Mrs. Barrie. A miracle. Another miracle."

"I've been called many things, Gwen Armstrong, but never a miracle. I rather like the sound of that, but I'll be asking you to call me Cora from now on, just the same."

47

"November 7, 1923—we'll remember this as the day I became your adoptive mother," Gwen announced happily, lifting her glass in a toast.

"November 7, 1923—the day I became your adopted son." Alistair responded in kind, then turning to Cora announced, "the day you became my adopted grandmother."

Cora laughed, delightedly, and raised her glass.

"So, what does this day make me?" Malcolm raised his own glass.

"What, exactly, do you want it to make you?" Cora asked as innocently as a child. "If there's a place you want in this family, you'd best speak up."

Gwen saw the color rush up Malcolm's neck as their glances collided. She felt that same heat rush up her own. Still, she wasn't sorry Cora had spoken. She only wished Malcolm would.

He was nearly a regular fixture in their home, at least a regular visitor. Sundays, he drove them all to church. Sunday afternoons Cora cooked for them all. Sunday evenings they attended church again. Midweek he picked them up for prayer meeting. They always sat together; sometimes they held hands during the prayer.

Is this enough for him? Is this all he wants?

Gwen knew he remained focused on gaining his American citizenship. It was a condition Dr. Callahan had placed on Malcolm's ability to buy the medical practice, eager as the older doctor was to retire, and thus on Malcolm's ability to provide for a family. They would have enough between them now to make a go of things, especially with the revelation of the trust Marion left for Alistair, but she knew Malcolm was determined to support them all.

His required residency for five years before petitioning for naturalization wouldn't be fulfilled for another year and some. He'd said he wouldn't feel certain of his ability to remain in the country until he became an American citizen. Gwen didn't know if that was a legitimate concern, but she wished he'd speak.

She'd grown not only to count on Malcolm, but to trust him fully, to love him, to love how he cared for each member of her small family. *What are your feelings toward me?*

Gwen did her best to keep busy, to focus her life on Alistair and his growing needs, marveling that in not quite a year since his first injection of insulin, he'd fully recovered, put on weight, matured, gained confidence. At fifteen he looked much the same as his peers. Even his hair had grown in. Since insulin had become commercially and more readily available, he'd been supplied the lifesaving injections he needed several times each day. Constant monitoring of his diet was a given for life, and it was crucial that he protect himself, as far as possible, against infection or cuts of any kind. But with those precautions and with those gifts, life for the most part went on apace.

As time went by, he began writing letters to Howard Carter, excited over his prospects in years to come.

"You can't expect Mr. Carter to respond. He's a very busy man. He must get hundreds of letters," Gwen cautioned, concerned he'd be disappointed and remembering Carter's lack of response to her.

"You're funny, Aunt Gwen. Of course I don't expect him to respond. I just want him to get to know me. I'll be over there working with him in a few years."

Gwen knew she looked dubious.

Alistair smiled, a smile Gwen could not resist. "Need I remind you about miracles? They may take time, but they're always in the making. We must watch for them, expect them."

She ruffled his hair; she couldn't disagree.

The afternoon of Tuesday, April 29, 1924, was another date neither Gwen nor Alistair would ever forget. Malcolm had gotten tickets for the three of them and Cora to hear Howard Carter speak at Carnegie Hall about his discoveries in King Tutankhamen's tomb.

Sitting in the great hall next to Gwen, awaiting Mr. Carter's lecture, Alistair thumbed through the twelve-page program. "There's only one column about today's lecture! Everything else is advertisements for cars and pianos and phonographs and such."

"Look at this," Cora exclaimed from Alistair's other side. "It says he opened the inner tomb little more than two months past. There was a mummy case inside the big mummy case—wood, all gilded with gold in a likeness of the king."

"That outer case is called the sarcophagus, Granny Cora." Alistair spoke with authority.

"So it is." She smiled.

Gwen and Malcolm exchanged a knowing glance. Cora would say anything to get a rise out of Alistair, leading him to call her Granny.

Malcolm squeezed Gwen's hand.

How easily we read one another's minds. Are you reading my mind now, Malcolm McNeill? Just how long are you going to dally with my affections? I love you, you know. Gwen pulled her hand away in frustration. *A man ought to speak his mind—if he's of a mind.*

Malcolm wrapped his arm around Gwen's shoulders as they waited for the lights in the great hall to lower and for Howard Carter to appear at the podium. He leaned closer and whispered in her ear, "I took my Oath of Allegiance yesterday."

"You what? You're just telling me this?"

"I'm a United States citizen now. I'll never be able to offer you the treasures of Egypt, or even New York . . ."

She leaned closer, felt her heart quicken.

"But if you'll allow, I offer you all that I have, Gwen Armstrong, all that I am."

She turned to face him. "You're all I'll ever want, Malcolm McNeill."

He pressed his forehead against hers. "Then will you do me the honor of becoming my wife?"

Her answer could not be heard amid the thunderous applause as Howard Carter took the stage. Their kiss may not have been noticed by most as the lights of the great hall lowered. But Gwen could have sworn she heard Alistair laugh, and stage-whisper, "Ha! About time!"

Epilogue

NEW YORK, 1935

Gwen plucked yet another gray hair from her scalp.

"You're going to have to stop doing that or you'll be bald as a new bairn's head," Cora observed. "Winter's coming and you'll find yourself chilled to the scalp. After all, it's not like Malcolm's kept the color of his hair. Growing old gracefully is a natural part of life."

Gwen sighed as she plunked in her seat nearest the fire. "I know. I just don't want Alistair's first trip home after all this time to find us so much changed."

"And you don't think he'll be changed after spending two years digging in the deserts of Egypt? Sunburned and spindly, that's what he'll be. We'll have to fatten him up."

"Gently, Cora."

"Yes, yes, I know, count every carbohydrate. I'll be careful, I promise." She put down her knitting. "That won't be so hard with the price of food. I'd surely like to see the end of this infernal Depression. Ach, but it will be that good to have him home again, no matter what, won't it?"

"Yes. A thousand times yes," Gwen agreed. "Dr. Alistair Bennett—a man fully grown with a life and adventures all his own—things we know nothing about. I hope he won't find us too prosaic."

Malcolm laughed as he entered from the next room. "I heard that. Imagine, Alistair finding you prosaic! I canna ken such a thing."

Gwen smiled. It seemed the longer they all lived together, the stronger Malcolm's and Cora's Scottish brogues emerged.

"He'll find his aunt as beautiful and charming as ever, and always his champion. Every man loves that, no matter his age." He tweaked her cheek.

"You too, Dr. McNeill?" she teased.

"Me especially, Mrs. McNeill." He kissed the top of her head.

Cora yawned. "Mercy me, look at the time. I'll be off to my bed, then. I'll see you both in the morning."

"Good night, Cora." Gwen shared a smile with Malcolm. Whenever he had a free evening at home and not on call, Cora excused herself to bed uncharacteristically early. Gwen loved her for it.

"Good night, Granny Cora," Malcolm chimed.

Cora shook her finger good-naturedly in his direction. "That's a title for one and only one to use."

"Just getting you ready. Thought you might be needing practice."

"Ha! Never!" She laughed and left the room humming.

Happily alone, Malcolm pulled Gwen to the sofa.

She leaned her head against his chest. "I can't believe it's been so long since we've seen him, and yet it seems like forever. I don't know how I'd stand it if he didn't write so often. It really is good of him."

"He loves you."

"He loves us all."

"Aye. We never gave up on him, not one of us."

"And now he's fulfilling his dreams . . . thanks to the trust Marion left for him. My sister showed such fortitude, secretly getting Mr. Whitfield to sell her jewelry to establish trusts for the children, even when she was so ill. He did well by her, keeping that secret from Russell."

"Mr. Whitfield's a good man. Russell Bennett was his client, but he didn't approve the man's tomfoolery. Relieved to see him gone, no doubt."

"He's certainly done well by Alistair." Gwen snuggled closer to her husband. "Things are not like he and Clara first dreamed them. They dreamed of working as a team . . . but he's really doing it . . . really digging in Egypt, exploring the past. The things he must be learning, seeing."

"Do you wish you'd gone with him? You planned grand adventures there, the two of you."

"In such detail!" She smiled. "Those plans, those dreams helped; they kept us both going through the darkest days . . . days we didn't know would have a dawn. Those dreams served a great purpose, but they were his dreams. He needed to forge a life without me, and he's done it."

"And what about now? Do you ever wish to go? I imagine he could find a fine camel for you to ride."

"I don't need to go there now. I'm precisely where I want to be, Dr. McNeill." She traced her finger down his nose. "I love you, you know."

He smoothed her hair, nestling her head beneath his chin. "Aye, and I love you. There's a poem for that . . . and a bit of a song."

"Hmm. Robbie Burns?" She smiled again, knowing the Scotsman in him could not resist.

"As fair are thou, my bonnie lass,
So deep in luve am I;
And I will luve thee still, my Dear,
Till a' the seas gang dry."

Gwen joined him for the lines engraved in her heart, lines precious for both the men she loved.

"Till a' the seas gang dry, my Dear,
And the rocks melt wi' the sun:
I will luve thee still, my dear,
While the sands o' life shall run."

A Note from the Author

My eight-year-old granddaughter's diagnosis of type 1 diabetes, her heroic journey, and the miraculous, lifesaving discovery of insulin inspired this story.

Type 1 diabetes (not to be confused with type 2 diabetes) is a disease in which the autoimmune system attacks and destroys beta cells in the pancreas that normally produce insulin, preventing the body from effectively regulating glucose (blood sugar). High glucose levels over time can lead to severe damage of body systems and organs, including kidneys, eyes, blood vessels, and nerves. It can lead to loss of vision, stroke, heart disease, nerve damage, and feet problems due to lack of blood flow. Cognitive impairment is possible.

Currently, while insulin is used to treat type 1 diabetes, there is still no cure for this disease. Left untreated, it is ultimately a death sentence. Anyone at any age can develop type 1 diabetes. Studies have shown that there can be a hereditary predisposition to acquiring the disease even when no one else in a family's history had it. Studies have also shown that environmental factors, such as viral infections, can trigger the disease. My granddaughter developed type 1 diabetes after a bout with Covid and a viral infection. There is no known family member who had type 1 diabetes.

Less was understood about diabetes in the early 1900s when my story takes place. It was fascinating to me that after the Spanish flu, as after Covid, there was a rise in diabetes among the population.

A few other aspects of the story that were based on actual people or events:

- Dr. Frederick Allen really did develop and publish a program he desperately hoped could keep patients alive until a cure could be found. Treating patients in his institute with a very strict starvation diet to keep blood sugar stable, he experienced varying amounts of success. Early diagnosis and strict supervision of their diet in some cases prolonged life two years or more. Every effort was made to keep the patients cheerful and the environment pleasant to avoid emotional stress, which could also raise blood sugar. Still, the children remained hungry and dreamed and spoke of what they longed to eat.
- The incident Alistair shares in his letter about the boy, Eddie, so hungry that he ate birdseed, which raised his blood sugar and led to his death, occurred at Dr. Allen's Physiatric Institute. After that, no children were allowed to keep birds as pets.
- Dr. Frederick Banting, a Canadian surgeon working diligently with medical student Charles Best at the University of Toronto under Dr. Macleod, first isolated the hormone insulin in 1921. But there were problems: The insulin wasn't pure, it wasn't stable, they had no idea of the correct dosage or how that differed from person to person, and they had no way to make it in quantity or commercially available. James Collip joined the team and helped to purify the pancreatic extract.
- In 1922, Dr. Banting and others at the Toronto General Hospital rushed the purified extract to a ward of mostly comatose children—children dying from diabetic ketoacidosis. Daring to hope, they rapidly injected the children with the new and purified extract of insulin. By the time they injected

> the last child, the first child to be injected had opened their eyes. One by one the children woke from their comas.

Each time I read of that scene, I think, *It must have been like watching a resurrection! Death hovered menacingly at the door, but insulin threw it wide open, and life walked in.*

Dr. Frederick Banting, Dr. James Collip, and Charles Best sold the patent for insulin to the University of Toronto for one dollar. Dr. Banting declared, "Insulin does not belong to me, it belongs to the world."

I needed to tell the story of one child's journey through this dark valley and that of the loved ones travelling with him. I needed to show the devastating loss of "normal," how a tragedy or the diagnosis of a serious or fatal disease can stop on a dime everything we know and plan in life.

Ultimately, I needed to show that there is one all-knowing, all-trustworthy, never-quit relationship that cannot die, that will see us through, even when we walk through the valley of the shadow of death—our own, or with those we love most. I needed to show how hard it is to surrender ourselves or our loved one to the care of almighty God, but how that is truly our lifeline, and the path to peace.

I hope you've enjoyed *Every Given Day* and found nuggets of truth and inspiration in this story. I hope Gwen and Alistair's journey gives you a better understanding of type 1 diabetes and those who live with this disease. I hope most of all that the story draws you even closer to our heavenly Father, and that you know how very much He loves you.

Staying connected with readers is a great joy for me. Feel free to stop by my website and sign up for my newsletter at cathygohlke.com. If your book club or reading group enjoyed *Every Given Day* or any of my books, I'd be happy to meet with you virtually. You can reach me through the Connect page at authorcathygohlke.com to schedule a date and time.

If you enjoyed *Every Given Day,* please consider leaving a review on Amazon, Goodreads, or your favorite review site. Reviews and personal recommendations are the best way others can find books you love.

Until next time, God's great blessings for you, and happy reading!

Cathy

Acknowledgments

I so appreciate you, dear reader, for sharing this story journey with me. I hope you have been blessed as you bless me.

Very special thanks to my daughter, Elisabeth, my son-in-law, Tim, and my granddaughter Aimee for sharing their family's journey through Aimee's type 1 diabetes and celiac disease. Your courage and fortitude inspire me daily. Participating in your homeschool field trip to the King Tutankhamun exhibit in Washington, DC, inspired the Egyptian portion of this story.

Many thanks to Roseanna White for sharing your experiences as a mother of a child with type 1 diabetes, and to the Moms of Type 1 Facebook group for all I've gleaned from your posts and heroic journeys. I stand in awe of each of you.

Many books have helped in my research of this story: *Breakthrough—Elizabeth Hughes, the Discovery of Insulin, and the Making of a Medical Miracle*, by Thea Cooper and Arthur Ainsberg; *The Discovery of Insulin*, by Michael Bliss; *Fred & Marjorie—A Doctor, A Dog, and the Discovery of Insulin*, by Deborah Kerbel; *Total Dietary Regulation in the Treatment of Diabetes*, by Frederick M. Allen, Edgar Stillman, and Reginald Fitz; *The Starvation Treatment of Diabetes*, by Lewis Webb Hill, M.D., and Rena Sarah Eckman, Dietitian; *The Earl and the Pharoah—From the Real Downton Abbey to the Discovery of Tutankhamun*, by the Countess of Carnarvon; *Aristocrats and Archaeologists—An Edwardian Journey on the Nile*, by Toby Wilkinson and Julian Platt; *A World Beneath the Sands—Adventures and Archaeologists in the Golden Age of Egyptology*, by Toby Wilkinson; *The Millionaire and the Mummies—Theodore Davis's Gilded Age in the Valley of the Kings*, by John M. Adams; *The Discovery of the Tomb of Tutankhamen*, by Howard Carter and A. C. Mace; *The Tomb of Tutankhamun, Volume II—Burial Chamber and Mummy*, by Howard Carter; *The Tomb of Tutankhamun, Volume III—Treasury and Annex*, by Howard Carter; *When You Pray—A Study of Six Prayers in the Bible*: "Session Five—How Long, O Lord—Prayers of Lament," by Jennifer Rothschild.

So much appreciation for Heather Tuller and the Sisters of our Bible study group. Your thoughtful insights, and your love and prayers, have kept me going.

Many thanks to Natasha Kern, my longtime literary agent and dear friend, for championing this story and for sharing my deep concern for loved ones challenged by type 1 diabetes.

Thank you to Karen Watson; to my editors, Stephanie Broene and Sarah Rische; to Dean Renninger for the beautiful cover design of this book; and to all the wonderful team at Tyndale House Publishers. Your encouragement and prayers mean everything to me. I could not ask for a better publishing team.

Very special thanks to dear author friends Carrie Turansky and Terri Gillespie for encouraging me in the writing of this story, and to Terri Gillespie and Natasha Kern for reading an early version of this manuscript. Your insights were pure gold!

Special thanks to my husband, Dan, and to all my family for encouraging and supporting the hours, days, weeks, months I worked to complete this book. I could not do this without you.

I'll always be grateful to my uncle, Wilbur Goforth, for encouraging me to make certain I'm working in the will of God by asking, "Do I have joy? Is this yoke easy? Is this burden light?" Yes—after all these years, writing still gives me joy—even when the subject matter challenges. Is it easy? Not always, but the writing lightens my heart and makes it sing.

Most especially, I'm thankful to my heavenly Father and Lord Jesus Christ for life, for salvation, for health and family, for the joy and gift of writing. My life verse has become, *"The Lord is my strength and my song; he has become my salvation"* (Psalm 118:14).

Discussion Questions

1. Gwen received her sister's invitation to come to New York City at a pivotal moment, one when she was eager for change. But when she arrived at Bennett Place, the scenario she'd expected no longer existed, and she had to adapt quickly. Have you ever experienced a sudden major change in life plans? How did you respond?

2. Given her history with Russell Bennett, Gwen knew she was running a risk by living in his home. Do you think she was wise or unwise to accept the position Marion outlined? Should she have stayed once she learned Marion was in a sanatorium?

3. Why do you think Russell treated Alistair so poorly? Why did he favor Clara?

4. Mrs. Barrie and all those at Bennett Place took great care during months the Spanish flu raged, both for themselves and to protect Marion, who was made even more susceptible by tuberculosis. Did you feel they were overly cautious, or should they have done more? What similarities did you see between the Spanish flu and the Covid pandemic?

5. Malcolm McNeill lost his young daughter to diabetes when he was away from home, serving in Egypt during the Great War. How did that fuel his passion to help Alistair? Besides advocating for Dr. Allen's diet, what did Malcolm offer Alistair? What did he offer Gwen and Mrs. Barrie?

6. Gwen frequently closed her eyes to Russell's business dealings, even when she believed he was operating in something dangerous and illegal. Do you agree with her motivations? Given the time and place, could she have done something different? What did you imagine Russell was involved in?

7. Following Dr. Allen's protocol helped prolong Alistair's life in the hope that a cure for diabetes would be discovered, but the diet was grueling and many considered it cruel. What do you imagine you would've done in Gwen and Mrs. Barrie's position?

8. Dr. Callahan prohibited Malcolm from sharing information about Dr. Allen's program with Gwen, believing it would give the family false hope. Why did Malcolm go against the senior doctor's wishes? Do you agree with Dr. Callahan's reasoning, or do you think Gwen was right when she wondered, *How can hope of any kind be false?*

9. Gwen feared God as a great puppet master who might punish her—or worse, punish Alistair—for her doubt and unbelief. What did Gwen learn about the power and practice of lament in the Psalms? What did she ultimately learn about surrender to God?

About the Author

Bestselling, Christy Hall of Fame, and Carol and INSPY Award–winning author **Cathy Gohlke** writes novels steeped with inspirational lessons, speaking of world and life events through the lens of history. She champions the battle against oppression, celebrating the freedom found only in Christ. Cathy has worked as a school librarian, drama director, and director of children's and education ministries. When not traveling to historic sites for research, she and her husband, Dan, divide their time between northern Virginia and the Jersey Shore, enjoying time with their grown children and grandchildren. Visit her website at cathygohlke.com and find her on Facebook at CathyGohlkeBooks; on BookBub (@CathyGohlke); and on YouTube, where you can subscribe to Book Gems with Cathy Gohlke for short videos of book recommendations. Cathy welcomes invitations to virtual book club meetings through the Connect page of her website.

CONNECT WITH CATHY ONLINE AT

cathygohlke.com

OR FOLLOW HER ON

CathyGohlkeBooks

cathy_gohlke

cathygohlke

cathy-gohlke